Literature, Gender, and Nation-Building in Nineteenth-Century Egypt

Literatures and Cultures of the Islamic World

Edited by Hamid Dabashi

Hamid Dabashi is Hagop Kevorkian Professor of Iranian Studies and Comparative Literature at Columbia University. Dabashi chaired the Department of Middle East and Asian Languages and Cultures from 2000 to 2005 and was a founding member of the Institute for Comparative Literature and Society. His most recent books include *Islamic Liberation Theology: Resisting the Empire; Makhmalbaf at Large: The Making of a Rebel Filmmaker; Iran: A People Interrupted;* and an edited volume, *Dreams of a Nation: On Palestinian Cinema.*

Published by Palgrave Macmillan:

New Literature and Philosophy of the Middle East: The Chaotic Imagination
Jason Bahbak Mohaghegh

Literature, Gender, and Nation-Building in Nineteenth-Century Egypt: The Life and Works of `A'isha Taymur
Mervat F. Hatem

Islam in the Eastern African Novel
Emad Mirmotahari

Urban Space in Contemporary Egyptian Literature: Portraits of Cairo (forthcoming)
Mara Naaman

Literature, Gender, and Nation-Building in Nineteenth-Century Egypt

The Life and Works of `A'isha Taymur

Mervat F. Hatem

LITERATURE, GENDER, AND NATION-BUILDING IN NINETEENTH-CENTURY EGYPT
Copyright © Mervat F. Hatem, 2011.

First published in 2011 by PALGRAVE MACMILLAN® in the United States—a division of St. Martin's Press LLC, 175 Fifth Avenue, New York, NY 10010.

Where this book is distributed in the UK, Europe and the rest of the world, this is by Palgrave Macmillan, a division of Macmillan Publishers Limited, registered in England, company number 785998, of Houndmills, Basingstoke, Hampshire RG21 6XS.

Palgrave Macmillan is the global academic imprint of the above companies and has companies and representatives throughout the world.

Palgrave® and Macmillan® are registered trademarks in the United States, the United Kingdom, Europe and other countries.

ISBN: 978-0-230-11350-3

Library of Congress Cataloging-in-Publication Data.

Hatem, Mervat Fayez.
    Literature, gender, and nation-building in nineteenth-century Egypt : the life and works of 'A'isha Taymur / by Mervat F. Hatem.
        p. cm.—(Literatures and cultures of the Islamic world)
    Includes bibliographical references.
    ISBN 978-0-230-11350-3
    1. Taymuriyah, 'A'ishah, 1840 or 41-1902 or 3—Criticism and interpretation.
2. Taymuriyah, 'A'isha, 1840 or 41-1902 or 3—Political and social views. 3. Women authors, Arab—Egypt—Political and social views. 4. Politics and literature—Egypt—History—19th century. 5. Literature and society—Egypt—History—19th century. 6. Women and literature—Egypt—History—19th century. 7. Sex role—Egypt—History—19th century. I. Title. II. Series.

    PJ7864.A53Z69 2011
    892.7'8509—dc22   2010040369

A catalogue record of the book is available from the British Library.

Design by Scribe Inc.

First edition: April 2011

10 9 8 7 6 5 4 3 2 1

Printed in the United States of America.

To Mona, Pamela, and Amal

Contents

Note from the Editor

The Islamic world is home to a vast body of literary production in multiple languages over the last 1,400 years. To be sure, long before the advent of Islam, multiple sites of significant literary and cultural productions existed from India to Iran to the Fertile Crescent to North Africa. After the advent of Islam in mid-seventh century CE, Arabic, Persian, Urdu, and Turkish in particular have produced some of the most glorious manifestations of world literature. From prose to poetry, modern to medieval, elitist to popular, oral to literary, these literatures are in much need of a wide range of renewed scholarly investigation and lucid presentation.

The purpose of this series is to take advantage of the most recent advances in literary studies, textual hermeneutics, critical theory, feminism, postcoloniality, and comparative literature to bring the spectrum of literatures and cultures of the Islamic world to a wider reception and appreciation. Usually the study of these literatures and cultures is divided between classical and modern periods. A central objective of this series is to cross over this artificial and inapplicable bifurcation and abandon the anxiety of periodization altogether. Much of what we understand today from this rich body of literary and cultural production is still under the influence of old-fashioned Orientalism or post–World War II area studies perspectives. Our hope is to bring together a body of scholarship that connects the vast arena of literary and cultural production in the Islamic world without the prejudices and drawback of outmoded perspectives. Toward this goal, we are committed to pathbreaking strategies of reading that collectively renew our awareness of the literary cosmopolitanism and cultural criticism in which these works of creative imagination were conceived in the first place.

—Hamid Dabashi

Foreword

This project took more than ten years to finish. This was not merely a function of the work ethic of the author, but it reflected the complexity of the deconstruction of the life and work of ʿAʾisha Taymur, who stands at the center of this book. First, there was the need to step back and evaluate the canonical narratives that historians had offered of Taymur's life, which made the father outshine his daughter as he stepped forward to support her childhood desire to learn how to read and write in opposition to the wishes of her mother who favored embroidery as a prized feminine craft. Next, there was the need to learn more about Taymur's life beyond this pivotal moment that could serve as the basis of an alternative narrative that reflected the complex life of this nineteenth-century Egyptian woman who emerged as a prominent writer and poet. Finally, there was the huge task of closely examining her published Arabic body of work, which included a work of fiction, a social commentary on the changing gender relations and roles that men and women played in the family, and her poetry. Taymur also published her Turkish and Persian poetry titled *Shekufeh*[1] in Istanbul in the 1890s, but its discussion was outside this book's examination of the emergence of the Arabic language as one of the cornerstones of the nation-building process in Egypt.

Taymur's body of work presented another huge challenge to this researcher. Even though she was acknowledged by her male and female peers as well as most historians of nineteenth-century Egypt to be the most prominent woman literary writer, her published works did not get the serious study that they deserved. Mayy Ziyada, the Palestinian-born Lebanese national and resident of Egypt, wrote a biography of Taymur that was unusual in its discussion of Taymur's works. Its attitude toward them was typical of the attitude that the Egyptian literary establishment had toward nineteenth-century literary production: she examined them through a modernist lens that categorized them as "traditional" in form and in content and as such deserving to be dismissed. Students of Egyptian women's nineteenth-century history were more partial in their approach to Taymur's works, largely focusing on her introduction of *Nataʾij al-Ahwal fi al-Aqwal wa al-Afʿal al* (1887), in which she discussed her experiences as a young girl who was interested in learning how to read and write and how it challenged the gendered norms and roles in nineteenth-century Egypt and the impact that seclusion and the veil had on her literary education.

There were some limited attempts by Egyptian literary critics to place Taymur's writings, her work of fiction and poetry, in the literary contexts of the time but these usually concluded that her works either imitated those of literary men or were limited by her narrow gender concerns. Despite their partisan views, they encouraged me to develop this approach further by placing Taymur and her works in the literary as well as the political contexts of her time, especially the preoccupation with nation-building reflected in the use of Arabic, not Turkish, as the language of the nation and its literary, social and political production.

Given the fact that I am a political scientist by training, this meant considerable retooling to examine the gray area in which literature, politics, and gender contributed to nation-building. To add to the complexity of this interdisciplinary enterprise, there was the added challenge of how to approach the nineteenth century literary Arabic language that Taymur used in her works. While I am a native Arabic speaker, the Arabic language that I was taught in school during the middle of twentieth century was a distant descendant of modern standard Arabic that developed a century earlier as the language of the press and the modern public schools. It was not the language of literary production. A lot of literary, colonial and national abuse has been inflicted on that old literary language that has been described as flowery, redundant and preoccupied with musicality and cumbersome multiple levels of meaning. These were only some of the reasons that led Egyptian nationalists to attack and dismiss it. Add to this the colonial attacks on this language as antithetical to scientific and clear thinking dooming Arabic speakers to backwardness. The result was a prevalent literary tendency to dismiss and/or to display impatience with the works that utilized it as a medium of expression.

In response to this complex and partisan nineteenth century history of the Arabic language, I have approached Taymur's work, which attempted to simplify but to maintain its aesthetic linguistic ideals of expression, as another language that I needed to seriously learn and appreciate. I spent many summers pouring over Taymur's works of fiction, poetry, and social commentary with the help of Hans Wehr's *A Dictionary of Modern Written Arabic* (1974) to make sure that I have understood what Taymur was intending to say and appreciate the elegance and economy of the language that could convey that many levels of meaning. Not only did I take into account the most obvious meaning that most analysts stuck to in declaring that there was nothing new or original in her work, but I also tried to appreciate the fact that all literary writers had multiple audiences in mind. In addition to the average reader who was interested in an entertaining narrative, there were also other readers including members of the literary and political establishments who were looking for something more in these narratives and judged them in accordance with complicated standards including the light they shed on the concerns of their time. If one stopped at the surface meaning, then one could understand how many critics were happy with the caricature that confirmed its traditional character without realizing that their superficial and flat reading was the more serious problem. I cannot deny that this more complex way of reading was accompanied by high levels of frustration that prolonged the writing of this book, but at the same time, it increased my enjoyment of her works.

My dual goals were to make sure that I understood what Taymur was saying and that I did not miss any of the multiple levels of meaning that she might have intended. When my spirits faltered because every time I went back over the original texts I found new meaning, I told myself that if the students of English literature never tired of examining the works of William Shakespeare as one of their most distinguished writers, why should I display any impatience with the work of the most distinguished nineteenth-century Arabic woman writer? I am not comparing Taymur to Shakespeare; I am referring that to the fact that her work was to me as significant as that of Shakespeare to some English critics and that this required painstaking readings of her works. This argument helped get me through the many rewrites; and now that the manuscript is done, I can honestly say that I have done my best in presenting the many-layered aspects of her work.

Such a large and time-consuming project could not have been completed without the support of a community of colleagues, friends, and family. If the alternative narrative I offer of Taymur and her work is also about an emerging small community of women who allowed her to eventually emerge as one of the leading women writers of her time, this manuscript carries the imprints of a parallel community of women who helped me along the way. My colleague, Professor Denise Spellberg, offered many suggestions and readings that helped the presentation and discussion of Taymur's life and work. It is a pleasure to acknowledge many of these contributions at different parts of the manuscript. Her support was also invaluable in the search for publishers and maintaining momentum in the final phase.

Next, there was another friend and colleague whose presence throughout the long march to finish this manuscript is a pleasure to acknowledge. Pamela Sparr, who is an economist by training and whose work is mostly concerned with the comparative study of feminist economics in the United States and the developing world, listened with a great deal of enthusiasm to my attempt to make Taymur's life and work accessible to students of gender studies everywhere. She also volunteered to be a time keeper, setting deadlines for finishing different parts of the manuscript. Without this strict, but kind, time keeper, I doubt if I would have finished this project any sooner. If illness and unexpected personal developments made the project take longer than expected, Pam was not responsible for this delay and in fact her unwavering support during these struggles was critical.

My sister, Mona Hatem, played a different crucial role in getting me back to health at considerable physical and emotional stress. To her, I will forever and gladly be indebted. There were many others who supported me in this long and complicated personal journey: Jane Flax, Lamis Jarrar, Lana Shekim, Amina Khalifa, Amal Mahfouz, Afaf Mahfouz, Carl Schieren, Julia Jordan Zachery, Joyce Zonana, Hoda Elsadda, Adib Jarrar, and Grace Said. Last but not least, there were the members of a group to which I belonged during this period who kept me focused. They are Ayana, Don, Dorothy, Denise, Susan, Lannea, Shirley, and Holly.

Hoda Elsadda's support of this project took the special form of encouraging the Women and Memory Forum (WMF) in Cairo, Egypt, to organize a conference celebrating the centennial anniversary of Taymur's death in 2001. The conference discussions and papers provided new views and debates that were very useful. She also arranged for me to write Arabic introductions to the reprinting of ʿAʾisha Taymur's *Mirʾat al-Taʾmu fi al-Umur*, which was published by WMF in 2002, on the occasion of the conference on Taymur and *Nataʾij al-Ahwal fi al-Aqwal wa al-Afʿal*, which was published by the Egyptian Commission on Women in 2003. For this effort and support, I am very grateful. Salwa Ismail was helpful in a different kind of way. In one of her research trips to Cairo, I asked her to purchase and carry the very heavy Arabic dictionaries, *al-Mawrid*, *al-Munjid*, and Wehr's *A Dictionary of Written Arabic* from Cairo to Florence in 2001 to which she generously agreed. These dictionaries became my intimate and invaluable companions in the long process of understanding and appreciating Taymur's contribution to the beautiful literary Arabic language.

Last but not least, Professors Jane Flax of Howard University, Dina Khoury of George Washington University, Amira El Azhary Sonbol of Georgetown University, Omaima Abou Bakr of Cairo University, Jennifer Olmsted of Drew University, and Peter Gran of Temple University read various parts of the manuscript and generously offered feedback and suggestions. Obviously, I bear ultimate responsibility for this work, especially for any shortcomings it may have.

I wish to give special thanks to Professors Zehra Arat, Afaf Lutfi al-Sayyid Marsot, and Judith Tucker for reading the manuscript and agreeing to endorse it. Their works have influenced me throughout the years and it is a pleasure to acknowledge it in this context.

Last but not least, I am grateful to my editor Brigitte Shull at Palgrave for her support of the project. I also wish to thank Joanna Roberts, her editorial assistant at Palgrave, for making the process of preparing the manuscript for submission less cumbersome and volunteering to help with important details. I am also grateful to Dr. Mary-Jane Deeb, Chief of the African and the Middle East Division at the Library of Congress for organizing a presentation on `A'isha Taymur and for pointing me to the right departments to facilitate the acquisition of a resolution map of Egypt. My graduate student Ms. Ravza Kan Kavakci helped with taking a picture of Taymur from a poster.

Introduction

Why Study `A'isha Taymur?

This book reflects my interest in the study of modern, national, and feminist constructions of Egyptian women's history and their impact on the consciousness of its target audience. My initial interest in the study of the life and works of `A'isha Taymur was partly motivated by a strong sense of unease regarding the paradox at the heart of the modern construction of Egyptian women's history, which presented the educator Shaykh Rifa` al-Tahtawi (1801–1973) and judge Qasim Amin (1863–1908) and their discourses on the education and the liberation of women as its most important starting points. This fraternal construction provided a very good example of a new form of male domination over women, one that relied on the modern relationship between power and knowledge. Not only have their discourses on education and the liberation of women positively influenced women's lives, but they also acquired the status of unquestioned truths or knowledge about the path that women needed to take to play an active role in society. Many generations of women have embraced these truths as part of their struggle for women's rights and those who have sometimes wondered about the reasons behind the slow progress of Egyptian women in the twentieth century seldom blame these discourses for this problem.

More recently, the works of Beth Baron[1] and Marilyn Booth[2] have contributed a countermodernist narrative that focused attention on women's journals, published largely by Christian and Jewish Syrian women in Egypt starting in 1892 and into the 1920s, as an alternative starting point for Egyptian women's history with its expanded discussion of the way the education of women could serve the interests of the family. This narrative represented a marked improvement on the dominant one in its representation of women's views and concerns contributing a modernist agenda for women that preceded that offered by Qasim Amin at the end of the 1890s. The new focus on the intellectual production of the largely Christian and Jewish Syrian minority women in Egypt remained nevertheless partial in its reinforcement of the general impression that

Muslim women in general and Egyptian Muslims in particular lagged behind their Syrian counterparts in their contribution to the intellectual history of the period. The attention given to Zaynab Fawwaz, a Shiite woman from southern Lebanon, whose biographical dictionary (*al-Durr al-Manthur fi Tabaqat Rabat al-Khudur*) was considered to be important, was a rare exception.

The narratives offered by Syrian women and the male reformers defined gender in one-dimensional terms, focusing on either what women said about each other or what men said about women. Gender as a relational category is missing from the views of al-Tahtawi and Amin, which were oblivious of the views of women who actively supported the education of girls thus influencing the emerging public debates about women's changing roles in the family and society. Al-Tahtawi's book on the education of women, titled *al-Murshid al-Amin lil Banat wa al-Banin* (the faithful guide for girls and boys) published in 1873, was commissioned by Khedive Ismail after Jesham Effet Hanum, his third wife, used her own money to establish the first general public school for girls at al-Suyufiya in 1873.[3] Similarly, Amin's book, *Tahrir al-Mar'at* (The Liberation of the Woman), developed many of the themes that the women's journals presented—especially the importance of putting women's education in the service of the family and the nation—but was silent on their contribution. Similarly, the Syrian women who founded the women's journals discussed Oriental women's views on important issues of the day and the more advanced roles that Occidental women played in their societies, devoting little attention to the patriarchal context of the 1890s within which they operated.

While 'A'isha Taymur's name appears in all the Arabic and English books that deal with nineteenth-century Egypt as one of the pioneering women writers of the time, neither Arabic and English books gave attention to her views about the changes taking place in Egyptian society and politics. All focused on how a young Taymur (1840–1902) rejected her mother's attempts to teach her embroidery and expressed a desire to learn how to read and write, which was supported by her father. From these beginnings, she was said to emerge as a prominent literary writer in the last two decades of the nineteenth century. This abbreviated construction of Taymur's life and work, which first appeared in Fawwaz's *al-Durr al-Manthur fi Tabaqat Rabat al-Khudur* has withstood the test of time. While Fawwaz cited Taymur's major works of fiction, poetry and social commentary, she also included the short newspaper article Taymur published in 1887, which was titled "Girls' Education was Beneficial to Families,"[4] a theme that the Syrian women's journals developed in the 1890s as part of their discussion of the cult of modern domesticity. Even though Taymur discussed education in 1887 long before the publication of any of these journals, Fawwaz did not comment on its critique of the modern education of girls, which emphasized domesticity. This left the reader with a distinct impression that

Taymur shared the thrust of the views of her Syrian contemporaries overlooking the fact that she offered a novel critical perspective that departed from the dominant position taken in the debates of the time. Mayy Ziyada, the Palestinian-born and Lebanese literary critic who resided in Egypt for several decades starting in the first decade of the twentieth century, published a more detailed biography of Taymur in the 1920s that paid attention to the author's major works of fiction and commentaries only to dismiss them because of their traditional forms and themes. This paradoxical attitude toward Taymur, simultaneously presenting her as a pioneering figure, but dismissing her work because of its form, which many took to mean that she added nothing new to our understanding of Egyptian modernity other than a basic faith in the importance of women's education also puzzled me for a long time. Why did not Fawwaz and Ziyada, who were familiar with Taymur's work, use it to add to our understanding of the contributions that women writers made to the larger intellectual and political debates of a turbulent period in Egyptian history when the early process of nation-building was unfolding? The answer to the question required an understanding of the increasing power of the modernist discourse and its narrow construction of the concerns of women coupled with an appreciation of the implicit and sometimes explicit competition between Syrian and Egyptian women in claiming credit for articulating the concerns of women during the last two decades of the nineteenth century.

The modernist construction privileged the focus on women's contributions to the discussion of gender issues paying less attention to their views on other social and political issues of the day. Because Taymur's works coupled an interest in broader political and social issues of the day with gender concerns, they did not fit neatly in this narrow construction of women's interests. Equally important, modern historians and feminist writers represented the last two decades of the nineteenth century period as one in which modernization and modernist discourses were triumphant. They considered the Islamic discourse used by Taymur and other writers as a throwback to older forms that were unfit for the discussion of the important problems facing their society. These assumptions developed into articles of faith that fostered a less-than-serious attitude to Taymur's texts. As example, Ziyada dismissed Taymur's poetry as largely traditional themes even though they were different in form and content, misidentified some of the key characters of her work of fiction, *Nata'ij al-Ahwal fi al-Aqwal waal-Af'al,* and flattening her tale by treating it as derivative of the oral narratives that women told their children.[5]

In approaching Taymur's works of fiction, poetry, and social commentary, I experienced the weight of these constructions as well as their emphasis on textual analysis and literal readings made popular by Orientalist writers. By placing them in the context of the changes taking place in Egyptian society and the literary arena, one could see the connections between them and the century-long process of nation-building including increased interactions with the West coupled with internal transformations of the Arabic language and literature into markers of an "imagined national community" with new linguistic and socio-logical landscapes, development of new solidarities, and new forms of literary expression. Seen in this new light, I could see how *Nata'ij al-Ahwal fi al-Aqwal wa al-Af'al* transformed the familiar story of the adventures of a misguided prince who lost his throne into a discussion of some real as well as imagined challenges facing dynastic Islamic government as it sought to develop into a modern and national state. In *Hilyat al-Tiraz* (1892), Taymur produced poetry that linked her difficult personal journey as a woman writer and the ups and downs of the Egyptian society and government and how they contributed to the changing definitions of Islamic femininity, modernity, and politics. Finally, Taymur's *Mir'at al-Ta'mul fi al-Umur* (1892) discussed the sacred aspect shaping the developing modern national community offering a novel interpretation of the Qur'anic verses that dealt with male leadership over women in the family. This important work brought important responses from Shaykh Abdallah al-Fayumi, a member of the ulema class, and Abdallah al-Nadeem, one of the leading nationalist writers of this period.

The public debate that Taymur's views triggered in 1892 represented what should be legitimately considered as the first national public debate on gender issues and concerns. What was novel and exciting about this early debate was that women were not the objects of the discussion; Taymur took the initiative of bringing the changing gender relations in the family to the attention of the readers and examining the impact of the new materialism that fuelled male greed had on the crisis of the family. Her critical Islamic discourse added a new layer to our understanding of the social and intellectual history of the period and its articulation of the concerns of women. Its examination of the changing roles of men and women in the family preceded the debates initiated by the women's journals. Hind Noufal's *al-Fatat* (the young woman), the first journal, published and edited by a woman, appeared in November 1892 at the heel of the debate that Taymur's work provoked. The journal tried to capitalize on the resulting public interest in gender issues and concerns by providing women with a forum that continued their participation in public discussion of gender issues and concerns. Last but not least, the debate that Taymur's book triggered preceded the debate that followed the publication of Amin's book, *Liberation of the Woman* (1899), which most students of Egyptian women's history mark as a turning point, by seven years.

As a result, what began as an interest in the life and work of 'A'isha Taymur as one of the pioneering women of her time has evolved into an attempt to study how literature (broadly defined as the study of language, fiction, poetry, and social commentaries) played a role in the process of nation building, expanding the knowledge and understanding of the unfolding changes. It allowed one to capture the lively debates taking place among writers—both men and women—who continued to use a changing Islamic discourse and local literary forms (fiction and poetry) to address the problems of their society and how their contributions differed from the discourses, forms, and perspectives espoused by their older and younger (modernist) counterparts. While our knowledge of the latter group and their views is developed, our understanding of the Islamic discourse and its writers is very ideological and underdeveloped. Suffice it to say for now that during 1887–92, Taymur's Islamic discourse was still prominent and identified with high culture, addressing itself to modernity as a new cultural project in confident and unapologetic terms. It did not falter in the face of the new modern discourses but successfully adapted itself to the demands of the time, that is, the critique of key institutions like Muslim kingship, the relations between men and women in the family and the public arena (which the development of a new national imagined community strained), and modern practices that were replacing the old Islamic ones. Rather than close itself to change, Taymur's discourse opened itself to the discussion of political reform and the emphasis on the regulation of individual behavior as the basis of Islamic modernity.

There will be some who will object to the idea that this privileged Ottoman woman writer, who wrote in three languages (Turkish, Persian, and Arabic), could be made to represent the perspectives of Egyptian Muslim women and men or the new national community. Taymur's privileged class background and/or her Kurdish-Circassian ethnic roots were not very different from those of other poets like Mahmud Sami al-Barrudi and Ahmed Shawqi or writers like Qasim Amin, whose Egyptianess (i.e., the right to speak for or about the problems facing Egyptian society) or right to speak for other Egyptians or the modern national community were seldom questioned on ethnic or class grounds. Our understanding of the writings of Christian and Jewish Syrian middle-class women's of the views and concerns of women at the time were also not devalued because of their cultural, religious, and regional differences, which were a feature of Egyptian society. Taymur's ethnic and class difference should add to the discussion of that period. More important than her ethnic and class roots was the fact that her views were unquestionably Egyptian in their sharp focus on and rootedness in the changes taking place in Egyptian society, including the Arabic language, literature, the family and, government.

The above discussion on who is or is not part of the Egyptian national community provided another reason for the importance of studying Taymur's life and work and their connection to nation-building. As someone who lived through the reigns of Muhammed Ali, Ibrahim, Abbas I, Ismail, Twefik, and

Abbas II, Taymur's work provided considerable insight into the major cultural and political debates regarding the old and new communities in Egypt. Up until now, those who study the transition from a religious to national community in Egypt draw on the important work of Benedict Anderson's *Imagined Communities* to *substantively* emphasize the contributions that print capitalism/the press made to the definition of its concerns including a public voice for women.[6] No one has examined the role of literature to the process of nation-building even though Anderson claimed that the novel provided another technical means for "'re-presenting' the kind of imagined community that is the nation."[7]

In the fusion of the world within and without, Taymur's novel, poetry, and social commentary (*Nata'ij al-Ahwal fi al-Aqwal wa al-Af'al, Hilyat al-Tiraz,* and *Mir'at al-Ta'mul fi al-Umur*) showed how the newly developing national community did not immediately break with the Islamically imagined ones but continued to engage its institutions and discourse. Some of the works that used Anderson's work to examine the development of the history of Egyptian nationalism during the last two decades of the nineteenth century were largely focused on how to politically characterize the new community: was it narrowly territorial and modern or was it supraterritorial and premodern in its preoccupation with Islam and later on Arabism?[8] In constructing these dichotomous definitions of the types of historical communities that existed and/or were developing in Egypt at the time, it was easy for some to argue that because of the prominence of other types of community that were old and new, one should dismiss the relevance of Anderson's work. I do not find this particular reading of Anderson's work and Egyptian history to be terribly useful or persuasive because it overlooked how his discussions of the different models of national community were less interested in the search for neat or abrupt breaks between the old and new types of communities and more interested in the hybrid dynamics of change. The Egyptian national community represented by Taymur elegantly captured the transition from the old to the new community including the convergence of Islam, Ottomanism, Arabism, and the more narrowly defined Egyptianess as overlapping currents that one would expect in a big picture. The silence of most historians, who deal with this particular historical period on the presence and participation of women of all classes in the events associated with nation-building, indicated that it was not the history of this period that was fraternal but our modern constructions of it.

There was some debate on the nature of the problems with this modern construction. Some of those whose work borrowed Anderson's emphasis on the role of the print media to suggest the women's journals were engaged in the rethinking of the roles that women and the family were to play in the nation,[9] made a similar observation. Baron noted that despite the contributions made by the women's journals, the nationalist narratives of that period continued to push women into the background or simply leave them out.[10] Jean Said Makdisi articulated the problem of omission in discursive terms, pointing out that "women in Arab society were active and present and that it is our modern reading that reduces their impact."[11] In this formulation, she rejected the assumption that modernity was postpatriarchal underlining its analytical tendency to devalue women and their activities in many different ways.

This presented one with yet another paradox in the discussion of nineteenth-century Arab women's history. Contrary to the widespread notion that modern society was sympathetic to women's emancipation, its construction of the older religious and dynastic communities in Egypt were problematic in their rendering of women as secondary actors, declaring them and their societies as traditional. A close examination of the well-documented Egyptian case suggested that there was nothing traditional in the way women of different classes participated in the social and the political ferment that accompanied the national revolution led by General Ahmed `Urabi from 1880 to 1882. Working-class women were visibly present in their assistance of the Egyptian army's effort to push the British back. Some middle-class women attended the speeches of Gamal al-Din al-Afghani, one of the political thinkers of the revolution.[12] Royal princesses were divided in their support of Khedive Tewfik and his nationalist rival, General `Urabi.[13]

Unlike many other women writers of her time, Taymur's engagement represented an expanded definition and discussion of gender roles during this period. She was not only interested in the critical discussion of the private roles that women played in that community but also insisted that they take on new ones in the literary and political arenas. She was as interested and preoccupied with the gender roles of men. In assuming the roles of writer and chronicler of the changes taking place in the community, Taymur devoted considerable attention to the old and new basis of fraternal relations among men. In *Nata'ij al-Ahwal fi al-Aqwal wa al-Af`al*, Taymur wrote very eloquently about the positive and negative aspects of these fraternal relations and their impact on the national community and women. While her work of fiction underlined the need for women to participate in the process of nation-building, Taymur was clear that the context within which this occurred was within largely horizontal fraternities that devalued women's contributions, denying them access to the important resources of the community including the right to guide and lead it.

In the chapters that follow, I hope to use the life and work of `A'isha Taymur to offer a different appreciation of the role that gender and literature played in the conceptualization of early nation-building. Chapter 1 will examine the way the history of the Taymur family, its men and women, was shaped by service in changing dynastic governments at the Ottoman center and its Egyptian periphery and how this shaped the aristocratic class within which she was born.

The construction of Taymur's life will follow covering her childhood and adult struggles to emerge as a writer and a poet.

Chapter 2 discusses the role that literature (language, translations, and *maqamas* [literary narrative]) played in the transition from an Ottoman centered community into an increasingly narrow national one in nineteenth-century Egypt. As part of this transition, there was a change in the power relations between Turkish and Arabic (and to a lesser extent Persian) as literary and official languages, the new importance accorded to European languages through translations, the debate on the need for the simplification of language and writing styles, and finally the experimentation with hybrid literary forms.

Chapter 3 examines how `A'isha Taymur's *Nata'ij al-Ahwal fi al-Aqwal wa al-Af'al*, used empathy and/or identification with its characters to examine the changing bases of Islamically imagined communities. It discussed the manifestations of the crisis of dynastic government and that of Islamic society, the reforms needed to develop new forms of solidarity between rulers and ruled including Islamic fraternal ones, and the use of heterosexuality to strengthen the government and the family.

Chapter 4 will turn its attention to *Mir'at al-Ta'mul fi al-Umur* and its use of gender relations to identify the changes taking place in the national community. It also addresses the sacred dimension of nation-building through its discussion of the Qur'anic verses that defined the rights that men had over women and those that women had over men. The booklet provoked a hostile response from Shaykh Abdallah al-Fayumi and a positive response from Abdallah al-Nadim, a nationalist figure and social commentator.

Chapter 5 will look at Taymur's collected Arabic poems titled *Hilyat al-Tiraz* and the way they connected her personal struggles with the larger forces of change and opposition within the community. In this discussion, Taymur identified herself as a member of the Arab literary community and its small sisterhood of prominent women poets. Her poems offered a window on the many changes taking place in poetry, Egyptian society and politics, the views of modernity, and the definition of Islamic femininity.

In the conclusion, I will discuss how Taymur used her work of fiction, social commentary and poetry to expand the definition of the nation-building process to include different social classes, ethnic groups and women of different generations and nationalities. In this sincere effort, she was able to transform her very narrow social class roots putting them into the service of the larger community. As such, she deserved, not just her poetry, the title of the "Finest of Her Class," which was one translation of the title of her poetry, *Hilyat al-Tiraz*.

CHAPTER 1

The Changing Islamic-Ottoman World of the Taymur Family

Historical Overview

Egypt became an Ottoman province in 1517 continuing to be formally part of the Ottoman world until military defeat in World War I, put a dramatic end to the Ottoman Empire. During these five centuries, the Ottoman system of government in Egypt relied on the appointment of representatives of the sultan whose primary obligations were to collect annual tribute[1] and the incorporation of the Mamluks—the militarily trained former white freed slaves whose political dynasty the Ottomans overthrew in 1517—in the new system as tax collectors. In contradistinction to this Turkish-speaking political elite, a local elite made up of ulema (learned men of Islam), large merchants, and affluent farmers had a limited degree of power over a largely peasant population.[2]

The eighteenth century witnessed the rise of internal and international actors that significantly changed the substantive operation of this Ottoman system. Early in the century, the Mamluks reclaimed their positions of military and political power effectively usurping the power of the Ottoman governor if not his title.[3] The competition among different Mamluk military households contributed to political instability and a weak decentralized form of government. Napoleon's French expedition to Egypt in 1798 contributed a further blow to this system. Not only did the French expedition militarily and politically challenge Ottoman claim to the province, but it also undermined the military and political position of the Mamluks. France's larger political goal was to establish an effective presence in the region that would get them to threaten British control of India, signaling French and British imperial competition in nineteenth-century Egypt. The British were responsible for the destruction of the French fleet leading to their withdrawal in 1801 but were unsuccessful in filling the chaotic political vacuum they left behind. Ottoman attempt to reassert control during the next four years of political chaos ended in 1805 with their consent to appoint Muhammad Ali, an officer in the Albanian Ottoman contingency, as viceroy (*wali*) with the support and pressure of a local coalition made up of large merchants, the ulema, and the urban poor.[4]

Once in power, Ali turned against his former enemies and allies, consolidating his control over the province and developing a centralized system of government that replaced the decentralized and feeble eighteenth-century government.[5] Despite the brutality of the new ruler, his dynasty gradually established bases for its legitimacy that were derived from an ambitious modernization project that reorganized the economy in the form of state monopolies (which were eventually replaced by private property), a strong army, and modern systems of education and health care. Muhammad Ali's political and territorial ambitions at the expense of the Ottoman Empire were frustrated by international powers, which used the treaty of 1841 to impose military, economic, and political restrictions on him in exchange for the right of the eldest member of his family to rule over Egypt as an Ottoman province. This dynastic rule was changed in the 1867, when Khedive Ismail successfully lobbied the Ottoman sultan to make succession hereditary among his children. The dynasty continued to claim the right to rule Egypt even after the British occupied Egypt in 1882 and exercised colonial control over the country until 1952 when a military coup abolished the monarchy and ended the system of colonial control.

The Taymur Family in the Nineteenth-Century Ottoman World

The history of the Muhammad Ali dynasty was of central importance for the understanding of the fortunes of the Taymur family in Egypt by providing a distinct political context within which `A'isha Taymur emerged as a prominent writer in the last two decades of the nineteenth century. The role that she played in the building of a modern national community distinguished her from other Turco-Circassian women who had played other key roles in the previous century. Elements of continuity and change will help one develop a nuanced appreciation of the gendered aspects of the complex transition to nation building reflected in Taymur's life and works.

In the far flung multiethnic Ottoman world of the early nineteenth century, Muhammad Ali (who hailed from Kavala in Macedonia) met Muhammad Taymur (who came from Kurdish Mosul in northern Iraq) in Egypt as members of the various Ottoman forces recruited to restore imperial control of the province. According to one source of the early history of Muhammad Ali's family, its ethnic roots could be traced back to the Anatolian heartland and Kurdistan,[6] establishing a loose Kurdish connection with Muhammad Taymur.

Ethnic roots aside, the Taymur family fortunes in Egypt were shaped by the alliance between the two men to ensure Muhammad Ali's ascent to and consolidation of his position of power. Personal loyalty to the new ruler simultaneously delivered great rewards and perils as the title *waliyy al-ni`am* (translated from Arabic to mean "the source from whom all blessings flowed") that Ali acquired during this period indicated.[7] The personal and the political relationship between different members of the Taymur family and rulers of the dynasty were key in shaping the careers of `A'isha Taymur's grandfather and father and her affiliations with the ruling family influencing her views of government and political reform.

Initial research into the Taymur family, its history, and its social standing yielded nothing. The biographical dictionaries of nineteenth-century Egypt did not shed any light on Ismail Pasha Taymur, `A'isha Taymur's illustrious father, whose name did not appear in any of them. While the biographies of `A'isha Taymur[8] and her younger stepbrother Ahmed Taymur[9] were prominently presented, they did not shed any new information on the family history. In one of the biographies of Ahmed, who became a prominent student of the history of the Arabic language and its literature in twentieth-century Egypt, a footnote reported that his grandfather was a member of the Ottoman army that arrived in Egypt following the end of the French expedition who quickly became a close associate of Ali and helped in the effort to physically liquidate the Mamluks. Later on, Muhammad Taymur was said to have been appointed as provincial governor and died in 1847, a year before Ali himself expired. The son, Taymur's father, was said to have served in various administrative positions in the governments of Abbas I, Said, and Ismail and died in 1872.[10]

A closer review of Ahmed's many publications yielded a relatively detailed history of the family tucked away in one of his obscure books titled *Lai`b al-`Arab* (The Pastimes of the Arabs). It situated the Ottoman history of the family in Arab cultural and historical contexts reflecting Ahmed's personal interest in the history of the Arabs, their language, and cultural history. This partisan construction was useful because it provided evidence of multiple definitions of community in nineteenth- and twentieth-century Egypt that was Ottoman, Arab-Islamic, and national. It also offered a somewhat reliable account of dates, places, and descriptions of the bureaucratic journeys that the men of his family took in the Ottoman imperial and provincial governments.

I will begin with that history, then turn to the discussion of `A'isha Taymur's biography: her early personal and social rebellion against the old definitions of femininity associated with an older definition of community and how she eventually emerged as a prominent writer in a new Egyptian national community of the 1880s and the 1890s. Finally, I will discuss Zaynab Fawwaz's canonical construction of her life and work, which Ahmed simultaneously relied on and selectively employed, to reveal some of the discourses of that period and the ambivalence that her family felt toward her distinguished status.

In the construction of the history of the family and that of `A'isha Taymur, a serious problem emerged relating to exact dates of important events. Zaynab Fawwaz, Ahmed Taymur, and `A'isha's grandson relied on dates that were derived from the lunar Islamic calendar, which was different from the solar Christian. Because knowledge of the month was often missing, precise dates could not be offered. The absence of precise dates for the birth, death, and marriage of key figures in her life signified that birth, death, and marriage certificates were not yet instituted leaving one reliant on the private memories of family members. With the exception of the dates relating to the birth and death of Ismail, Ahmed, and `A'isha, all the other dates relating to Taymur's grandfather, husband, and daughter (Tawhida) were approximate dates.

There was also confusion about the dates of some of her publications. On my copy of *Nata'j al-Ahwal*, there was a library call number that listed the date of publication as 1887. Another copy of this work that was reprinted in 2003 by the National Commission for Women in Egypt listed the date of original publication as 1888. In addition, there was no information about when Taymur's collected Turkish and Persian poems, *Shekufeh*, was printed. One can assume that it was printed before 1894 because Zaynab Fawwaz's *al-Durr al-Manthur fi Tabaqat Rabat al-Khudur*, published in 1894, reported it was already out at the Ottoman center.

Another problem emerged in the construction of a family tree for the conjugal families of `A'isha Taymur, her father and grandfather. She was said to have had a large family with many sons and daughters. Yet one is only able to identify the roles played by Tawhida (her eldest child) and Mahmud (her youngest son), because they played important roles in her personal history. One does not also know how many wives and concubines her grandfather, father, and even her husband had. With modernization, there was increased silence on these perceived, premodern practices resulting into what could at best be a partial family tree where some useful personal information was missing.

A Nineteenth-Century Taymur Family Tree

Muhammad Taymur (1767/8?–1847/8?)

|

Ismail Taymur (1814–72)

|

`A'isha Taymur (1840–1902), `Iffat (n.d), Ahmed Taymur (1871–1930)

A List of `A'isha Taymur's Publications and Their Dates

1. *Nata'ij al-Ahwal fi al-Aqwal wa al-Af`al,* a work of fiction, published in 1887/88
2. *Mir'at al-Ta'mul fi al-Umur,* a social commentary, published in 1872
3. *Hilyat al-Tiraz,* the collected Arabic poems, published in 1892
4. *Shekufeh,* the collected Turkish and Persian poems, published before 1894 without any exact date.

The Taymur Men's Careers in the Ottoman Military and Bureaucracies

At the outset of this section, let me elaborate on the approach that I used in developing the history of this family and the periods within which they lived. I have collected as many basic facts as are presently available. Because there were only few primary sources provided by Ahmed and `A'isha Taymur, I have also had to exhaustively examine many secondary sources with the hope that they might provide some useful leads or details that can be helpful in fleshing out the author and her life. Needless to say, I am aware of some of the perils associated with this secondary data. For example, there were claims that after Taymur's marriage, the couple settled in Istanbul for a while returning at a later date. I was inclined to dismiss this claim because if it were true the accounts provided by Ahmed and his sister would have mentioned it.

In putting this material together, I have opted for the development of an interpretive reading of her life and that of her family that coupled what was explicitly mentioned along with some of the significant silences that underlined the blind spots of dominant constructions and narratives. For example, the dominant construction of Taymur's life gives great importance to the negative role played by her mother, who was a white freed slave concubine, in opposing her ambitions, but there was no serious attempt to understand how her slave status might have offered a rational understanding of her and her daughter's histories. Her mother's slave status provided one with an opportunity to shed light on the complicated histories of women in aristocratic families. In this interpretive reading, my primary goal was to provide as many layered explanations as were possible for understanding what was specific about these nineteenth-century figures capturing elements of continuity and change. Similarly, there was very limited discussion of Taymur's husband and their relationship. So one was left with the need to try to make sense of this silence.

I am not oblivious to the hazards of this interpretive approach. In a review of an early chapter that I contributed on ʿA'isha Taymur to an edited volume, one critic pointed out that I have no *empirical* way of knowing what were the motives behind the actions of Taymur's mother.[11] It is true that very few slave voices were ever allowed or able to speak to us directly and hence the historical exclusion of their voices from history. For a long time, the lack of empirical evidence and/or primary sources led to the silence on slavery as a local institution and the voices of slave women in particular. I am happy to report, however, that there are presently many innovative approaches that attempt to use census figures and missionary accounts to indirectly reconstruct some of the lives and voices of African slave women in Egypt.[12] I would like to add to them the vast feminist literature that examines the psychodynamics of mothering as the historical task that patriarchal societies have assigned women,[13] making sure that such interpretations were placed in the context of this period, culture and family to shed light on various dilemmas and views. Whenever "reliable empirical" evidence was available I stuck with it and when the evidence became murky, I offered the best interpretation that fit the material. Whether or not this interpretive reading worked will be up to the reader to judge.

The biography of al-Sayyid Muhammad Taymur al-Kashif, the founder of the family in Egypt, provided sketchy but essential information about the ethnic and geographic roots of the family. He was born to a Kurdish family from the town of Baqarat Gulan that was located in the Ottoman province of Mosul in the north of modern day Iraq. Ahmed Taymur suggested that the fortunes of the town and the family declined in the eighteenth century following the building of the city of al-Sulaymaniya. During this period, Muhammad Taymur had a serious falling out with his older brother and joined the Ottoman army.[14] There was little else that was said about the nature of the conflict or the family he left behind. In an attempt to fill in the blanks in this family history, Ahmed claimed that the Kurds were known for their pride in Arab ancestry, a trait that Arab historians, like Ibn al-Kalbi (819), Ibn Khallikan (1211/12),[15] who were masters of Arab genealogies, pointed out their continuous ancestral links to Qahtan in the Arabian Peninsula as descendants of Ibn `Amer Ma' al-Sama' of Aden.[16] In contrast to this view, contemporary students of the Kurdish history offer an alternative construction of their ethnic roots suggesting that the "the Kurds have claimed kinship with the ancient Medes, one of the founding races of the Persian Empire and their language with its many dialectics, is related to Persian."[17]

Ahmed claimed that his Kurdish family maintained another honorable link to Arabness (`uruba) and that is that the names of the different family members in old papers and and important documents appeared with the title of al-Sayyid attached to them. This identified them as members of the al-sadda—that is, those who claim to be descendants of Prophet Muhammad's family. Taymur's grandfather reinvented this bit of family history by carving his name as al-Sayyid Muhammad Taymur on the marble door of the mansion he built for his family in the neighborhood of Darb Sa`ada in Cairo in 1814–15.[18]

Recent studies of the history of Ottoman Mosul shed more specific light on this period that might help explain the changing fortunes of the ancestral town that influenced Muhammad Taymur's decision to join the "Ottoman" army. According to Dina Rizk Khoury's study of Mosul, its Kurdish tribes were located in frontier areas representing the eastern boundaries of the Ottoman Empire constantly contested by the Ottoman and Persian armies. In the eighteenth century, major confrontations between the two armies took place in Kurdish territories. There were also many campaigns that were conducted by the governor of Mosul to control the tribal populations in the mountains and plains around the city.[19] This contributed to the militarization of rural frontier population and opened up seasonal employment opportunities within different armies for young men with few or limited prospects.[20]

This background history explained Ahmed's elliptical reference to how the rise of the city of Sulaymaniya contributed to the decline of Baqarat Gulan as an important fortress town where the military contracted rural soldiers for the defense of Ottoman lands. According to Khoury, the increased level of militarization throughout the eighteenth century established the partial Ottomanization (i.e., control) of Mosuli frontier.[21]

While Muhammad Taymur's birth date was not known, his grandson claimed that he died in 1847–48 at the age of 80. This indicated that he might have been born around 1767–68 and became an adult during 1780s. While there was no specific data to help one reconstruct his early military career, it was safe to assume that he joined some of the provincial armies in the Mosul prov-ince gaining military experience in the activities that Khoury described.[22] Other sources on the history of the family suggested that he then acquired a position in the army of the viceroy of Acre (Ottoman Palestine)[23] before going to Egypt in 1802. His service in these different provincial armies served the interest of their rulers by helping them control their subjects and defending their lands against local and external threats proved helpful to his Egyptian experience. According to Ahmed, his grandfather was a member of the Ottoman force that was sent to Egypt following the departure of the French expedition in 1801. Afaf Lutfi al-Sayyid Marsot's discussion of this period mentioned that Khurshid Pasha who was appointed as the Ottoman governor of Egypt then "called in around 5000 troops from Syria, the redoubtable Delhis or 'madmen' who were notorious for their high astrakhan bonnets and their ferocity. Kurdish, Druze and Matawilla in origin, they were dreaded by the local population and by the Albanian troops as well."[24] Because Muhammad was in the service of the vice-roy of Acre during this period, there was a strong possibility that he was among the forces that were sent to Egypt.

There he met Muhammad Ali, who was a junior officer of the Albanian contingent sent from Kavala[25] and become close friends with him. When Ali was appointed viceroy, he promoted Taymur to a variety of military positions becoming one of his senior loyal officers playing a prominent role in the bloody liquidation of the leaders of the Mamluks, the former military rulers of Egypt and political rivals of the new viceroy, which took place in the citadel in 1811. He participated in putting down other popular rebellions (*fitan*) during this period. Other military exploits included serving as one of the experienced senior officers of the army led by Toussun Pasha, one of Muhammad Ali's sons, to fight the Wahabis in the Arabian Peninsula. The defeat of that army provoked the anger of the viceroy, who refused to grant his son's army permission to return to Egypt leaving it stranded until he pardoned its members.[26]

Taymur also held a variety of administrative positions including being the police chief of a subprovince in al-Sharqiya eventually becoming administrative governor (*kashif*), a title he retained even after he left that position.[27] When al-Hijaz was finally brought under Egyptian control by Ibrahim Pasha, another one of Muhammad Ali's sons and eventually his crown prince, Taymur was appointed as the prince of al-Medina, where he stayed for five years. Upon his return to Egypt, he retired from government service. By then, he was of advanced age so the state assigned him an adequate pension. Despite his retire-ment, his grandson claimed that he remained on friendly terms with the viceroy and his heir who continued to turn to him for advice. During this period, he developed a new reputation for being devout and desirous of God's forgiveness after his long (very bloody) military career. While he was considered to be a just governor, his grandson conceded that he was also known for his severity, which his grandson rationalized as a characteristic of the rulers of this period.[28] At this point in the narrative, Ahmed chose to comment on the meaning and ethnic roots of the surname of the family. He stated that Taymur was a Turkish word that meant iron and that the common folk (al-`amma) in Egypt had difficulty correctly spelling it. He included in his definition of common folk who had problems with the name prominent Egyptians like the historian Abdelrahman al-Jabarti, Ali Mubarak Pasha, and the editors of the *Egyptian Gazette (al-Waqa'i al-Misriya)*. Al-Jabarti referred to the role of Tamer *kashif* in the massacre of the Mamluks in 1811.[29] Similarly, Ali Mubarak Pasha, who was the minister of education and public works and also the author of an important book about Cairo, listed his father's mansion with its big garden as the belonging to Ismail Pasha Tamr.[30] Finally, the *Egyptian Gazette* also misspelled his grandfather's name when it announced on that "Muhammad `Ali Pasha convened a Council that included the literary men in official positions, the ulema and the heads of all the sub provinces and the provincial leaders to consult them in government matters . . . The Council included Tamur Agha, chief of police (ma'mur) of a county in al-Sharqiya province."[31]

After having initially put considerable emphasis on the family's Kurdish-Arab ancestry, this discussion of its Turkish surname set it apart from other Egyptians providing Taymur with a way to suggest that the family was identified by others, not to mention identified itself, as part of the Turco-Circassian elite. His grandfather's advancement in bureaucratic ranks clearly depended on his Turkishness and/or membership in Turkish-speaking aristocracy or ruling class.

Ismail Taymur's mother was `A'isha al-Siddiqa (the truthful one or the true friend), the daughter of Abdelrahman Effendi al-Istanboli, who was one of the senior clerks of Sultan Selim III's Imperial Ottoman Council (al-Diwan al-Sultani). `A'isha al-Siddiqa was also the name of `A'isha bint Abi Bakr, the wife of Prophet Muhammad, and the daughter of the first caliph of the Islamic state who became a leading authority on the prophetic tradition. This provided another opportunity for Ahmed to emphasize the religious standing of his family through his maternal grandmother. Her father was described as a nobleman from a good family who shared the sultan's interest in reform, was treated as a confidant, and was someone whom the sultan could depend. When Sultan Selim was deposed and killed, al-Istanboli became a political fugitive who was forced to flee to Egypt. This harrowing experience took a toll on his health. Upon reaching Egypt, he was well received by Muhammad Ali, who hosted him in one of his palaces. Soon thereafter, Sultan Mustafa, Selim's successor, was deposed and replaced by Sultan Mahmud, who invited the supporters of Selim to return to government. Al-Istanboli politely declined, citing ill health and the benefits it derived from Egyptian climate. The sultan excused him and ordered that he be given a salary by the Egyptian provincial government.

Muhammad Ali expected al-Istanboli to work for the salary, offering him different public posts in his government, but al-Istanboli again declined citing his health and pointing out that it would be inappropriate to accept a position in provincial government after turning down the sultan's offer. He petitioned the viceroy to bring his family (wife and two children) from Turkey. This request coincided with the viceroy's plan to send for his own family and so it was that the two families were brought to Egypt together on the same ship arriving in May 1809–1810.

When an imperial decree ordered the marriage of al-Istanboli's daughter to one of Ali's trusted men and for the Egyptian treasury to bear the costs of setting up the new household, Ali chose Muhammad Taymur al-Kashif as a husband to al-Istanboli's daughter. What Ahmed did not discuss, as part of this account was that his grandfather must have been at least 42 years old at the time and most probably already married with children. His history as a soldier of fortune added other reasons for al-Istanboli's displeasure. His death shortly before the wedding of his young daughter to Taymur was attributed to ill health, but it was not much improved by the choice of a son in law who was much older than his daughter and the social disparity in the backgrounds of the bride and groom. This cast a gloomy cloud over the occasion.

For Muhammad Taymur, marriage to the young daughter of a former official of the Ottoman Imperial Council enhanced his status. The couple soon had a son, Ismail, who was born on November 8, 1814. While his son had other brothers and sisters, confirming the speculation that his father most probably had other wives and children, Ismail was said to be the only one who survived. He was brought up in an affluent environment and showed an early interest in learning and literature. His father hired tutors to teach him Arabic and Islamic sciences. Ismail Taymur also learned Turkish and Persian with the help of Abdelrahman Sami, a member of one of the large groups of ambitious young Turks who came to Egypt in search of their fortune in the early years of Muhammad Ali's modernizing government. Later on, Sami became a cabinet minister at the Ottoman government after the exodus of many members of that cohort during the reign of Abbas I. Ismail also learned different types of calligraphy from the Egyptian Ibrahim Effendi Mu'anis, showing a particular aptitude and excellence in this field. Because of his education, which mixed important regional and local languages along with the skill of Turkish composition that surpassed most of his peers, Ali appointed Ismail as his private clerk or secretary whose duties included the review of the important documents, correspondences of the viceroy, and passing on orders to the members of the royal council (*diwan*).

Thus began Ismail's extended journey within the Egyptian bureaucracy, which was facilitated by Turkish ethnicity and language that confirmed his membership in the Ottoman political community in Egypt. While knowledge in Arabic language did not provide a significant stepping-stone, it must have proved useful when Ismail went on to become deputy governor of al-Sharqiya province and then governor of other provinces including al-Gharbiya, the largest of all provinces, which was his last assignment. Despite the importance of these administrative provincial positions contributing to the expansion of family wealth and landholdings, Taymur decided to return to Cairo and government service.

His decision coincided with the retirement of Muhammad Ali from government service and the transfer of power to his son Ibrahim. Ahmed described this period to be particularly difficult with the government facing multiple problems including the accumulation of court cases at the Legal Society (*al-Jam'iya al-Haqanniya*) created in 1842 to prosecute senior government officials charged with legal offenses and other crimes that the governing council referred to it.[32] As such, it served as the highest legal body in the land. When the society was reorganized and renamed the Second Legal Society (*al-Jam'iya al-Haqanniya al-Thaniya*) in 1847–48, Ismail was appointed as its president.

With the ascent of Abbas I (1848–54) to power, Ismail was promoted to a more important government position: becoming a deputy of the royal council of the ruler (*Diwan Katkhuda*), which placed him close to the center of power. It should be remembered here that according to Ahmed, his grandfather fought alongside Prince Ahmed Toussun, Abbas's father, in the Hijaz. It was not surprising, therefore, that his father would reach new heights under the reign of the new ruler. Ahmed opined that the position held by his father during this period was equivalent to being prime minister (i.e., having the most important say in government after the viceroy). Unfortunately, Ismail's fortunes changed as a result of a slander by another bureaucrat that contributed to his dismissal from the council. When the falsity of the slander was exposed, Abbas asked him to return to government service but to a less prestigious position: manager of his royal personal finances (*Khasatuhu al-Musamah al-Da'ira al-'Asfiya*).[33] He remained in that position until the death of Abbas and was able to rise even further during the reign of Sa'id (1854–63) becoming the head of the royal council in 1858–59. When the viceroy publicly scolded him in the presence of other members of the council on some issue, Ismail took offense and resigned his post. Despite the repeated attempts by the viceroy to make him reconsider his resignation, he declined government service.

During the reign of Khedive Ismail (1863–79), Ismail Taymur was not able to secure a suitable government position because he suspected the khedive harbored an ill opinion of him. This led to his effective retirement: spending his time managing his many farms and enjoying his large collections of books. A chance encounter with the khedive changed all this when the khedive bestowed on Ismail the title of Pasha and asked him to be part of the personal entourage (*al-Khasa*) of crown prince Muhammad Tewfik. According to Ahmed, his father reluctantly accepted the post even though he no longer enjoyed government service, preferring instead to enjoy his books and relative isolation (*al-`Uzla*). He denied the rumor his father had said when told of his new appointment: "Is it possible that after [distinguished] government service that included being the head of the Royal Council that I be made a babysitter of children!"[34] He acknowledged his ambivalent connection with the crown prince by naming his only son—born on November 6, 1871—Ahmed Tewfik. Ismail was reported to have died while praying at the palace of the crown prince on December 27, 1872.

In addition to this distinguished history of government service, Ismail was said to have had a reputation for eloquence in more than one language that led to his being seconded more than once to publicly read imperial decrees and important government announcements in the gatherings of the notables. He also enjoyed the frequent company of learned men and possessed many valuable books.[35]

With this detailed family background, it is possible to turn to `A'isha Taymur's autobiographical discussion of her life, which appeared in the introduction to *Nata'ij al-Ahwal fi al-Aqwal wa al-Af`al* (1887) describing the internal and external journeys that led to her interest in literature, access to an unusual education and the complex adult struggles that shaped her emergence as a leading woman writer and poet in the 1880s and the 1890s. This section will also use the translation of Taymur's introduction to her Persian and Turkish poetry titled "Shukufeh," included in Mayy Ziyada's biography of the author along with the personal account of Taymur's grandson of her seven years of mourning her beloved daughter Tawhida, as multiple primary sources for the construction of her life.

In Her Own Words: `A'isha Taymur's Personal and Public Journeys

Childhood

`A'isha Taymur was born in an affluent and cultured environment in 1840. She was the eldest of three daughters that her father, Ismail Taymur, had with her mother, a freed white Circassian slave. One of her sisters died at an early age as one of Taymur's elegies indicated. There was no discussion of other children in her family until 1871 when a very elderly Ismail fathered a son, Ahmed, before his death in 1872. At the time, Taymur was 32 years, indicating that her brother was most probably from a different mother about which we know very little.

The fact that her father did not have a son until late in his life affected Taymur's upbringing entitling her, as we shall see, to the status of an honorary son explaining her access to the very unusual literary education reserved to males. Because of the limited knowledge that students of nineteenth-century women have of the way young girls were socialized in the Egyptian upper class, I will rely on extensive quotes from Taymur's introductions to her books in the description of her family environment that influenced early interest in literature.

Said the broken-winged `A'isha-`Asmat, daughter of the late Ismail Pasha Taymur,

> When my cradle days were over and I began to move around, to distinguish the sources of temptation from those of rationality and to be aware of what was forbidden by my father and grandfather, I found myself fondly preoccupied with suckling the narratives/accounts (*al-akhbar*) of nations (*al-ummam*). My maturing energy tended towards investigating the accounts (*'ahadith*) of those who preceded us a long time ago. I was enamored of the nightly chats of elderly women [in my family] who recounted the best stories/histories (*al-akhabar*). I was fascinated by the strange twists of fate. To the best of my abilities, I contemplated their meaning whether it was serious or funny. I also selected and committed the best of them to memory. At that age, I had no other capability but listening. I [also] did not have access to other forms of enjoyment and entertainment.
>
> When my mind was ready to develop and my capabilities were receptive, my mother, the goddess of compassion and virtue and the arsenal of knowledge and wonder, may God shelter her with his grace and forgive her, approached me with the tools of embroidery and weaving. She was diligent in teaching me. She worked hard to explain things cleverly and clearly. But I was not receptive. I would not improve in these feminine crafts. I used to flee from her like a prey seeking to escape the net.
>
> [At the same time] I would look forward to attending the gatherings of prominent writers without any awkwardness. I found the sound of pen on paper the most beautiful . . . and I became convinced that membership in this group was the most abundant blessing. To satisfy my longing, I would collect any sheets of paper and small pencils and then I would go to a place away from everyone and imitate the writers in their scribe. Hearing the sound of pencil on paper made me happy.
>
> When my mother would find me, she would scold and threaten me. This only increased my rejection and inadequacy at embroidery.[36]

The first story Taymur shared with the reader in her book of fictional tales was her own. Her recollection of her childhood indicated that members of her family were collectively engaged in teaching its young girls different things. While her father and grandfather taught her what was forbidden (ethical rules), the elder women of her family piqued her imagination with their oral narratives that explored *al-akhbar* (popular histories of ancient nations). She owed her interests in these two blended genres (history and literature) to these women who were skilled storytellers, entertainers, and transmitters of cultural history. Their tales were specifically concerned with the accounts of nations (*akhbar al-umam*), which is different from the "political chronicles" of the eighteenth and the nineteenth centuries. While the latter is explicitly political and concerned itself with dynastic history, the former is concerned with the nation's cultural history as well as that of other ancient societies that shared similar values and social wisdom derived from their lived experiences. In addition to providing a source of entertainment, these tales led Taymur to carefully listen and reflect on their meaning. This early appreciation of storytelling as a source of meaning, learning, and entertainment prepared her for a more adult interest in fiction and social commentary.

During this early period, Taymur's childhood was happy and problem free. As she grew older around the age of eight, her interest in tales as artifacts of feminine cultural production was redirected by her mother to the learning of another set of skills identified with femininity in upper-class families: embroidery and weaving. This was a very unhappy experience for both mother and daughter. The mother's serious attempt to teach her daughter embroidery did not meet with much success. Taymur was not particularly receptive and showed little promise. Her mother did not relent making it clear that she was disappointed in the feminine capabilities of her eldest daughter.

Having failed in the feminine crafts, Taymur developed a more confident interest in attending her father's literary gatherings that included male writers who were engaged in a different form of cultural production—that is, writing poetry and prose. Taymur described the sound that their pens made on paper as the most melodious tune. It led her to collect bits of paper and discarded pencils to pretend that she too could write. Her mother's scolding fell on deaf ears. The stubbornness of mother and daughter regarding which one of those activities was appropriate for her education set the stage for the father's intervention.

Taymur provided two sets of descriptions of the role that her father played in resolving the conflict between mother and daughter that shed a complex light on the motivations of mother and father in supporting these different types of education. In the Arabic introduction to *Nata'ij al-Ahwal*, she offered the following account:

> My father, may God rest him in heaven, told my mother: "Leave me this girl [so I can train her] for the pen and paper. You can have her sister to train in whatever wisdom you desire." He then took my hand and led me out to where the writers were gathering. He arranged for 2 tutors to educate me: one in the Persian language and the other in Arabic. Every night, he would review with me what I learned. Gradually, I became more discerning deciding that I was inclined to

poetry. My first poems were recited in Persian. I worked very hard at my education and never missed a day or stopped [my pursuits].[37]

In the eyes of the child Taymur, her father emerged as a heroic figure who settled the struggle with her mother in her favor. This entitled him to a very special place in her heart. She remembered his exact, important words to her mother: "Leave this girl to me so I can train her for the pen and paper. You can have her sister to train in whatever wisdom you desire." With those fateful words, he led Taymur to the place where the male writers were gathered as though she belonged there. Then he arranged for two tutors, who might have been in attendance in those meetings, to begin her education. With this real and metaphorical initiation of the daughter by her father to the literary world of men, Taymur became the ward of the father who supervised her progress every night.

This arrangement had a profound impact on Taymur. Realizing that access to this male literary world was an unusual privilege to members of her gender, she felt great gratitude to her father. In an attempt to show her promise in this new type of education, she picked poetry, the most demanding and valued form of literary production in this part of the world, as her particular area of interest. To succeed, Taymur did what most women trendsetters were known to do: working much harder at her studies than any boy her age. To demonstrate the seriousness with which she pursued her new preoccupations, she stated that she never missed a day's work and that she never stopped studying. As part of her strong desire to please her father, she wrote her first poem in Persian, the language that only her father knew.

In the introduction to the Persian and Turkish poems, *Shekufeh,* Taymur offered a more detailed account of her struggle with her mother and the negotiations that took place between mother and father to settle the question of her education.

Even though I was genuinely inclined towards [literate] learning, I also tried to win my mother's approval. But I continued to dislike the feminine occupations. I used to visit the reception area [*slamlik*] past the writers who were there and listen to their melodious verse. My mother—may God rest her in the heavenly gardens—*was hurt by my actions* [italics mine]. She would reprimand, warn and threaten. She also appealed to me with friendly promises of jewelry and pretty costumes.

[Finally], my father reasoned with her, quoting the Turkish poet who said: the heart is not led, through force, to the desired path. So do not torment another soul if you can spare it. He also cautioned: Beware of breaking the heart of this young girl and tainting her purity with violence. If our daughter is inclined to the pen and paper, do not obstruct her desire. Let us share our daughters. You take

`Iffat and give me `Asmat [another of `A'isha's names]. If I make a writer of her, then this will bring me mercy after my death.

My father, then, said: Come with me `Asmat! Starting tomorrow I will bring you two tutors who will teach you Turkish, Persian and *fiqh* [jurisprudence] and Arabic grammar. Do well in your studies and obey my instructions and beware of shaming me before your mother.[38]

Taymur's dislike of the feminine crafts did not lead her to reject or dislike her mother. On the contrary, she wanted the mother's approval but was unable to overcome her dislike of the feminine crafts. She noted that her disobedience hurt her mother's feelings, which she regretted. While nobody questioned a mother's right to determine the education of her daughter including the father who used Turkish poetry to persuade her to change her mind, her wishes were disregarded.

Taymur's Slave Mother: Egyptian Slavery in Black and White

Her father's use of Turkish poetry to reason with her mother was the only piece of information that Taymur ever volunteered about the ethnicity of her mother. Fawwaz stated that she was a freed Circassian slave and concubine (*jariyya*).[39] The exception was Mayy Ziyada, who used the slave status of Taymur's mother to explain why "she could not comprehend her daughter's interest in book learning, possibly thinking that Taymur was abnormal and praying to God for assistance in dealing with her."[40] Here, Ziyada seemed to be suggesting that slave women reflected their backward social backgrounds in dealing with their children's needs, in this case Taymur's interests in literature and poetry. This dismissive modernist view of slaves reflected in denying them any understanding of their environments was problematic because the most vulnerable members of any community were usually aware of their status as well as that of others in developing their own strategies of survival and resistance. While Taymur's mother did not leave any record of her views of slavery or her relations with different members of her family, her daughter's accounts revealed that she lacked freedom to raise her daughter as she saw fit in the face of her husband's wishes. She conceded defeat in that struggle with Taymur's father, who was also her master, feeling hurt and rejected by her daughter. As a mother, she could have subverted her daughter's endeavors in a variety of other ways, but she refused to take that route.

At this point, I wish to briefly historicize our understanding of slavery in Egypt by looking at the differences between the Western and Middle Eastern institutions as contexts within which slaves had to survive. Next, I wish to examine the traffic in white slave women underlining the brutalizing aspects of their experience, which they shared with other slaves as well as some of the differences. My goal is to demystify the institution for both the general and specialized readers examining some of the representations of slave women. The fact that Taymur was the daughter of a freed slave woman who eventually rose to literary prominence writing about the institution provided examples of the links and the breaks between the eighteenth and nineteenth century histories of this segment of the population of slave women.

I have already mentioned that there was an exciting new research being done on the institution of slavery in Egypt, especially in deconstructing the lives of African slave women and to a lesser extent those of their white slave counterparts. For Western readers who associate slavery with blacks or Africans, the existence of white slaves will—at first glance—make little sense because the history of the Atlantic slave trade in the West has shaped our understanding of slavery. It transformed West African men and women (some of whom were most probably Muslim) into a primary source of coercive labor for the capitalist world economy in the eighteenth- and nineteenth-century plantation economies in the Caribbean and Americas.[41] The use of slave labor to satisfy the demand of the capitalist world economy was different from the demand for slavery that existed in the Middle East before and after the advent of capitalism.

The old slave institutions of the old world had multiple histories that could be traced back to Greek, Byzantine, and the Islamic worlds with their distinct social and political economic systems. The three shared, however, traffic in both African and white slaves. The Egyptian political economist Samir Amin used the comparative scales of precapitalist (small) and capitalist (large) slavery to suggest that the former was associated with luxury consumption in social formations that were very different from those in the latter that relied on slave labor for the production of varied export commodities for profit in the eighteenth- and the nineteenth-century world market.[42]

As part of the study of these Middle Eastern precapitalist or premodern social formations, the Mamluk dynasty in Egypt (1250–1517) added distinct political military dimensions to slavery. The Mamluks (Arabic for being owned) were young non-Muslim white men (and women),[43] from the Eurasian steppe region extending from the east of the Caucasus, with Circassian and/or Turkish ethnic roots. They were captured in war or kidnapped then sold into slavery, forced to convert to Islam, and trained in military arts to become skilled fighters. After the completion of their training, they were freed joining the ranks of numerous Mamluk military households that became engaged in the internal and regional political struggles for power.

The Mamluk dynasty rose to power in response to two crises facing the Egyptian Islamic political community: the incursion of Louis IX's crusade army in Mansura, Egypt, in 1250 followed by the Mongol invasion of Syria, which posed a threat to Egypt in 1260.[44] Their role as defenders of the Islamic political community contributed a conflicted basis of political legitimacy, that is, as freed Muslims slaves they were part of the community, but as former slaves their right to rule over free Muslims was always a source of contention.[45] The result was an interesting paradox: when these young white men and women were enslaved, their status, lives, and deaths were under the complete control of their masters just like slaves of other ethnicities; but with freedom, few of them rose to the apex of political power ruling over never-enslaved Muslims. The power and privilege that these former slaves could exercise over the free challenged many assumptions associated with the modern-capitalist institution of slavery.[46] Equally significant, this particular political history provided the basis for arguments made about the benevolent character of Islamic slavery. If freed Muslim slaves could eventually reach the highest political positions in the community, then slave status in lands of Islam was not as dehumanizing an experience as was reported in other cultures.

The gender component added other complicating layers to the benevolent view of Islamic slavery. The first Mamluk (freed white slave) ruler in Egypt was a woman, Shajarrat al-Durr. Her name, which literally meant tree of pearls, indicated someone with wealth and high status belying her original slave status. Metaphorically, it referred to a fecund tree (woman) that gives abundant fruits or flowers. As it was, Shajarrat al-Durr had one son, whose name she took after she was declared queen. The emphasis on wealth and reproductive capacity showed that Mamluk gender expectations were simultaneously traditional and unusual, allowing a freed Muslim slave woman to become the only Muslim queen.

Her rise to power occurred when her husband, the last Ayyubid ruler al-Saleh Najm al-Din Ayyub (under whose rule the numbers of the Mamluks multiplied) died suddenly as his Mamluk army was engaged in battle with the seventh crusade.[47] She kept the news of his demise from the troops and coordinated the war effort with Beheriyya Mamluks, who served as al-Saleh's bodyguards, until Turanshah, her husband's son, arrived to take charge. The assassination of Turanshah by his father's Mamluks led their leaders to choose Shajjarat al-Durr as queen, whose status as the widow of Ayyub gave her and the Mamluk leaders a basis of political legitimacy. The political role given to the widow of the deceased ruler represented a new political practice for the transfer of power from one Islamic dynasty to the next. In addition, it recognized the important role she played in managing the war against the crusaders and their eventual military defeat.

Initially, al-Durr wanted to rule alone taking on titles that offered complicated arguments in favor of this new political role for a Muslim woman ruler. By calling herself "al-Musta`simiyya," "al-Salihiyya," and "walidat al-Sultan Khalil Amir al-Mu'mininn," she sought to define her relations to the key male political figures of this period. Al-Musta`ssimiyya was the feminine form of the name of the Abbasid caliph of the time, headquartered in Baghdad, al-Musta`ssim, whose support she needed to confirm her legitimacy in this new position. The title could be interpreted as a form of flattery designed to express her loyalty.[48] It could also be taken as a reference to her equanimity in the face of danger following the death of her husband in the middle of a serious military battle. The Mamluks acknowledged this important political quality in choosing her as their queen. Lastly, this title was designed to underline her virtuousness (`isma`), a quality not associated with slave, but free women. This also offered a second reference to a form of independence that only free, married Muslim women exercised: the right to `isma` (i.e., to divorce) their husbands, which accorded them freedom.

The title of al-Salihiyya underlined her position as the widow of the previous ruler al-Salih Ayyub and her legitimate right to succeed him. It also added the claim that she was religiously devout (*saliha*) as another quality that made her suitable for political rule. Last but not least, she included a reference to her son in another claim for the right to govern on his behalf as the prince of the faithful. Despite all of these complicated arguments and claims, one historian suggested she still represented two problems to Islamic political theory and practice: as someone who was once a slave, she was not qualified to rule over free Muslims; and as a Muslim woman, she had no right to rule over Muslim men. The Abbasid caliph refused to confirm her claims to power, sarcastically remarking in his response: if you lack qualified men in the country, let us know and we will send you one.[49]

So, after eighty days in power, she was forced to step down entering into a political marriage with al-Mu`izz al-Din Aybak al-Turkumani. This kind of a political marriage followed the Saljukid precedent for the marriage of an *atabeg* to the widow of his former master.[50] This political marriage lasted for seven years in which she served as coruler with Aybak, with both of their names appearing on coins and mentioned in the Friday sermons.[51] When he decided to take another political wife, she had him killed and was in turn killed.

The details of this early phase in Mamluk dynastic history left its imprints on Mamluk political and social practice during the next three centuries of their rule and also their political struggles for power after the Ottomans put an end to their rule of Egypt in 1517. Under the Ottoman system of government, the Mamluks took on the important but subordinate role of tax collectors, which allowed them some degree of economic influence. In the eighteenth century, however, they recovered considerable economic and political influence.[52] The Mamluk princes continued the practice of inheriting the property of their former masters coupled with marrying their widows to establish some form of legitimacy.[53] This type of political marriage represented a form of coercive heterosexuality in which these freed slave and privileged Mamluk women had no choice but to marry those who were responsible for the death of their husbands or risk violence to their families and the loss of their property and position. So even though by then they were free, they were not free to refuse to engage in these political marriages. As such, one could argue that they were still treated as property passed from one Mamluk leader to another.

As a result, Mamluk women found in the accumulation of wealth a "hedge against the death of a protector a patron or a husband."[54] Because of the political instability under the Mamluk rule, it was not surprising that the marriage institution within that class was equally unstable. Constant military competition among Mamluk military households shortened the life span of men imposing emotional and social burdens on their women. In this light, the studies that deal with the economic power and wealth of this group[55] acquire a different meaning. While the archival research provided very valuable details of how freed white slave women accumulated and managed their wealth, challenging the association between slavery and destitution in the Middle East, this bird's eyes' view of their world ignored the fact that accumulation was not merely a sign of privilege but an acute reflection of the lack of security in the very insecure Mamluk world.

The studies that emphasized the wealth of some Mamluk women also provided further evidence of the benevolent character of Islamic slavery reinforcing "the rags to riches"[56] stories that were ideologically successful in the reproduction of slavery in general and white slavery in particular. As Madeline Zilfi suggested most slave women, whether or white or black, were not destined to an easy but a difficult life.[57] Unfortunately, this view was not prevalent in the discussion of white slavery in Egypt. Typically, white and black slavery were split from each other: the harshness of the institution is assumed to be the lot of the African slave while white slavery is treated as a vehicle for the advancement of white men and women. This discursive strategy, which pitted white and black slaves against each other, undermined our understanding of the harsh and brutal effects of bondage experienced by the two groups. While white and black or African slaves were part of a very complex hierarchy of prices offered for them as commodities subject to supply and demand, this did not necessarily reflect a difference in treatment since members of both groups were treated as properties by their masters. It also ignored the fact that these racial divisions operated as part of a powerful ideological structure that contributed to the reproduction of slavery in the region for more than five centuries. It explained the silence that existed on the traumas and pains experienced by most white slaves including the freed ones, like Taymur's mother, which the poet partially unlocked in the elegy of her mother.

Did the conditions of white slaves improve with the liquidation of the Mamluks by Muhammad Ali, the abolition of slavery, and the modernization of society? This was a very difficult question to answer because there were very few accounts that attempted to connect the eighteenth- and nineteenth-century fortunes of white slave women, with the exception of Afaf Lutfi al-Sayyid Marsot. She provided very strong arguments in support of how modernization and the centralized state power of the Muhammad Ali dynasty had negative consequences for this class of women. She suggested that during the eighteenth century, there were smaller educational and age differentials between men and women in Mamluk families. Both men and women married young, spending limited time in education. Wives outlived their husbands because of the violence that characterized Mamluk competition. This gave elite Mamluk women a greater opening in the economic arena, which explains their successful accumulation of wealth. The physical liquidation of the Mamluks led to the building of a strong state whose monopolies of agricultural landholding were used to reward loyal men, denying women access to this source of income. In the nineteenth century, men had to work longer through the state ranks before marriage, creating larger age and educational differentials between spouses. Even when women had access to wealth, new modern economic institutions, like banking, gave men a new role to play in the management of their wives' fortunes. Finally, elite women were encouraged to adhere to the modern rules of domesticity, in which one of the consequences was to leave the management of their businesses to their husbands.[58] Taymur indirectly addressed these developments in her booklet, *Mir'at al-Ta'mul fi al-Umur*, which will be discussed in Chapter 4.

In her insightful article on servants and slave women at the center and the periphery of the Ottoman Empire, Madeline Zilfi also suggested that "in the later Ottoman century female slaves became an even higher proportion of slaves taken into household employment . . . [reinforcing] the association of household work and slavery itself with, women."[59] For this general population whether one was a concubine or a slave servant, both were treated as properties[60] and most slaves, white or black, were not destined for an easy life. Furthermore, even freed slaves were treated as minors regardless of their age.[61] While distinctions between Mamluk (white) and `abd (African) slaves[62] reflected the existence of racial divisions and attitudes toward different races, it was a mistake to assume—as the general literature on the region did—that white slaves escaped the racism. In Taymur's work of fiction, *Nata'ij al-Ahwal*, she described the contempt with which black and white slaves were treated within the Egyptian ruling classes. She described Prince Mamduh's (the hero of her tale) initial haughty disdain for any contact with Africans whose color was given negative connotations associated with misfortune and anyone who was captured at war (i.e., the white Mamluk slave) even if he were to become a prince, could never escape the stigma of having been bought and sold as property or as an animal.[63]

Ziyada did not discuss the local contempt with which white slave women were held in Egypt at the time, but her comment about Taymur's mother not being able to comprehend or appreciate her daughter's wish to learn how to read and write was reflective of this attitude. At the same time, she addressed the Orientalist claim that because many kings in the region married their freed slaves, the majority of Oriental populations had slave blood. She thought that theirs was a superficial view not because the majority of the population in Egypt was never enslaved but because of the equally ideological narrative that some concubines were either captured at war or kidnapped from noble families. She listed the influx of Greek slave women following the war in Morea, Greece, where Ali's army was sent by the Ottoman government to put down the Greek insurrection.[64] She also listed the Circassians as representing an older complex historical model of slavery in the Ottoman world.[65]

Ziyada claimed that "Circassian families sold their children into slavery in the hope of their advancement outside of the Caucasus Mountains." This frequently cited claim in the literature, regardless of its veracity, made the blow of bondage even more severe for the purpose extracting obedience from these young men and women. It also sought to distract attention from the present painful effects of the experience by focusing on the promise of a better future. Ziyada said that she did not seek to justify the actions of these families because most of these slave children ended up working in small homes, freed late in life, marrying poorly, and accumulating modest assets. Still she said Sharia (Islamic law) was most gentle with slaves along with some opportunities whereby boys could become Mamluks (i.e., members of the political elites or the royal courts) and young girls could become *hanims* (i.e., rich ladies), provided members of both genders with dreams of royalty.

For would-be husbands or masters who had an interest in these slave women, their only requirements were that they be healthy, pretty, and well built. Ziyada seemed to be oblivious of how offensive this discussion of women was stating uncritically that their worth depended on how much of these qualities they possessed and whether or not they were trained in household management (*tadbir al-manzil*), needle work and the arts like dancing, playing an instrument, and singing. They had to be socialized into the customs of these notable families that required developing the key quality of mixing obedience with pride. For a long time, I could not understand what this quality was about. How could a white slave woman be trained to be obedient and proud at the same time? And what pride was she expected to declare? A possible answer had to do with pride in being Turkish or Circassian—even if one was a slave—which the aristocracy valued as a central component of their identity.

According to Ziyada, a concubine had the added advantage of being completely devoted to her new family because she lacked one in her new setting.

Some men humorously claimed that Adam was the happiest man because Eve had no family to meddle with him or to inconvenience him with their many visits. Ziyada viewed slave women's lack of connection to their original families as leading to the independence of the conjugal family, establishing the sacred boundaries of the household and women's complete devotion to the care of their families. She declared that this was "the reason behind the advancement of most English families and the backwardness of most oriental ones."[66]

Finally, she cited Niyya Salima the pen name of the French Eugenie Le Brun who was married to Husayn Rushdie Pasha and wrote a book on the social customs of Egyptians to show the influence that slave women had on the lives of their children. An "Egyptian woman who was herself a freed slave told her [in the 1890s] that she was going to shop for a slave wife for her son in Istanbul because the daughters of the local aristocracy were spoiled and that the benefit of having a concubine was that she would have no kin of her own guaranteeing his happiness."[67] This might explain the isolation and the lack of support that Taymur's mother experienced in the conflict on how to raise her. Taymur acknowledged the hurt that she unintentionally inflicted on her mother even if she could not completely understand it. To the shame of this slave mother who had to obey others, her daughter refused to obey her as well. Worse, her daughter's dislike of embroidery frustrated the mother's attempt to pass on to her daughter one of the skills that some slave women had.[68] More alarmingly, her daughter's rejection of feminine arts in favor of reading and writing trespassed on activities, which were associated with maleness, would set her daughter up for major disappointment. Later on, Taymur would confess her frustrations during her marriage at the unfulfilled hope of being a poet and a writer. So, despite Ziyada's claim to the contrary, this slave mother showed foresight in anticipating the unhappy consequences of her daughter's rebellion against existing social rule.

A Patriarchal Bargain

The arrangement Taymur's father negotiated with her mother regarding the education of his daughters was a mixed one. He would guide Taymur's education in reading and writing while the mother initiated her sister `Iffat into embroidery and the other feminine crafts. In this bargain, it was understood that he would shoulder the responsibility for the consequences of supporting the unusual interests of his daughter. What led the father to contemplate this unusual arrangement? One can only speculate. As already mentioned, the father had no sons at this pont. With one daughter showing an interest in what would have been a proper education for a son, the father might have taken some satisfaction from Taymur's unexpected interest in this area. He was willing to put some of the family resources into his daughter's literary education as a surrogate son. For those, like Zaynab Fawwaz and Mayy Ziyda, who read in the father's actions feminist tendencies, there were serious problems with that interpretation. First, the only reason he mentioned behind his action was the belief that God will grant him mercy after death for having educated one of his daughters. This was a reference to a well-known Hadith, a statement reported by the prophet that stated the following: "Anyone blessed with 3 daughters raising them well and educating them (*adabahun*) will find out that they will provide him with a protective barrier (*satran wa hijaban*) against the fires of hell. A man then asked the prophet: what if they were only two? He replied: even if they were two. The narrator of the Hadith concluded that if someone had said to the prophet, what if it was only one daughter, he would have said even one [educated] daughter would have provided a father with this kind of reward."[69]

The Hadith was explicit enough in its support of fathers investing time and energy in the upbringing and education of their female children. This was not surprising for the prophet had many daughters and only one son who died in infancy, which must have influenced his view of how important a father's engagement, was in the upbringing and education of his daughters. In promising those who follow in his footsteps heavenly rewards, he was encouraging other men to develop the same commitment. This was the mercy that Ismail wished for in exchange for his support of Taymur's education following his death. Contrary to the Hadith, which mentioned involvement in the lives of two or more daughters, he followed the bare minimum requirement of educating only one of his two daughters. The agreement he reached with their mother stipulated that his other daughter would be brought up in the usual conventional way. Still Islam was represented in the mid-nineteenth century as sympathetic to the education of women. During this period, literary women did exist and there were at least three who were well known for their literary expertise and skill. An adult Taymur was to call on two of them to tutor her in poetic meter and Arabic grammar.

Despite the above, the father was clearly worried about the ominous effect of a prolonged confrontation between mother and daughter. He alluded to this concern in the exchange with his wife suggesting that in dealing harshly with the daughter's unorthodox interests, the mother might break Taymur's heart and drive her to a more serious rebellion against other social rules, especially those that affect her purity. This stood as the more ominous scenario. He was afraid that this small rebellion would develop into a more serious challenge of patriarchal expectations of early marriage and domesticity. It explained his unusual intervention on behalf of his daughter. His support for change was designed to contain its subversive effects through making minor concessions to this limited rebellion to avoid a potentially major one.

In exchange for assisting Taymur in her new area of interest, her father asked her to "do well in your lessons, follow my instruction and make sure I am not shamed before your mother." Taymur, in turn, promised to "obey him, do her best to gain his trust and realize his hopes."[70] Lest the reader miss what the father had in mind, Taymur provided valuable information. When she began to read and then write love poetry, her father frequently criticized and discouraged her. He opined, "If she read much of this type of poetry, it might lead her to neglect her other lessons." In a practical attempt to steer her in a different direction, he insisted that she follow the popular Ottoman literary ideal of writing poetry in Turkish, Persian, and Arabic. Otherwise, he insisted one could not possibly enjoy them.[71] Her father used this ideal to insist that she concentrate on the linguistic aspect of poetry at the expense of the expression of feelings, which he deemed undesirable.

Ismail commissioned two male tutors to instruct his daughter in Turkish, Persian, *fiqh*, and Arabic. The ranking of importance given to different languages reflected the literary ideals of the time and the history of the family. While Turkish was the language of government, it was also the spoken and the written language of the aristocracy and the family. Persian was considered to be an important language for anyone who had serious literary aspirations, not to mention its closeness to the Kurdish roots of the family. Arabic was taught as a third language. The father's recruitment of male tutors, not female ones, to assist his daughter in this intensive program of study supported the view that the existing rules of sexual segregation was flexible and/or that families, like the Taymur, employed elderly male teachers to provide a safe education to their female children. The study of *fiqh* represented a novel addition to the Islamic ideal of education given to upper-class girls that most probably emphasized the learning of social and future marital obligation of young girls. It provided another means by which the father ensured his daughter's socialization into the patriarchal norms that stressed female virtue.[72]

Analysts have for most part assumed that the father's support of his daughter's education including the commitment of necessary resources contributed all the necessary conditions for successfully initiating Taymur into this field. Absent from this discussion was the mother's cooperation and how initial opposition did not continue providing a hospitable climate for change. If the mother had continued to subvert the efforts of father and daughter, then this early stage would have been much more difficult. There was no evidence of such continued opposition in any of Taymur's accounts. Despite her early opposition, Taymur's mother chose not to undermine her daughter's accomplishments whether she agreed with them or not.

Even though Taymur excelled in her studies, this stage with its unique type of literary education for a young aristocratic girl ended with her marriage at the age of 14. As her father predicted, the containment of her modest challenge of patriarchal rules regarding what young girls should or should not learn contributed to her acquiescence to the prevailing social rules that included early marriage and domesticity. Although much is made of Taymur's early education and how her father's support contributed to the rise of a new generation of women whose options and social standing were different from those that preceded them, Taymur's life during the next twenty years was not very different from other free women of her class whose roles as wives and mothers consumed their time.

Marriage, Motherhood, and the Challenge of Patriarchal Rules Through an Alliance between Mother and Daughter

Ahmed's only contribution to Zaynab Fawwaz's biographical profile of his sister, which he largely copied in his history of the family, was to correct the misidentification of his sister's husband. Fawwaz had stated that Taymur married Mahmud Bek al-Islamboli when her husband was al-Sayyid Muhammed Tewfik Bek, the son of Mahmud Bek al-Istamboli and the grandson of al-Sayyid Abdallah al-Islamboli, a former clerk of the Ottoman Imperial Council.[73] The marriage took place in AH 1271 (1854–55).

This correction raised more questions about her husband's family. For example, given the fact that her husband's grandfather was a former clerk at the Ottoman Imperial Council, when did the family settle in Egypt? Some accounts suggested that the couple got married at the Ottoman center and lived there for a while before settling in Egypt. Ahmed did not mention the occupation of Taymur's husband. Her grandson volunteered that he was minister of the treasury (*nazir bayt al-mal*).[74] Mayy Ziyada mentioned that he was the son of the governor of Sudan.[75] If he or his father had occupied ministerial positions in government, Ahmed would have included this information in his family history, which celebrated the accomplishments of the men in the family. It was most probable, however, that he was a high-ranking bureaucrat at the ministry of the treasury. One thing that Ahmed made clear was that his sister's husband and his grandfather belonged to the religiously distinguished al-Sadda class with the religious title of al-Sayyid attached to their names. Ahmed had strongly emphasized the importance of this title in his construction of the Arab history of the family. Not only did his sister's husband hold that religiously prestigious title, but her husband and his father also held the equally prestigious aristocratic title of Bek enjoyed by members of that class.

While Taymur's in-laws clearly added to the class and the religious stature of the family, one had to wonder whether the combined religious and class background of that family contributed greater social conservatism and critical intolerance of Taymur's unorthodox interests. One thing was clear: while Taymur used elegies to offer us a window from which to examine her relations with her sons, daughter, sister, brother, and parents, there was no elegy of her husband in her collected poems. Her silence on this dead husband of close to twenty years spoke volumes about the problems she must have faced in that relationship. There was the possibility that he was much older than she was. He died three years following the death of her father in the mid-1870s when she was about 35 years old. She lived to be 62. Lutfi al-Sayyid Marsot had suggested that in contrast to the eighteenth-century marriages, where the age and educational differentials were small, nineteenth-century marriages were characterized by larger age differentials. In Taymur's case, one could speculate that her husband was much older than she was and her literary education was more sophisticated than his. However young or old he was, she did not remarry choosing to remain single and independent in a society that did not support either of these situations.

Her brother stated that she had a very large family including many girls and boys. Tawhida mentioned a sister and many brothers.[76] This suggested that Taymur became a very busy young mother looking after a relatively large family as well as managing the affairs of her household. This changed when her eldest daughter came of age leading mother and daughter to make a fateful decision.[77] The following quote described the evolution of Taymur's complex relationship with her daughter.

> After ten years [of marriage], the first fruit of my heart, Tawhida, who is part of my self and the spirit of my joy, reached the age of nine. I enjoyed watching her spending her days, from morning till noon, between the pens and the inkbottles and weaving the most beautiful crafts during the rest of the day and evening. I prayed for her success, feeling my own sadness regarding what I had missed when I was her age and repulsed by the latter activity.
>
> When my daughter was twelve years of age, she began to serve her mother and father. In addition, she managed the household including all of the servants and the dependents. It was then that I was able to find spaces [zawaya] of relaxation.
>
> At this point, it occurred to me to resume what I had missed as a youngster learning poetic meter. I brought a woman instructor to teach me . . . But she passed away six months later. My daughter, who attended these lessons, was able to excel in that art more than I did because of her youth and sharp intellect.[78]

Tawhida was Taymur's eldest child: she was nine years of age after ten years of marriage. Her mother clearly loved her very much describing her as "a part of my self and the spirit of my joy." Like her mother before her, Taymur was in charge of her daughter's education when she turned nine but approached it in a way that was different from her mother. She did not pressure Tawhida to learn any particular set of skills available to girls of her age and social class making it possible for her to take equal delight in writing and in embroidery synthesizing both the new and the old. While Taymur took pleasure in being a good mother who did not impose her preferences or experience on her daughter's learning, the boundaries between mother and daughter were sometimes blurred predicting serious trouble ahead. For example, Taymur reported feeling sad because her own experience led her to oppose writing to embroidery denying her the kind of pleasure that Tawhida enjoyed. She also felt competitive with her daughter who got more out of the lessons with the tutor Taymur employed to teach them poetic meter. Ziyada suggested that the reason Taymur and Tawhida seemed more like sisters, not mother and daughter was due to the small age difference between them (15 years).[79] The problem was, however, less related to age and more connected to the confusion of boundaries in this close mother-daughter relationship. While Taymur was able to maintain these boundaries in approaching her daughter's education, her acceptance of what she described as Tawhida's desire to "serve" her mother and father was problematic. In describing what this service included, she suggested that Tawhida began to manage their big household with its many servants and dependents. While Taymur was silent on how her daughter served her father, it was likely that Tawhida also looked after her father's daily needs.

In describing the transfer of her domestic duties to Tawhida, Taymur implied that this was her daughter's decision, which raised the question of how Tawhida reached that decision and why Taymur was willing to go along. Because Taymur continued to feel frustration on her unrealized aspirations, the transfer of her domestic duties allowed her for the first time, since her marriage, to find time to relax and to entertain the idea of resuming her education. At the age of 12, Taymur had spent her time studying languages and writing poetry and continued to do so until she married at the age of 14. There was clearly no social expectation that she take on the huge responsibility of the management of her family's large household before her own marriage. If this was not part of Taymur's preparation for marriage, what made Tawhida think of volunteering for it? Taymur provided the answer herself, when mother and daughter took lessons in poetry writing, Tawhida, who was at the time dividing her time between learning how to write and to embroider, was able to learn much faster than her mother. Sensing her mother's disappointment and desire to devote more time to learning, Tawhida volunteered to help with the domestic tasks.

Even if a talented 12-year-old had the illusion that she could juggle her mother's duties and her other interests, it was a mother's role to correct that misconception and refuse that sacrifice. In this case, a conflicted Taymur, who was both tired of her domestic obligations and frustrated with her inability to resume her studies, did not make the more difficult decision of declining her daughter's offer.

There was no indication that Tawhida's father was involved in that decision, confirming the fact that the mother determined her daughter's education and the role she played in the household. Unlike Ismail Taymur, Muhammad Tewfik Bek was clearly less involved in the important decisions affecting his daughter's life. As a high-ranking bureaucrat, he either had little time to spare on the affairs of the household or paid more attention to his sons. If he noted that Tawhida had taken over her mother's duties in the household, he either did not care or chose not to intervene between mother and daughter. Zaynab Fawwaz claimed that Taymur's husband died three years after her father. While Ahmed gave an exact date of his father's death on December 18, 1872, we have no way of precisely dating the passing of Taymur's husband, leaving us with 1875 as an approximate date.

This left other female members of the household as bystanders who did nothing even though Taymur's poetry made clear their displeasure with Taymur's unconventional interests. Their unwillingness to intervene could be explained by their expectation that Tawhida would surely fail in carrying this heavy burden. Unfortunately, Tawhida did not fail and was as committed as her mother to the completion of the latter's literary ambitions.

With free time on her hands, Taymur recruited two women instructors who helped to complete and polish her literary skills: Fatima al-Azhariya and Setita al-Tablawiya. The first was a writer who taught her Arabic grammar and the second was a poet who taught poetic meter. Under their guidance, she began to compose long verse and the lighter literary form of *zagal*, establishing a growing literary reputation. As a result, Taymur confidently began to experiment with novel roles during this period of great social change initiated by Khedive Ismail and the women of his family. For example, Taymur cited her involvement in the royal court of the queen mother (*al-Walda Pasha*) of Khedive Ismail.

> I was invited by her royal highness, the mother of the khedive Ismail, to the palace whenever the relatives of the Persian king visited . . . I stayed with them during their visits, entertained them and inquired about their customs and their moral habits.[80]

So in addition to spending considerable time learning the tools of literary writing, Taymur's knowledge of other languages opened new doors for her. Facilitated by the death of both her father and her husband, who died three years apart, she assumed new roles that took her outside of her secluded household: as a court translator and companion of the women of visiting dignitaries. The death of these patriarchs gave her new freedoms taking her away from home and increasing her disengagement from its affairs. In both her literary studies and her new public ventures at the royal court, Taymur became dissociated from feminine gender roles, which primarily stressed women's private availability to the needs of others in the family. The shedding of the feminine roles reinforced her social identification with masculinity, identified with the satisfaction of one's individual needs unencumbered by the needs of others as reflected in her single-minded pursuit of literary learning and the embrace of public roles.

As a result, Taymur was caught off guard by the late discovery of Tawhida's declining health. This serious turn of event was complicated by the fact that Tawhida's pride in her mother's new accomplishments led her to hide the signs of her illness treating it as a "silly matter."[81] So Taymur's transformation into a public figure had the effect of making Tawhida think of her, not as a mother, but as someone involved in grand endeavors that were more important than the personal or mundane needs of a daughter. Taymur's belated attempt to use all the family resources to enlist the help of many doctors to arrest the illness did not succeed. Her daughter died at the age of 18 (1875–76) and, according to family members, on her wedding night.[82] This indicated not only that Taymur and the family misjudged the seriousness of Tawhida's illness but also that they did not entertain such a dramatic ending to the illness. These circumstances clearly made Tawhida's death doubly tragic and emotionally debilitating.

Tawhida's Death and Taymur's Breakdown

Tawhida's death had a crippling effect on Taymur and her work. Her most immediate response was to burn most of the poetry she had written up to that point. While some of her Arabic and Turkish poetry survived the burning rampage, her Persian ones did not: "As for my Persian poetry, it was in my daughter's folder, which I burned just as my heart burned over her [loss]."[83] Finally, Taymur began seven years of actively mourning Tawhida (1876–83), which had more serious physical and emotional effects. Her grandson described her deterioration in the following quote:

> [Taymur's] sadness over the loss of her daughter was great. She mourned her for seven years leading to weakened eyesight that suffered from opthalmia. She also no longer enjoyed life choosing to spend her days alone and in a wild manner. She boycotted poetry and literature with the exception of her elegy of her daughter, which she used to describe her pain, tribulations and suffering. This prolonged sadness led her children to *isolate her* [italics mine].[84]

Taymur's literary, emotional, and physical breakdowns were interconnected. First and foremost, she felt enormous guilt for having disengaged from her maternal role in pursuit of her literary aspirations and other public activities, which she expressed by burning most of her poetry and completely destroying her Persian poems. While the role of court translator and companion of the Persian dignitaries represented the epitome of Taymur's public achievements during this period, it took her away from the family at the time when Tawhida's decline occurred. At the same time, Tawhida's pride in the poetry her mother wrote as a result of this interaction with members of the Persian royal family was made apparent by her keeping it in a personal folder reminding Taymur of how much her daughter was "a part of herself," as she had previously stated, sharing her own interests and making her own sacrifices for them. As Taymur put it, burning the Persian poems graphically captured the burning of her heart.

Because her childhood and adult struggles to become a poet were difficult, Taymur's destruction of the hard-won fruits of these struggles represented a most severe punishment. Because she continued to channel her creative energy in the writing of an elegy mourning the loss of her daughter, it would seem that she did not denounce poetry per se but the social strategy she used to pursue the goal of becoming a poet. Rather than challenge patriarchal rules that defined her only as a mother and a wife, she used the path of least social resistance (i.e., relying on other women, in this case her daughter) to escape the social burdens that restricted her ability to resume her literary studies. It pitted the needs of mother against daughter and Taymur's role as a poet against that of a mother. Both had very tragic consequences for mother and daughter.[85]

Taymur's prolonged and painful mourning provided her with an opportunity to reflect on the tensions that resulted from her attempt to single-mindedly pursue literary interests without integrating them with her caretaking role. The failure to integrate the new role with the old one put them on collision course by making her less available to and aware of her daughter's needs when it most counted. Her attempt to integrate these roles was evident in the writing of the long elegy of Tawhida, in which the literary and the maternal parts of her wounded self came together. This particular Arabic genre had historically recognized women's gender difference (their emotional connectedness to others), giving them particular skills in the poetic expression of the loss of loved ones. It was this poetic tradition that Taymur fell back on[86] as she attempted to integrate her gendered and nongendered roles.

Complicating the mourning process and contributing to its length was the social criticism that Taymur faced from within and outside her family blaming her for Tawhida's death. It alienated her, which explains why she mourned alone and for a long time trying to prove her critics wrong and demonstrate her love for her daughter. Those same critics blamed her crying for her weakened eyesight and the onset of opthalmia, which in nineteenth-century medical discourse was used as a catchall category for eye disease. As a result, she struggled with the periodic loss of the ability to see allowing her to block out a bitter reality, which her critics used as evidence of divine punishment for the role she played in her daughter's death.[87] Blindness served as a good metaphor for Taymur's loss of her sense of direction in a very hostile environment deepening her sense of injustice and depression.

Within the family, Taymur's children, including many of her sons and another daughter, reacted to their mother's struggles in two different ways: First, there were those who were largely unsympathetic to her plight feeling that she had proved to be a bad mother twice. The first time was when she abandoned their care to resume her literary studies; and second, by persisting in their neglect through this prolonged mourning of Tawhida. Angry they turned against her, questioning her actions, decisions, and sanity. In an indirect attempt to explain why her children made these painful charges, her grandson cited the following pattern behavior: (1) her unusually long mourning of Tawhida, (2) her rejection of the family's advice to stop crying making her a danger to herself, (3) the loss of any interest in living, the boycotting of the company of others and maintaining a wild lifestyle, and finally (4) her destruction of the poetry she wrote and the sudden loss of interest in what had been a budding literary reputation.

Her youngest son, Mahmud, represented a more sympathetic second reaction to his mother's woes. His role in her recovery from depression and eye disease will be discussed in greater detail in the discussion of the next section. Taymur suggested in *Hilyat al-Tiraz* that her "enemies" enlisted the help of modern doctors to challenge her sanity and the doctors treated her as someone who was hysteric.[88] Other prevailing views of mental illness argued that women were prone to mental imbalance as a result of biological changes in their life cycle.[89] In response, her grandson reported that her sons decided to *isolate* her. Isolation was the new medical approach used to treat mental illness in the 1870s and the 1880s reversing earlier approaches that integrated these groups into the social fabric.[90] It was not clear from the grandson's cryptic reference to isolation if she was hospitalized or if her isolation took place in a separate quarter at home. Being locked up in the family home had the advantage of allowing the family to exert social and psychological pressure on the offending member.

Recovery and Rise to Prominence

Not all her children opted for this punitive and coercive approach to their mother's complex struggles. With a different set of needs and without the resentment felt by his older siblings, Mahmud, Taymur's youngest son, showed empathy toward his mother, helping to nurse her back to health. Taymur offered the following description of the role he played:

My weak body felt lifeless because of its many aches and grief. Then, God blessed me with recovery and lit the darkness of my depression with the bright presence of my son Mahmud who became the joy of my house of sadness.
[He asked to collect my Arabic poems and to publish the Turkish ones] as a marker of my cleverness and eloquence.[91]

As her youngest son who still needed her, he understood that she could not be available to him without regaining her health and hope in the future. Like Tawhida, Mahmud adopted a caretaking role toward his mother. It was facilitated by his youth, which made dependence on his mother acceptable and taking care of her, an appropriate task for a daughter, was not a serious threat to his masculinity. At the same time, Mahmud's need for his mother offered Taymur a final opportunity to prove that she was a good mother responsive to the needs of her children. Mahmud's interest in his mother's poetry and promise to support its publication as a marker of her achievement reinforced the association between him and his sister Tawhida. So Mahmud succeeded where his older brothers, sisters, and the doctors failed. Taymur agreed to end her mourning, treat her eyes and begin a slow return to normalcy. Initially, she agreed, without much enthusiasm, to collect her remaining poetry for publication.

My son, your mother no longer has the desire to read any literary books. I would like to direct my attention to the interpretation of the Qur'an and reading the prophetic tradition. I will give you my books and papers to do whatever you wish with them. If you find any trace of excellence in them, then you can publish them.[92]

Taymur's interest in Qur'anic interpretation and the prophetic tradition was for the purpose of solace signaling a break with literature. Interestingly, she found in religion and its texts a source of renewed interest in both literature and poetry. According to Mahmud, up until then Taymur had only written poetry, which he promised to publish. In 1887, his mother published a work of fiction titled *Nata'ij al-Ahwal* and on February 12, 1889, she published an article in *al-Adaab* newspaper that was critical of the way modern education for girls' emphasized child rearing and domesticity.[93] In 1892, she published a social commentary titled *Mir'at al-Ta'mul fi al-Umur* and *Hilyat al-Tiraz*, her collected Arabic poems. "Shukufeh," her collected Turkish poems, were published afterward, but the specific date was not available.

The chronology of these publications with her Arabic and Turkish poetry published later than earlier indicated the family's ambivalence toward Mahmud's promise to publish his mother's poetic production. The publication of her Arabic and Turkish poetry a decade later in the 1890s indicated the strong resistance the project faced. Meanwhile, Taymur's numerous publications that preceded that of her poetry established the bases for an illustrious literary reputation that enhanced the social standing of the family. Given the spread of education among some women of the affluent classes and the public debates on women's education taking place in the 1870s and the 1880s, the opposition exhibited by the family gave way to the desire to benefit from Taymur's pioneering role as the leading woman poet and writer of her time. It helped to realize their promise to publish her poetry.

The Canonical Construction of Taymur's Life

Zaynab Fawwaz's Contribution

Taymur's inclusion of the story of her life as part of her introduction to her book of fictional tales emphasized the importance of the subjective and the constructive character of any life. She seemed clear that her personal struggles were also part of the cultural history of the nation. Fawwaz offered a different construction of Taymur's life biography using it in support of the development of an Arab-Islamic national community.

As already mentioned, Zaynab Fawwaz was Taymur's contemporary who provided the earliest construction of the author's life and accomplishments in her *al-Durr al-Manthur fi Tabaqat Rabat al-Khudur*. Despite Fawwaz's access to Taymur's autobiographical introduction to *Nata'ij al-Ahwal* (published in 1887), her construction of the identity of the author and her personal history were markedly different. I will treat the omissions and the distortions of that biographical profile as part of the social and discursive history of that period whose critical appreciation should shed light on the cultural and social climates of the time and the desire to appeal to and shape the identities of the reading public and/or developing communities. As the prototype of the canonical construction of Taymur's life and work, it presented a socially sanctioned definition or view of women's relation to the community.

Fawwaz began by transforming Taymur into an Arab poet and prose writer claiming that she learned Arabic before Turkish assigning her a significant position among the prominent women poets of that tradition like Walada [Bint al-Mistakfi], Leila al-Akhiliya, and al-Khansa'. This construction purposely ignored the fact that Turkish was Taymur's mother tongue, not Arabic. It was the language spoken by both of her parents and within the household. It explained why even Fawwaz's account of the tutors Ismail employed for the education of his daughter largely taught her Arabic and Persian, not Turkish.

In dealing with the Turkish aspect of family history, Fawwaz focused on the fact that Taymur's mother was a freed Circassian slave. She then proceeded to discuss the struggle between Taymur and her mother as a metaphor for the conflict between different generations of women that represented different ideals of femininity and community. This ignored the important role that Taymur's autobiographical introduction to *Nata'ij al-Ahwal* assigned to the elder women of the family whose oral narratives stimulated her early interest in literature. In choosing to start with the struggle between the freed slave mother and daughter in which the father emerged as the supporter of his daughter's aspirations rescuing her from the reactionary tendencies of her mother, Fawwaz underlined the important role that men played in the struggle for the rights of women. She did not criticize Taymur's father for disrupting his daughter's education by marrying her off at a young age even though she considered his death and that of the husband in 1872 and 1875, respectively, to have allowed the poet to finally become "self governing" and to resume her literary studies.

Finally, Fawwaz represented Taymur's relationship with her daughter in functional terms: Tawhida spared her mother the trouble of taking over the task of managing her household. The problem with this construction was that it failed to explain the profound sadness that the mother felt over the loss of favorite daughter. The functionalist view flattened the complex emotional relationship between mother and daughter that was characterized by both deep affection and conflicting interests. If Tawhida were born after the first year of Taymur's marriage, then Taymur became a mother at 15—an age at which one could not expect her to be either a mature or an experienced mother. In fact, Taymur described her daughter as a young companion who shared many of her interests. The enormity felt at the loss of such a cherished daughter, who was a loving ally, explained Taymur's prolonged mourning, which lasted seven years, disrupting her world and dwarfing her grand aspirations for herself as a writer and poet. Fawwaz's functionalist construction failed to provide an adequate explanation of the complex relationship between mother and daughter that led to the emotional breakdown.

Fawwaz's profile ended with a broad review of Taymur's prose and poetry. It included the full text of her article on the modern education of young girls and broad selections from her Arabic poetry. In addition to the full text of Taymur's first poem that praised the virtue associated with veiling and the development of a new definition of Islamic femininity that emphasized the education of women, Fawwaz also offered examples of Taymur's poetry that dealt with religious themes, courtship, important private and public social occasions and the elegy of her daughter.

The above construction became canonical for several reasons that deserve discussion. First, it nationalized Taymur's Ottoman identity making her a member of the regional Arab-Islamic and Egyptian national communities whose mother tongue was Arabic. Fawwaz was a member of both communities by virtue of being born in Jebel 'Amil in southern Lebanon, then settling in Egypt on and off from the 1870s onward.

Next Fawwaz represented Ismail Taymur, `A'isha's father as a progressive agent of change in his support of his daughter's right to education and presented her slave mother as an obstacle to it. The backwardness of the Turkish slave mother contrasted with the supportive, forward-looking Egyptian-Arab father in their aspirations for their daughter. As a modernist writer, Fawwaz discounted the lasting inspiration that the oral narratives of illiterate women had on her young imagination. She ignored them in her construction because these women, who lacked formal learning, could not be seen as having a lasting positive effect on a prominent writer. The dismissal of the effect that "traditional" mothers or mother figures had in the lives of their children was sacrificed in the focus on the "modern" or scientific definitions of mothering. This construction was used as part of an appeal to men to support a new type of education for their daughters without the fear that it might threaten patriarchal privilege.

Finally, while Fawwaz saw marriage as an obstacle to women's nondomestic aspirations, she did not directly attack the institution that left women with limited time and energy to pursue other activities. Fawwaz, who was married more than once, seemed convinced of this. Yet she only hinted at this critique by declaring that the death of both father and husband freed Taymur from significant social constraints.

In short, Fawwaz's profile of Taymur appealed to the community's new nationalist or linguistic definition of itself. It presented Taymur's father and men in a flattering light and in this way hoped to convince the readers to emulate him in their support of the education of women. It presented the older generation of slave or free women in a less flattering way beginning with Taymur's mother opposition to her daughter's desire for education to Taymur's incomprehensible collapse following the loss of her daughter reinforcing belief in women's emotionality. In short, this construction of Taymur's life as a pioneering woman suffered from the misdirection of blame and credit contributing to the distortion of her life and the lessons to be derived from it.

Ahmed Taymur's Biography of His Sister

The canonical status of Fawwaz's construction of Taymur's life and work was confirmed by Ahmed Taymur's decision to selectively paraphrase and/or copy sections of her biographical profile in his history of the Taymur family. His reluctance to offer any personal insights into his sister's life was puzzling because most of his biographers pointed out that his sister and her husband brought him up following the death of their father in 1872 when he was a little over a year old.[94] Nothing was known about his mother, but one biographical sketch suggested that he lost both parents at an early age making it possible to speculate that his mother died at childbirth and his father a year later leading to the dramatic decision that he be brought up by his sister and her husband. Taymur was said to have been responsible for the decision to send him to a French school as well as his learning of Turkish, Persian, and Arabic.[95] Despite this very close and intimate relationship with his sister, his heavy reliance on Fawwaz's construction of his sister's biography was interesting. It might mean that Fawwaz got the most important details correctly limiting his task to correcting some of the obvious mistakes. Other omissions provided the reader with insights into his historical project as well as his ambivalence toward his sister.

For example, he dropped Fawwaz's description of his sister's mother as a freed slave of his father. He also omitted Fawwaz's explanation of how the death of Taymur's father and her husband gave her greater independence and her long mourning of her daughter, who helped her resume her literary studies. These omissions clearly suggested that Ahmed's borrowing from Fawwaz's biography was guided by the desire to develop a sanitized account of his family's history and his sister's life. He did not want to present his father as the owner of slave women or that he was less than supportive of his sister's literary aspirations after her marriage. He also did not want to discuss how his sister's sons were among her opponents and her critics during her long mourning for Tawhida. While Fawwaz's biography of Taymur ended with a wide selection of her poetry that dealt with social, religious, courtship, and elegiac themes[96] that highlighted the broad scope of her poetic production, her brother chose to end his sister's biography by citing the first two stanzas of her earliest poem in which she defended veiling and female virtue. The result was a very narrow and conservative construction of his sister's poetry.

When Mayy Ziyada interviewed Ahmed for the biography of his sister, his most frequent answer to her questions was "I do not know." The physical description he gave of his sister was interesting: "She was neither tall nor short, nor white or brown, or fat or thin."[97] The emphasis that Ahmed put on the connection between his family and al-Sadda (i.e., the descendants of the prophet) was echoed in this description. In a Hadith (the prophetic tradition) attributed to Ali Ibn Abi Talib, he also described the prophet as neither tall nor short, avoiding extremes in his physical attributes. Here, Ahmed chose to reverentially describe his sister in the same way as Ibn Abi Talib described his revered cousin, the prophet of Islam. Equally important, Taymur's attempt to avoid any discussion of her physical attributes was an attempt at preserving her modesty and/or emphasizing that her literary skills, not her looks, were what mattered. The only substantive comment he made to Ziyada about his sister was in line with the above saying that she was a devout woman who performed all the important religious rituals.

Ziyada attributed Ahmed's inability to provide important information regarding his sister to the big age difference between them, which is more than thirty years, but Ahmed was at least 31 years old when his sister died, casting doubt on age as an excuse for his inability to be more forthcoming. He seemed reluctant to add to his sister's burgeoning reputation in the 1920s and a manifestation of sibling rivalry. During this period, Ahmed had already established a prominent literary and linguistic reputation for himself[98] and his two sons: Muhammad and Ahmed were developing literary reputations as play and short story writers. This might have made him reluctant to share the family limelight with his older sister. It added a generational layer to the Taymur family's ambivalence to Taymur's literary reputation and standing.

His competition with his sister did not negate his affection for her. According to Mahmud, one of Ahmed's sons, who was an award-winning writer of novels and short stories, his father felt a great deal of gratitude to his sister who encouraged his interest in reading and learning. In addition, the son described a very dramatic scene in which his father introduced him to his aunt's poetry when he was very young. He recalled his father approaching him one day with a sheet of paper on which some poetry was written in red ink and commanded him: "Read!" The scene derived its power from its association with the first Qur'anic verse revealed to Prophet Muhammad by the archangel Gabriel, who also commanded him to Read. The parallel between his father commanding him to read his aunt's poetry and Gabriel doing the same with the prophet must have had a powerful effect on his young mind. The association between the Qur'anic verse and his aunt's poetry resonated with power and influence. The poem that his father had asked him to read was the first one she had written in which she described her pride in her veiling and her virtue and how she represented a new definition of Islamic femininity in which her ideas and literary skills were also important sources of her pride.[99]

It was important to situate what I have described so far as the emotional ambivalence of her brother and/or the punitive attitude of her sons as part of the emergence of fraternal forms of control that were different in their operation from older forms of socially sanctioned patriarchal control exercised by fathers and husbands over daughters and wives. In discussions of the social advances made by modern society, the overthrowing of the power of the father who directly exercised power and authority over women and sons in the family by the sons who instituted fraternal relations as part of a modern civil order where equality was a formal right for all. The new society was seen as heralding the triumph of anti and postpatriarchal relations. Feminists were very skeptical of this claim;[100] and in Taymur's biography, one could see the vindication of their view in how her sons banded together as brothers, with the help of the doctors, to discipline their "bad" mother. Later on, their uncle, Ahmed, in withholding positive public valuation of his sister's work, joined them. In theory, neither the sons nor the brother were expected to exercise the kind of power that their fathers had over Taymur, but the new fraternal relations exerted indirect collective influence on her life and work. Ahmed, in particular, used the modern literary discourse and his position as a respected student of the Arabic language to compete with his prominent sister by devaluing the quality of her poetic production and its accomplishments.

CHAPTER 2

Literature and Nation-Building in Nineteenth-Century Egypt

In this chapter, I examine how the literature produced in nineteenth-century Egypt played an important role in the nation-building processes at both the Ottoman center and its periphery reflecting the social and political changes taking place and also helping to develop new forms of solidarity and models of community. This discussion will provide a context for Taymur's study of the relationship between literature, gender and nation-building within which the analysis of ʿAʾisha Taymur's work of fiction titled *Nataʾij al-Ahwal fi al-Aqwal wa al-Afʿal* (The Consequences of Change in Words and Deeds), published in 1887/88[1] will be offered in the next chapter. As part of the analysis of nation-building, I will pay special attention to the way language, translation, and the changes in the old literary forms and themes offered prisms for capturing the homogenizing dynamic in the construction of a modern national community in Egypt and its relations with the Ottoman and European ones. Equally important, I will show that this dynamic privileged the narrative structures, new thresholds of meaning, and prescriptive models of community of a new emerging middle class. The result was the development of horizontal and fraternal bonds of community that gave the emerging middle class an important role to play in the shaping of these communities.

The Role of Print Language and Capitalism in the Construction of a National Community

Nineteenth-century Egypt witnessed a redefinition of the hierarchal ordering among the multiple regional languages identified with the Ottoman community and the development of new relations of power between them and European languages. The Ottoman linguistic system, which reflected the defining political and cultural characteristics of the community, relied on Turkish as the official language of government, Persian as a literary language, and Arabic as the language of religion. In nineteenth-century Egypt, Arabic, the spoken language of the majority, gave way to a new form of social solidarity as the new language of government and literary production. What is often overlooked in the discussions of the nineteenth-century revival of Arabic as the new national language was the parallel reliance on the knowledge of European languages creating a bilingual intelligentsia that played a central role in the region's massive translation project and reform as the cornerstones of modernization.

An examination of the books published during this period in different languages provided a quantitative measure of the changing balance between the languages associated with the multilingual Ottoman system and those associated with the national. The earliest official figures available for published books in Egypt deal with the 1820s. There were one hundred books published during that decade: 49 books were published in Arabic, 43 in Turkish, and 8 in Persian.[2] The functional division of labor between Turkish as the language of government, Persian as a literary language, and Arabic as the language of religion[3] and the number of books published in each language provided a base line for the Ottoman-Egyptian community.

In the 1830s, the opening of modern state schools associated with the modernization project had mixed effects on the fortunes of the Arabic and Turkish languages. It did not immediately challenge the linguistic hierarchy between the two even though the schools heavily recruited Arabic speakers among its student and instructors resulting in a demand for Arabic textbooks—giving the language a new role to play and explaining the jump in the number of published Arabic books to 186. Because these schools also used Turkish to teach administration and military sciences, they also contributed to a parallel jump in the demand for Turkish textbooks (148). The technocratic bent of the modern schools explained both the drop in the number of literary books published in Persian to 5 and the publication of 19 books in what were identified as "other languages,"[4] most probably European ones, which suddenly emerged as new linguistic players during this period.

This early trend, which maintained the relative power of Turkish vis-à-vis Arabic, Persian, and European languages did not continue into the 1840s and the 1850s. In the 1840s, the number of published Arabic books (244) continued its rise in comparison to Turkish (122), Persian (12), and European (26). The educational and fiscal retrenchment that characterized the 1850s did not affect the continued rise in the number of Arabic books (345) but contributed to the decline of the number of all books published in local and European languages: 66 books published in Turkish, 9 in Persian, and 23 in European languages.

In the 1860s, a qualitative change in the fortunes of these languages occurred that was reflected in their publishing record. The reign of Ismail (1863–79), characterized by a simultaneous commitment to maintaining a degree of independence from the Ottoman center and the formation of new alliances with European powers, provided a political framework for accelerating nationalization and internationalization. The adoption of Arabic, instead of Turkish, as the official language of government in 1869 represented a new degree of linguistic and national independence from the Ottoman center. Paradoxically, it was coupled with an increase in the number of European residents and interests in Egypt. The result was that the number of published Arabic books in 1860s skyrocketed to 1,199 with the number of Turkish and Persian books declining further to thirty and three, respectively. In contrast, the number of books that were published in European language (identified as French, English, German, and Italian) rose to 159,[5] signaling a new configuration of languages of (economic and cultural) power. During the turbulent 1870s, the nationalizing and internationalizing trends continued with 1,405 books published in Arabic, 28 in Turkish, 5 in Persian, and 159 in the European languages. While the books published between 1872 and 1878 largely dealt with scientific and technical topics, ones with Islamic titles also increased in numbers.[6]

Most discussions of nineteenth-century nationalism in Egypt and the Arabic-speaking Middle East focus on the rise of the Arabic language as the language of power and cultural production as an important marker of the rise of a new national community. They overlooked the fact that the new community was not monolingual reflecting the international influences (translation, missionary, and state schools, banks and private enterprises) that shaped its early development leading to a multilingual coupling of Arabic with other European languages. While Arabic was the language of the majority, many segments of the middle class became identified with the use of modern standard Arabic as well as at least one other European language.

The onset of British occupation did not reverse the general trends that dominated the second half of the twentieth century. The two-track education system supported by British colonial policy, which on the one hand emphasized basic education for the majority that was largely in Arabic and on the other emphasized the use of Arabic and English for the education of the elite, prepared them for service in the colonial bureaucracy serving as cultural mediators between the speakers of Arabic vernaculars and its British personnel. This system explained the doubling of the number of books published in Arabic with a noticeable increase in European languages in the first decade of British education. Whereas 2,774 books were published in Arabic, 25 in Turkish, 5 in Persian, and 217 in European languages (English, French, and German) in the 1880s, the number of books published in the local and regional languages in the 1890s, including Arabic (2672), Turkish (18), and Persian (4) dropped slightly and those published in European languages (392) nearly doubled.[7]

While the publishing market throughout the nineteenth century was dominated by the school system's demand for textbooks, literary books emerged as a distinct genre that had its own niche. During the first half of the nineteenth century, these books produced in the languages associated with the Ottoman system included: 64 books in Turkish, 12 in Persian and 33 in Arabic.[8] The large number of literary books written and published in Turkish indicated that it was not only a language of government but also the language of literary expression, with Arabic and Persian lagging behind.

During the second half of the nineteenth century, published literary books were more likely to be translated from other languages, be they Turkish, Persian, or European. The important difference here was that regardless of the original language from which these books were translated, 84 percent of them were translated into Arabic underlining the strengthening of the linguistic nationalizing trend and the way print capitalism benefited from the new market for Arabic books. Translations into Turkish represented the next largest category of works at a very modest 14 percent[9] representing the needs of the Turkish speaking elite to which the market continued to respond.

Finally, translated literary works represented a sizable portion of the non-student market establishing literature as an important genre that attracted the interest of the adult reading public. The numbers of fiction that were originally written in Arabic during the second half of the nineteenth century were not available. There were, however, some very important literary works that were written and published in Arabic during this period by leading public figures—like Abdallah Fikri, Ali Mubarak, `A'isha Taymur, and Muhammad al-Manfaluti—that attracted considerable attention.

The expansion of print capitalism was clearly fueled by an increase in literacy, which ceased to be the monopoly of the few (namely, the bureaucrats, the merchants, and the ulema) and reached new social groups like the shopkeepers' apprentices and the sons of village headmen.[10] The primary catalyst in this change was the doubling of the numbers of Qur'anic schools between 1869 and 1878[11] where the Qur'an provided the basis of all learning. Students learned not only the principles of Islam and the basis of Islamic society but also Arabic reading, dictation, simple composition, and basic arithmetic.[12] Along with the modern schools, which remained the preserve of a small segment of the population, they have contributed to the rise of the literacy level from about 5 percent to 8.3 percent in 1880.[13] These percentages were comparable to those that paved the way for the development of modern national communities in Europe.

The new reading public provided a strong stimulus for other forms of print capitalism. During the reign of Khedive Ismail, there were 27 Arabic papers and another 30 published in European languages[14] catering to international residents with economic and political interests. They provided social, economic, and political accounts of the community, its activities, and relations to important European states. They also reported on the corruption of the police and high-ranking provincial officials[15] and commercial information like the prices of exports (especially cotton) and imports.

As the press became the medium of the new national community, it also reflected the important changes in the view of the Arabic language. The Ottoman view of Arabic as a religious language was increasingly challenged as misrepresenting the history of the language in that part of the world and the role it played in the community. Unfortunately, this view persists in some recent reconstructions of the language and its history in Benedict Anderson's *Imagined Communities*—which suggested that Arabic was, like Latin, a sacred language—ignoring the fact that Arabic was spoken long before the advent of Islam by the different peoples of the Arabian peninsula whether they were desert nomads, poets, merchants in trading stopping stations, or the settled peasants communities in Yemen. These early Arabic speakers adhered to many different religions including Christianity, Judaism, and polytheism. During this early period, Arabic poetry emerged as the most developed standard of its literary traditions establishing the ability of the language to give expression to the experiences of its speakers regardless of their different religious traditions.[16] With the advent of Islam, Arabic gained a new sacred status as the language in which the Qur'an was revealed contributing to the development of a body of Islamic knowledge and acquiring Islamic idioms. In playing this new role, it continued to be the spoken language of Arab Muslims, Christians, and Jews. The expansion of the Islamic empires made Arabic the language of administration and education giving new importance to Arabic prose alongside poetry.

The Qur'an, the sacred text of Islam, eventually became a central source that set the standards for the study of grammar and linguistic forms of expression, with religious poetry constituting only a small portion of the prodigious Arab poetry produced by Islamic societies. To be sure, there was a genre devoted to the praise of the prophet that pursued some religious themes, but Arabic poetry remained by and large a wordily alternative to the discourse of religion. Even the study of elegy (*rith'a*), a genre where religious themes and imagery could be expected to dominate, the afterlife was very rarely evoked in Arabic literature as a form of consolation or solace to loss. Such references to the afterlife were employed only when the person mourned was the son of a leader.[17]

Anderson ignored this complex history of the language because he was a student of Indonesian politics where Arabic was not the native language. He made no distinction between the Islamic societies where Arabic was the native language and the places in Asia and Africa where it was identified with religion but where other languages were spoken. In these specific cases including the Ottoman center and the European parts of the empire, Arabic became a religious language separated from the language of daily life.

In the nineteenth-century Arabic speaking world, language clearly emerged as an arena of political struggle and a medium for including different groups into the emerging national community. During this period, the translation of the bible into Arabic represented an attempt to nationalize the language and put it in the service of the Christian subjects and to secure them a place in the new community. Similarly, the `Urabi revolution tried to use the colloquial language in some of the national Arabic press increasing their circulation for the purpose of mobilizing the working classes in support of the revolution.[18] With modern standard Arabic serving as the language of the modernizing state, the middle-class graduates of modern schools, and the colloquial representing the language of the rural and urban majorities offering a more populist definition of the community, the attempt to use of both vernaculars during the `Urabi revolution reflected a radical attempt by the nationalist elite to unify these two segments of the Arabic-speaking community against the Turkish-speaking elites allied with the Europeans. The widely reported social practice of reading the newspapers during the revolution to assembled crowds[19] also signified this emerging alliance between the literate and the illiterate classes.

The failure of the revolution and the expulsion of the working classes from politics settled the outcome of this social linguistic struggle for power in favor of modern standard Arabic and the middle class. Many literary critics who examine the changes taking place in the Arabic language during this period do not pay attention to this social and political history. They also do not acknowledge the important role that print capitalism played in providing the basis for a larger Arabic speaking community that transcended national boundaries and the fragmenting effects of different vernaculars.

The Effect of Translation on Literary Production and the Definition of Community

I have already mentioned that a lot of the literature produced in the second half of the nineteenth century was translated from other languages into Arabic. Rather than deal with these translations as representing the cultural effects of external forces on local literary production, I will offer the alternative view that they were transformed by local writing styles and the politics of the period into regional artifacts. As such, they showed continuity in change. Among the most important translated literary works of the second half of the nineteenth century was Abbe Fenelon's *Les Aventures des Telemaque*, which stood out because it was translated into both Turkish and Arabic providing a vehcicle of the critique of old style autocracy practiced by Ottoman and Egyptian dynastic governments.

Its translators—two leading figures of the Egyptian modernizing elite—were Yusuf Kamil Pasha, one of the ambitious young Ottomans who sought their fortune in Muhammad Ali's modernizing project and Shaykh Rifa` al-Tahtawi, the Egyptian director of the state's translation department.

The Turkish Telemaque (1862)

Serif Mardin's study of the Young Ottomans (an important group of cutlural and political reformers at the Ottoman center) provided a useful context for locating the mature Yusuf Kamil Pasha, the Turkish translator of *Telemaque*. He pointed out that Egypt's reform program, begun by Muhammad Ali (1811–41), preceded the reform effort of Sultan Mahmud II and went further in its Westernization attracting the attention of many Ottoman young men at the center.[20] For these ambitious men, the fact that the Egyptian program was implemented with the aid of Turkish and French staff offered appealing employment opportunities. Unfortunately, the rise of Abbas I to power was accompanied by a conscious effort to purposely disperse members of the upper Ottoman elite in Egypt to distinguish his regime from that of his predecessors.[21] As a result, many of these men returned to Turkey in the 1850s carrying with them new ideas and an abiding interest in reform.

One of these men was Yusuf Kamil, whose career in Egypt offered an interesting case in point. There was some confusion about when and how the younger Yusuf Kamil Effendi (the title used by the educated members of the new middle class) arrived in Egypt. Did he make his way there in 1833 as a young man seeking to make his fortune?[22] Or was he sent in 1841 as a low-level emissary of the Ottoman government?[23] According to family chronicles, Yusuf Kamil took the gamble of coming to Egypt and petitioned its ruler for work.[24] Since Kamil could speak and write in Turkish, Arabic, and Persian, Ali appointed him to a series of clerical positions. Meanwhile, Kamil also learned French during his stay in Egypt.[25]

In 1845, Muhammad Ali surprised his family by selecting him as a husband for his youngest daughter Zeyneb Hanim. From the very beginning, most members of the royal household were opposed to the marriage because they did not think that Kamil had a high enough rank, but Ali ignored their objections. As a result of his services as a representative of the Egyptian government during this period, the sultan bestowed on him the more exalted title of Pasha. Upon Ali's death and the rise of Abbas I to power, the couple were ordered to divorce. They refused, and in response, Kamil was exiled and imprisoned in Aswan close to the Sudanese border and Zeyneb was confined to her palace. She employed the good offices of an elderly female relative traveling to Istanbul to ask the Grand Vezir to intervene. An Imperial Writ was issued securing the release of

Kamil and his guaranteed departure from Egypt. Zeyneb was not allowed to accompany him and her freedom was made contingent on her divorce. The couple pretended to submit to Abbas's wish, sending the divorce papers to Egypt. Once she was set free, she asked for permission to go on the pilgrimage to Mecca and when it was granted, she traveled to Istanbul where she and Kamil remarried.[26] Meanwhile, Kamil had a brilliant career at the Ottoman center occupying several high positions including that of grand vizir.[27]

Upon his return to Istanbul, he completed the Turkish translation of Fenelon's *Telemaque* in 1859. It circulated in manuscript form in Ottoman salons until its publication in 1862—five years before the publication of al-Tahtawi's Arabic translation. The publication of the Turkish translation provoked debate in Istanbul, creating a considerable stir among the Ottoman literati as the first work to carry Western political overtones.[28] Ibrahim Shinasi Effendi, the important poet and a member of the Young Ottomans, stressed that the novel dealt with "all the arts of government that have as their purpose the justice and the happiness of the individual."[29] The Ottoman audience interpreted the work by Fenelon, the tutor of the Duke of Burgundy, the son of Louis XV as charting the path that a just prince should take. The novel focused on Telemaque's search for his father with the help of a wise companion, Mentour, whose advice outlined the bases of self-government and good dynastic rule. Some suggested that this aspect of the novel made it very similar to the Islamic mirror for princes' genre that provided counsel to princes, facilitating its reception by Ottoman readers.[30]

Other commentators examined the translation in relation to the ongoing debate on the change of the Turkish language and its writing style. In the 1850s, Munif Pasha, another Ottoman figure who started his career in Egypt, began to advocate a writing style "accessible to as wide an audience as possible."[31] His call influenced the subsequent review of many translated and other literary works. Namik Kemal, another member of the Young Ottomans, was critical of the Turkish translation of *Telemaque* because it did not have a "popular-enough style."[32] Kemal employed the same criticism of the work of another Young Ottoman writer, Ziya Pasha, who he thought represented the "old school and of the type of literature which the Young Ottoman's had earlier criticized as overloaded and empty."[33] It was Ibrahim Sinasi, another member of that group who led the effort to perfect a clear, concise and simple journalistic Turkish language.[34] He spearheaded the journal *Tasviri Efkar* (1862) to do battle against the advocates of classical Turkish style.[35] Finally, Ziya Pasha later started to argue in favor of the unspoiled Turkish of the pre-Islamic era, thus suggesting the beginnings of a challenge to the Ottoman literary ideals based on the premise of the integration of different languages that provided the basis of the imperial community.[36]

Finally, the Turkish translation of *Telemaque* also drew a conservative Muslim response from a member of the ulema in the form of an anonymous manuscript circulated at the time and titled *Tanzir-i Telemak* (the Rebuttal of Telemaque). This work protested the Tanzimat, the reformist reorganization of the Ottoman bureaucracy, for overlooking religion and Islamic principles as bases of civilization. According to the author, this oversight led to the reformers' failure to cure the evils within the empire like the decline of morals and the neglect of its pious foundations. Equally important, the author faulted the Tanzimat for not according the ulema the importance they were due in defining change in general and for not implementing the Islamic value of "consultation," which was deemed crucial in the discussion of an Islamic form of representative government.[37] It is interesting to note that the so-called conservative Muslim response did not reject or oppose the drive to reform but rather wanted to secure a bigger role for religion and/or Islamic principles. This idea was not without its supporters. In fact, some of the members of the Young Ottomans shared this goal; Namik Kemal, in particular, worked toward the development of a modern-Islamic synthesis.[38]

Commentators on the Turkish translation of *Telemaque* pointed out that its themes were largely concerned with the reform of dynastic Islamic forms of government, emphasizing the ruler's need to look after the interests of his subjects (*reaya*), the importance of subordinating his base animal pleasures to the pursuit of knowledge, the abandonment of political intimidation, corruption, graft and despotism, and the management of the affairs of state "in council."[39] Just as Fenelon felt a "yearning for the reestablishment of a perfect bygone order of state that lived in his imagination," the Young Ottoman's couched their demand for representation through the return to the Islamic-Ottoman governmental principle and practice of *meshveret* (consultation).[40] These different Turkish views regarding the need for reform to arrest the decline of the Ottoman dynastic form of government introduced modern forms of discipline in the debate. It advocated changes in the "government of others" with a redefinition of the relationship between the Muslim ruler and those that he led (*raeya*): he was expected to protect them and to pursue their "interests," which were elevated to a new level of importance. In addition, the modern Muslim ruler was expected to exercise "self government"—that is, subordinating base pleasures to the pursuit of knowledge. One could detect here the effect of the utilitarian discussion of the hedonistic pleasure versus more superior pleasure like knowledge and education. Self-government and the government of others met in the admonition for the prince to give up intimidation, corruption, graft, and despotism.

To what extent did the Egyptian literary and political establishments including the the Taymur family follow this debate? During the early part of Ismail Pasha's reign (1863–79), an intense rivalry between Ismail and his half brother—Prince Mustafa Fazil, who was next in line to inherit the Egyptian throne—that played itself out at the Ottoman center. Fazil had spent most of his life at the Ottoman Porte where he got his education eventually becoming minister of education in 1862, minister of finance in 1864 and then chairman of the council of treasury in 1865.

Ismail used money and the fact that his mother was the sister of Sultan Abdel Aziz's mother to alter the principle of Egyptian dynastic succession, giving his descendants direct access to the throne in May 1866. This was followed by the declaration of an Egyptian constitution in November 1866, which established Ismail's modernist and constitutional credentials. In response, Fazil embraced the Young Ottomans' reform agenda as a means of politically reinventing himself at the Ottoman center. As the self-described leader of the group,[41] Fazil submitted a letter to Sultan Abdel Aziz that argued in favor of the introduction of changes in the political system that would pave the way to a modest constitutional-representative government. The letter, published in the French daily (*Liberté*) on March 24, 1867, was also translated into Turkish with fifty thousand copies distributed in the Ottoman capital where it created a sensation.[42] It was followed by the establishment of the Young Ottoman Society on August 10, 1867, in Paris, which adopted the principles of reform outlined in Fazil's letter as the basis of its program.[43] To popularize their ideas and their criticisms of the Ottoman government, the society published its views first in *al-Muhbir* (1867) and then in *Hurriyat* (1868), which were both published in London with Fazil's financial backing.

One can assume that the views of the Young Ottomans on reform during the 1860s and the 1870s spread to Egypt given their connection to Prince Fazil whose actions were of interest to members of the Ottoman-Egyptian class. Turkish language journals found their way to Egypt[44] allowing many Egyptians to follow these developments. Not only were these publications of interest to Egyptian readers, but they were also followed by the Egyptian government. When Fazil's support for *Hurriyat* waned in 1868, Khedive Ismail stepped in his shoes and supported the newspaper's continued critique of the Ottoman government with the proviso that they exonerate him from blame in the struggle with his brother and other Ottoman officials.[45] Prince Fazil eventually broke with the Young Ottomans in 1874 and died shortly after in 1875.

The Arabic Telemaque (1867)

Shaykh Rifa` al-Tahtawi brought his stature and political struggle with injustice to the Arabic translation of Fenelon's *Telemaque*. Next to the Albanian Muhammed Ali, who founded a new dynasty in Egypt that represented itself as the advocate of modernization, the Egyptian al-Tahtawi was the pioneering intellectual and romantic figure of that period. An Azharite shaykh appointed to give moral guidance to the Egyptian students who were members of the largest educational mission sent to France in 1826, al-Tahtawi displayed an impressive aptitude in learning French eventually becoming one of the illustrious students of that mission. Upon his return to Egypt, he became a state functionary for a long period (1838–73) who was responsible for the translation of many scientific, historical, legal and geographic works from French to Arabic. Al-Tahtawi was credited with making European modern works and approaches available to an Egyptian public eager to embrace them.[46] In general, he was seen as the creative mind behind the development of the indigenous "enlightenment" project.

When Abbas I closed the state's translation department in 1851, he sent al-Tahtawi (who was its director) to Sudan to serve as the principal of its first primary school. Al-Tahtawi considered this appointment to be a punishment and/or a form of exile. Some historians speculated that he was punished for some of the views included in the second edition of his popular book, *Takhlis al-'Ibriz fi Talkhis Pareez* (The Extraction of What Is Prominent in the Description of Paris), whose discussion of the French monarchy emphasized that it shared power with representative institutions and ruled in accordance with the law and the constitution[47] ideas that an autocratic ruler, like Abbas, found threatening.[48]

Most literary critics draw a connection between al-Tahtawi's experience of exile in Sudan and his selection of this novel to translate. They based themselves on his introduction to the work in which he explained his state of mind and the reasons why he selected Telemaque to translate:

> When destiny landed me in the Sudan, I did not resist the will of God . . . For a while, I was inactive and my intellect was paralyzed in the face of this catastrophe. The oppressive heat of this province with its toxins practically destroyed me. I felt as though its ferocious elephants came close to swallowing me. Then, I decided that if I were to have a share of happiness [or hope in] the future, some form of useful activities and justice, I needed to distance myself from this far away place. I told my heart this translation will provide me with a sense of security to be found in its valuable stories from European kingdoms upon which education depended. More than any other book, [this one] is concerned with literature and the discussion of the best royal ethics and policies . . . It was then that I decided to entertain myself by translating Telemaque and strengthening my hope that the stars will turn.[49]

Al-Tahtawi clearly experienced his transfer to Sudan (1849–54) as a catastrophic turn of events. His representation of Sudan was bleak: it was a place whose heat, toxins, and ferocious animals threatened and sapped one's energy, making it impossible to be creative. The only way he could protect himself from the deadening effects of the place was to distance himself from it through the translation of a literary work that brought him closer to Europe and its culture and narratives, which discussed the "best royal ethics" as part of an ideal form of government. Because opposition to Abbas's decisions was a form of political suicide, al-Tahtawi bid his time hoping for a change in the stars or fortune placing his faith in his destiny and God's will as the title of the book indicated. Most literary critics who discuss al-Tahtawi's Arabic translation of *Tele-maque*, titled *Mawaqi`a al-'Aflak fi Waqa`i Telemaque* (The Position of the Stars and the Adventures of Telemaque), consider it to be the Arabic reader's first introduction to a new genre, a novel that broke away from the existing literary forms, themes, and even the beliefs of the time. Paradoxically, they note that the translation was written in the familiar rhyming style of the *maqama*, which was the local literary form. The old rhyming style employed in the translation led some critics to say that it was responsible for its inexactness.[50] All defended his translation, however, by suggesting that he was obliged to write in this style in order to appeal to his readers' sensibilities.[51] Most were unwilling to concede that al-Tahtawi's Islamic and cultural perspectives as well as the maqama writing style distracted from the modern character of the translation.

This was an interesting reading of the work because it differed from the way the translator viewed it. In the introduction, he did not stress any radical break between the French work and Arabic literary tradition. On the contrary, he drew parallels between the importance of Greek mythology from which Fenelon drew inspiration and the pre-Islamic traditions that were important for Arabic poetry. As for the moral lessons learned from Greek mythology in *Telemaque*, they were not very different from the parables offered by *Maqamat al-Hariri* (*al-Hariri's Maqama*) and the *One Thousand and One Nights*.[52]

Even though the Arabic *Telemaque* was published in Beirut and therefore was not immediately available to Egyptian readers, it eventually became very popular. A young Shaykh Muhammad `Abdu, who was actively involved in 1881 in the `Urabi national revolution, reviewed the most popular books of the time in an article published in *al-Ahram* daily newspaper on May 11, 1881. He pointed out that the reading public "preferred works of history, articles dealing with moral subjects and novels."[53] The latter he called *rumaniyat* (romances) and included among them *Telemaque* and *Kalila wa Dimna*, a book translated from Persian by Ibn al-Muqaffa` (died in 727).

The joint popularity of *Kalila wa Dimna* and *Telemaque* indicated elements of continuity and change in literary tastes and sensibilities. The public continued to enjoy Persian literature translated into Arabic well into the last quarter of the nineteenth century. It also enjoyed *Telemaque*, which in the turbulent 1880–81 acquired a new national meaning and content. With one khedive deposed in 1879 and another under severe nationalist attack, *Telemaque's* critique of royal autocracy resonated with the general public accounting for its popularity. Even though Shaykh `Abdu categorized the work as a romance novel, he was emphasizing the connection between the literary and the political with the former used to camouflage the latter.

Finally, al-Tahtawi mentioned in the introduction to *Telemaque* that he had heard about, but not seen, the Turkish translation by Kamil Pasha. This reference was designed to separate his work from the one that preceded it and had such a great reception at the Ottoman center. When al-Tahtawi praised the Pasha for having strong skills in both the Turkish and the French languages, he seemed to stress his authority over Kamil who was a student at the School of Languages where al-Tahtawi was the preeminent teacher and translator of French.

Several questions remained about how and why Kamil and al-Tahtawi selected *Telemaque* to translate. Was there any connection between Kamil's and al-Tahtawi's decisions to translate this work into Turkish and Arabic, respectively? Was *Telemaque* part of the French curriculum at the School of Languages? If the answer is yes, then were they influenced, for example, by the popularity of the book? Did their exile by Abbas I explain why this work with its critique of old style autocracy resonated with them?

It is difficult to answer any of these questions definitively. It seems reasonable to assume though that Kamil and al-Tahtawi were acquainted with each other and that their decisions to translate the same novel were shaped by their connection to the School of Languages, conflict with Abbas and the way literature was used during this period as a venue and cover for voicing political criticism of government. All of the above showed the contextualization of the French work, which neatly fit into the discussion of the nature of government in Egypt and the interest in reform. Instead of highlighting the comparative differences between the French and Ottoman and Egyptian communities and governments, the translation underlined their common interest in the critique of autocratic government.

The *Maqama* and the Novel as Markers of Tradition and Modernity in Nineteenth-Century Discourses on Egypt

In contrast to al-Tahtawi's stress on the comparable similarity of the French and Arabic literary traditions, most of the students of nineteenth-century Egypt, who focus their study on the development of modern national communities, utilize the binary opposition between tradition and modernity to offer a linear account of how Arabic literature abandoned the maqama, an indigenous premodern narrative form considered to be inferior to the modern novel as a measure of successful modernization of Arab literary forms of expression appropriate for the modern nation.[54] In fact, the discussion of nineteenth-century literary production is dominated by a huge debate focused on which Arabic work qualified as the first novel.[55]

The binary opposition between tradition and modernity is an important intellectual assumption in the discussions of the development of modern national communities. Some students of European societies suggested that the use of archaic images and/or forms provided means of distinguishing what was historically new about modernity.[56] In the same vein, some theories argue that *tradition was a modern construct* used to highlight what was appealing about its social and political projects.[57] In contrast, there was a second view that occupied center stage in the study of non-European societies, treating tradition as a defining characteristic of the Orient that explained its essential backwardness and opposition to the modern Occident. It represented the institutions of Oriental society as static, inferior, and unable to adjust to the demands of change making modernization or modernity the only available societal option. The literal interpretations of that opposition were both sweeping and misleading in their claim to describe and explain the diverse premodern formations

The last construction influenced nineteenth-century appreciation of the maqama, a narrative form that emerged in the fourth Islamic century. It had four constitutive pillars: "(1) the presence of a narrator and a hero who sometimes were one and the same, but sometimes were separate, (2) the employment of a literary writing style that emphasized rhyme, ornamental words and imagery, (3) the exploration of a class, economic, religious or linguistic problem and (4) the choice of a specific topical concern or moral lesson. While the first three requirements never changed, the choice of topic usually reflected the influences of the time."[58] As such, the maqama could be described as a short story with an elegant writing style that focused on a specific problem with its own moral lesson.[59]

Of the above characteristics, most literary critics focused on the maqama's preoccupation with rhyme, ornamental words, and imagery as its most serious flaw. Not only was this writing style considered to be cumbersome, but it also was considered to be an obstacle to the exploration of issues and the development of characters. In the assessment of the literary production of the nineteenth century, invoking the maqama writing style or form became sufficient grounds for dismissing a literary work, focusing one's attention on form rather than content and maintaining silence on the possible contributions that a narrative might make to our understanding of the specific historical concerns of a particular period.

The above attitude to the literary language used in nineteenth century reflected a lack of appreciation for its multiple levels of meaning used to entertain and to instruct the reader. Flowery language did not conflict with serious concerns. They provided something for everyone: for the average reader, they offered the beauty of expression; and for the more discerning one, they elegantly posed thoughtful issues. In addition, there is the amazing skill involved in the wordplays that have more than one meaning, allowing the writer a certain economy of expression. In the next two sections, I will demonstrate the complexity of this discredited language in the translation of titles and passages from Taymur's work. For most part, I have opted for the less obvious literal meaning, making sure that the one selected is also in line with the intellectual concerns of the work.

The discussion of Abdallah Fikri's maqama offered a good case in point of the limited approach. Fikri, the deputy director of the department of private schools, was the author of a maqama titled *al-Maqama al-Fikriya al-Saniya fi al-Mamlaka al-Batiniya* (*Fikri's Royal Maqama in the Kingdom of the Unconscious*) that was published in Cairo in 1873. He claimed that he translated it from a Turkish work that was, in turn, copied from a European one, which he found when he traveled to Constantinople.[60] Curiously, he did not mention the titles of either the Turkish or the European originals; only that he was translating their work. Despite the absence of these important references, the maqama reflected the cultural and political concerns of the period: the influence of translation, the important role that Turkish and European literatures played in Egypt, the reliance on the maqama to make a translated work familiar to the reader and the question of political reform.

Fikri's maqama had a narrator, whose name was Abu al-Maqal Ibn Thakir (literally "father of the article and the son of memory") and the hero was al-Khayal Ibn Khater (imagination the son of thoughts). Both represented the important role that prose and fiction writers played in the understanding of the human world. The allegorical names also suggested that the narrative had an instructional goal based on the adventures of travelers in the relatively safe imaginary world.

Imagination traveled with a guide called tact. They saw king reason with his vizier (advisor) called foresight and a treacherous companion named emotion (*al-hawa*). Imagination meditated some of the contradictions he observed within the boundaries of this kingdom. Reason occasionally submitted to foresight and frequently to emotion. Throughout the journey, imagination asked tact to explain these contradictions and tact obliged.

On one level, the allegorical characters engaged in abstract discussion of the interplay between reality and imagination or fantasy as well as emotion and reason. On another, they offered a critique of how royal figures did not listen to rational counsel and more often than not fell prey to fickle feelings and treacherous characters. As such, it offered a critique of the personalized aspect of dynastic government by a prominent functionary, who had good knowledge of its operation. His suggestions for reform were in line with the Young Ottomans' call for the rationalization of dynastic rule and Fazil's critique of the tyranny and corruption within the higher circles. Because these political views would expose the author to punishment, Fikri paired imagination and tact in this effort to critique. In case that failed, he could claim that this work was a translation from other languages as Yusuf Kamil and Rifa` al-Tahtawi did before him.

The maqama ended with the following interesting conclusion: "I returned to where I came from and after consciously understanding what I saw and desired, I wanted to share my enlightenment with the common folks and to narrate what I observed."[61] If the kingdom of the unconscious was where these events occurred, then the hero had not really traveled at all but realized the connection to a real place, making the lessons learned from this short story beneficial to other readers. Not only did the maqama describe themes and problems with which Egyptians were historically familiar, but it also provided them a culturally specific form that they recognized.

Fikri's creative attempt to work within the literary tradition to capture the changes taking place within the community provided a contrast to Kamil's and al-Tahtawi's attempts to employ imported forms. It was also different from another work written by Ali Mubarak who was trained as an army engineer in France for a number of years. With this technical and military background, he was appointed numerous times as the minister of education, founding the journal of that department, *Rawdat al-Madarass* (the play on the word *Rawdat* allows him to refer to a garden where these schools flourished and the training these schools provided), which served as a vehicle for spreading the use of modern standard Arabic as a functional language of education and state administration. He also wrote a 13-volume set of the history of Egypt and its major cities.

Given these many nontechnical writing interests, it was not surprising that Mubarak dabbled in fiction. The result was `Alam al-Din, which was published in 1882. Most literary critics found it very difficult to categorize because while it was not a maqama, it was also not a novel. It used the writing style frequently employed in the press: it had a central idea, but very few unfolding events and finally the work stopped without having a proper ending. As a result, the effort by some to classify it as the first Arabic novel[62] was not widely accepted.

In the introduction to the work, Mubarak observed the very slow change in peoples' literary tastes and hoped to use `Alam al-Din to offer an alternative. The following were his views on this subject:

> I observed that many people preferred to read biographies [*siyar*], stories [*qissas*], and *bons mots* [*mulah al-Kalam*]. The opposite was true of pure arts or the sciences that [readers] often boycotted when feeling bored . . . or worried. This led me to write book that included many benefits [*al-fawwa'id*] in the form of a nice story. My goal was to stimulate [people] to read it . . . and unconsciously without much effort reap these benefits. [All this] was done in the pursuit of generalized manfa` [utility]. [It] included [the discussion of] religious *shari`a*, sciences, industrial arts, the secrets of the universe, strange creatures of the sea and land,

the change of the human species in the ancient past and the present, its progress and its regression . . . It offered multiple oppositions and comparisons of habits during different periods of time and in diverse locations.

[The story line revolved around] the imaginary travels of an Egyptian Shaykh named `Alam al-Din, who was employed by an English orientalist, to go to France. Their exchanges serve as a basis for a comparison between Eastern [Oriental] and European [Occidental] conditions.[63]

In the above quote, Mubarak acknowledged the failure of the new writing style and genres to appeal to most readers who preferred the old literary forms, including biographies and narratives (*qissas*), with their decorative writing styles and elegantly written tales of wisdom (*mulah al-kalam*). Lack of general interest in what Mabarak identified as new forms, which he categorized as pure art or science, led him to offer a modern narrative that emphasized instruction, utility, and benefits couched in the form of a travel narrative (*qissa*) that provided a comparison between the "Orient" and "Occident." The title happens to be the name of his leading character, `Alam al-Din (literally the flag scholar of religion), whose services were employed by an English Orientalist requiring `Alam al-Din to travel with him to France—one of the most modern centers of the world. Through the lengthy exchanges (125 conversations in total) with the Englishmen sightseeing in France, `Alam al-Din became persuaded of the inferiority of the Orient and the superiority of the Occident, transforming him into a spokesman of the new order.

Recent analyses of this novel emphasized its Benthamite (utilitarian and modernizing) message and the connection it provided between spatial order and personal discipline in France and their lack thereof in Egypt.[64] As an articulation of the new order, most modernist literary critics admired the work and especially its break with the maqama writing style, but they faulted Mubarak for paying less attention to the structure of the narrative including the absence of an ending. Mubarak's political views proved to be another serious problem. Some analysts criticized the way he "appeased the English and the Europeans."[65] Others pointed out that *`Alam al-Din* offered an apologetic view of British occupation claiming that the English "did not fight us on religious grounds nor did they expel us from our land, [but] stood with us against our enemies"![66] In this minority view, there was no need to reject British occupation because it could be represented as a new alliance between English and Egyptian modernists against the forces of tradition. Finally, some critics pointed out that an examination of the content of the exchanges between the English Orientalist and `Alam al-Din showed an uncritical acceptance of the Orientalist discourse and its problematic representation of the "Orient" as static and barren. It catalogued the manifestations of the inferiority of Islamic societies seeking to persuade the Orientals that they could only develop by opening themselves to the "Occident"[67] whose superiority was made evident by modern institutions and modes of expression. His characters, both Muslims and non-Muslims, traveled to the West and treated it as a standard by which they were to judge themselves, each other, and their respective societies.

In light of the above, `Alam al-Din proved to be a difficult sell. Its length (1,486 pages), its offensive representations of Western and Oriental civilizations, its date of publication (1882) in the middle of the events leading up to British occupation, and the cost of its four-volume set explained why one thousand sets were collecting dust in a Cairo warehouse two years after its publication.[68] Meanwhile, the publishing market continued to sell Arabic readers popular Islamic classics, like *The Travels of Ibn Battutah* and collections of the prophetic tradition.[69]

It is clear that the intellectual class of the second half of the nineteenth century played a critical role in the attempt to nationalize and homogenize the community through the reform of the spoken language of the majority and its use in the discussion of the primary concerns of the community in old and translated literary works. These attempts occurred both at the center and the periphery of the Ottoman community. Yusuf Kamil, Rifa` al-Tahtawi, Abdallah Fikri, and Ali Mubarak represented prominent members of a rising middle class who were rewarded with honorary titles in recognition of their contribution to the community. As titled individuals, they established new links between middle and upper classes in this important period.

Taymur's Perspectives on Literature, Gender, and the National Agendas as Markers of Community

Taymur's introduction to her first published work, *Nata'ij al-Ahwal fi al-Aqwal wa al-Af`al*, outlined the intellectual framework that guided her writing delineating the connections between religion, literature, gender, and the nation as markers of community. In addition, she was concerned with the development of a societal and literary synthesis that integrated old and new agendas.

In the opening paragraph that was almost always ignored by the critics as flowery and formulaic, she discussed the connection between human and divine knowledge in literary production and explicitly referenced al-Hadith (the prophetic tradition and also prose writing) as parts of the work. The prophetic tradition's concern for guiding the words and deeds of ordinary Muslim was explicitly part of the title, indicating a desire to examine the impact that change had for the articulations and actions of of Muslims as members of the community.

In one of the pioneering works about cultural production in nineteenth-century Egypt, which for most part situated itself within an Islamic framework,

Peter Gran differentiated between two approaches to writing, its relationship to the world and change. On the one hand, there were Hadith studies whose attempt to understand the actions and utterances of the prophet encouraged a positivist attitude to the world that took into account the logic of context and induction lending itself to critical consciousness.[70] It paid attention to "language sciences" but more broadly to literature and history. Within that tradition, there was already an exploration of comparative definitions of history that included *al-akhbar* literature that offered chronicles of events and deeds, middle class history in its interest in explaining change and finally a move toward "a holistic understanding of the human condition."[71] The merchant classes also relied heavily on this tradition in their attempt to address its changing needs.

On the other hand, there was the approach represented by *fiqh* (jurisprudence) that was identified with Aristotelian logic and deduction with an emphasis on the abstract and the universal.[72] This particular form of writing was employed in state administration and legislation seeking to adapt the modernizing blueprints to local conditions.[73]

Because *Nata'ij al-Ahwal* belonged to prose writing of this period, Taymur saw no problem in situating herself within Hadith studies with its openness to induction as part of the study of the changing world and better human knowledge. The prophetic tradition inspired reflective thought and human knowledge, and literature added to the understanding of the divine message: "Human truth benefited from this divine gift"[74] and the speaking self was able to use this religious advantage to excel. Those interested in literature enjoyed the privilege of having divine talents (the knowledge and the beauty of the Arabic language), making understanding the focus of their thought, reflection their long term quest, determination and generosity their companions, and careful examination their source of guidance.[75] The beauty and writing styles of the Qur'an and the prophetic tradition were sources of literary inspiration allowing those interested in literature to develop the divine gift of language. As the reader of *Nata'ij al-Ahwal* was to discover, the religious message was not crudely offered; it combined the understanding of issues with thoughtfulness, an appreciation of the values of society, and social guidance cum regulation.

Next, Taymur introduced gender as a novel marker of community by discussing how her personal experience and education reflected the old and new roles of women. She identified herself as the "broken winged" 'A'isha Taymur, a popular social idiom of the time that stressed a woman's seclusion within her home and the inability to venture to the outside world with its broad interests. She quickly challenged this view of women's limited horizons by sharing with reader how the oral stories narrated by the older women of her family, a familiar social activity within most families, were not handicapped by seclusion and the resulting broken wings. Their imaginations soared beyond the mundane demands of their household reflecting an interest in an informal or popular type of history (*akhbar*) that helped stimulate and develop Taymur's imagination and early interest in the literary world: the mysterious play of fortune, the mixing of the serious and the light in entertaining the listener and reflecting on the meaning behind the narratives.

Next, Taymur mentioned the moment in her childhood when she learned about gender as a marker between the cultural worlds of men and women. When she was old enough, she learned that written literature produced by men was not open to members of her gender. Thus began an unusually long and active history of struggle to overcome social and institutional barriers, which made her quest to become a literary writer difficult. First, she learned that she was expected to learn embroidery and crafts. Next, the desire to learn how to read and write was defined as a violation of the social rules that separated the gender roles of men and women. Through stubborn determination, she succeeded in gaining the support of her father for a private education that allowed her to learn Turkish, Arabic, and Persian, which formed the basis of Ottoman literary learning.

While she did not mention that her private education was disrupted by marriage, she informed the reader that she also continued her literary learning on her own. In her secluded world, the Qur'an emerged as an important religious and a literary text. It provided moral guidance, a source of appreciating the beauty of the Arabic language and the art of storytelling. As a result, Taymur credited God through the Qur'an with teaching her "what man [woman] had not known." This last point was borrowed from the first Qur'anic verse revealed to Prophet Muhammad, which begins, "Read in the name of God . . . who taught man what he did not know." In this case, the Qur'an taught Taymur what "no woman had known"—that is, an appreciation of language, literature, and religious knowledge. What Taymur did not mention was that she employed the literary services of two capable women tutors to learn about grammar and poetic meter. While this kind of education fell short of the formal literary education that her male contemporaries enjoyed, Taymur underlined its superiority by virtue of the fact that God and Islam's divine text guided it.

In addition to the Qur'an, Taymur developed a strong interest in formal history (*al-tawarikh*) as distinct from the more informal history (*al-akhbar*) that the older women of her family incorporated in their oral narratives. She declared that she read as much history as she could. This offered a very explicit indication that history in general and Egyptian history in particular influenced her narrative.

Taymur then asked her reader to take her gender difference into account in their evaluation of the work. She did not have access to the knowledgeable circles of the ulema or the gatherings of literary men. While she resented her exclusion and educational deprivation simply because she was a veiled and secluded woman, she used this to beg the reader's indulgence for any slight errors the readers may find in her text.

Seclusion affected Taymur's writing in another way: it made her rely more heavily on reflection (*ta'mul*) in the development of her narrative and its message. While she was aware of the history of her society, she was not an active participant in that history. As a result, the reflection born of that seclusion became a hallmark of her work and it was the approach that she frequently mentioned in describing her work. She also included it in the title of her other important work *Mir'at al-Ta'mul fi al-Umur* (A Reflective Mirror on Some Matters). This reflective quality distinguished her writings from those produced by other men and women of different generations.

While many literary critics dismissed *Nata'ij al-Ahwal* as another traditional work because of its maqama writing style, those who have paid close attention to her use of language credited her with introducing major innovations in the literary language of her time.[76] While she did not use the journalistic language used by different newspapers and/or by Ali Mubarak's `Alam al-Din*, she used an Arabic language that struck a middle ground, retaining some of its images, musicality, multiple meanings, and sacred references (including verses from the Qur'an and reference to the prophetic tradition) but simplifying the writing style so that it was not cumbersome to the reader. This provided additional evidence to support the claim that reform was a major and complex theme in her writings, including the development of a literary synthesis.

Did the introduction describe her work in those terms? In a very brief summary of the content of her narrative, she informed her reader that she combined the past traditions of women with those written by men relying on the use of informal and formal history to reflect on the *course and history of nations* (*umam*). In this regard, she was convinced that fortune and misfortune followed each other. She stated that her personal experiences confirmed that view. While she did not elaborate on how her personal experience mirrored the course and history of nations, her Egyptian readers most probably understood her reference to their changing national fortunes: the ambitious and promising modernization led by Khedive Ismail (1863–79) was followed by increased indebtedness, the deposition of the khedive and British occupation in 1882.

Because censorship accompanied British occupation, freedom of literary expression continued to be restricted during the 1880s. Only a few newspapers were allowed to operate: prominent among them was *al-Muqatam*, owned by Syrian Christians, which emerged as the legitimizing voice of British rule and its colonial agenda. As a result, Taymur couched the theme of her narrative in the traditional terms of fortune and misfortune. If she had explicitly stated that her narrative was preoccupied with the national crisis of dynastic government that rocked Egyptian society in 1879–82 and its reform, the censors would not have permitted her to publish the work. So she followed in the footsteps of Yusuf Kamil, Rifa` al-Tahtawi, and Abdallah Fikri, who camouflaged their political views by using what, looked on the surface to be innocuous literary works that adhered to traditional literary forms.

In developing her study of national issues and agendas, she added an indirect gendered twist to the discussion that was typical of the maqama writing style where the language was typically used to imply different levels of meaning. Because the root Arabic word for nations (*umam*) and the word for mother were the same, Taymur connected her experience as a bereaved mother to that of the wounded Egyptian nation subjected to occupation. Just as the history of nations affected the development of its members and their important social activities including mothering, women, through their caretaking activities had an important contribution to make to the transformation of the nation and its members.

While the loss of her daughter initially plunged her into the depth of despair, writing provided her with a way to heal the loss and make sense of it. Taymur described *Nata'ij al-Ahwal* as written for all those who suffered from misfortunes, injustice, or felt isolated and alienated from their surroundings. It sought to entertain, help them overcome their isolation and loneliness, explaining the way to happiness and pleasure and outlining the religiously sanctioned straight path.[77] The last point combined interest in the secular notion of happiness with the religious view of correct behavior as part of the instructional message. In its quest for both of these goals, the nation acquired a new hybrid character.

Taymur shared with Mubarak a utilitarian view of literature where entertainment was a way of engaging the reader and instructing him. As if to reinforce the utilitarian and educational concerns of the narrative, she proceeded to explicitly state the themes of each one of her chapters. Chapter 1 discussed the methods for awakening the ignorant from the duplicity of hypocrites, how they tricked their victims and how the ignorant eventually realized the negative consequences of a life that they had mismanaged. Chapter 2 developed a proscriptive approach that discouraged arrogance and rebelliousness in words and in deeds through discipline. Chapter 3 dealt with a cultural understanding of the anatomy of approach and withdrawal as central themes of any life.[78] In experiencing the withdrawal of fortune, one's faith and patience were tested. In contrast, those who deal with life's approach needed *brotherly or fraternal support* and the ability to express their gratitude. Chapter 4 explored the delights of friendship and how to coolly nurture it and use it to learn about "good management." Finally, Chapter 5 examined the good rewards due to those who were patient and the realization of their hopes and the terrible consequences of betrayal and how deceit undermined its perpetrators.[79]

The utilitarian themes aside, the outline also underlined some of the important old and new cultural vices and virtues in nineteenth-century society with an emphasis on personal responsibility and the development of a new type of social education needed for individual growth. As far as Taymur was concerned, the struggle between virtue and vice continued to be entertaining to adult readers as well as useful in understanding the challenges one faced in the education of the young. The list of vices discussed in the narrative included hypocrisy, deceit, immodesty, rebellion, and betrayal, which emerged as social problems and/or challenges to personal growth and learning. The virtues included the ability to appreciate failure and achievements as integral parts of an individual's life cycle along with patience, faith, friendship, and fraternal support. In the above one could see the influence of the old Islamic ideal of the avoidance of vice and the learning of virtue coupled with the modern goal of the management of the self.

In the concluding section of this introduction, Taymur turned her attention to literature, good manners, education, and gender as important parts of a national agenda that *Nata'ij al-Ahwal* advocated. This was how she described it.

I want to state (and upon God I depend and with the prophet in mind) the [following] self-evident/Muslim and certain truth: literature/good manners [*al-adab*] represents an axis [*qutb*] upon which a lived and a familiar life revolve. It is a source of culture and education that can reform deviance . . . Whoever leans on the cane of literature/good manners is safe from false steps. Those who benefit from it are able to clothe their flaws from others.

Good education [*husn al-tarbiya*] is the most wonderful thing to present to an audience. It brings one closer to human truth and shows how the goodness of a child depends on education because if left to himself, he will not tend to discipline [*tahtheeb*]. He will avoid good manners as a sheep would a wolf. He whose reins are left to the whims of childhood will surely destroy the future solidity of his masculinity [*rujulatih*] and his virtue [muru'atih]. The leniency of a caretaker can easily lead [a child] to evil. This is not a surprising conclusion for it has been said that he who grows up accustomed to something will grow old with it.

Those with foresight are certain that the most serious struggle [*jihad*] is that which concerns the education to male children [*al-'awlad*]. It includes politically/diplomatically *bi al-siyasa* preventing them from mingling with foolish and lowly people. Beware of having a knave lead [your child], covering his eyes with the veil of trickery or distracting him through hypocrisy from the source of good manners, which serves his best interest [*maslaha*]. [Without it], he will be condemned to loss . . . and to burn with the fire of regret and anxiety. From bad manners, he will derive a deadly salt that will transform his [original] good intentions into habitual deceit and hypocrisy.[80]

Taymur began by playing with the Arabic word *adab*, which stood for good manners and literature. Adab, a "complex of valued dispositions (intellectual, moral and social) appropriate norms of behavior, comportment and bodily habitus,"[81] was a long standing cultural and Islamic tradition that was represented by proper behavior[82] and legal manuals[83] that minutely discussed the responsibilities of mother and father toward their children in the family and also the process of their separation. According to the articulations of these traditions in the nineteenth century, women were responsible for the upbringing of their children (*hadhana*, which refers to the process of bonding with a child by literally "holding him/her to one's bosom") until the age of seven; after which, a father will participate in the education and the discipline of his children, especially sons.[84] This stressed the shared responsibility that mothers and fathers had in the upbringing of children.

Some suggested that this Islamic tradition influenced the debate on education in nineteenth-century Egypt and competed with modern discourses on the subject.[85] Unfortunately given the polarized representation of nineteenth-century social debates, the advocacy of Islamic reform in education was considered to be part of old cultural traditions or the *salafiyya* movement as articulated by Jamal al-Din al-Afghani and Muhammad ʿAbdu.[86] This view overlooked the important works of ʿA'isha Taymur and Abdallah al-Nadeem that had explicitly made reference to the *adab* tradition seeking to adapt it to the needs of society that were clearly not part of the *salafi* social or political projects.

For example, Taymur added discipline to the emphasis on good manners as central concerns of Islamic literature. By making both self-evident Islamic truths, she nationalized them with literature, as a source of culture and education, serving an important regulatory function from which individuals derived important benefits. According to Taymur, literature and good manners could reform deviant behavior, protect oneself from moral failure, and present oneself appropriately to the world. It made an important contribution to society bringing one closer to human truth. Finally, Taymur inserted the education of children in the discussion of literature, implying that the instructional benefits reaped by its adult readers eventually filtered back to the children.

This theme, which *Nata'ij al-Ahwal* developed in some detail, emphasized the modern view of childhood as the crucial period for the development of sound adult character: early self-discipline was a complement to educational achievements and discipline was connected to a well-developed masculinity. Because fathers, not mothers, were associated with discipline in the family, Taymur seemed to be suggesting that the new emphasis on discipline in early childrearing was likely to contribute interesting changes in the roles that men and women played in the family. On the one hand, it was an argument for greater involvement of men, the disciplinary agents in all families, in the early care and/or the education of children. This was not a new idea to Taymur, who mentioned how her father and grandfather's early involvement in teaching her right from wrong. The obvious benefit that this had in defining fatherhood was relieving adult women from the overwhelming demands of managing the household and also being the primary caretakers of children, which contributed to Taymur's unfortunate arrangement with Tawhida. On the other hand, if men were reluctant to become actively engaged in the childrearing, it was necessary for women to also play a role in the discipline of children through education. This meant that women were to play an important role in the development of masculinity and its virtues (*muru'a*). By adding discipline to the responsibilities of women in the family, it challenged a major distinction between their gender roles in the family. It also gave women considerable power over the socialization of young boys potentially allowing them to introduce changes in the way future men defined their roles and approached their responsibilities in the family.

Muru'a represented the culturally specific Arab definition of the virtuous ideals of manhood familiar to most nineteenth-century readers. This concept was partially derivative of the pre-Islamic chivalry (*mur-uwa*), which was the "ideal of the ancient Arab tribal ethos that comprised of [*sic*] cardinal virtues such as bravery, equanimity and generosity."[87] Islam added to this definition of male virtue belief in God and the hereafter.[88] The prophetic tradition and social customs provided other definitions of a virtuous man like the importance of living a pious life, serving as an example to others, the serious attitude to one's social responsibility, finding glory in protecting and serving the community and developing an awareness of the 'arbitrariness of fate' and one's mortality. Armed with these heavy obligations, a Muslim man courageously faced hardship, curbed his desires and acknowledged divine supremacy.[89]

By adding modern forms of discipline and education to this culturally specific ideal, Taymur was not embracing modernity as a source of cultural values; rather she wanted to put it in the service of the development of Islamic definition of masculinity (*muru'a*), which remained at the center of discussion. While the development of Islamic masculinity was to benefit from the modern insights regarding the evils of permissiveness and the way bad childhood habits tended to survive into adulthood, the cultural core of that concept and role was to be preserved. The early learning of these cultural definitions of masculinity was to take place in the family under the supervision of the mother.

Taymur viewed the cultural education of male children to be the most the serious struggle (*jihad*) facing the national community. In this discussion, she clearly relied on the classic Islamic understanding of this concept found in many heroic literary narratives that viewed the struggle against an external enemy as less important than that against base human tendencies. In support of this view, the prophet was reported to have said, "Your greatest enemy is between your two sides."[90] This made character building and the psychic arena part of the important internal struggle that took precedence over the struggle against an external enemy. Taymur concurred with this view by placing the fight, to prevent the corruption of the young boys, their masculinity and their virtue at the center of community development. This might be the reason Taymur was conspicuously silent on the topic of external *jihad* against British occupation and Western domination. The latter was obviously secondary to the internal and national struggle to build and maintain the cultural integrity and character of Islamic masculinity, which will be put in the service of the defense of the community. The most important tool used in this education was persuasion (*siyasa*) and its most primary goal was to devise social strategies that separate the children of the better classes from dangerous social elements like fools, swindlers, cheats, and hypocrites. The class enemy within was more dangerous than the enemy without represented by the British and other Europeans.

This discourse on education was clearly different from that which was produced by others in the 1890s in more than one way. Rather than embrace the goal of modernizing Islamic society and providing a modern education to its children, it sought to Islamize the ongoing modernization through the incorporation of Islamic definitions of virtue and vice in this education. Unlike the modernization discourse espoused by Ali Mubarak, it did not render Islamic society and its value system as having nothing to contribute, but maintained the central role that the Islamic moral code played in the new social order. She also did not posit an opposition between Islam and modernity but saw Islamic society as hospitable to the modern regulating functions of literature and education. Both were utilized in the development of the education of children in general and of young boys in particular in which men and women participated. In both of these projects, masculinity with its culturally specific emphasis on Islamic *muru'a* was to occupy a privileged position as a public and a private concern. It was part of a complex synthesis of the old and the new associated with the process of nation-building that was Islamically based helping to identify the community from all others.

One should not interpret Taymur's interest in the education of young boys as lack of interest in the education of young girls. She published an early article on that subject in *al-Adaab* newspaper in 1887 in which she supported the education of young girls but offered one of the earliest critique of the modern emphasis on women's looks, domesticity, and childrearing, activities about which they knew a lot. In supporting the education of girls, men stood to directly benefit from the advantages it bestowed on their future partners. The emphasis on looks, fashion, and jewelry encouraged women to be vain instead of being interested in general and religious knowledge.

Next, Taymur reviewed what secluded women, who have not had access to modern education, knew about childrearing. It included the interpretation of the physical needs of infant children, knowledge of their developmental stages, their ability to nurture, anticipate and satisfy their emotional needs, and the use of early methods of discipline. The point of this detailed review of what young girls learned about childrearing in their family was designed to provide support for their access to a less gender specific education. Other advantages of giving young girls a very broad type of education was to satisfy some of their ambitions for themselves and to channel their restless energy into protecting their families from destructive tendencies and helping their husbands carry on their responsibilities. The reasons why men remained opposed to this less gender specific education overlooked this view and focused instead on their worry that women will know as much or more than men and/or that teaching women to read and especially to write would corrupt their morals by facilitating contact between them and men. As far as she was concerned, this was a very shortsighted view of the long-term needs of nation-building that required women's participation with men in the affairs of their society.[91]

Taymur's discussion of gender was a complex one referring to the sociological roles that men and women played as means of identifying or "imagining the community." She also acknowledged fraternity as having played a role in the old and the new changing Islamic communities. While the old definition of fraternity was part of the Islamic value system, modern fraternity, brotherhood, friendship represented the horizontal bonds of solidarity among men. Mothers and fathers were to play new roles in the socialization of male children in these roles as part of the learning of the cultural definition of masculinity.

CHAPTER 3

The Crisis and Reform of Islamic Dynastic Government and Society

> Your highness, he who wishes to evaluate
> the advice given to him by others, must
> accept as truthful that which is familiar
> to the common folk [al-`amma] . . . Whatever
> is met with the peoples' [al-nas] approval
> should be followed and that which is censured
> should be avoided. A rational man is he who
> follows the examples set by others.[1]
>
> —Nata'ij al-Ahwal

This chapter will offer a study of the only work of fiction that Taymur published in 1887/8. Rather than focus on where *Nata'ij al-Ahwal* stands vis-à-vis the modern Arabic novel, I wish to emphasize its use of the form of Shahrazad's *One Thousand and One Nights* to address the concerns of the newly emerging national community. While Benedict Anderson treated the modern novel as the only literary form capable of representing the "nation," Taymur's use of the structure of *One Thousand and One Nights*, which included a frame story coupled with a "story within the story," successfully accomplished this goal through the use of what I categorize as a hybrid narrative that used an old literary form to analyze many of the changes taking place in the different arenas of the community and their connections to each other. In the process, she offered readers ways of recognizing and understanding old cultural bonds they shared with one another as well as their present concerns as members of an imagined national community.

Before I embark on this discussion, I wish to share with the reader the plan I followed in making this presentation accessible. Taymur used this fictional work to articulate her ideas about "the course and history of nations" by which she meant the study of the past and present politics of dynastic Islamic governments. A careful reader of the Arabic work cannot but note her interest in the history of these governments, and the mirror of princes' literature (a body of work that discussed the rules of Islamic princely government) that guided and left its imprints on her attempt to make sense of the complex world of politics, which fascinated her. While she was not a political theorist, she was brought up in a political family with long careers in government service. She was also most probably married to a prominent civil servant. While this background might have influenced her initial interest in politics, it was clear that her interests in politics took a different direction after the death of both her father and husband in the mid-1870s. As illustrated in *Nata'ij al-Ahwal*, Taymur emerged as an astute observer of the turbulent politics of the 1870s and the 1880s raising many questions about the political future of dynastic government. I have tried to do justice to her unusual political interests, which were articulated in literary form. Fortunately, her exploration of the nation-building process benefitted from her use of literary writing to engage the readers by drawing on their shared experiences as members of the community.

In what follows, I wish to begin with a discussion of how Taymur used the frame story of her narrative to outline the nature of the political crisis of the community, establishing it as the context within which the economic and cultural crises explored in the story within the story could be placed and understood. One of the main goals of *Nata'ij al-Ahwal* was to evoke what it was like to live in this community to the nineteenth readers so that they could be persuaded of the desirability of the reforms she suggested. For the twenty-first-century reader, the presentation seeks to examine Taymur's success in this task so that they could appreciate an insider's view of that society that counters the very prevalent clichéd assumptions about what it was like. In the discussion of this period of Egyptian history, there is a great preoccupation with the signs of a developing modern society with less attention given to the political, social, and economic dynamics of the one that preceded it. The presentation in this chapter hopes to correct this imbalance without forgetting that Taymur's gender, social class, and ethnic backgrounds obviously left many of its prints on her reconstruction.

Literary Forms, Narrative, and the Representation of a Changing Community

The narrative structure of *Nata'ij al-Ahwal* bore a striking resemblance to Shahrazad's *One Thousand and One Nights*. It started off with a frame story followed by a story within the story and then an epilogue. Unlike the classical work with its series of stories whose primary intent was to protect the narrator—that is, Shahrazad, from the murderous rage of her misogynist husband—*Nata'ij al-Ahwal* stood very well on its own. Through the frame story and the story within the story, the readers were able to simultaneously observe and connect the changes that were unfolding in the political, economic, and the social arenas of the narrative with their membership in a new national community. As such, *Nata'ij al-Ahwal* provided more than a "technical means for 'representing' the kind of imagined community that is the nation,"[2] as Anderson suggested. It presented a culturally specific articulation of the community that relied on older forms of narrative that connected the past to the present in a novel way.

Like the Egyptian modernists who were engaged in the search for the first modern novel in Arabic literature, Anderson exhibited a similar preoccupation in his study of Southeast Asian literature's contribution to the imagining of the nation. I am not persuaded that this exercise is the only fruitful approach to the discussion of nation-building. It may be one of many possible approaches as the study of Taymur's work will show. In this regard, Sugata Bose suggested, "One way to disturb the essentialized views of India and Islam that had been colonialism's legacy to area studies is to unravel the internal fragments, the other is to render permeable and then to creatively trespass across rather rigidly external boundaries."[3] *Nata'ij al-Ahwal* offered a culturally specific fragment, whose interpretation could be liberated from the essentialist construction imposed on it, to present a cogent representation of the nation and its content. In this rich literary part of the world, the representation of the nation did not have to wait for the development of the modern novel before it could be successfully articulated. Older literary forms proved to be very capable of adapting to the new historical demands and conditions.

Instead of being disjointed parts of the narrative, the frame story and the story within the story emerged as two devices that provided the readers with means of simultaneous examination of the changes unfolding within the political community and its relationship to changes in other arenas. In this exploration, the readers, who were never going to personally know one another, were encouraged to consider their shared past and the effects of the resulting political, economic, cultural, and gender changes in their community whose steady anonymous development they could identify with and observe.[4]

Taymur's nineteenth-century discussion of nation-building was unusual by Western and Arab standards because of its exploration of the gendered aspects of this process. Anderson characterized the new national communities as horizontal fraternities but remained silent on the implications that this had for the discourses that were developed to understand them. As one critic pointed out, "Theories of nationalism have tended to ignore gender as a category constitutive of nationalism itself."[5]

Taymur was aware of the exclusion of her gender from Arabic literary writing and the writing on the nation. In choosing the literary structure of the *One Thousand and One Nights*, which guided her chronicle of the changing community, one could argue that she sought to establish an important connection with Shahrazad, the only other woman narrator or storyteller in the Arabic writing tradition. As one literary critic pointed out, women writers were largely excluded from the writing of Arabic prose in the classical and medieval periods.[6] Because "prose by its nature permits a clearer representation, a more elaborate reformulation and a restructuring of the world,"[7] the exclusion of women from prose writing denied them the right to intellectually shape their societies.

This characterization of the Arabic writing tradition overlooked the work of the *al-muhadithat*, the female interpreters of the prophetic tradition, whose contributions influenced the interpretation of the important social and political norms that guided Islamic societies. Zaynab Fawwaz, Taymur's contemporary, documented the existence and the contributions made by this community of women interpreters of the Islamic traditions in her important work *al-Durr al-Manthur fi Tabaqat Rabat al-Khudur*. Taymur acknowledged her debt to this body of literature and the role that women played in it including `A'isha Bint Abi Bakr, her namesake and the most important woman interpreter of the prophetic tradition and the only one to emerge as a commentator on and a participant in Islamic politics of her time,[8] in her choice of the title *Nata'ij al-Ahwal fi al-Aqwal wa al-Af`al*, with its direct reference to the prophetic tradition's interest in the deeds and statements of Muslims.

The dual influence of Shahrazad and *al-muhadithat* on this work indicated that literature, religion, gender, and community were clearly on Taymur's mind setting her narrative apart from others. At the heart of *Nata'ij al-Ahwal*, there was also the discussion of the crisis of the paternal and absolutist forms of dynastic government and the rise of competitive mercantilism, whose ideals of unbridled individualism undermined Islamic fraternal solidarity. While she acknowledged the contribution that Islamic fraternal relations could make to the formal and informal resolutions of the crisis of community, she also discussed how the changing relations between men and women provided ways for a better restructuring of the community and its government.

In the next two sections, I wish to examine Taymur's analyses of the political then the economic and cultural manifestations of the crises of the community. In each section, I will examine Taymur's views on how the responses to these crises contributed to the development of a fraternal reconstruction of the community through a redefinition of the relations that men have with each other as representatives of different segments of the community. Then I will examine how she addressed herself to the roles that women and heterosexuality can play to further nationalize the community. I think it is fair to say that while Taymur did not challenge the fraternal character of the new imagined communities, she sought to use her voice to critique the old gender discourses on women in Islamic government and society, giving them new roles to play and making room for their perspectives.

Literary Representations of the Political Crisis of Community and Its Reform

Taymur classified *Nata'ij al-Ahwal fi al-Aqwal wa al-Af`al* as an *uhdutha*, a specific narrative form that focused on a central *hadath* (an event, incident, occurrence, or happening)[9] in the frame story: Prince Mamduh's loss of his throne and the personal and social journeys he had to take to regain it and restore political legitimacy to dynastic governments. Only one critic examined the significance of Taymur classifying her narrative as an *uhdutha*. He suggested that when Taymur stated that she "creatively developed this *uhdutha* to entertain the readers," she was also indicating her interest in action and entertainment rather than character development.[10] This view overlooked how Taymur's narrative, like others produced during this period and reviewed in the last chapter, had multiple purposes and meanings: it provided entertainment through the adventures of its characters and used empathy with them to offer a political commentary on a fictional main event (that mirrored real ones) developing new interpretations of the changing literary writings and societies.

Because the author lived through the dethroning of one khedive by international interests and the near overthrow of another by a nationalist revolution, the challenges to dynastic government emerged as her main event or concern. In her own words, *Nata'ij al-Ahwal* provided a long reflection on the consequences of this event or development for "the course and history of nations." The frame story supported this specific reading and outlined the multilayered crisis of political community. Its central figure was the popular but ailing king, al-'Adil, who was left to care for his young son, Mamduh, following the death of the mother. Unfortunately, those who were expected to discipline the prince (*al-mu'addibun*), his father and members of the court, indulged him. Malik, the capable vizier, and `Aqeel, the trusted courtier, felt compelled to warn the king about the ill effects that this lack of discipline had for the future of the dynastic order (*nizam al-mulk*). Because they feared the king's displeasure and rejection, `Aqeel indirectly articulated their concern through a story. He described how he entrusted the vizier with the care of a rare and a special tree, which he neglected contributing to its crooked development. `Aqeel's description of the rare tree as one that grew in the valley of "elevation" recalled the founding myth of the Ottoman Empire, in which Osman dreamed that a tree sprang out of his naval and shaded the entire world[11] predicting the development of his empire.

The king understood `Aqeel's reference to his son and the future of the dynasty and agreed with his royal advisors that the paternal bond did not provide the best means for providing the discipline necessary for the education of the prince. He put Malik and `Aqeel primarily in charge of his son's education. The ulema and the philosophers played a secondary role in this process, which suggested that the discipline associated with modern education was critical. This development provoked the envy and anger of Dushnam and Ghadur who served as ministers of treasury and the army, respectively,[12] begrudging Malik and `Aqeel their new positions. A power struggle ensued between the ambitious bureaucrats, who sought to satisfy their self-interests through the corruption of the prince and Malik and `Aqeel who hoped to serve the long-term interests of the dynasty through teaching the prince the art of self government (i.e., discipline).

Dushnam and Ghadur's hypocrisy and their indulgence of the prince's pride and vanity won the day. Mamduh acquired a reputation for arrogance and cruelty that made him unpopular among his subjects. In a last ditch effort to arrest the accelerating moral corruption of the prince, Malik and `Aqeel arranged his marriage to the Persian king's daughter, Boran. They hoped that a good wife could provide a powerful correction of his character flaws. When Malik was sent to Persia to arrange for Mamduh's marriage and `Aqeel to China to purchase the needs of the new royal household, Ghadur and Dushnam used the untimely death of the king and the unpopularity of the prince to usurp the throne. They ordered two slaves to kill Mamduh and sent messages to Malik and `Aqeel designed to keep them away. Malik was told that the prince had become infatuated with a young European woman (*min banat al-ifrnj*), but knowing that his father would never accept her, had fled with her to her country. He was dispatched there to look for them. `Aqeel was told that Mamduh was kidnapped during a hunting trip by slaves, who recognized him as the brutal prince who mistreated their kind, ending up in Sudan. `Aqeel was asked to travel to look for him. These multiple plots were fatally undermined when the slaves, ordered to kill Mamduh, took pity on him and set him free.

Mamduh's exile and the life-transforming experiences among his subjects taught him the error of his old ways. His successful reuniting with `Aqeel provided another important source for Mamduh's personal and social education. As part of this instruction, `Aqeel employed a story within the story that traced the ups and downs of the careers and lives of two Egyptian merchants, Bahram and Farhad, to instruct and familiarize Mamduh with the changes taking place in the culture, politics, and economy of the community and to demonstrate the importance of continuing to adhere to Islamic value system of fraternal solidarity. In the epilogue, `Aqeel and Mamduh were reunited with Malik who successfully engineered Mamduh's return to his throne. Mamduh was also reunited with his intended bride, Boran, who became his queen.

Taymur and the Political Discourses on Islamic Dynastic Government and Community

The above discussion of the changing nature of Islamic dynastic government was different from the Islamic and European discourses of Taymur's time. The Islamic works on Muslim kingship focused on the religious bases of government and its political practices. As "the successor of God on Earth," one brand of Islamic political theory offered an intriguing parallel to the European divine right of kings, with the caliph as the source of supreme earthly power.[13] They were complemented with medieval discourses that accepted the coercive powers of the caliph in a Muslim polity rooted in a pessimistic anthropology that assumed men to be violent and rapacious.

Last but not least, there were the genres of political wisdom and "mirror for princes," first cultivated at the Ummayad Court and developed by the Abbasids,[14] that sought to instruct the prince by example,[15] providing a mirror that he could use to judge his performance. This large political literature recognized justice as the central principle that provided the Islamic state its basis of legitimacy. Justice was conceptualized as a "circle" where "power was sustained by men, men by wealth, wealth by prosperity and prosperity by justice."[16] This circle did not eliminate inequality of power or wealth, but it saw the promise of prosperity as the source of the stable equilibrium that held the Islamic community together.[17] Malik and `Aqeel, the loyal bureaucrats and courtiers, mentioned Nizam al-Mulk (died 1092), the chief minister of the Seljuk Sultan Malikshah, who wrote one of the most important medieval political manuals: the Siyasat-nama or Siyar al-Muluk (Book of Government). As a source of political inspiration for Taymur's discussion, it identified the royal delivery of unmediated justice as the primary obligation of Muslim kings,[18] royal restraint as the basis of general prosperity, and the commitment to justice as deterrence to the misdeeds of the maleficent elements.[19] The manual also discussed the important character traits, good character and sound judgment, required of the vizier, who provided important counsel and the personal skills and wisdom needed in the boon companions of the king.[20] Finally, the manual reinforced the Islamic exclusion of women from government.

In contrast, the European discourses on dynastic government emphasized the separateness of their institutions from those operating in the Islamic-Ottoman world. The origins of this intellectual divide could be traced to Niccolò Machiavelli who stated that the existence of a class of slave officials and a large standing army contributed institutional differences that separated Ottoman autocracy from European forms of dynastic (princely) government.[21] Nineteenth-century Orientalist analysis reconfigured these historical differences into the essential and radical category of "oriental despotism."[22]

Against the medieval Islamic, modern/realist and Orientalist discursive backdrops, *Nata'ij al-Ahwal's* "meditation on the course and history of nations"[23] underlined the changing nature of Islamic dynastic governments and its ability to adjust to new social and political contexts. According to Taymur, al-`Adil ruled over an imperial dynastic community whose capital was Baghdad where the Abbasids governed for centuries.[24] Because its political system was described as both the caliphate and a sultanate, it was obvious that the tale was specifically focused on the late history of the Abbasid political community when "the caliph ruled in Baghdad besides a Seljuk sultan,"[25] signaling the ascendance of the Turks in Islamic dynastic governments and eventually the rise of the Ottoman Empire, whose rulers held both titles.

Why did not the Ottoman-Egyptian Taymur choose to explicitly locate *Nata'ij al-Ahwal* within the Ottoman imperial community? Because this work was written in Arabic, Taymur rightly assumed that the Arabic reader in the last quarter of the nineteenth century was more likely to have an interest in Arab Islamic history and hence the choice of the Abbasids. In other words, the nationalization of language influenced the cultural and historical choices that writers, who operated within the new national communities, made. While the narrative recognized the continued existence of a multilingual Islamic *umma*, whose influence could still be seen in the travels of the different characters, it also acknowledged the political fragmentation of the Ottoman political community and the national competition it faced. The many characters of this narrative provided differentiated pictures of Islamic and non-Islamic dynastic political communities. They belonged to Islamic dynasties/nations in Algeria, Egypt, Iran, al-Sind (the Muslim name for present day Pakistan), and some non-Islamic dynastic states in India and China.

Because Sudan and its African inhabitants lacked their dynastic government, Taymur considered this as a marker of their lack of civilization and community. As such, she treated them as providing a southern boundary for Islamic communities in that continent. Taymur's description of `Aqeel's adventures in the Sudan bore a striking resemblance to the Turkish account offered by Selim Qapudan, the naval officer who conducted explorations in Sudan in the middle of the nineteenth century (1838–42) making contact with its different tribes. [26] For example, `Aqeel used flashy beads, Ivory bracelets, and some silver rings to elicit information from members of these barbaric tribes reflecting a popular condescending attitude toward them. If as Mayy Ziyada suggested Taymur's father in law was a high-ranking official there, this could reflect some state views of that population. In *Nata'ij al-Ahwal*, the Africans were represented as scary, barbaric, and gullible heathens, who were fierce haters of whites in general, which hinted at the degradation they suffered at the hands of the Egyptian army led by Turkish, Egyptian, and international ethnicities.

In this discussion, the dynastic rulers, their representatives, geography, and history provided very specific markers of modern nations. In the epilogue, Taymur also invoked old and new political invented rituals as well as symbols of Islamic nation-building in the description of the celebration of Mamduh's return to his throne. The flag of al-`Adil, his crown, sword, and royal gown of succession (*kiswat rasm al-khilafa*) served as political symbols, recognized by the commoners, the army and the political class, as aspects of the legitimate transfer of modern dynastic power. Mamduh's investiture with political power was also formally sanctioned by the ulema, the learned religious scholars of Islam, who represented the religious-political consensus of the community.

Nata'ij al-Ahwal also offered a novel definition of "good" Islamic government, which King al-`Adil (*al-Malik al-`Adil*) represented. His kingdom was characterized with improved coercive capacity manifested in its defensive and offensive capabilities along with tight control of its territories. Justice remained as a personal quality of the ruler and a marker of his adherence to the Islamic code of ethics and faith as bases of community. In addition, a just ruler (also literally *al-malik al-`adil*) was now closely associated with interest in reform (*bi al-salah mathkur*), [27] which the nineteenth-century Ottoman and Egyptian dynastic bureaucracies as well as nationalist movements identified with improved economic and political performance.[28] To reinforce this point, Taymur described the vizier who presided over the state machinery as a modern day bureaucrat cum manager. He ran the government efficiently set and implemented its policy goals, which had indirect positive effect on the Islamic circle of justice. A well-run government increased prosperity, which in turn enhanced the delivery of justice, popular support, and political stability.

The above changing face of Islamic dynastic government retained some premodern political concepts and practices. At the beginning of the narrative, Malik and `Aqeel continued to identify themselves as "slaves of the monarchy."[29] This notion emphasized the absolute obedience owed to the ruler reflecting the long history of Islamic reliance on a slave military corps in governments that started during the Abbasid dynasty.[30] While slaves no longer played a direct role in government, relations between the ruler and his bureaucrats continued to be defined as slave-master relations.[31] The transition from household to complex bureaucratic government[32] explained the new emphasis that bureaucrats and courtiers put on discipline as part of the education of the prince and as a new governmental ideal that replaced the principle of absolute royal privilege and loyalty. The tension between the desire to return to the old form of royal absolutism, which Dushnam and Ghadur encouraged, and the need for disciplined government, which Malik and `Aqeel pushed for, represented the primary struggle in this political narrative.

Because the common folks (al-`amma) were the first to suffer at the hands of a brutal and an undisciplined prince, like Mamduh, the demand for justice in popular rebellions during this period was increasingly identified with governmental restraint.[33] It explained why in the narrative they maintained a healthy interest in the education and the character of the prince. Mamduh's brutality and lack of discipline were interpreted as an inability to run an efficient government leading them to withdraw their general approval and support, which left him an easy target for those who usurped his throne at a crucial point (i.e., succession). As far as Taymur was concerned, justice, disciplined government, and popular support were not just desirable as modern political principles but as crucial measures to secure the survival of dynastic government.

Divine support continued to provide a basis for political legitimacy. As the successor of God, an Islamic ruler was obliged to embrace and deliver some important divinely sanctioned principles. Malik summarized this view of Islamic dynastic government at the ceremony held to celebrate Mamduh's return to his throne, which was attended by members of the army, the political class, and the general public. It provided an explicit statement about the bases of reformed Islamic government that emphasized justice, royal stock, and discipline.

> O worshipers of God, this is your king Mamduh, who is the legitimate successor to your caliph. God has returned him to you with the best character exemplifying justice and the treatment of all without discrimination (al-insaf). You can be assured of his high morals. His previous evil deeds were not his own, but the result of the hypocrisy of his guardians whose trickery backfired on them . . .
>
> O people, God [one of whose names is] the Just has encompassed us with his fairness and returned the government of al-`Adil/the just to his son. God, one of whose attributes is truth and rightfulness (al-Haq) has delivered [both] to him. The evil and the deceitful got what they deserved. God almighty has elevated the fortunes of our king and now it is possible for this Sultan, who is the son of a Sultan, to enjoy his crown and throne. God ordained, rightfully guided and cared for him [so that] he found his way back to the true path. The divine revelation states: "Does man think that he will be left to no end?" This is your caliph, Mamduh who is of pure royal stock. He promises to uphold the firm grip of justice and good behavior. Muslims have pledged allegiance to him (baya`tehu al-muslumun). Victory is his crown as the successor of God. Right has come and falsity has been defeated.[34]

Islamic dynastic government was the only legitimate type of government because it enjoyed divine approval represented by God's intervention to return

Mamduh to the throne of al-'Adil. As the Qur'anic verse stated that God frowned on the uselessness of man, it identified an ideal ruler as one who was of royal stock, with a firm grip on justice and good behavior, and deserving the pledge of allegiance of his Muslim subjects. Justice acquired the modern connotation of fair treatment of all without discrimination as well as the succession of a legitimate ruler to his throne. It was connected to *al-haq* (truth and rights), another divine quality, which rulers needed to observe. It suggested the importance of a government doing "right" by its people even if it did not yet recognize their political rights. The political right of a ruler to his realm (i.e., the hereditary right to succession from father to son) was the only right that was fully developed in the previous speech. Even though Taymur also acknowledged the pledge of allegiance given by Muslims to their rulers as a requirement for Islamic government, she treated it as a formal requirement and not a basis for new political rights for Muslims. Mamduh acknowledged other rights when he asked the attendees of this ceremony to articulate the grievances they suffered at the hands of Dushnam and Ghadur. In response to complaints of lost property under the previous government, Mamduh pledged to safeguard the property rights of his subjects as a basis of his rule.[35] In short, modern dynastic government recognized and promised to protect the economic rights of its subjects provided they respect its political right to govern.

In the above alternative discourse, Taymur attempted to present a view of Islamic dynastic government that was different from the dominant Islamic and European discourses on the subject. It attempted to move away from personalized rule and the old notions of master and slave as a political model of government, embracing the need for a disciplined and efficient management of government affairs. It also employed some notion of "right," if not rights: the implication being that government needed to do right by its people, who it represented as having a healthy interest in government and guaranteeing its political legitimacy. Even though, *Nata'ij al-Ahwal* could be read by some as a more developed form of mirror of princes literature, its counsel seemed to be closely based on the reading of the public debates on the nature of government that took place in Egypt in the reigns of Khedives Ismail and Tewfik. As such, it offered a different approach to the discussion of Islamic kingship.

The Reproductive and Heterosexual Roles of Women in the Reform of Dynastic Government

The leading characters in the frame story in *Nata'ij al-Ahwal* provided other insights regarding the changing gender bases of Islamic dynastic politics. All the characters in the frame story were men, who established the exclusionary and masculine character of Islamic politics. The only reference to Mamduh's mother in the introduction of the royal characters and members of the royal government was oblique, suggesting that al-`Adil suffered from a broken heart presumably because of the death of his wife, which forced him to raise his son alone. Women were not supposed to matter in government and Taymur adhered to this assumption by not formally mentioning them. Interestingly enough, even after Malik and `Aqeel were put in charge of Mamduh's education and upbringing, his schooling was continued within the harem, suggesting that the early education of young princes typically took place in that feminine space, allowing mothers and/or mother figures to influence and to take care of the royal sons.

Recent studies of the role that women played in early Ottoman governments revealed the informal roles that mothers, wives, and concubines played in the upbringing of their sons and the safeguarding of their interests before and after their ascent to political power.[36] No such comparative insights were available into the working of the early history of the Muhammad Ali dynasty in Egypt. Anecdotal evidence exists that supported the important role played by royal mothers in securing the fortunes of their royal sons in political succession during the second half of the nineteenth century. Khedive Ismail's mother, who was the sister of Sultan Abdul Aziz's mother, was influential in lobbying the sultan to change the Egyptian system of succession so that it is limited to her son's line.[37] Her court, *al-Walda Pasha* (the khedive's mother), was said to be larger and more prominent than that of any of his wives.[38] Abdallah al-Nadeem, whom the khedive tried to briefly co-opt, described the head eunuch of *al-Walda Pasha* as having more influence than the prime minister.[39] Finally, most reports suggested that she was the only family member who was with him when he received the Ottoman decree that deposed him.[40]

Khedive Tewfik's mother also exerted considerable influence on him emerging as his staunch defender as the royal family split on the `Urabi revolution. A. M. Broadly, the British lawyer who defended General `Urabi, described the way she subjected the princesses of the royal family who supported the leader of the revolution to a tongue lashing for their disloyalty and promising to severely punish them.[41] These anecdotes suggested that royal mothers were not removed from the political affairs of government and that the princesses of the royal family were also politicized taking independent political positions regarding the `Urabi' revolution.

In *Nata'ij al-Ahwal*, Taymur seemed to suggest that the solution to the political dissention that royal mothers brought to dynastic government was to put the early socialization and education of Mamduh in the hands of men: first his father, then Malik, `Aqeel, as well as Dushnam and Ghadur. Equally important was the fact that al-`Adil did not take another wife or concubine suggesting that kings, who presided over disciplined government extended that discipline to their sexual lives indirectly repudiating the polygamous heterosexual ideals that had prevailed up until then. In short, the allegorical death of Mamduh's mother clearly signaled a break with old style Ottoman dynastic sexual politics serving as a starting point for other changes in the harem as a social and a political institution.

While Taymur's narrative underplayed women's involvement in politics through reproduction, her discussion of Boran's role, the intended wife of Mamduh, who was the daughter of the Persian king, served to outline an important political role for the princes' wife. Boran was named after the only queen to assume the throne of the Sassanid dynasty in pre-Islamic Persia.[42] She died after ruling for over a year[43] an already declining empire. Upon hearing of her ascent to the throne,[44] the prophet was reported to have said in a hotly contested Hadith: "No people will be successful if they put a woman in charge of them." Since then, Muslim conservatives have used this Hadith to justify the exclusion of women from politics and political leadership positions. The fictional Boran reminded the informed reader of a time when women's involvement in politics contributed more to government than the reproductive capacity to bear future heirs. According to Malik, she had mature opinions (*saddad al-ra'iy*), intelligence, good management skills, beauty, and grace, which were going to influence her husband in some important ways. If she loved Mamduh and was, in turn, loved by him, she could serve as a catalyst in encouraging him to give up bad habits (*al-nahy `an al-su'a*) and to embrace the imperative to reform (*al-amr bi Al-islah*).[45]

According to Malik, marriage was a complex social institution, which served as an Islamic marker of male adulthood (*al-hilm*) enhanced by the selection of a mature wife. This offered an interesting qualification to the medieval Islamic view offered by Imam Abu Hamed al-Ghazali, which discussed how wives distracted their husbands from religious and public duties.[46] In allowing the character of the wife to have an effect on her husband, it was possible to present a differentiated view of women. Malik anticipated that Boran would make a positive contribution to the moral and political development of her husband. Despite her youth, she was the more mature partner who was to guide Mamduh to a virtuous life. Later on, after Mamduh and Boran were united, the couple was described as not only satisfying each other sexually but also relating to each other as human beings, which implied that they shared complex interests and concerns. All this explained why Boran was expected to play an expanded role in her husband's government through the commanding of right and the forbidding of wrong, which was the primary obligation of all members of the Islamic community.[47]

In the epilogue, Mamduh went further in the representation of the important counseling role of a royal wife suggesting that it contributed a third pillar in the reform of dynastic government. Mamduh publically recognized the importance of the counsel given to him by three important figures: in addition to Malik and `Aqeel who provided political and social and cultural counsel, Mamduh implicitly acknowledged the political counsel and support given to him by his wife, Boran. She was not mentioned by name, but the reader recognized her as the only other character that could act in that capacity in relation to the king. Like Malik and `Aqeel, she stood by him when he lost his throne and refused to marry others disobeying her father and fleeing their country. This, coupled with her life experiences during exile, entitled her to positively influence him. Already, members of his government and the general public could see the good effects that she had on the king. Because Mamduh considered her as both a human being and a sexual partner, this entitled her to a role in his agenda, which included the administration of justice, avoiding discrimination, and even defense. As far as Mamduh was concerned, the commitment of the above three figures to his dynastic government made them as worthy of obedience by other members of the community.

While Taymur's discussion of the importance of the roles played by courtiers and advisers in the operation of Islamic dynastic government was in line with that of Nizam al-Mulk, her support of Boran's involvement in government dramatically departed from his strongly held position regarding the disastrous consequences of women's involvement in government. Nizam al-Mulk had run into conflict with Turkhan Khatun, the wife of Sultan Malik Shah over the question of succession,[48] which made her a dangerous opponent who threatened his position in the Seljuk court. It was not surprising that he devoted a chapter in his political manual titled "On the Subject of those who wear the Veil" that listed several historical and religious examples of the negative consequences that resulted from women's access to political power. He also cited another Hadith that counseled "Consult them [women] then oppose them."[49] Among the reasons he offered for repudiating the advice given to kings by their wives was that women had incomplete intelligence, lacked the experience that men had with the world, and had limited social circles.[50] Taymur's epilogue represented an attempt to overcome these objections and push for the transformation of Islamic tradition with regard women's involvement in politics. As an intelligent and educated woman who had independent experiences, views and opinions and as a wife who shared the political interests of her husband, Boran had valuable knowledge that her husband could draw on.

In choosing Malik and Mamduh as the spokesmen for this complex representation of women's gender roles, Taymur employed the male voice in support of a more expansive definition of femininity correctly assuming that her male readers were more likely to pay attention to this view if a male character articulated it. The male voice also helped legitimize Taymur's reinterpretation of the well-known Islamic injunction that required all Muslims to command right and forbid wrong (*al-amr bi al-ma`rouf wa al-nahy `an al-munkar*). In response to the dramatic social and political upheavals taking place in this fictional Islamic society, like the emphasis on individual self-interest, competition, and the challenge of the political power of the prince, Taymur reversed the order of the above injunction emphasizing the abandonment of bad practices (*al-nahy `an al-su`*) first and then observing the imperative of reform (*al-amr bi al-Islah*)—that is, the support of socially and politically worthwhile causes. In Taymur's opinion, the success of the Islamic reform project clearly depended on the recruitment of royal or elite wives who supported their husbands in the implementation of the principle of just government.

So Taymur's exclusion of royal mothers from the affairs of dynastic government was not an indication of her acceptance of the masculine character of Islamic politics. By undermining the politicization of the reproductive role of women, she offered companionate marriage as providing another type of less hierarchal relations crucial for the operation of a reformed dynastic government. The bond between royal husband and wife, reinforced by love and respect, made it possible for them to operate as a political couple. This offered a qualitative shift from the classical and medieval literary traditions that exclusively represented women as sexual beings[51] in favor of more complex definitions that combined the sexual and the nonsexual in the discussion of the roles that men and women played in the family and political arena.

While Taymur viewed heterosexual love between Mamduh and Boran as the basis of new roles for women in government, heterosexual love between the prince and European women was seen as major harbinger of disaster. In trying to hide the fact that they got rid of Mamduh, they claimed that he had fallen in love with one of *banat al-ifranj* (a European woman) and that he abandoned country and duty to settle in hers. Clearly, European women were seen as a threat to the community with influence that could separate the prince from his *umma*.

Finally, the modern heterosexual couple served to balance the influence of the new fraternal relations of power that served as a basis of modern Islamic dynastic government. The allegorical death of Mamduh's mother not only cleared a new political space for the couple but also indirectly cast doubt on the paternal bond and the involvement of the father in the personal and political education of his son. Al-`Adil was guilty of indulging his son and, therefore, not fit to enforce the discipline that he needed. To deal with this problem, Taymur suggested the replacement of the paternal-kinship bond with fraternal relations developed between the prince and members of key social groups that constituted the political elite. The education of the prince provided an important opportunity for the development of important political ties among the prince, his courtiers and his bureaucrats. They were better equipped, than mothers and fathers, to enforce the necessary discipline and their involvement in the training of the prince served to nationalize dynastic government.

Fraternity and the Nationalization of Islamic Government

Taymur turned next to the discussion of the development of fraternal bonds as basis of national government. For her, this required movement away from the premodern vertical and hierarchical dynastic political community, which in an Egyptian context referred to the Mamluk master-slave model, with its definition of the relations between the prince and king, the political class and the larger population that he ruled. This transition was a difficult one because it seemed to be fraught with potential political threats from these groups. Yet failure in this transition posed equally serious dangers. So Taymur began to discuss in great detail the process by which the relations among three important political actors (the prince and king, the political class—which helps him to govern—and the rest of the population) could contribute to the development of horizontal national fraternities.

The discrediting of the kinship (maternal and paternal) bonds as a basis for the political operation of government, which served as the starting point of the story of Prince Mamduh, was generally associated with the rise of civil forms of modern government characterized by the more egalitarian fraternal relations among men of different classes. Mamduh's changing relations with Malik and `Aqeel as well as those with his subjects offered insights into the nationalization of dynastic government. While the narrative began with Malik and `Aqeel defining themselves as slaves of the monarchy, al-`Adil's decision to put them in charge of the prince's education signaled the beginning of the abandonment of the old master-slave model that guided the absolute form of dynastic government in favor of a more fraternal model. Dushnam and Ghadur's negative influence over Mamduh was also part of this transition to the fraternal mode, underlining some of its sources of dangers. By encouraging Mamduh to resent the power and authority of any counselors, they hoped to improve their position with him and/or eventually usurp his throne. The result was a return to personalized or absolute rule in which Mamduh was contemptuous of all the members of the political class as well as most of his subjects. He refused all contact with anyone who was enslaved, be they white or black. He considered it to be beneath his dignity as a prince to deal with freed white slaves who attained high status because that did not wipe out the fact that they were bought for a price like animals. He was also brutal in his treatment of African slaves considering their skin color to be akin to misfortune. Finally, Mamduh was also cruel to the needy (*arbab al-hajat*), who approached him with petitions to redress acts of injustice, treating them as low lives, and common criminals only worthy of more punishment.[52] Under this extremely hierarchical dynastic form of government, it was very easy for Dushnam and Ghadur to usurp the power of the politically isolated prince who had no other basis or source of political support. In one of the most significant political speeches in the frame story, Malik sought to offer Mamduh his views of how general public can provide him with a reliable frame of reference in evaluating the advice offered by his counselors and courtiers. The following was the most important fragment of the long speech:

> He who wishes to evaluate the advice given to him by others, must accept as truthful that which is familiar to the common folk [al-`amma] . . . Whatever is met with the peoples' [al-nas] approval should be followed and that which they censure should be avoided. Ar rational man should follow the examples set by others.[53]

Malik gave the social standards of al-`amma and al-nas a paramount role to play in the social education of the prince and his ability to evaluate the advice he received from his counselors. To protect himself from the hypocrisy of friends and foes, the prince needed to test their views and opinions against the sensibilities of the masses and/or the people to distinguish good from bad counselors and right from wrong. As such, the masses were the arbiters of proper behavior and the prince had to conform to the standards they set for the community. Following the social practices of the majority provided the basis of rational ideological and political behavior because of the social injunction to benefit from the experiences of others. This was an interesting theoretical role reversal, which transformed the nineteenth-century assumed passive role of the masses (al-`amma) and the people (al-nas) into a more active one that set ethical and social standards of royal behavior. In emphasizing these new linkages between the prince and his subjects, Malik offered the bases of modern princely government, which redefined the relations between the prince and his subjects transforming the monarchy into a national institution. Modern dynastic government sought to make itself part of the social fabric. The ability of the prince to see himself in al-`amma and al-nas and vice versa contributed a major departure in the definition of Islamic dynastic government.

So which arenas provided Prince Mamduh with access to people so that he could learn their social standards? In the frame story, Malik and `Aqeel proposed that al-`Adil reward his son's educational progress by building him four new palaces where he would engage in activities that would bring about his personal and political maturation. One palace would serve as the residence for Mamduh and his future wife, Boran; a second would serve as the seat of his government; a third would be used as the residence of his royal guests and the fourth was a place of worship (khaniqah) for al-`abbad (worshippers) and ascetics. This last venue was put to multiple uses: in addition to the religious rewards to be reaped from building a place of worship, the prince was to learn the importance of charitable behavior and moral lessons from the informal accounts (*akhbar*) offered by its visitors. The old emphasis on the religious bond between the rulers and the ruled was given a new populist content, suggesting that the prince could personally benefit from the contact with his Muslims subjects. In the context of this period, this was a radically new social idea in its emphasis that the rulers and the ruled shared the same moral code and definitions of good behavior as bases for the imagined communion between the privileged and the underprivileged as members of the Islamic community. It served as a first approximation of the development of social bonds that contributed to the rise of horizontal fraternities.

In cementing the ties between the rulers and the ruled, Taymur turned to the expansive Islamic category of *al-ra`iya* to capture the existence of layers of government that was spread throughout society, bringing men and women of different classes together. *Al-ra`iya* were the political subjects of an Islamic system of government and it could also literally mean the social flocks spread throughout society. A well-known prophetic Hadith stated, "You are all shepherds and responsible for your flocks. The ruler is a shepherd and is responsible for his *ra`iya* (subjects). Man is a shepherd and is responsible for his kinfolk/family (*ahluhu*). Woman is a shepherd and is responsible for her husband's household inhabited by his kinfolk and his children (*'ahl bayt zawjiha wa 'awladuhu*)."[54] Through the use of this Hadith, government was not the sole preserve of the ruler but was shared by men and women throughout the society in their responsibilities for others especially in patriarchal families. At the apex, the ruler was responsible for the welfare of his subjects, then, a man for his kinfolk (or family) and then a woman for her husband's family and children. The ruled, whether they were men or women, assumed responsibility only in the social and the familial arenas, but not in government. Only the ruler had political responsibility to all his political subjects. Next, individual men bear responsibility for their kin and family and women were held responsible for their husbands, his family, and kin. Only men were able, however, to have legal claim to both the family and the women. By taking care of their husbands' family and kin, women contributed to the reproduction of these social networks deriving some form of social authority, but not legal acknowledgment of this role. Instead, they were treated as double subjects of the rulers and of men. In this discussion, neither the *ra`iya* nor women were passive objects of government, but rather as interested participants in government affairs following the affairs of state because of their awareness of its effects on them and their society.[55]

Malik's extended discussion of how to best distinguish right from wrong was not completely religious but combined pre-Islamic and popular concepts and knowledge in the development of a long list of virtues and vices that one recognized as offering the cultural bases of community consensus. Using the notion of *al-dahr* or the unpredictable fate, he reminded Mamduh as well as other Muslim and the non-Muslim readers of this pre-Islamic concept, which Arabic literature and poetry prized. Malik put it in the service of the government of the self by suggesting that acceptance of the vicissitudes of life was part of the wisdom of the ancestors that provided deterrence to princely arrogance by acknowledging the limits of individual control.[56] Another was the paradox that Arabic culture, poetry, and literature used to good effect (i.e., the awareness of death as a precondition of virtuous or good life).[57] Finally, there was stress that Malik put on equanimity in dealing with fate, which contributed to the ability of the prince to bear the burden of his office.[58]

There were, however, certain vices and virtues, which withstood the test of time. Pride destroyed any hope in a productive life. Arrogance showed the lowliness of one's race. Hypocrisy lent itself to falsity, had a poisonous effect on life, and served as a trap. In contrast, setting one's sight on lofty goals proved the honor of one's character. Friendship was a valued social resource in the attempt to distinguish truth from falsity. A true friend derived joy from his mate's success and was always dependable. In contrast, a hypocrite could easily lead a friend to loss, breaking all acceptable social rules in the attempt to hide his falsity. For that reason, the choice of one's friends had serious consequences. This list of vices to be avoided and virtues to be sought were generally accepted by the prince and his subjects as important providing another basis of communion between the two.

Malik's discussion of false and true friends or brothers was intended to be a direct reference to the new fraternal relations that Mamduh was encouraged to have with Dushnam, Ghadur, Malik, `Aqeel, and himself. As a metaphor for the new fraternal relations, friendly relations between the prince and his counselors and/or courtiers were respectful, less hierarchal and even somewhat intimate. The equalization of the relations between the rulers and those who assisted them in government was not without perils. Hypocrisy and individual self-interest allowed Dushnam and Ghadur to pose a significant threat to dynastic government. In contrast, Malik and `Aqeel were role models of how fraternity sacrificed self-interest in the service of nationalized dynastic government and protected it from the threats posed by serious challengers. Mamduh's exile also served to equalize his relations with the masses among whom he lived. He was sold into slavery and bought by a Turkish soldier who wanted to marry him off to his daughter from an Abyssinian slave woman to improve her social standing. After purchasing his freedom back, Mamduh also worked as a hired hand in a bakery and was confined with the insane and treated like them. These experiences made him empathize with the woes of the most vulnerable and poor segments of the population, influencing his future views and relations with his subjects.

The only subaltern or marginal element to have a specific role to play in Mamduh's new government was the African slaves who had saved him from death and were in turn tortured by Dushnam and Ghadur. They were to serve as Mamduh's enforcers (i.e., those who meted out punishment to his enemies). The rationale seemed to be that because they had been subjected to brutality, either they were fit to play this role or they were given a crude form of justice by meting punishment to their previous tormentors. Even though they were considered to be members of the community, African slaves were clearly locked into being the objects of either brutality or its delivery. The modernization of dynastic government stopped short of introducing significant change in the roles of or the prospects for members of that group.[59]

Finally, the major characters in the frame story offered an interesting commentary on the class alliances and tensions that shaped modern dynastic government.[60] Taymur clearly favored heavy dynastic reliance on the aristocracy. Even though the king entrusted both Malik and ʾAqeel with the education of the prince, ʾAqeel—whose name means virtuous in Arabic and wisdom and intelligence in Turkish[61]—emerged as the one most singularly equipped to communicate with and guide the young prince. ʾAqeel emerged as the central player in this narrative, saving the prince from despair, dynastic government from political decline, and single handedly supervised the personal and cultural education of the prince during his exile. In fact, one could argue that ʾAqeel, not Mamduh, was the hero of this tale in that his loyalty, wisdom, and instructional skills were largely responsible for nurturing the prince to maturity and thereby guaranteeing the survival of dynastic government. The relationship between courtier and prince also exemplified the informal and intimate nature of the fraternal bond as a political bond.

Malik, whose name meant owner or proprietor, had the characteristics of members of the propertied class. Not only was he broad minded and a good manager (*mudabir*), but the king also entrusted him with the reins of government. Malik gave the king's roving thoughts focus and proved to be a good judge of the consequences of change. He also was skilled in security affairs, guarding the state secrets. As representative of the propertied class, he provided the monarchy with another important social and political ally. His political advice, organizational, and executive skills secured the successful return of the throne to its rightful heir.

Through the examination of the political actors who were part of the ceremony celebrating Mamduh's return to the throne, Taymur used proximity to King Mamduh to offer a glimpse of the relative importance of the key characters and classes in modern dynastic government. While the ulema, the learned religious scholars of Islam, sat in a row to Mamduh's right signifying their formal importance, Malik sat at the beginning of that raw putting formal (executive) power ahead of religious power. To Mamduh's left, other princes of the royal family sat with `Aqeel occupying the first seat in that raw. Because `Aqeel was not a member of the royal family, his elevation indicated that courtiers were to play a more important role in government than other princes who represented the declining importance of the kinship bond.

The frame story made clear that the threat to dynastic government came from ambitious civil servants recruited from the new middle class. Ghadur (whose name means treacherous in Arabic and ruthless in Turkish) and Dushnam (whose name was neither Arabic nor Turkish perhaps signifying the involvement of foreigners in the affairs of dynastic government) possessed important managerial skills but they also demonstrated the perils of the individualism promoted by modern education, which made them politically untrustworthy. Their ambition, self-interest, greed, and quest for power drove them to hypocrisy, deceit, the corruption of the prince, the discredit of the dynasty in the eyes of the ra`iya, and usurping the throne.

The ra'iya emerged as a guard against this class threat. Taymur offered two novel approaches to this discussion of the link between this general population and Islamic government. She portrayed Dushnam and Ghadur as the advocates of the realist Machiavellian approach to politics and government: they not only placed their individual self-interests above their loyalty to the king but also employed whatever means necessary to gain access to political power. The theory of government they taught Mamduh was also Machiavellian in that it advocated cruelty to the subjects and argued that leniency and good nature were political liabilities that undermined the subjects' obedience and their respect to the rulers. In addition to fear that was necessary for governance, Dushnam and Ghadur advised Mamduh to periodically purchase his subjects' support by lowering or forgiving their taxes since only a prince who could dispense such favors can gain him the support of his subjects.[62]

Orientalists and modernists alike confused these practices with Islamic autocracy or the legacy of Oriental despotism when these, in fact, were compatible if not derivative of Machiavelli's modern realist approach to princely government with its preoccupation with how to attain power and maintain it. According to this early modern approach, brutality and cruelty were justified as effective means of holding on to power. In contrast, Sugata Bose pointed out that precolonial sovereignties were seldom unitary, allowing the ra'iya to escape into autonomous social spaces that were outside state control.[63] If this were the case, then the concept of Oriental despotism confused the improved coercive capacity of the modern state with its premodern precursor. What Taymur proposed was the replacement of the modern realist approach to government with the nationalizing one, developing important linkages between it and a populace.

Finally, Islamic masculinity provided another source of enhanced forms of solidarity among men in the ruled and the ruling classes. As mentioned in the last chapter, Taymur's introduction to *Nata'ij al-Ahwal* emphasized that the education of young male children was both a general concern of the reading public and also a specific concern of dynastic government. This conceptualization set aside the old assumption that what was relevant to the education of the prince could not apply to his male subjects. While the prince's corruption by ambitious politicians demonstrated that competition and conflict existed among men, Mamduh's exile and encounters with his male subjects reinforced Malik's advice that he follows the values shared by other men. Discipline, responsibility, and obedience emerged as part of the social definition of Islamic masculinity as well as the basis of fraternal solidarity. The African slaves ordered to kill Mamduh mistook him for a disobedient white slave and proceeded to instruct him on the importance of loyalty and the evil of disobedience. They advised him against rebelliousness, which they defined as flouting social and cultural conventions, and following one's own whims.[64] In this instructional role, slaves were members of the community who shared in the obligation to command right and forbid wrong.[65] When Mamduh was sold as a white slave, his new owner, a Turkish soldier who purchased him to marry his mixed-race daughter, promised him access to his property if he obediently followed his wishes. Even though Mamduh did not wish to marry his master's daughter, he did not flee his service, indicating his acceptance of obedience and responsibility as adult male values. Instead, he sought to purchase his freedom back rejecting rebelliousness as part of a dangerous individualism that flouted the rules defining a community.

What about rebellion against the colonizers as part of the defense of the community and its rules? Taymur's was conspicuously silent on this issue. British occupation of Egypt took place in 1882, five years before the publication of *Nata'ij al-Ahwal*. It was very likely that Taymur viewed national rebellion against this new enemy as a double-edged sword: resistance against this external enemy coincided with a challenge of the old dynastic order. Because British occupation eliminated the nationalist threat to the latter, which Taymur considered to be the primary cause of the political crisis facing the community, she might have approved of it as a welcome temporary development that gave the dynasty a new lease on life to reform itself. Since she emphasized dynastic government as the only legitimate government, it was safe to say that she would come to see colonialism as an eventual threat to the community.

The Transition to Capitalist Mercantilism and the Crisis of the Cultural-Economic Community

Benedict Anderson identified the religious and dynastic communities as examples of communities that preceded the rise of the modern national one. The latter defined itself in relation to the former in its definition of its cultural roots.[66] The simultaneity of continuity and change was used in Taymur's narrative to encourage readers, who might not individually know one another, to recognize old and new elements at work in their community. While the first two chapters focused on the corruption of Prince Mamduh then his dramatic exile leading to a journey of self discovery, the third chapter of *Nata'ij al-Ahwal*, which was the longest one in the book, devoted itself to the development of a "story within the story," which discussed the important changes taking place in the loosely structured economic community about which Anderson was silent but which Taymur saw as having dramatic effects on old values as well as the emergence of new ones.

In this discussion, the author focused her attention on what Bose identified as the Indian Ocean Rim as an example of an "interregional economic and cultural arena" where different civilizations in Africa, the Middle East, India and China interacted. Bose suggested that the rise of a capitalist world system and colonialism did not immediately lead to the collapse of the older economic communities or subsystems. Chapter 3 focused the reader's attention on the examination of how the economic arena was responding to capitalist influences by pointing out that long-distance trade was no longer focused on luxury goods (silk and precious stones) but now dealt with bulk items (sugar, salt, herbal dyes, and medicine). The old economic elite shared formal and informal rules regarding how to handle oneself, wealth, and social relations,[67] which operate within what Bose described as a "religiously informed universalism . . . an overarching unity in its varied regional and cultural settings."[68] In contrast, the new capitalist elite was engaged in stiff economic competition and the pursuit of individual self-interest, undermining the formal and the largely informal rules represented by the old Sufi, ascetic, and mystic ways of life that constituted according to Bose the basis of this region's religious cosmopolitanism.[69] While some parts of this value system survived, they were no longer uniformly appreciated, facing competition against more crude forms of entertainment like drinking, gambling, and the consumption of drugs.[70]

Taymur significantly avoided the use of the categories of East versus West that were central to the dominant Orientalist discourse of her time in the discussion of the changes taking place in the economic community. Despite British occupation of India and Egypt, her narrative had only a few minor European characters that were categorized as *al-afrinj* (Franks). In her contemplation of "the course and the history of nations" in the ancient world, they do not figure prominently perhaps reflecting her belief that Egypt, India, and China were going to survive the effects of capitalism and European colonialism. The continued reference to these old cultural traditions and economic systems reminded the reader of their long-shared economic and cultural histories as a counter weight to the new dominant culture of European modernity, which some local literary works, like Ali Mubarak's `Alam al-Din, have described. The primacy of the Mediterranean world with Europe, Europeans, their lives, thought, and economic and political institutions were not the center of discussion here but the older regional frames of reference.

The Roles of Male Friendship (Brotherhood) and Faith in Changing Capitalist Economies and Societies

Like in the frame story, the story within the story was also concerned with the theme of "friendship among men" and how it strengthened or undermined fraternal solidarity. While the reuniting of `Aqeel and Mamduh demonstrated the emerging belief in male friendship as a bond that had its rewards, the characters of the story within the story were divided in their view of friendship or brotherhood as a guard against economic insecurities of the time. In the introduction to the book, Taymur described the concerns of the chapter in the following way: "There were two things that friends needed as they experienced the approach and the retreat [of life]. The one who goes through the retreat needed to hold on to both his piety and patience as means of handling misfortune. The other one who experienced the approach [of life] needed to support *his brothers* [*ikhwanuha*] and also to give thanks to [God] for his blessings."[71]

In coupling the roles played by friends and faith in good and bad times, Taymur added an Islamically specific dimension to the definition of fraternity and community Loss and prosperity tested one's faith and fraternal bonds in different ways. She elaborated on this theme through the examination of the ups and downs of the friendship between two Egyptian merchants (*tujar*) who were also neighbors. Farhad, who traded luxury goods like jewelry and textiles, became one of the wealthiest merchants in the land whose trade was never affected by loss. He lived in a big and well-built house with two wives named *Khiyana* (treachery) and *Sharassa* (maliciousness) and a sister called Sa`ada (happiness). He indulged himself in several pleasurable activities like listening to music, attending frivolous gatherings, and drinking heavily.

Farhad's next-door neighbor, Bahram, who could barely make ends meet, was a small merchant trading in bulk items like wheat and salt. He had four wives: *Sadaqa* (friendship), *Balagha* (eloquence), *Hiyla* (trickery), and *Shattara* (cleverness) and a sister called *Nehusa* (misfortune). A pious man who spent most of his days fasting and his nights working, Bahram tried every year to do well in his business, pay alms, and generate enough income to support his children. Guided by the Qur'anic verse that warned "the spendthrifts were the brethern [*sic*] of the devil," he tried to avoid being one.[72] Even though a responsible member of the community who respected the rights of others and managed his trade well, Bahram could not understand why he, the pious one, was not wealthy while his morally flawed neighbor was. His speculative answer to this paradox was that Farhad must have a good conscience of which only God was aware.

When Farhad decided go on a trading trip to India, Bahram solicited his neighbor's financial help so that he could join him, but he was met with rejection. After borrowing to finance the trip, he planned to take his wife Sadaqa and his sister Nehusa with him. Bahram's good friend *al-Sabr* (patience) advised against the trip predicting that profits and happiness were fated in every occupation and since Bahram had his sister Nehusa with him, he was not likely to succeed. He asked Bahram to wait until God separated him from his sister quoting the Qur'anic verse "victory can only come from God." Bahram disagreed and cited another verse that advised "walk in the highlands and eat from what you earn" pointing out that he had four wives to support and whose good qualities he wanted to put to use. In particular, Bahram hoped that his wife Sadaqa would protect him any of his sister's missteps.

Despite Sadaqa's good advice and Bahram's hard work, Nehusa's carelessness ruined Bahram's chances to make any material gain. In contrast, Farhad's deviousness and the treachery of his wife, Khiyana, were positively neutralized by his sister, Sa'ada. Farhad and Bahram's next two business trips followed the same scenario with Farhad refusing to financially assist Bahram who found other ways to go on these business trips with his sister Nehusa accompanied first by his wife Balagha and then Shattara, whose skills were helpful, but not enough to counter the undisciplined, and unethical actions of Nehusa. In contrast, the treacherous and malicious advice given to Farhad by his wives were balanced by the well-intentioned, principled, and thoughtful Sa'ada. In the middle of the fourth trip, Nehusa and Sa'ada, who disapproved of their brothers' actions, decided to leave them. While Nehusa married Farhad, Sa'ada, in protest, offered herself to Bahram as a concubine. This signaled the reversal of fortune of the two merchants with Bahram finally able to reap the rewards of his pious behavior and hard work with support from Sa'ada and Farhad, directed by Nehusa, began a downward spiral. In contrast to Farhad's earlier behavior, Bahram consistently stood by his friend and his own sister who continued their devious and thoughtless behavior.

The above narrative focused its attention on the changing socioeconomic contexts within which these merchants operated and definitions of acceptable business and social practices. Bahram and Farhad functioned within an economic arena where small and large scale merchant capital competed with each other and developed different work ethics, value systems, and consumption habits. Large-scale capital replaced the generally accepted Islamic rules of commanding right and forbidding wrong (*al-amr bi al-ma`ruf wa al-nahiy `anal-munkar*) with the pursuit of individual self-interest. Farhad, representing the new entrepreneurs, did not necessarily work hard for his rewards but used whatever means necessary to maximize his wealth. Within this economic environment, Bahram representing the tremendous pressures faced by small-scale businessmen, increasingly questioned why creativity, goodness, and hard work were no longer rewarded with fortune and why greed and treachery increasingly won the day. His continued adherence to the old moral code in the face of the harshness of stiff competition became a solid expression of his faith and/or the old value system that eventually bore fruit.

The injunction to command right and to forbid wrong, which is repeated in seven Qur'anic verses, served as a major organizing mechanism defining the duty and/or the obligations of the economic actors in the community. A particular verse stated, "Let there be one community of you (*ummatun*) calling to good and commanding right and forbidding wrong."[73] "Doing right" was generally interpreted to include religious observances as well as the general acceptance of established social standards. "Forbidding wrong" was associated with deviation from these practices and engaging in activities like singing, wenching, gambling, and drinking linked to lack of self discipline.[74] This commitment to commanding right and forbidding wrong, which had served to distinguish the Islamic community from all others, was increasingly under attack by capitalist business and consumption practices that diluted the distinct moral character of the *umma*. Farhad's behavior provided many examples of threats they posed to the social cohesion of the community, patient conduct of business and the pursuit of happiness (*al-sa`ada*). In the early 1880s, the Egyptian press especially the journal of *al-Tankeet wa al-Tabkeet*, edited by Abdallah al-Nadeem the nationalist writer and social critic, singled out the discussion of these threats that the wealthy young members of the community imported through the mimicking European business and social mannerisms, like singing, drinking, and gambling. He argued that these social practices were markers of Westernization that were contributing to the corruption of Islamic society.[75]

Polemics aside, Taymur was also concerned with how the above practices led devout Muslims, like Bahram, to question the moral economy of faith—that is, the belief in God's direct rewarding of the pious and penalizing of the errant members of the community. Nizam al-Mulk's book began by explicitly asserting the unambiguous belief in this direct religious explanation of an individual's fortune and misfortune.[76] Such a belief could no longer be sustained in a new economic system whose rewards were increasingly reaped by those who worried less about the morality of their practices and more about how to secure material gains. The response of the devout Bahram to this paradox contributed to a tortured belief that Farhad must have a good conscience of which only God was aware. Fearing that the confidence of the less devout in Islamic social and economic prescriptions would waver, Bahram's friend, al-Sabr recommended the separation of fortune and misfortune from divine actions and thinking of them as parallel forces beyond individual control. While God had the power to end misfortune and bring about fortune, these nonreligious forces were not always divinely sanctioned, but indirectly tested both. In counseling the acceptance of the capriciousness of fortune and misfortune, he echoed the views and the assumptions made by the early Arabs with their pre-Islamic notion of *al-Dahr* (time with its vicissitudes) and the need to stoically accept whatever it brought as a measure of the strength of one's character.

Whereas al-Sabr cited a Qur'anic verse that advised patiently waiting for divine intervention to end the capriciousness of misfortune, Bahram quoted another verse that advocated combining religious reflection with activism in seeking one's fortune. This suggested that the quest to understand the socioeconomic changes that resulted from ruthless competition and the loss of moral certainties led some Muslims to reflect on how to reconcile Qur'anic messages that embrace individual agency with an appreciation of forces outside one's control. The notion of fortune and misfortune as nonreligious forces outside one's (but not God's) control helped Bahram to maintain his faith in the moral relevance of the Islamic code and hard work in the face of his competitor's unethical successes. Bahram and Farhad represented the options available to individuals who operated in this new uncertain economic world: one could embrace a "commerce without conscience" as the new morality dictated by individual self-interest, or one could continue one's faith in the divinely sanctioned Islamic social rules to command right and forbid wrong, which were tried-and-tested rules that served the interests of the community.

In the face of forces outside one's control, moral ambiguity and economic uncertainty, Taymur put greater, not less, emphasis on individual choice and agency. Farhad and Bahram chose the moral code that suited them best and enduring the tests offered by the rotation of fortune and misfortune. Despite the presumed arbitrariness of fortune and misfortune, Taymur represented them not as supernatural forces like the jinn, which thwarted human actors, but as human actors with human motives that explained the resulting outcomes. They represented clusters of human qualities that enhanced or undermined the short- and long-term interests of the different characters taking into account the messiness of human interactions and relations that sometimes led to unintended outcomes that were the result of incomplete information, human misunderstandings coincidence/chance on human outcomes.

This definition of human agency was different from the very form of instrumental logic produced by capitalism, which stressed individual control and human intentionality and ignored the messiness and the complexity of human interactions, including the gap between what is intended and what actually happens. In one of the rare discussions of Europeans in the story within the story, Taymur used the minor character of an *afranki* (European) king to comment on the inadequacy of this type of logic. He had advertised in different places that he was searching for a stone that had medicinal value and assumed when he saw Bahram with the stone that he had seen the advertisement, went out and looked for it and had come for the reward. The reality was altogether different. Bahram had inadvertently found the stone, did not know anything about its use or who needed it and fortuitously met the king who recognized it and rewarded him. Instrumental logic offered a flat explanation of the messy complicated courses of human action.

Only the Islamic moral code had an effective social mechanism that protected the individual from the painful effects of misfortune with its appreciation of social solidarity in the face of the uncertainty of the outcomes of partial human decisions. The emphasis on the friendship and/or the brotherhood of men provided a means of cushioning the harsh effects of economic and social uncertainty. Taymur's conception of brotherhood bore a significant resemblance to the views of the medieval theologian Abu Hamid Muhammad al-Ghazali who offered the most detailed discussion on the subject. He defined the community of Muslim believers as a brotherhood[77] and likened the Islamically sanctioned "contract of brotherhood" to that created by the marital contract. Brotherhood in religion was stronger than that based on kinship[78] obliging Muslim men to extend material and emotional support to each other. The strength of this bond was measured in different ways: Responding to another Muslim's request for support was the weakest commitment that a Muslim man could make to the welfare of another and as such was a fulfillment of that contract in the third degree. Placing one's brother at the same footing as one's self-interest represented a higher level of commitment in the second degree. Finally, elevating the brotherly relationship between two Muslim men to the status of *siddiq* (a true friend) included putting the needs of one's brother ahead of one's own and contributing a "faithful witness to the truth"[79]—that is, the highest fulfillment of that brotherly contract.[80]

Al-Ghazali was aware of the difficulties that his views regarding the strength of Islamic brotherhood will meet from the market folk and their unwillingness to accept their material responsibility to help a brother.[81] To overcome some of their resistance, he cited another Hadith that suggested that the economic support of a brother was a worthier activity than giving alms to the poor, which was one of the cornerstones of the Islamic faith. By suggesting that extending material help to a brother was more desirable than giving alms, al-Ghazali sought to provide well-to-do merchants with incentives to invest in the development of brotherly relations. This whole discussion suggested the existence of an early Islamic precedent to using brotherhood as a means of counteracting the economic tensions generated by competition in the market place.

In Taymur's tale, `Aqeel qualified as a siddiq, who not only spent whatever he earned on Mamduh but also served as his guide in understanding the intricacies of human relationships and truth. Similarly, Bahram's defense of Farhad against his enemies, providing him with a safe environment where he was protected despite his faults offered another example of a friend and a brother whose fulfillment of the contract of brotherhood was of the highest order. In this way, the narrative sought to both instruct by example and to persuade (*bi al-siyassa*) Farhad, and the reader who identified with him, of the need to rationalize conflicting economic interests by placing them in the context of the Islamic moral code that bridged the divisions within the community. `Aqeel summarized these lessons in the following paragraph:

> The Qura'nic verse stated that he who violates [the confidence or a contract of] another, violates himself. He who does good does it for himself. The lesson to be learned is that he who enjoys happiness shall not be arrogant about it. He shall be modest and shall be kind in his interactions with his kin and his brothers. He shall extend support to whoever needs it among his family and neighbors. He shall daily express his gratitude to God and trust in him. He shall hold on to the bond of friendship in his words and deeds. As a proverb . . . states, if happiness is to shine on you, then you shall use it to provide mercy to your neighbors and friends. If it passes you by, then they will be there for you. A happy man can do right by endeavoring to pursue all that appeals to rational [men] which is everything that is moderate and consistent with the transferred tradition. He shall know that wealth is like a meal to be shared with the loved ones. Hardship is the test of the experiments of the brothers. If one is generous with his wealth, he can count on the sincerity of people in difficult times and their support and rebuke of one's enemies and those who envy him.[82]

The Qura'nic verses cited by `Aqeel clearly supported individualism and individual responsibility by stipulating that good actions benefit their individual owners, but he sought to temper the individualist drive by underlining the social nature of success and happiness. Instead of being overly happy or proud of one's own accomplishment, one should be modest about them, sharing his good fortune with his kin, "brothers," and neighbors. In putting individual achievement in the service of existing social groups and one's faith, one clearly served one's long-term interests in this world and the next. A popular proverb reinforced this social message by highlighting the importance of sharing one's happiness with neighbors and friends in the hope that they would support one should one's luck change. Tradition and individual rationality supported this view of the utility of friendship and brotherhood in the face of uncertainty.

In this discussion, the obligation to support one's friends received more discussion than that of the support of one's kin. Supporting one's family during good times was recommended, but the passage repeatedly stressed the importance of nurturing fraternal bonds with neighbors and friends (including one's business associates) through words, deeds, and affections. The motivation behind the attention given to these fraternal ties was to guard against the increase in risk taking, which was the hallmark of Farhad's actions and the advice that Nehusa gave him, which left them economically vulnerable. As the true individualist in this tale, some of Farhad's risks sometimes were rewarded at the expense of others, especially Bahram. In contrast, Bahram provided an alternative entrepreneurial model that combined an interest in the accumulation of wealth with social responsibilities: he not only supported the increasingly impoverished Farhad and Nehusa but also built a mosque in his community[83] and then purchased a bigger home for his family. The order of these activities emphasized the diverse social obligations that successful members of the community owed others and themselves.

Fortune and Misfortune in the Articulation of Islamic Femininity and Heterosexuality

In the previous section, Taymur used the chronicle of the relations between Bahram and Farhad to criticize the way competitive mercantilism undermined the relations of solidarity among men and to encourage men to depend on each other for social and economic support. In the discussion of Farhad and Bahram's relations with women, she simultaneously highlighted male emotional and practical dependence on women in the family, their inability to control them, and women's mediating roles in the nurture or subversion of the fraternal bonds among men. The resulting discussion of Islamic femininity and heterosexuality was unlike any other produced in the second half of the nineteenth century.

It was significant that Taymur chose to represent happiness or fortune and misfortune as female characters in the discussion of forces beyond the control of individual men. Three centuries earlier, Niccolò Machiavelli identified fortune with femininity in his discussion of sixteenth-century Florentine politics, justifying the exclusion of women from politics and public life and stressing the importance of male autonomy and agency. Machiavelli inherited the figure of *fortuna* from a long political tradition that was both Roman and Christian.

He used it to examine the possibilities and limitations of human action. Very specifically, he defined politics as a manly occupation that pitted the uncontrollable feminine character of fortune against male *virtus* and suggested the need for the sexual conquest of fortune.[84] "Fortune was a 'cruel goddess' who is 'demanding and injurious' towards men; she 'gives commands and rules' and 'commands them with fury.' She is 'shifting,' 'unstable' and 'fickle,' never keeps her promises and acts 'without pity, without law or right,' often depriving 'the just' and rewarding 'the unjust.'"[85]

In contrast, Taymur conceptualized femininity as a much more complex source of happiness or fortune and misfortune. While the Arabic word for happiness was a feminine word (*al-sa`ada*) and the word for misfortune (*al-nahs*) was masculine, Taymur purposely transformed the masculine *nahs* into the feminine *al-nahusa* to explore its effects and that of *al-sa`ada*, as two faces of female agency. Sa`ada and Nehusa, Farhad and Bahram's sisters, had positive and negative capabilities that affected their contributions to their families. Rather than discussing happiness and misfortune as representing innate feminine qualities, Taymur offered relational explanations of these qualities through an examination of the important roles that women could play in their families. Nehusa brought misfortune to her brother's family because she was careless, a reckless risk taker who mishandled his affairs, unappreciative of his good qualities, betraying him to his competitors, displaying bad judgment, fostering discord in the family, and breaking socially accepted rules. In contrast, Sa`ada, balanced of the short- and long-term interests of her brother, was a good judge of character and seriously accepted her obligations as a good Muslim. In embracing these different forms of social behavior, sisters, wives, and concubines shaped the fortunes of men.

As representatives of forces beyond the control of men, Taymur used Sa`ada and Nehusa to offer an unorthodox view of the brother-sister relations in which the sister had power over her brother and not vice versa. Farhad and Bahram were socially bound to their sisters even though their personalities were mismatched. Bahram could not cast Nehusa aside even after he was convinced that her actions and views were the cause of his failures. While he was financially responsible for her welfare before and after her marriage, he also could not influence her choice of a husband. This was an important right that she exercised, along with all Muslim women, without the assumed deference to her brother's wishes. Even though Sa`ada was a good sister and a model Muslim woman, she also made that decision alone and her choice of Bahram was contrary to the wishes of Farhad. While this was a right, which the Islamic religion gave to women, clearly families of this period exercised undue influence over women in their choice of husbands. Taymur's prominent emphasis on this right leads one to wonder if she regretted not having this right in her own unhappy marriage.

In choosing to break with her brother Farhad over his decision to marry Nehusa, Sa`ada reflected the interest that family members had in these important decisions. In this case, she also saw it as a means to exercise another right, that is, the obligation of a Muslim woman to command right and to forbid wrong. This was a right, which most Islamic interpreters gave Muslim women, but whose application they restricted to family life—that is, providing moral guidance to one's kin, husband, and children.[86] Sa`ada extended this right to include the break with one's family or brother and his determination to do wrong by marrying *Nehusa* and all the evils she represented. Even though this break put her in a vulnerable economic and social position, explaining why she had to offer herself to Bahram as a concubine, she clearly saw this position as preferable to residing with *Nehusa*, *Khiyana* and *Sharassa* in her brother's harem.

Within extended Muslim families that included multiple wives and unmarried sisters, the latter exerted more influence over the actions of the male head of the household because kinship relations between brother and sister were stronger and more stable than the marital relationship between husband and wife. At the same time, because a sister eventually married and became a member of another family, her influence over her brother eventually weakened but his responsibility for her continued.

While the men could not choose their sisters, they chose their wives and sexual partners whose character represented qualities that they admired or shared. For example, Nehusa's suggestion that Farhad collect her brother's reward appealed to Farhad's greed making her as an appealing addition to his harem that included other wives, who represented treachery and maliciousness as acceptable means in his determined pursuit of self-interest. Similarly, Bahram's wives represented allegorical qualities that were in tune with his personal inclinations and value system—that is, friendship, eloquence, and cleverness, which also distinguished his approach to business from that of his competitor and made him an appealing partner to Sa`ada.

By equally representing women as possessing positive and negative qualities that they shared with men, Taymur turned her back on the long Islamic and European male literary and political representations that treated women as the source of evil and/or negative influences over men. She also suggested that rather than having a monopoly on good or evil, they combined a host of very human qualities that included friendship, eloquence, cleverness, trickery, treachery, and maliciousness. While the company of women, whether that of a wife or a sister, also had the effect of giving their men the good or bad qualities they possessed, they were not essential feminine qualities but qualities that they shared with men.

Thus, the dependence of men on other men, which Taymur advocated as a source of social and economic security, was complemented with the reciprocal dependence of men on women as compatible marital partners seeking the same economic goods. Men did not just depend on women to run their households but they were swayed by their advice on what to do in the marketplace and in the political arena. Bahram purposely took one wife in each one of his business trips intending to explicitly benefit from each of their social skills (friendship, eloquence, and cleverness) in his transactions with other people. The same was true of Farhad. Their wives and sisters were very interested in enhancing the business and political interests of their men and placed their ideas at their service. For example, treachery advised Farhad to undermine the position of one king and his son and in this way make their throne available to the Egyptian king who would then generously reward him. Nehusa/misfortune suggested that they increase their wealth by diversifying their investments in urban real estate and agriculture. She also advised him to buy businesses that were in distress because they would be offered at cheap prices. Finally, she stressed that they use their economic wealth to gain political access, consider making alliances with the military, and eventually usurping the power of the king.[87]

The association of Nehusa and Khiyana with the rough and tumble aspects of politics was not designed to discredit women's involvement in politics. Most of the female characters of this narrative, from Boran, Sadaqa, Balagha, Shatarra, Nehusa, Khiyana and Sharassa, were active companions of men, sharing their woes as well their rewards. They suffered from the economic instability and the poverty that the new market system inflicted on their families. They also had to bear the consequences of their men engaging in drinking and gambling as new popular consumption activities. Farhad was engaged in these activities when thieves descended on his ship stealing his goods and killing two of his wives making him an inadequate patriarch.

Wives and sisters also emerged as clear beneficiaries of their husbands' pursuit of wealth and economic self-interest. They enjoyed the comforts that came with wealth including big houses with big gardens and many servants. As the wife of a wealthy man, Nehusa desired to travel for pure enjoyment as a new consumption activity enjoyed by women of that class. The Chinese princess that Bahram encountered in one of his trips coupled her interest in travel with the desire to learn about the comparative norms that governed heterosexuality and how women viewed marriage in other cultures.

Taymur did not treat women's economic and political involvement as qualitatively different from that of men: she supported it when it was identified with reform and condemned it when it was largely guided by greed and ambition. For example, Malik, 'Aqeel, and Boran's active participations in politics were commended because it served as a means of strengthening and reforming dynastic government, but the political ambitions of Nehusa and Khiyana, Dushnam, and Ghadur were denounced because they contributed to the degradation of political life and undermined Islamic government.

Finally, the story within the story shed light on the differing perspectives that men and women had of heterosexuality and marriage. Taymur's tales were littered with many references to the increasingly important sentimental side of marriage treating heterosexual love as a contested ingredient of formal and informal marital unions. While Malik's view of heterosexual love presented women as the saviors or caretakers of men, some of the female characters were skeptical of marriage and heterosexuality as social arrangements that served their best interests. In his third trip, Bahram encountered an Algerian prince who fell in love with a Chinese princess who swore off marriage. In an attempt to help the Algerian prince, Bahram, disguised as an old ascetic woman, learned that the princess was affected by the experience of an Iraqi merchant's daughter who devoted herself to nursing an ailing cousin whom she loved only to have him betray her, steal her jewelry, and marry another. In response, the princess declared her hatred of men and the rejection of marriage as an institution that made women the caretakers of treacherous men whose roving eyes made them untrustworthy and the marital union a trap to be avoided. Women of the ruling classes, who had these critical views, emerged as independent actors in the political arena because their decisions to marry or not to marry gave them power over sexual politics of the dynastic governments that needed them to cement their blood ties with other rulers. Weariness about the treachery of men and the denunciation of heterosexuality and marriage provided women with new bases for independence.

The way Bahram got the princess to change her mind was one of two instances in which he was less than admirable: Bahram tricked and lied to her. Even though Bahram borrowed trickery from one of his wives, who allegorically carried that name, he put it into masculine use. Not only did he try to explain away the infidelity of the Iraqi woman's cousin, but he also tried to rehabilitate the idea of marriage by appealing to the maternal instincts of the princess. He quoted the Qur'anic verse that described money and children as the finest ornaments of earthly life, emphasizing the regrets of old women about not having children when they were younger. Bahram's trickery worked; the princess overcame her dislike of men and started to see children as the most important reward of a marriage, not heterosexual love or fidelity.

Despite the success of Bahram's elaborate ruse in changing the princess' mind, the readers knew he lied about the sincerity of men and that the princess or women had valid reasons for resisting marriage. To reaffirm this point in the reader's mind, Taymur's narrative made many references to the existence of ascetic women who used religion to opt out of the marriage institution. Bahram had disguised himself as one these women. Even though this old Islamic tradition allowed women to reject heterosexuality and domestic roles for a life of worship, it was not a widely chosen path. It was certainly a path that Taymur took following the death of her husband when she was in her thirties by staying unmarried for the next 30 years.

The new stress on capital accumulation provided a material context that supported the rise of smaller families and heterosexuality. At the beginning of the tale, Bahram's poverty was not simply a function of having misfortune as a sister but also the result of having to support four wives. The wealthy Farhad only had two wives and a sister to support, contributing to greater prosperity. As Bahram's fortune began to turn, the size of his household grew smaller. Two of his wives Balagha and Hiyla died and Shattara asked for divorce. This left Bahram with one wife, Sadaqa, and one concubine, Sa'ada, in a much smaller family or harem. It would appear from this discussion that Taymur considered large harems, with three or four wives, as contributing to diminished prosperity and that a two-woman harem was a more economical model for Muslim households. The view of large households as a mark of wealth was clearly changing leading the well to do to consider them to be a social and economic drain on their wealth. So while polygamous marriages continued, the number of the wives was sharply reduced to two as an ideal. At the same time, as Farhad's wealth diminished so did the number of his wives. When his two wives died following the raid on his ship, he was only left with Nehusa. Here, Taymur seemed to suggest that monogamy was appropriate for the poor Farhad.

Bahram's desire to add *al-Qana'a*, whose name meant contentment, to his harem showed that the transition to smaller polygamous marriages was more of an ideal than a reality. When Bahram apologetically confessed to Sa'ada his infatuation with al-Qana'a, she laughed at him stoically and asked him to wait for fortune to hand her to him. Woman readers recognized in this advice her attempt to delay the inevitable addition of yet another woman to her household to share the affection of her man. Bahram's addition of al-Qana'a to the household provided evidence that the promises and affections of men were not to be trusted.

Because Bahram served as a model of the virtuous Muslim man, the names of his wives shed light on the qualities that were identified with heterosexual intimacy in the changing Muslim family. Friendship, eloquence, cleverness, and trickery showed that men and women began to have different expectations of each other. As indicators of the development of companionate marriage, all the wives in this tale wanted to be appreciated and respected by their husbands and engaged in the different aspects of their lives. The happiness of women and the contentment of men were to contribute to the rehabilitation of the marriage institution and overcome elite women's skepticism of marriage and heterosexuality.

The new emphasis on heterosexual love and intimacy was accompanied by the muting of homosocial and homosexual relations.[88] The Chinese princess' declared hatred of all men did not imply that she was in love with women rather it stressed her strong identification with the experience of other women. It offered an example of homosocial relations that the systems of sexual segregation fostered among women in that part of the world. There was very little evidence in *Nata'ij al-Ahwal* that relations among women were ever sexual. The only reference in the narrative to homosexual attraction or demonstration of such tendencies occurred among men. When Mamduh was enslaved during his early exile and was brought before a prince to defend himself against the charge of adultery, the prince proceeded to admire Mamduh's beauty, expressing a reluctance to harshly punish him.[89] Mamduh's success in proving his innocence put an end to the exploration of these relations among men.

Conclusion

The narrative of *Nata'ij al-Ahwal* was primarily concerned with the dynamics of the nation-building process, and it contributed to the reestablishment of new bases of dynastic government and its Islamic society. Its analysis of the changes taking place in Islamic society provided a means of engaging the readers in the imagining of where the community was and where it hoped to go in light of the many challenges it faced. What emerged out of its detailed discussion were societies that were in flux but were also capable of utilizing their extensive literary, social, cultural, economic, and political resources to adapt to change in ways that preserved the integrity of their institutions and ways of life.

CHAPTER 4

From Fiction to Social Criticism

> The lion was enraged by the disrespectful
> behavior of his wife who dared to leave him
> the leftovers of her hunt . . . He reminded her
> of the inequality of their status . . . The lioness
> laughed at this reminding him: "this was
> when you were you and I was me. Now,
> Our roles are reversed: you are me and I am
> you."
>
> —*Mir'at al-Ta'mul fi al-Umur*[1]

The year 1892 witnessed the publication of `A'isha Taymur's *Mir'at al-Ta'mul fi al-Umur* (a reflective mirror on Some Matters), a 16-page booklet and *Hilyat al-Tiraz* (the finest of its class), her collected Arabic poems. In this chapter I will examine the first of these two publications where Taymur turned her attention to social criticism—that is, the changing gender relations between men and women in the family and its effects on the representation of the national community. In the process, she offered a novel interpretation (*ijtihad*) of the contingent nature of the religious and social bases of male leadership over women in the family. Taymur's work elicited critical responses from Shaykh Abdallah al-Fayumi, a member of the ulema and Abdallah al-Nadeem, the nationalist writer, who offered two perspectives of her work and views of gender as a marker of the community. This early debate underlined the contested character of gender relations and roles as features of the community in the early 1890s long before the work of Qasim Amin's *Tahrir al-Mar'at* (The Liberation of the Woman) in 1899.

The publication of *Mir'at al-T'amul fi al-Umur* in 1892 was important because that year witnessed the confluence of political and social developments that established its importance in Egyptian national history. The unpopular Khedive Tewfik died in January 1892 and was succeeded by his young son, Abbas II, who quickly clashed with Lord Cromer, the British consul general, transforming himself into a unifying national figure around which the divided nation was finally able to rally. In an early demonstration of his desire to heal the national divisions unleashed by the ʿUrabi national revolution, the new khedive pardoned Abdallah al-Nadeem, the orator of the revolution on February 3, 1892, paving the way for his return to Egypt on May 9 of the same year and the publication of his new magazine, *al-Ustaz* (the teacher), which became a forum for his nationalist social and political views.[2] For the next two years, *al-Ustaz* inspired young Egyptian nationalists, represented by the graduates of the modern schools including Mustafa Kamel, who demonstrated against *al-Muqattam* newspaper, owned and run by Syrian journalists, for serving as the voice of the British occupation.[3]

Also in 1892, British colonial government marked the anniversary of its first decade in Egypt with the publication of *England in Egypt* by Alfred Milner, the director-general of Egyptian accounts, which celebrated British accomplishments justifying its continued occupation.[4] When that book was translated into Arabic, it had the opposite effect demonstrating the extent to which the occupation usurped khedival economic and political powers fueling greater support for a khedive led nationalist opposition.[5] The anniversary motivated writers, like Taymur and al-Nadeem, to discuss the negative consequences of colonial modernization.

Along with the publication of ʿAʾisha Taymur's *Mirʾat al-Taʾmul fi al-Umur* and *Hilyat al-Tiraz* in 1892, the first women's journal titled, *al-Fatat* (The Young Woman) also appeared. It was edited by Hind Noufal, a young Syrian Christian woman. The three publications established 1892 as an important marker of the active efforts by Egyptian and Syrian women to influence public debate. It is probable that the publication of Taymur's *Mirʾat* preceded the publication of *al-Fatat*, whose first issue appeared on November 30, 1892.[6] While the journal sought to encourage women's participation in public debates, it also emphasized the modernist ideals that emphasized women's domestic concerns as part of a sexual division of labor, which it does not question.[7] In contrast, Taymur's *Mirʾat* sought to initiate public debate on the significant changes in the roles that men and women played in the family. With Taymur sending a poem to celebrate the publication of *al-Fatat*, which the journal published, the journal's second issue included some of Taymur's poems from *Hilyat al-Tiraz*. What this made clear was that women writers of this period took an active interest in each other's work, offering support and building a loose sisterhood and/or community. The latter was loosely defined because it included women of different generations, ethnic groups, discourses, and social agendas.

With this context in mind, it was possible to turn to Taymur's *Mir'at al-Ta'mul fi al-Umur*, which attracted considerable critical attention to the changes taking place in the family and what to make of them.

Next, I will examine two of the responses to Taymur's work by Shaykh Abdallah al-Fayumi who focused on its religious interpretations and Abdallah al-Nadeem who focused on the social importance of the changes she noted and what to do about them. In the conclusion of the chapter I will discuss the importance of the debate.

Mir'at al-Ta'mul fi al-Umur and the Crisis of the Family

Taymur's booklet was indirectly critical of the social effects of colonial modernization including a new materialism that undermined the Islamic social and religious consensus that defined the "rights that men had over women and that women had over men."[8] Up until 1892, no other Muslim woman had dared to publicly address the religious bases of male leadership in the family transforming Taymur into a Muslim social critic commanding right and forbidding wrong. While Michael Cook suggested that "Western penetration of the Muslim world had little visible impact [on the discussion of commanding right and forbidding wrong],"[9] Taymur clearly used it to denounce Muslim men, whose adoption of Western social practices led to their abandonment of their responsibilities in the family.

In the brief introduction to this booklet, Taymur outlined the features of the Islamic-rationalist approach she was going to use with its emphasis on allowing reason to guide faith and employing human understanding to strengthen religious knowledge. While Islamic male scholars have historically contributed to the development of this approach, Taymur intended to use her access to a different kind of learning to rationally analyze the "strange and problematic social practices"[10] spreading in Egyptian society. Her decision to take on this sensitive topic sharing her views with a reading public that was largely composed of men was not an easy one. She hesitated and agonized over it feeling like a cat imprisoned within the walls of her secluded household by pouring rain, thunder, and lightning outside. As these manifestations of continued crisis persisted, her courage triumphed because she felt that the Islamic divine tradition was founded on justice and sympathy for the underdog. She also drew support from a prophetic statement, "Peace and goodness are to be found in me and my [Islamic] community until judgment day,"[11] which she interpreted as an invitation to speak out on matters of "right and wrong" directly addressing social problems taking place in the family. The prophetic statement, which located goodness in all the members of the Islamic community, provided support for her desire to bring these matters to the attention of the public. Taymur's reference to feeling like a cat imprisoned within her secluded household in the middle of inclement weather indicated that opposition to the voices of Muslim secluded women continued in the more conservative post revolutionary social climate reinforced by British occupation.

She employed an interesting literary device to provide herself with the courage she needed in tackling her sensitive religious and social topic: she referred to a hypothetical discourse she had with a scholar of the Islamic tradition (`alama) whose duty was to answer the questions of the devout and those who wanted to do good. The reader understood that as a veiled woman this was the only kind of dialogue that Taymur could possibly have with any member of this group. She explained to this interlocutor that she had spent a very long time thinking and investigating the causes of [the present social] malady and its cure and was told that she will get the support and guidance of intelligent and principled persons. In *Hilyat al-Tiraz*, published in the same year as *Mir'at al-Ta'mul fi al-Umur*, Taymur revealed that the hypothetical `alama was none other than the respected Shaykh Ibrahim al-Saqqa. In her elegy of the shaykh, she mentioned the assistance he gave to her *Mir'at*. While al-Saqqa might have helped her in selecting and interpreting the intent behind some of the Qur'anic verses she discussed, it was clear that her interpretations of male *quwamma* (leadership) were her own going beyond the conventional religious views of the time.

While Taymur's publication of *Nata'ij Al-Ahwal fi al-Aqwal wa al-Af'al* in 1887/8 followed by her collected poems *Hilyat al-Tiraz* (1892) contributed to her distinguished literary standing, *Mir'at al-Ta'mul fi al-Umur* was to break new grounds with its discussion of the collapse of social consensus, the exploration of the corrupting effects of new consumption patterns, the increasing materialism and the intense and continuing divisions among the different classes and among men and women in the new colonial society. Taymur's analysis of these problems was motivated by a desire to restore equilibrium to a society that had lost its social and economic balance.

The following quote explained the nature of the crisis, its underlying causes and her novel response to them:

> God instructed me/the believers to follow the correct path through the recitation of the Qur'anic verses. These explicitly identified the bases of the rights that men had over women and those that women had over men. It stated that 'men had leadership over women by virtue of the advantages that God gave them over one another and by what they spent of their money.' A man provided for the needs of his wife striving to protect and look after her. God explained his judgment [with regards male privilege] by citing their access to affairs/activities [*umur*] that enhanced reason and religion. This was why he gave them a monopoly of political and religious leadership positions (*al-wilaya wa al-imama*). They also had a legal advantage in having the testimony of one man equal that of two women . . . These advantages/privileges were coupled by [divine expectation of] justice guided by

faith. Male privilege over women [in the family] was also premised on 'spending of their money' on such things as *al-mahr* [dowry], their food, clothing and housing in accordance with their status. Finally, Men were to economically provide for their infant children so that a mother, who just gave birth, would not be asked to do more than she could (*la tukalif nafsn 'ila wis`aha*). These obligations were required by Qur'anic verse (*al-nus*) and community consensus (*al-ijma*).[12]

It was significant that Taymur focused her attention on the question of "rights," which the `Urabi revolution sought to politically redefine and British colonialism effectively curtailed. The ascent of Abbas II to power in 1892 and the friction between him and the British Consul, Sir Evelyn Barring, added fuel to this debate by focusing attention on the rights of the dynastic ruler vis-à-vis the British and his own subjects. Taymur had already discussed the question of the political rights of the ruler and the economic rights of his subjects in *Nata'ij al-Ahwal*, she used *Mir'at al-Ta'mul fi al-Umur* to examine the question of "gender rights" that Muslim men and women had in the family, which were *indirectly* affected by colonial modernization.

She chose as framework for her discussion the crucial Qur'anic verses that described the "rights that men had over women and women had over men."[13] The Qur'an offered a twofold discussion of the bases of male leadership over women in the family: the advantages that God gave men and women over each other and then the economic contractual relations that bound the two in marriage. In discussing the advantages that God gave men, Taymur underlined the fact that men's monopoly of religious and political leadership positions enhanced their experience, reason, and religious knowledge explaining the legal privileges that they had over women with the testimony of one man being treated as the equal of that given by two women. In terms of the leadership that men had over women in the family, Taymur suggested that it was derived from the fact that men spent money over women from *al-mahr* (a one-time financial offering a man makes to a woman before marriage) to clothing, housing, and food to support them while they nursed infant children.

On the surface, this presentation of the bases of male leadership appeared in tune with the mainstream understanding of male privileges in Islamic societies. On closer examination, Taymur was, in fact, offering a rereading or reinterpretation (*ijtihad*) of the Qur'anic verses, suggesting that male leadership over women was *doubly contingent* on specific political and economic conditions. First, men enjoyed the advantages of having access to religious and political positions, which represented one source of male privilege. Muslim women generally lacked access to these arenas even though they historically played an important role in the interpretation of the prophetic tradition leaving Qur'anic exegesis to the *ulema*. By attempting to offer her own reading of the Qur'an and articulating it publicly, Taymur was challenging both the religious and political bases of male privilege. Through access to literary education, with its emphasis on the complex study of language, Taymur could approach religious texts with a degree of confidence that Muslim men had up until 1892 exhibited. Through extending religious and political advantages that enhanced the knowledge and experience of men to women, some of the bases of male privilege changed contributing to the equalization of gender roles. Secondly, Taymur represented the relations between men and women in the family as largely contractual ones in which male leadership was contingent on their economic support of their wives and failure fulfill this obligation ended the basis of that leadership. Qur'anic verses and community consensus, of which women were a part, were the sources that shaped the understanding of these relations and rights.

Next, Taymur turned to the description of the new problematic social values and practices associated with modernity and the way they undermined the above understanding of the gender rights of men and women and created new sources and forms of marital discord.

> It is odd that most young men of our time have refrained from reading the above verses and pondering their latent and manifest meanings. Ignorance is responsible for their arrogant willingness to overlook God's injunctions. At present, every man who ponders marriage, whether he is a person of low or high status, lazy or bright, is generally after jewelry, pots, farms and real estate-not a good family, religiosity, virtue and modesty . . . This conduct represents the onslaught of heartbreaking failure, blinding darkness that misleads the thoughtful, the decline of the honor of nations (*umam*) and the destruction of what [their national] energies has built . . .
>
> [While,] this description does not include noble and powerful men who boldly continue to uphold the ideals of masculinity (*al-futuwa*) and its virtues (*al-muruwa*) . . . , its targets are the men who consider dimness insignificant, robbery an art and cowardice a lucrative craft. The desire of these young men to marry is not inspired by protection of the self or religious injunction, but by greed and the possession of wealth. Their intent is to waste what their ladies own, satisfy their base needs and exercise fiscal irresponsibility.
>
> Once one of these young men gets a hold of an obedient wife and her wealth, whether she is from the lower or the upper classes, he is intent on enjoying himself and avoiding any kind of exertion, responsibility or gainful employment . . . He spends his time in bars with friends of fair weather listening to music, gambling and drinking . . . These excesses lead each to return home in a sorry state: unable to stand up straight and/or to make sense. This behavior has become a permanent manifestation of their impaired [capacity], illness, injustice and evil. When the money is spent, the so-called friends vanish. Distress, grief and panic follow.
>
> [In this situation], a wife feels alienated from her husband and serves him with a broken heart. It becomes extremely difficult to manage the affairs of the household.

She will take whatever thrifty measures she can manage. Unfortunately, the husband's excuses will not cover the costs of running a household or hide the resulting economic hardships.

As wives take over the responsibilities of these households and resolve to resist hardship with patience, authority passes to these goddesses of management and the source of resourcefulness. Men give up the leadership that entitles them to respect and dignity and wear the veils of surrender, cowardice and shame . . . Their situation is depicted well by a popular parable that describes a lion that was too lazy to hunt so he orders his lioness to hunt in his place. She obeys him, but with the passage of time, she begins to treat herself to the prey first leaving him the scrapes. When he objects reminding her of his power and authoritative status, she laughs and reminds him that this was all in the past and that since she took on his role, she deserves to enjoy his authority and power. The lion is dumbfounded, but realizes that he can only blame himself for his plight and swears never to ask for her assistance in hunting even if it means dying of hunger.[14]

At the center of the above account, Taymur discussed the social features of a colonial modernization that was associated with economic greed, materialism, and a lifestyle that treated drinking, gambling, and frequenting nightclubs as signs of one's status. This new lifestyle undermined the Islamic definition of the roles that men and women were to play within the marriage institution and familial rights. It contributed to the development of a new type of masculinity that was less guided by religiously inspired definitions of the bases of male leadership and influenced by the rise of the values and lifestyles associated with the colonial setting. Afaf Lutfi al-Sayyid Marsot added another explanation for the ease with which these young husbands got a hold of the management of their wives' wealth. Unlike the Islamic institution of *Waqf* (endowments) that accommodated the many needs of secluded women to control their wealth in the eighteenth and the nineteenth centuries, these same women were disadvantaged when it was necessary to open, let alone have an easy access to, bank accounts, investment companies, and the stock market. For these new economic activities, they needed a male agent, most frequently, the greedy husbands described by Taymur as only too happy to get their hands on their wives' wealth. The modernization of the economic arena, which disadvantaged women in Europe, could be seen to yield similar effects to secluded women, who suddenly were made dependent on men in the management of their economic affairs.[15]

For Taymur, it was the demise of the balancing of virtue, modesty, and the religiosity with other economic concerns that contributed to the serious crisis in the family. The decisions of who to marry were increasingly solely focused on the economic resources that a wife brought into marriage, including jewelry, pots, clothing, farms, and real estate. The mention of pots, clothing, and jewelry as forms of property indicated that the new pattern of male behavior was not only restricted to the middle- and upper-class families but also extended to working-class families where women typically brought such items to their new families. Where did Taymur get knowledge of the changes taking place in working-class families? Taymur provided an answer to this question in another section of *Mir'at al-Tamul fi al-Umur* through the discussion of how working-class women replaced slave domestic household labor in upper-class families. These new domestic workers provided Taymur and other upper-class women with windows on the lives of urban working-class families, which had to deal with the same social phenomenon—that is, the greed of their men and their failure to provide for them. In Taymur's opinion, this signaled the general decline of honor and hard work as public ideals that contributed to important national accomplishments. These younger, cowardly men, who parasitically lived off the wealth of their wives to satisfy their base needs, represented the general crisis of Islamic masculinity.

While Taymur suggested that older noble men continued to adhere to their role as breadwinners and providers, there was a generational divide between them and their irresponsible younger counterparts. Another aspect of the crisis of masculinity included the development of superficial and exploitative relations between these foolish young men and the men they encountered in bars and night clubs who hypocritically presented themselves as friends, but actually participated in the dissipation of family wealth and disappearing when it was spent.

The changes that affected the definition of masculinity contributed to parallel changes in the definition of femininity. Even though minority of women continued to perform the roles of obedient wives vis-à-vis these irresponsible husbands, the majority had to shoulder the social and economic responsibility of their strapped households assuming the authority that used to belong to their husbands. One could argue that the latter group of women took on these new roles in their families out of necessity, reflecting their understanding that their relations with their husbands were contractual in nature and hence the change. According to Taymur, even the minority wives who continued to obey their husbands felt alienated from their husbands because of their failure to perform the socially prescribed roles. Men also had difficulty accepting the consequences of their actions especially the loss of their leadership roles in the family. A minority surrendered their leadership but many persisted in demanding their leadership positions even though they had abandoned their duties. The parable of the lion, which surrendered the obligation of hunting to his lioness and yet expected the same privileged status and treatment, was very instructive here. The lioness explained that the role reversal entitled her to the privileges that used to me owed to the male of the species.

After making a powerful argument to support the contingent nature of male leadership and the reasons behind its present decline, the next segment of Taymur's text seemed to paradoxically support patriarchal privilege.

> O men why do you not appreciate the unlimited blessings God have [*sic*] given you and comprehend the obligations [that go with it]? How could such a privileged group not understand the seriousness of this matter or not express gratitude for the divine favor given to them?
>
> It is popularly said that women can be snares for all devils. [Given] this evil description and reprehensible title, [it was] determined that their education should be left to Islamic scholars and that their discipline be delegated to the resolute and the just. Because a wife followed the commands and prohibitions of her husband upon whom her worldly possessions depended, the Qur'anic verse recommended, "[T]hey should get as much as they were owed in kindness." Women had rights over their husbands, which they should preserve and observe like good companionship, the service of their needs and the abandonment of harm. [In fact,] these conjugal rights were not complete until each [spouse] observed what they owed and were owed by the other. A husband was obliged to look after [his wife] and her interests. [In exchange,] she was obligated to obey him. If the situation was reversed and the man's elevated position was lowered with the woman becoming his guardian, why should she not set aside the rules that governed her seclusion and not throw away the veil of her modesty![16]

On the surface, Taymur seemed to be extolling the benefits of Islamic masculinity and patriarchy, encouraging men to appreciate their privileged status and the serious obligations that came with it. Her apparent goal was to ensure that women's old rights, which were the main justification for male privilege, were observed. She was clear that the abdication of the old ideals of Islamic masculinity undermined these rights leading to the abuse of women. For the wives who were faced by economic ruin, the return to the old rules of the marriage contract—which gave men privileges over women but saddled them with many social and economic obligations[17]—was preferable to the modern masculine ideals, which encouraged men to expand their privileges by using duplicity to take over their wives' property and shirking all their responsibilities toward them. Taymur suggested that there was no Islamic justification for this type of male behavior. Despite popular claims that women were the companions of all devils, Islam did not consider them to be innately or hopelessly evil. It did not deny them their rights or treat them in a punitive way. It advocated that they be educated by Islamic scholars and disciplined by their *just* husbands. A husband did not need to use much discipline to sway his wife for she knew that her interests were tied to his. The Qur'anic prescription was even more generous in outlining the many rights that a husband owed his wife, including companionship, caring treatment, the service of her needs, and looking after her rights and interests. In exchange, women were to obey them. In contrast to the many obligations that a husband owed his wife, obedience was the only duty required of her.

Because men have failed to honor their obligations toward women, their elevated status was understandably lowered and women assumed the role of the guardians of the family. Under these conditions, Taymur wondered out loud: why should not women set aside the old roles that required them to be obedient and modest?[18] As a literary writer, Taymur used this very provocative statement for maximum effect and as part of a complex strategy that she developed to address the pressing needs of women and their families. The statement underlined how the actions of men contributed to women in setting aside their old roles and social rules. It argued that under the present circumstances, women's actions were logical and rational. Finally, it attempted to harness male anger over the gender role reversal in many families to persuade them of the need to reclaim their marital obligations as a means of rectifying the present situation.

Taymur's defense of the old paternalist views of Islam and its marriage contract offered an indirect defense of women's rights in the turbulent first decade of colonial rule that undermined the old rights, which women had enjoyed, without replacing them with any new ones. In response, Taymur defensively used many of the male arguments as a means of persuading Muslim men to return to the old rules. In a recent paper, Omaima Abou-Bakr suggested that Taymur's emphasis on the rights that men owed women was consistent with the dominant Islamic view of male privilege that emphasized its attendant responsibilities. Contrary to the popular views of modernization as favorable to women, Abou-Bakr suggested that the views of Shaykh Muhammed 'Abdu, the key modernist figure, did not improve the lot of women; they exempted men from all responsibilities and saddling women with all the obligations.[19]

Relying on a Qur'anic verse that clearly described married women "as having [rights] just as they owed others in kindness,"[20] Taymur stressed the reciprocal obligations that both spouses had vis-à-vis each other: he was required to provide for her and protect her interests and she, in turn, was obliged to obey and respect his commands. When their relations were reversed, he owed her loyalty and she did not need to obey him.

Taymur described in some detail the emotional and physical toll that economic ruin had on the lives of women and their families. Some of the virtuous secluded women, who dealt patiently with (their men) closing their eyes to their ugly behavior and hiding the details of their misfortunes, were largely unappreciated by husbands who persisted in their destructive path until their wives met an early death, leaving behind orphaned children whose fathers took whatever was left of their wives' inheritance to wed other victims. In contrast, there were women with sharper tongues and weaker natures who did not keep silent, blamed their husbands for their woes, and quarreled with them in loud and heated exchanges that took place in the morning and at night. Those who were far and near as well as friends and foes heard them. These discordant relations led women to disobey their husbands. A man caught in this situation could no longer discipline his wife because she would threaten to take him to court where he would be held accountable for his actions and ordered to provide for her. This forced him to accept the loss of status and what he used to consider as unacceptable behavior by his wife. In response, some of these men chose to spend most of their days at the shops and the nights at parks or bars listening to music and watching the dancing girls and only going home to sleep.

As a result, many healthy young wives found themselves having to deal with both marital desertion and financial ruin. These high levels of frustration led each to consider her mansion as a prison seeking solace and advice from their neighbors. Sometimes, they got good support from virtuous women who advised patience and its short- and long-term rewards. A particularly bad source of influence over these vulnerable women came from the working-class women who served as their maids. According to Taymur, this base element had restricted access to wealthy households, which were served by slave women who treated their mistresses with a great deal of reverence, kept their secrets, and obeyed them out of fear or mistreatment. When the doors of freedom were opened to slave women, Taymur claimed that their barbaric nature was revealed when they chose freedom to frequent bars to drink with other slaves rather than accept the promises and/or threats of their former mistresses. As a result, these houses were emptied of this reliable work force, leading their mistresses to replace them with women of the rabble (*al-ri`a*).[21]

As far as Taymur was concerned, the recruitment of working-class women into the service of middle- and upper-class women was far from satisfactory. She clearly preferred slavery and slave women's complete subordination to the needs of their mistresses. Working-class women, who were new recruits to domestic work, fell short of subservient and discreet slave labor. Not only did they maintain their freedom of movement outside of the household, which challenged the rules of feminine seclusion, but they also dared to believe that their worldly experience were relevant and even helpful to their mistresses. They meddled in the personal affairs of their mistresses, encouraging them to follow their vile moral code. For instance, a maid would tell her mistress: why do you lock yourself up in your house? You only have one life to live so why should you accept desertion with all your beauty? You should go out to the parks or go to the shops.[22] If the mistress resisted because people would criticize her, the maid would reassure her that she would accompany her in these trips and point out that other princely women, who found themselves in a similar situation, exercised these freedoms that restored their bloom, escaping censure because many women were resorting to them. Taymur considered this advice to be ill intentioned, mercenary, designed to rob the mistress of her remaining wealth,[23] and contributed to the slander of respectable women. Unfortunately, some mistresses followed it first shyly, but eventually got accustomed to this ignorant behavior.

In this part of the discussion, Taymur's social conservatism was made abundantly clear. While she understood and sympathized with the high levels of emotional and sexual frustrations felt by these aggrieved women, she disapproved of their responses to these problems, which ranged from reprimanding their husbands, airing their problems with the neighbors and listening to the abhorrent advice of their maids. She clearly believed in a conservative definition of marital relations that prevailed within the upper class and that required secluded women to tolerate their husbands' misdeeds in the name of protecting the honor of the family and in the hope that their husbands would eventually see the error of their ways.

Next to irresponsible husbands who were the primary villains in this narrative, Taymur reserved her harshest condemnation to slave and working-class women who she accused of betraying their mistresses. The fact that Taymur was the daughter of a freed slave woman complicated her response to the different choices made by freed slave women and their working-class counterparts. When Taymur's mother was freed because she bore her master three daughters, she chose to stay rather than leave her master's family. This was a complicated decision that weighed the cost of giving up her new freedom with the insecurities of being a freed white slave, who like "many harem women of the nineteenth century could barely speak any Arabic at all,"[24] and had no resources or a family to make this new freedom viable. If she decided to leave, she would also have had to abandon her children, a difficult choice in the best of times. Some would also point out that freed white and African slaves, who bore their masters' children, could look forward to a more secure existence and therefore were less likely to exercise their newly won freedom. The stress often put on economics as the only consideration in a slave's decision to stay or leave her master's house once slavery was abolished was too crude and did not appreciate the complicated weighing of many concerns, which these women had to consider including economic, emotional, and social consequences of that important decision.

As the daughter of a slave, Taymur's lack of sympathy for those slaves who chose to leave their masters and their families was emotionally understandable. If her mother had chosen to exercise her right to freedom by leaving them, then she would have been lost to her daughters, undermining the safety of their world. Because even the domestic slave women were part of the complex emotional world of secluded women, their quest for freedom was viewed as a threat to the needs of the women in the harem. Taymur explicitly stated that they were better caretakers of the needs of their mistresses and were also discreet in protecting their families. Unfortunately, this meant that Taymur could only see these slave women, including her mother, as an extension of the needs of their families reflecting the social climate of that period. What made these views puzzling was that she also recognized that a slave existence was associated with fear of mistreatment and abuse. Yet she could not or would not understand the refusal of many to stay in service after they were freed. This confirmed the view that her reaction to the abolition of slavery was an emotional one related to loss, not just of property, but of emotionally significant others on whom the world of the harem depended.

What made her reaction worse was that she chose to fall back on the racist beliefs circulated by members of her class that represented the slave women who chose to be free as demonstrating their barbaric nature, that is, their loose morality demonstrated by their preference to work in bars, drinking and/or dancing with other slave men. The self interest of members of that class made it impossible to understand the difficult decisions freed slaves made. Finally, while Taymur complained in some of her other writings about the restrictions of the lack of freedom associated with seclusion, she could not see any similarities between her and their desire for freedom.

Taymur's discussion of working-class women who stepped into domestic service showed contemptuous fear of this group and their moral code. She described them as completely immoral because they had no shame in disregarding upper-class rules of seclusion. Yet she clearly thought they were clever in devious sorts of ways as they convinced respectable upper-class women to exercise new illicit freedoms. Their pragmatic sensibilities were demonstrated in the way they dealt with irresponsible men, they shamed them by taking more liberties using the visits to the parks and shops to feel better. These strategies appealed to some upper-class women more than the accepted social norms of the upper class, which recommended a stoic acceptance of the misdeeds of their husbands. Taymur was so thoroughly convinced that rabble women were trying to either corrupt their mistresses or take economic advantage of them that she never seriously considered that the practices they recommended to their mistresses were coping mechanisms that some have also used to deal with similar problems in their families. She also dismissed the idea that these women were sincere in sharing their experiences with their mistresses in the hope that it would relieve their distress. What was curious here was that even though Taymur started *Mir'at al-Ta'mul* by stating that women of all classes suffered from the greed of their husbands, she considered working-class women's responses to their husbands' misdeeds to be immoral and below the dignity of upper-class women. When upper-class women embraced the new liberties by venturing into the parks and visiting the shops, Taymur considered their actions to be unacceptable because they removed the existing social barriers between working- and upper-class women and provided another source of discord to upper-class family life. Finally, Taymur was afraid that the new liberties, which challenged the rules of social seclusion, would be used by these men to denounce their wives, deflecting attention from the root causes of the problem (i.e., male greed and irresponsibility).

Taymur's ambivalence toward the new liberties that women have taken in response to the crisis of the family was connected to the fear that it would undermine female virtue. She was keenly aware that women of distressed families were more likely to be taken advantage of by their servants and others they encountered in this unfamiliar world. In an attempt to protect these women, she condemned these new social practices that did not address the root cause of the problem. In the very orderly and protected world of upper-class women, the disorder—unleashed by their irresponsible husbands and their working-class maids—was to be condemned in favor of the return to older social rules. As far as Taymur was concerned, the collective suffering of women of different classes in the face of the new economic greed and materialism did not merit the overlooking of class divisions that separated them. While she acknowledged the sisterhood of women that resulted from the abuse they suffered at the hands of their greedy husbands, it did not extend to benefiting from each other's experience, especially when upper-class women began to imitate the behavior of their working-class counterparts.

Finally, Taymur asked contemplative readers to rationally consider the reasons that led many prominent women to marry these irresponsible men. She suggested that a new generation of men in the affluent classes, who had wasted their wealth and/or were too lazy to work, used their good name or ancestry to entice women of wealth to marry them for largely mercenary reasons. How could women have anticipated this deceitful behavior from men of supposedly good families? Even if one agreed that men and women of good families lost faith in the old virtues observed in selecting a spouse (like good name and behavior), the materialism reflected in their marital choices led to family ruin.

In the concluding pages, Taymur directed her attention to the `alama, with whom she was sharing this account, in a clear attempt to pacify her potential critics, anticipate their objections, and deflect them.

I ask for God's forgiveness if I have made claims to knowledge that intruded on the debates that preoccupy the luminous [scholarly] gathering of men. I am well aware of the feminine viewpoint, but I also acknowledge the weakness of my [gendered] group's (`asbati) capacity in this [religious] area. I do not deny my seclusion within these walls and [how it contributed to] my apparent disadvantage. I am ahead of all others, however, in warning and reminding people of these dangerous matters. I have approached them shyly, leaning on the cane of hope and petitioning you to save my gender from blame, to support them against public and private false accusations and to prevent [the reproduction] of these problems through securing the attention of men of decision, discipline and insight. I have no doubt of the benefits to be derived from your enlightened directions. The mirror of the age is clearly polished, its moons are set in the elevated horizon and its men enjoy reverence for careful formulations that exhibit justice and artistry . . .

[To them], I say: benevolent and outstanding men, let us thank God for his blessings and knowledge. He taught the human being (al-'Insan) what he did not know and made religion the most honorable blessing . . . I have upheld [what you consider to be] noble deeds and respectable directions. So, do not reject the discourse of this weak woman and do not confuse [it] with the silly statements of women. Do not consider who speaks and observe what is being said.

If truth be told, you are more vigilant about your kinfolk than I am and you are also more capable and fit in protecting your companions. God has expanded the arenas of your strength and ambition, paved your roads to glory and honor, invested you with rhetoric and logic and endowed you with eloquence and cleverness. Do not shy away from using your capabilities for reform. Your determination gives substance to the belief of this weak woman of your vast capabilities. . . .

You have the means to pull men who are restless, lazy, and misguided leading them away from the abyss of injustice and evil. My most fervent request of you is that you generously advise those in need and charitably preach to those who lack insight. You are better suited to inspect and investigate what I have just outlined. Your thoughts are sharp, [can examine] without incitement the consequences of these changing conditions and guide the blind from the many pitfalls.

Our age is filled with many sources of light especially those derived from the capabilities of the rulers of a magnificent state, whose government is characterized by justice and care. [Khedive] Tewfik and his son, Abbas II, have divinely sanctioned talents and are descendants of courageous and distinguished grandparents. Abbas is the God of fear and happiness and the light of the cosmos. May God support his reign and sanctify it with the tradition of the master of all prophets and the Imam of all believers.[25]

The conclusion showed Taymur's use of a very clever discursive strategy that reflected a clear understanding of the constraints under which she operated: how they were going to influence the reception of her work and ways of going around them. Taymur knew she was attempting to challenge rigid gender boundaries concerning the interpretation of religion and the Islamic injunction to command right and forbid wrong. She summarized some of the objections that will be used by her critics against her work, like, she intruded on the social and religious debates that were the proper domain of men and the limited capacities of members of her gender due to lack of education and knowledge. She tactfully responded to these objections by modestly refraining from any reference to her standing as a published poet and writer, which clearly undermined the grounds that men had used to exclude women from public debates. To further underline her modesty, she recognized the disadvantages that seclusion imposed on her as a member of the female gender. Then she turned this weakness into an advantage by suggesting that seclusion allowed her to do what no man could do—that is, provide the feminine viewpoint of the problems facing women in many families. She also claimed special credit for naming and addressing a new set of problems of which the public was unaware. Finally, she argued that the violence and the seriousness of the social matters or problems she addressed should excuse her transgressing the rigid boundaries that defined the public roles of men and women and that her goal was to protect members of her gender from private and public criticisms.

No man was able to know the nature of the familial problems facing women in the family because of seclusion. Just as she was trying to explain the feminine viewpoint and to protect women from public censure, she appealed to men to pay attention to what members of their own gender were doing and its impact on women. To avoid a confrontation between the two genders, Taymur tried to appease her male critics by suggesting that she desired to forge an alliance with concerned men in addressing these problems. The goal of *Mir'at al-Ta'mul* was to draw the attention of wise and determined men to these problems so that women could benefit from their enlightened intervention. While the present age witnessed the disappointing behavior of many young men, there were also many great men who were capable of employing justice to address these social problems. She specifically turned to the religious scholars, reminding them of the Qur'anic verse that stated that God taught human beings (i.e., men and women) what they did not know through the medium of the religious message. As someone who upheld prescribed religious practice and instructions in both her life and analysis, she hoped that religious scholars would not reject her work. In an unexpected discursive twist, she asked the members of the religious establishment to ignore the gender of the author and to concentrate on her discourse and its content. If they were to judge what was being said without reference to her gender, then they would agree with her and would not confuse her views with the silly ones held by some women. Rather than defend the silly views held by some members of her gender, she thought it was more important to create a new public space for the views of a new generation of women writers.

This represented the earliest attempt by a woman writer to negotiate an alliance between men and women based on education and knowledge in addressing important social problems. It was attempted from a position of strength because Taymur was using her inside knowledge of the feminine world and her education to diagnose the causes of a social problem that was of general interest to women and men. At the same time, in the absence of a community of educated women who addressed these issues and establishing their legitimate right to deal with them, she was faced with the general patriarchal prejudice against her gender. As a result, she had to dissociate herself from the patriarchal representations, which devalued women and their views. In fighting against this view, she represented herself as a new kind of woman who not only shared with men many skills and perspectives but also was concerned with the problems women faced, bringing these issues to the attention of men so that they would address them and suggesting her own solutions.

Finally, Taymur appealed to the paternal sentiments of men by suggesting that they shared her desire to protect their womenfolk (sisters, daughters, mothers, and wives) from the abuses she described. She also pointed out that men had an interest in reinforcing male solidarity by protecting other men, who were their companions, from the pitfalls she described. As a privileged group endowed with power and determination, she instructed all good men to put their energy in the service of reform. Even though she exhorted them to take on this important task of advising the misguided among men and women who lacked knowledge and insight, she was equally clear that they were to follow in her footsteps investigating her account of familial problems and developing her solutions. In other words, despite the emphasis she put throughout this work on her modest capabilities, she also believed that her perspective on how to proceed was the best.

In concluding, Taymur described the age within which she lived as an enlightened one, using terms like "dawn" and "light" to suggest the need for tolerating her novel views and her role of public commentator. She praised the modern state as another agent of enlightenment under the stewardship of Khedive Tewfik and his son Abbas II, who were committed to Islamic justice and the modern principles of order and happiness. This not only reinforced the dominant view of the Muhammed Ali dynasty as an agent of enlightenment but also paradoxically whitewashed its coalescence with British occupation and the project of colonial modernization, some of whose indirect social effects Taymur just addressed.

Responses to *Mir'at al-Ta'mul fi al-Umur*

Shaykh al-Fayumi's Lisan al-Jumhur fi Mir'at al-Ta'mul fi al-Umur

Taymur's booklet attracted considerable attention within the literary, religious and social circles. *Al-Nil* newspaper published a serialized critical response to it by Shaykh Abdallah al-Fayumi in 1892 that represented the views of the literary and religious establishments. This response must have, in turn, triggered additional interest in the work. This section will begin with a detailed discussion of Shaykh al-Fayumi's account of the literary establishment's views of Taymur's latest work and then discuss his religious objections to her views. Abdallah al-Nadeem's views will add another layer to this discussion of the reception of her work.

Taymur as Viewed by her Contemporaries

Shaykh Abdallah al-Fayumi was a member of the ulema class who also had an active interest in literature reflecting earlier ideals of learning, which grounded all forms of literary writing in the study of the Qura'nic text as the paragon of the Arabic language. In the long introduction to his response to Taymur, titled *Lisan al-Jumhur fi Mir'at al-Ta'mul fi al-Umur* (the public has its say in *Mir'at al-Ta'mul fi al-Umur*), he offered the following interesting account of how the literary circles reacted to Taymur's work and the effort to recruit him for a response.

> I attended a literary gathering with many others discussing lofty issues that were both old and new. As we began to disperse, a sincere friend approached me and shared an "amazing report." He said: "I had read a beautiful work titled *Mir'at al-Ta'mul fi al-Umur* written by `A'isha Taymur, the daughter of Ismail Pasha Taymur, whose poetic and fictional works established her reputation as a model for others. Many of her peers acknowledged that if all women were like her, then they would be preferred to men . . . While her literary skills and accomplishments could not be disputed, [her latest work] showed that this acclaim had gone to her head leading her astray into areas where she should not have ventured. While it was the duty of the literary writers and the men of religion to give advice and to guide the community, God singled out the wise men of each generation for this important obligation. These men struggled to advice the nation, help it reach happiness and develop its sources of wealth sacrificing their souls to the comfort of the public.
>
> A Qur'anic verse that underlined the importance of counseling the community stated: "let there be among you a community (*umma*) that calls for goodness, commands right and forbids wrong." The prophet reiterated this theme describing "religion as advice. People asked him: who should deliver it? He answered: God, the prophet, religious leaders and the ordinary Muslims." It was particularly important to speak out about matters which if not addressed would lead to the violation of the sacred canon and practice. At the outset [of *Mir'at al-Ta'mul fi al-Umur*], Taymur engaged an imaginary learned religious man (`alama) in the explanation of her views. We waited for a member of the `ulama to respond to her call [for an exchange,] but no one has bothered to draw their swords in response. [The friend] declared he was too busy with other serious battles and appealed to me to take on that burden."
>
> I declared myself to be similarly occupied and added that I had despaired of worldly preoccupations, separated myself from both the riffraff and the astute

and gave up on people [observing how] a brother [could not be trusted] and friendships turned sour. Mountains of ignorant men, who occupied the place of honor in government agencies, became fat and arrogant overshadowing those who were learned filling these different arenas with multiple expressions of diseased brotherhood.

[The friend] answered that matters have reached a climax and you must answer this call [issued by Taymur] offering effective medicine to this general malady. I said that I feared that I might [in going after her] face an early death, but he reassured me that in this case I was going to be rewarded against my will.[26]

Even though Shaykh al-Fayumi did not mention the name of the friend who drew his attention to Taymur's work and recruited him to respond to it, one can safely assume that it must have been the owner of *al-Nil* newspaper, which published his response to Taymur first in serialized form and then produced them in a book. Here it is useful to remember that the spread of print capitalism in Egypt made newspaper owners on the lookout for topics and authors that would increase the circulation of their publications and businesses. There was evidence to suggest that some of these owners approached writers with ideas that they felt were of interest to the community publishing their work in articles and books. In this way, print capitalism helped develop the definition of community and its interests. For example, Yaqub Sarruf, the owner of *al-Muqtataf* asked Mayy Ziyada in 1918 to write an article about Malak Hifni Nassif, whose death contributed to a national debate on how her agenda for women, which was both Islamic and modernist, bridged the partisan divide between conservatives and modernists, providing incentive for them to work together after World War I in negotiating Egyptian independence from Great Britain. The publication of Ziyada's articles, first in serialized form and later on as a book,[27] in 1919 indicated that this was a long established business practice among publishers.

As an independent woman of wealth, Taymur did not wait for an invitation to write and/or to publish her work. While her works reflected concerns that were of national interest to the community, she could afford to publish them on her own even when they touched on sensitive religious and social issues like the changing relations between men and women in the family in *Mir'at al-Ta'mul fi al-Umur*. The owner of *al-Ni,* newspaper wanted to capitalize on Taymur's daring subject and the interest it provoked, picturing an unprecedented debate between a secluded Muslim woman writer and a member of the ulema that would capture and sustain his readers' attention over several issues. This indicated that both the gender of the author and the topic of changing gender relation in the family were already foci of general interest. In this regard, it was useful to point out that while Taymur's *Mir'at al-Ta'mul fi al-Umur* was 16 pages long in large print, Shaykh al-Fayumi's response was 35 pages long using small print. The goal of the latter was to sell more issues of the newspaper and eventually the book based on them. Not only did the articles and the book generate revenue for the publisher, but they also established the public reputation of Shaykh al-Fayumi, whose two other book titles indicated a very specialized interest in the study of logic. While very little is known about the shaykh, one biographical dictionary identified him as a member of the ulema at al-Azhar, the prestigious institution of Islamic higher learning in Egypt, who also worked as an instructor in one of the modern state schools.[28] We do not know which school employed him or which subjects he taught at that school even though it was very likely that he taught logic, Arabic, and religion.

According to al-Fayumi's friend, *Mir'at al-Ta'mul fi al-Umur* represented an "amazing development"[29] because of the stature of its author and topic. Taymur was already well known both as a writer and the daughter of Ismail Pasha Taymur, whose skills in prose writing and poetry were widely acknowledged. The well-written *Mir'at* was also well received, reinforcing her excellent literary standing and breaking new grounds by venturing into social commentary and religious interpretation. It shocked some readers because it sought to instruct and guide the public regarding problems unfolding within the family and in the process addressed topics reserved for men (i.e., the tasks of interpreting religion). Members of Taymur's gender were usually excluded from these debates even though *al-muhadithat* have long interpreted the prophetic tradition instructing students in that field. The task of Qur'anic exegesis remained limited to men. While the religious sources cited by al-Fayumi suggested that any Muslim could publicly guide the community on matters of commanding right and forbidding wrong, it was customary to only consult the ulema on religious matters that "violated the sacred canon and its practice." Taymur seemed to acknowledge this by consulting Shaykh Ibrahim al-Saqqa, who appeared in her text as an imaginary 'alama, who legitimized her views and opened the door for al-Fayumi, as another member of that group, to subject her work for inspection. This was not going to be a friendly exchange because al-Fayumi's friend imagined the response to her work to be disciplinary in nature like the drawing of the sword of religion to correct the breach of the sacred canon and practice.

Al-Fayumi was not eager to take on that responsibility, but he did not specifically explain why. One could, however, speculate on his reasons. First, Al-Fayumi could have been apprehensive about reactions of members Taymur's class and the literary circles to his attack. Not only were relations between the upper Turco-Circassian class and Egyptian-middle classes badly frayed by the 'Urabi revolution, but the exile of its nationalist leaders was used to silence middle-class critics of this aristocratic class. Given the wide respect for Taymur's literary works, which were declared to be superior to those produced by many of her male peers, al-Fayumi expected the literary establishment to side with her. As it turned out, al-Fayumi's fears were unfounded because members of

Taymur's class were not supportive of her pioneering views and very few male literary writers shared her concern for women and/or were willing to defend her against an attack from a member of the religious class.

Interestingly enough, al-Fayumi's description of the divisiveness of Egyptian society was very similar to that offered by Taymur in both *Nata'ij al-Ahwal* and *Mir'at al-Tamul fi al-Umur*. It was deeply divided making one suspicious of his brothers and souring many male friendships. He also described how the modern education system introduced a major division within the learned middle class by producing graduates at the modern schools who competed with the graduates of al-Azhar in employment and status. The result was what al-Fayumi described: a "diseased brotherhood" with the ignorant, arrogant and lazy graduates of the modern schools who usurped important positions of government from the learned ulema leading to the corruption of society.[30] Like Taymur, al-Fayumi used the concept of "diseased" brotherhood as an explanation of social malaise that led to and resulted in the collapse of social consensus and the social divisions of society.

Taymur's breach of gender boundaries was represented as another threat to this brotherhood. Al-Fayumi's friend described it as the climax of this corrupting trend because her *ijtihad* potentially violated the sacred canon and opened up the field of religious interpretation to anyone who had an education be it a man or a woman. In telling his readers that he has consulted many virtuous and honest men (a reference to the ulema) in developing his response to Taymur, al-Fayumi was appealing to fraternal solidarity that connected members of the ulema class with the majority of male readers, giving his views collective religious and social weight. He also added that the interpretation of the religious tradition required a particular training in which male scholars spent their productive intellectual lives[31] and that it was unwise for any educated man or woman to attempt it on their own.[32] At the same time, the fact that al-Fayumi consulted others in writing his response indicated that its topic was not his particular area of expertise, adding another reason for his worry about becoming the target of criticism. I will return to this point later on in this section.

By choosing the title of *Lisan al-Jumhur `ala Mir'at al-Tamul fi al-Umur* (the public has its say on *Mira'at al-Tamul fi al-Umur*) for his response, al-Fayumi was reclaiming the ulema's historical right to speak for the community and to serve its religious and social interests. Yet his description of the concerns of the ulema in advising the community was very modern and, therefore, could not have been the dominant view within the religious establishment. He suggested that the ulema were committed to "help the nation to reach its happiness."[33] Like Taymur, he underlined a modern concern with happiness; but whereas Taymur associated it with order, al-Fayumi saw it as part of the development of sources of wealth including self-improvement.

The title also allowed al-Fayumi to claim familiarity with the views of the majority of the reading public (*al-Jumhur*), putting Taymur on the defensive. As a woman writer who had an aristocratic background, she was not in a position to compete with al-Fayumi in claiming to represent the Egyptian majority. Yet if Taymur's social commentary was out of touch or did not register with the public in its discussion of the deteriorating relations between men and women in Egyptian families, the shaykh's response to her *Mir'at al-Ta'mul fi al-Umur* would have made little sense. Why would anyone take the time and invest energy in addressing a commentary that was either not well received or ignored by the public? In fact, al-Fayumi gave Taymur credit for beginning this important discussion and admitted that in responding to her he wanted to share some of the religious rewards she was going to reap for counseling the community regarding these problems. He asked Taymur not to reproach him for taking her on because both of them were interested in reaching what is "right." As a member of the ulema, he was obliged not to engage a woman in any arena, but in this case he was drafted into this discussion by what he described as the "cane and sword" of Islamic law, which demanded from those in his position to respond to claims made by outsiders with their own agendas. He reassured her, however, that he shared her interest in reform.[34]

Next, al-Fayumi identified two contributions he claimed to make to the debate initiated by Taymur. As a graduate of al-Azhar, he was someone who understood how the mind made use of theoretical and experiential capabilities. Through theory, the mind or the self (*al-nafs*) was able to distinguish between the whole and its parts and the mind with experience, the senses, and the body as additional uses and sources of knowledge. The study of religious interpretation relied heavily on rational and theoretical skills that were less prone to the limitations of experiential knowledge. Here, al-Fayumi established a hierarchal relationship between these two approaches to Islamic learning with the rationalist-theoretical knowledge that he appropriated for himself and declared superior to that produced by experience and the senses, which he attributed to Taymur and her experiences with other women in different families. In support of this view, he quoted a couple of poetic verses indicating an interest in literature: the first verse encouraged one to "develop the soul/mind because they, not the body, made one human and the second stated when God gave man a mature mind, his ethics and goals were complete." Al-Fayumi added two prophetic statements that reaffirmed these views: (1) "the descendents of Adam had nothing better than the mind to guide them to faith and to divert them from destruction" and (2) "wisdom was the goal of the believer who should embrace it wherever he found it."[35]

A bit later, al-Fayumi recognized that theoretical knowledge, which he had emphasized as the main pillar of reliable religious interpretation, also had its own limitations: it was governed by the text, rationality, and knowledge of the Arabic language. The uninitiated was advised not to simply give an opinion based on personal views because the result could easily lead to heresy (*hawa*), which (1) the Qur'anic verse warned against ("Do not follow your whim/passion/desire [*hawa*] that could lead you away from God"), and (2) the prophetic tradition that commanded, "Disobey your passions and women and obey whomever else you want."[36]

This section made clear two discursive strategies that al-Fayumi was going to use against Taymur: First, he paraded his abstract and philosophical skills as a way of intimidating Taymur and the readers. Second, he was purposefully evasive in his presentation of the issues as a means of confusing both. For example, he emphasized the limitations of the experiential approach that he attributed to Taymur, implying that the theoretical approach he utilized was immune to its problems only to admit later on that theoretical knowledge had its limitations. The success of this strategy was enhanced by the use of the old style Arabic language whose use of repetition, archaic words, and imageries often had the effect of losing even the most determined reader. Additionally, these devices were designed to discourage the average reader from attempting ijtihad, privileging only the most informed or specialized ones.

Al-Fayumi ended this section by identifying Taymur with whim and passion as threats to the faith because of what he claimed was the intellectual liberty she took in interpreting the Qur'anic text. As a way of hammering the point home, he quoted a dubious prophetic statement that commanded men to disobey both passion and women then to obey whatever or whomever else they pleased. This use of the prophetic tradition to exclude women from ijtihad was ironic because it purposely ignored how women had played a leading religious role in the development of this field. `A'isha bint Abi Bakr was the greatest Hadith narrator of her time and the prophet called on Muslims to take half of their religion (i.e., prophetic tradition) from her. Moreover, if the Hadith cited by al-Fayumi were reliable, surely women *muhadithat* (interpreters of the prophetic tradition) would not have been permitted to historically excel in this area.[37] In attempting to reestablish the connection between women and passion as the two most important dangers to the religion, al-Fayumi sought to rewrite the history of that tradition by collectively denying women's rationality. So what started off as a call for both rigor and rationality as characteristics of a desirable analytical, approach fell back on the polemical equation of passion/woman/error/false knowledge versus the mind/man/rationality/reliable knowledge.

Given the misogynist implications of this construction, al-Fayumi spent the next two pages elaborating on his second contribution to the debate (i.e., his support of women's roles in society). He dissociated himself from the conservatives within the literary establishment who offered poetic verses that declared that women should have nothing to do with writing, work, or public discussion. One verse declared that all that men owed women was the privilege of lying next to them. The ultraconservative writers and poets went further by declaring, "Even though women were known for some virtue, they were decaying cadavers encircled by vultures. Today, you [any man] have her neck and conversation and tomorrow someone else may have her affection and hand."[38]

After having introduced his readers to the most negative social views of women, al-Fayumi tried to prove his liberality by supporting women's education as a means of improving marital relations. While he did not mention the modernist Shaykh Rifa` al-Tahtawi's al-Murshid al-Amin lil-Banat wa al-Baneen (1873) as the source of his view, it was al-Tahtawi who popularized it two decades earlier. Whereas al-Tahtawi was open to teaching women literature and other less-gendered forms of knowledge,[39] Shaykh al-Fayumi put singular emphasis on the conservative modernist emphasis on training women in the science of home economics (tadbir al-manzil) as the science that channeled women's labor in the advancement of society.

Next, al-Fayumi indicated his awareness of Russian and French women's active participation in political and economic life citing the examples of members of the Russian Nihilist Party who preferred to die rather than reveal the secrets of their organization and French women running the railroads and telecommunications during the Franco-German War. He concluded, however, that Western and Islamic societies were alike in their exclusion of women from positions of power to preserve the stability of social order and the foundations of civilization. In explaining this position, he suggested that even though women lacked the physical strength of men, women were skilled in the use of emotions rendering men unable to resist them because of the laws of natural desire. Women's wiles (kayd), a reference that drew strength from the Qur'anic story of the Prophet Yusuf's seduction by the wife of al-Aziz, were capable of giving them a negative source of power over men. By denying women access to positions of power (religious preaching, political leadership, prophecy, and war), which they could use to challenge existing social taboos, religious, and political laws, Western and Islamic societies sought to neutralize their destabilizing effect. This clashed with the prophetic statements he cited declaring "women as deficient in mind and religion" and that "Muslims need to obey God with regards [sic] looking after two weak groups: slaves and women."[40]

While al-Fayumi clearly privileged the misogynist views of women's illicit power over men as the reasons for their exclusion from public life, he argued that the exclusion of women from religious, political, and military power in European societies provided support for the universality of the Islamic position. His conclusion went against the grain by arguing that the expanded modern roles of women did not reverse the need for the patriarchal control of power in modern societies. Having established the universality of male leadership in all societies, al-Fayumi contested Taymur's attempt to argue in support of the contingent character of the Islamic definition of that role. He claimed that her linguistic skills acknowledged by all her contemporaries, including al-Fayumi, could not have prepared her for navigating the complex exegetic traditions that male scholars spent their intellectual lives deciphering. If the interpretations of male scholars sometimes fell short, how could average men and women hope to succeed in such an enterprise? He went further by describing Taymur's belief that she could interpret the Qur'an and the prophetic tradition on her own as reflecting a certain insolence that violated the sacrosanct status of the word of God. Given the canonical focus of her discussion, she should have consulted male scholars in that area and should not have dared to publish them. Yet publish them she did, implying that her modest ijtihad was inspired by God giving her words and views a prophetic feel.[41] Finally, al-Fayumi claimed that Taymur thought that she could engage us like she had done in her other works and in the process add religious fame to her prodigious literary reputation but instead her rusty *Mir'at* or mirror misrepresented Islamic views and showed the narcissism of the author.

Al-Fayumi's Religious Responses to Taymur's Definition of the Rights of Men and Women

Al-Fayumi summarized his religious objections to Taymur's ijtihad in three sections: (1) the meaning of the Qur'anic verses she used, (2) her claim that the marriages based on greed were problematic, and (3) the reasons she offered for the corruption of the morals of married couples. In what follows, I will not only summarize his objections but also describe how they were far from traditional constructions of important Islamic concepts and institutions.

On Male Leadership

In explaining the religious misinterpretations he found in Taymur's work, al-Fayumi addressed himself first and foremost to her contingent view of male leadership. He claimed that Taymur was ignorant of the specific reasons for which the Qur'anic verse that discussed male leadership was intended. Because early Muslim women had questioned the prophet about why God advantaged man in inheritance, the verse explained that man had leadership over woman because God ordered him to provide her a dowry and financial support. These obligations completely erased any economic advantages man had over women.[42] It was not intended, as Taymur had claimed, to explain the illegality of marriages in which a husband did not support his wife. Male leadership was not just a function of economic support of a woman but was placed second behind the advantages that God gave man, which included rationality, management skills, maturity, strength, and his monopoly of prophecy, political and military leadership.

Next, even though Taymur suggested that the verses she quoted explained the rights that men had over women and those that women had over men, al-Fayumi pointed out that the verses did not include the word "rights." One could deduce them from the verses that discussed the two advantages that man enjoyed over woman: leadership and economic provision, which were divinely sanctioned characteristics of masculinity (*kul minhoma zati lil rajul*). Economic support or its lack thereof did not affect male leadership because whereas men had "rights in themselves and in women," women only had rights to things like dowry, economic support, and kind treatment.[43]

Men and women also had interconnected rights, that is, the husband had the right to be a prince or a shepherd of his wife who served as his subject. He looked after her rights and interests, and in exchange, she had to obey him. He should adorn himself for her just as she had to do the same. Finally, when a woman returned to her husband following a divorce, the husband should endeavor to change the behavior that led to the separation just as she had to be honest about the paternity of any child conceived during this period.

After admitting that women had rights over men as Taymur had argued, al-Fayumi sought to minimize the point by stressing the huge gap between the rights enjoyed by the two and the plural advantages that men have over women in rationality, religion, inheritance, and competence for political and judicial office (including testimony in court), multiple wives and concubines and divorce. The net effect of all these advantages enjoyed by man transformed a woman into a handicapped captive in the hands of a man (*al-mar'at kal aseer al-`ajiz fi yadd al-rajul*). Paradoxically, because of these privileges, man was delegated by God to generously guarantee woman her rights.[44] He who harmed or hurt a woman was threatened with religious sanctions because the sins of those who enjoyed God's blessings were grave and worthy of severe reprimand. These religious obligations of male leadership were said to ensure the joint utility and pleasure that both men and women derived from marriage (e.g., tranquility, intimacy, comradeship, companionship, love, pleasure). Men and women could not achieve these important ends alone and so had to accept their mutual dependence on each other. Women were said to be the beneficiaries of this arrangement because whereas their husbands were obligated to work outside the family to provide dowry, economic support, and to look after the interests of their wives, women were not. In exchange for the many rights women were entitled from men, they were obliged to serve them. Al-Fayumi ended this section by quoting the prophet as saying, "If I were to order anyone to bow before any other being than God, then I would order a woman to bow to her husband."[45]

The divine-like position of man was enough to reject Taymur's claim that male leadership was contingent on economic support. In addition, he sought to deemphasize the obligations that this position imposed on man by claiming that as a shepherd of a woman, his failure to look after the rights or interests was to be lamented, but it was not *obligatory* because a woman was free to give up these rights in which case a man did not have to provide them. The leadership enjoyed by man was an absolute masculine quality. A woman's obedience of her husband was in recognition of the fact that men, as a group, had a higher rank above women that reflected the sexual privileges of masculinity (*al-jinsiyya*)—that is, rights they had in women, which women did not have.

So this section began with al-Fayumi, underlining the historical context within which the verse that discussed male leadership was revealed, highlighting the activism of early Muslim women who objected to the unequal shares that men and women had in inheritance, and the divine explanation that the leadership of men (their divinely sanctioned obligation to provide women with dowry and economic support) wiped the economic advantage given to men in inheritance. It ended, however, with an attempt to underline the profound inequality that existed between men and women in Islam. Only men enjoyed individual rights (the right to leadership and economic provision), which were specific to masculinity and only men had "rights in women." Women lacked personal autonomy and/or reciprocal "rights in men."

Al-Fayumi offered a reference to the Hadith that discussed the roles of men as shepherds of their families but he was silent on how it also accorded women a similar status toward family members excluding men. The silence allowed him to speak of women as subjects of men in the family, which contrasted with Taymur's use of this Hadith in *Nata'ij al-Ahwal* to suggest that the practice of governance was spread among ordinary men *and* women through their roles as shepherds of the family and its members. Al-Fayumi not only characterized woman as the subject of man in the family but went further by characterizing her as "a handicapped captive in the hands of man."[46] This came close to speaking of her as a slave of man with its reference to captivity and the expression (*ma malikat yaddah*), which specifically meant the ownership of slaves. For al-Fayumi, women's subordination to men was unequivocal and for Taymur their equality was signified in their status as human beings (*insan*).

Al-Fayumi introduced a new emphasis on autonomy in the definition of Islamic masculinity and its loss in the definition of femininity, adding a new modern layer to the Islamic definitions of gender. As far as al-Fayumi was concerned, the fact that men had property in themselves entitled them to enjoy advantages in the areas of marriage, divorce, inheritance, legal, religious, and political monopoly of power. This coupled with the claim that male leadership or male rights were not linked to what they delivered but were masculine attributes that provided a short cut to the modern notion of "men as a fraternity" whose privileges were derived from membership in that group.[47]

At the same time, al-Fayumi sought to deemphasize the obligations that medieval Islamic scholars required of men in exchange for their privileges and to guard against the abuse of their power. His use of the Hadith that drew a parallel between God and man suggesting that women should bow deferentially to both supported the construction of an absolute masculinity that was as autonomous as the divine being. The idea of taking that Hadith seriously in a literal or a suggestive sense was undercut by the fact that it smacked of idolatry in requiring women to bow to men alongside God, which Islam strongly condemned. Finally, al-Fayumi suggestion's that God delegated to men the task of guaranteeing women's rights without obliging them to do so because women were free to do whatever they wanted with these rights, including give them up in which case men did not have to observe them, was equally dubious. He allowed very exceptional cases of some women giving up their rights to invalidate a divine rule supported by the majority of male scholars.

In this modernist construction of Islamic femininity, women were *only free* to give up their rights in marriage and the only right they had vis-à-vis men, according to al-Fayumi's modern definition of masculinity, was the right to obey the husband as a ruler. While al-Fayumi pointed out that actual male leadership over all women was not possible and that there were certain conditions under which it did not apply, he did not elaborate on these conditions and argued that exceptions in this regard do not invalidate the general rule

To reinforce the loss of rights that women had historically claimed as a manifestation of this expanded modern definition of masculinity, al-Fayumi expressed his astonishment of Taymur's expansive definition of economic support that a wife and mother were entitled of a husband. She included in that definition giving a wife a dowry, providing her with food, drink, shelter, and clothing in accordance with the capabilities of both husband and wife. She also suggested that men were obligated to provide a birth mother and her child additional material and spiritual possessions during this important part of their life cycle. While al-Fayumi acknowledged that this topic was the focus of considerable religious debate, he took issue with Taymur's generosity even though her views were supported by those of the prominent Imam al-Shafi`i, one of the four founders of the Sunni schools of law. In contrast, al-Fayumi took the position that a husband or father was only obligated to support his offspring, but not his wife. While a nursing mother deserved economic support, only those who were divorced were entitled to it.[48] In this very restrictive definition of economic support, wives and nursing mothers alike did not have clearly defined rights that entitled them to be compensated for either role. All of this represented a dramatic departure from the divine equalizing strategy, which al-Fayumi said was behind the verse that described male leadership. More significantly, it denied wives and mothers of economic rights that the Egyptian legal system historically recognized and protected.[49] The fact that al-Fayumi's views were so out of touch with the legal realities that Taymur and other women understood leads one to believe that this was not al-Fayumi's area of expertise or that his views, if coupled with those of Muhammed ʿAbdu's emphasis on the obligations of women, but not their rights,[50] were part of a modernist call to roll back some of the rights women had and enhance male privilege.

On Marriage

Al-Fayumi began this section by reiterating that the true nature (*haqiqat wa sha'n*) of men entitled them to assume leadership over women even if some individual men were not able to play that role.[51] As a group, the nature and/or the true essence of men was better than that of women. This did not negate the existence of some individual women who were superior to many men like Khadija bint Khuwaylid and ʿAʾisha bint Abi Bakr who were wives of the prophet. These exceptional women did not negate the characterizations of women as a group. After having spent the last section establishing that male leadership was not tied to their economic support of women, he surprised his readers by stating that it was the nature of men to be leaders of women because of the fact that they provided them with economic support even if some men deviated from that norm as discussed by Taymur.[52] These deviant men, who did not support their women, did not change the nature or the essence of men so they were still entitled to leadership. Al-Fayumi not only reversed positions here by conceding that Taymur's interpretation of the basis of male leadership was conditioned by economic support but also maintained that the men who did not adhere to it provided evidence that male leadership should hold regardless because a general rule could not be invalidated by the behavior of a few.

As for the legal validity of a marriage in which a man did not support his wife, he suggested that one must rely on what the leading imams of the different schools of Islamic law said about marriage in general. Again, he acknowledged that there was considerable debate on this topic. Most imams consider dowry obligatory to a legally valid marriage contract. They maintained that it provided compensation for sexual access to a woman, but al-Fayumi did not consider it to be a basis of male leadership as Taymur had alleged. A wife could release a man from these financial obligations without annulling the marriage in which case you have male leadership despite the absence of a dowry. While male economic support of a woman in marriage was required to ensure exclusive access to a woman, again a woman could release a man from this financial obligation in which case it would not be treated as a debt owed to the wife. If she did not consent to this release, economic support should be treated as a debt that she could retrieve through the court system.[53]

While al-Fayumi claimed that this provided ample Qur'anic evidence in support of women's right to give up their dowry and economic support, he misrepresented the verses he cited, which specifically stipulated that the only financial obligations that could be forgiven had to be above that required (*al-Farida*) of payment of dowry and a minimum of economic support. Finally, he confessed that some of the verses he cited to support his views concerned what was known as marriage of desire (*nikah al-mut'a*), which was legal in early Islam but was generally struck down by the Sunnis and was now only accepted by the Shi'a.[54] He, nevertheless, asked rhetorically: "If God permitted this practice (where a woman could forgive both dowry and economic support in marriage), was it his intent to challenge male leadership and to recognize women's leadership over men?"[55]

In a final attempt to settle this matter, he suggested that the legality of the marriages in which men abdicated all financial responsibility for their family depended on how one answered the following question: were these marriages forced or chosen by the parties involved? If a woman was forced, then the marriage contract could not be legal because it must be consensual. If a woman consented to marry a man whose economic capabilities were limited, then she could only blame herself. If he had lied to her, she could be justified in annulling the marriage, but if she chose to stay in the marriage, then she should take responsibility for her decision and treat him with respect. There was no justification for the rebellion of a woman against her husband, her contribution to the deterioration of conjugal relations, or the contestation of her husband's authority just because of lack support. A husband must preserve his rights to leadership and command his wife as a ruler irrespective of whether or not he supports her and a wife must either choose to stay as a test of her contentment or leave him.

Al-Fayumi conceded that legal jurists recommend that men and women steer clear of a marriage in which the woman had more money than her husband on the grounds that this might cause her to look down on him. The prophet also discouraged Muslim men from such a marriage, but he did not forbid it. In another statement by the prophet, he recommended that young women be made pretty with jewelry and clothing so that men would find them desirable. Al-Fayumi interpreted this as providing a basis within the prophetic tradition to justify the decision by young men to marry for mercenary reasons. Then, he wondered how one could forbid young men to marry for these material things even though they were deemed perfectly understandable by legal tradition and the customs of marriage? In Egypt, fathers of young girls purchase jewelry and clothing for their young girls at an early age to make them ready for marriage when the time comes. He took this to mean that Taymur forbade what God had permitted when it was not categorically outlawed.[56] In fact, it could serve a good purpose if it provided legal means to satisfy the sexual desires of the parties involved and protect them from other corrupting behavior. How could these marriages be compared to other horrors that were presently committed, which undermined the foundations of good breeding and important social customs and laws before the eyes of those in authority positions?

On the Corruption of the Morals of Married Couples

Even though Taymur claimed that these flawed, unequal, and unhappy marriages were structurally responsible for the corruption of the morals of married couples, al-Fayumi argued that the ill character of these couples was the product of poor upbringing, education, social class, national influence, the social climate of a country, and the family.[57] One's basic character structure was shaped during childhood and external factors, like who supported whom or a husband's release from the payment of dowry or economic support, were irrelevant. If one compared the behavior of couples with good or poor breeding in which husbands supported their wives, one will observe a great variance in their behavior. So economic support or lack thereof could not account for corrupt morals or poor conjugal relations.

There were many examples of husbands who fulfilled their marital obligations toward their wives with the latter persisting in their ignorance and capricious and shameless behavior. At the same time, there were devout wives who served their husbands even if they could not offer them what others had because they were intent on keeping their marriages going out of compliance with religious injunctions. Finally, the abilities of a man or woman to protect and respect themselves and each other were shaped by their understanding of the legal and religious obligations irrespective of any causal connection to abundant, limited, or absent support.

Literary Critique of *Mir'at al-Ta'mul if al-Umur*

In the last section of his booklet, al-Fayumi addressed himself to what he described as "flawed parables" and grammatical and linguistic errors in Taymur's work. He began by referring the reader to his book titled *al-Usul al-Wafiya fi al-Qaw`id al-Sarfiya* (the Comprehensive principles of Arabic grammar) whose pedantic theme indicated that it was most probably a textbook used in the modern school system where he taught. It colored his attitude toward and assessment of Taymur's *Mir'at al-Ta'mul fi al-Umur*. First, he took issue with her use of a parable that described how a proud lion that depended on his lioness to hunt lost all pride and was humiliated by her. He claimed that because the lion was a symbol of courage and nobility, it was counterintuitive to present him as a coward without ambition. On this point he clearly overlooked the effectiveness of this image as a warning to proud greedy young men of the loss of respect that awaited them if they did not give up their shameful behavior. Al-Fayumi also cast doubt on the effectiveness of another parable that included a pigeon, a crow, and a hawk claiming it made no sense and then admitted that the famous al-Asbahani used it but with better effect.

In all of this he offered an unfair assessment of Taymur's literary skills and clearly showed himself as a traditionalist faulting Taymur for not sticking with the stale and familiar expressions and style of writing. He used these so-called errors to argue that someone with such a modest facility with language, like Taymur, should never have taken the liberty to produce a book in religious sciences. He faulted her for writing a critical *Mir'at* at a time during which foreigners were eyeing Egypt and Egyptians and looking for faults.[58] Finally, he asked the Egyptian government to take action to discourage writers who presume to write in the area of religious sciences or language without adequate preparation through the establishment of an association of knowledgeable experts, along the lines of the French academies, whose goals would be to accept or reject such works giving prizes to those that excel.

To sum up, al-Fayumi's text offered a prototype of some religious and literary arguments used by conservative modernists to discourage any ijtihad that would challenge gender inequality and/or any innovations in writing style. While it relied heavily on modernist arguments to support gender inequality, this did not discourage him from claiming that her interpretation of many religious views was not in line with the general good established by the long line of past male interpreters (*salaf*), which he claimed to also represent. Her views were declared to be an example of the evil associated with innovation (*bida'*) that breaks with the good male traditions.[59] The shaykh was invested in protecting both the old patriarchal rules in the family with Western and modern views that defended the superiority of men as a fraternity. At the same time that he implied that he was in line with past tradition, he incorporated modernist concepts of male privilege as an essential quality that belonged to men as a group, minimizing their responsibilities to women and the family. Finally, he used the specialized weight of the Islamic tradition to discourage educated women and men from future participation in the discussion of religious matters.

Even though Taymur's interpretations of important Qur'anic verses, which dealt with the rights of men and women in the family, were clearly in line with the spirit and the practice of Islamic law upheld by the court system, hers was the only voice in support of a woman's right to interpret the religious tradition and to make it sensitive to women's gender needs. As a result, al-Fayumi was successful in silencing her. She did not comment on his response. The unwillingness of the educated men of her time to support her right to interpret the religious tradition meant that they too lost the right to participate in this inter-pretive enterprise leaving a largely conservative religious establishment with a monopoly over it.

Abdallah al-Nadeem's Praise of Mir'at al-Ta-mul fi al-Umur

The effect of al-Fayumi's condemnation of Taymur's work was diminished by the positive recommendation of the work from a significant unexpected source. Abdallah al-Nadeem, the orator of the `Urabi national revolution and its lead-ing political and social critic, noted the publication of the work in his magazine, Al-Ustaz (April 4, 1893),[60] praising its important social themes. With the onset of British occupation, the Egyptian government successfully arrested all the leaders and/or the key national figures associated with the revolution. It exiled the particularly important ones with the exception of al-Nadeem, who success-fully escaped the watchful eyes of the state for more than nine years with the help of well-to-do and ordinary Egyptians who hid him in their homes, ignor-ing the huge reward of one thousand Egyptian pounds for his capture.[61] When he was finally apprehended, Qasim Amin, the prosecuting attorney who later on emerged as a leading intellectual whose views on the liberation of women made him a celebrated figure, treated him with great respect[62] as the living symbol of that revolution. He gave instructions to the prison officials to keep al-Nadeem's cell clean and to let him smoke and drink coffee at his expense. Finally, Amin contacted M. Legrelle, the prosecutor-general, trying to influence the way his case would be handled, but was told that the matter was going to be settled administratively.[63] Al-Nadeem was exiled to Yaffa on October 12, 1891. He was eventually pardoned by the new young khedive returning to Egypt in 1892 founding a new journal, al-Ustaz, which enjoyed the financial support of his new national mentor.

Al-Ustaz introduced Mir'at al-Ta'mul to its readers in the following way:

> Mir'at al-Ta'mul fi al-Umur is a witty account written by the aristocratic and virtu-ous `A'isha Hanim Al-Taymuriya that condemns the many habits of women and some of the catastrophes that result from their [decisions to] venture outside [of the homes] as well as the moral corruption of [freed] slave women who are left to pursue their sexual desires. [The work] represents the greatest moral lesson from a superior woman writer with a long distinguished record in literature and ethics. We congratulate our age for her presence and hope that God benefits from her writings and prolongs her good and blessed life.[64]

According to al-Nadeem's journal, Taymur's work condemned the many bad habits of women, which she did. He was conspicuously silent, however, on Taymur's condemnation of the greedy and irresponsible actions of men. This was most probably his attempt to recommend Taymur's work to thin-skinned men who could be turned away by her criticisms. He positively described the book as providing the "greatest" moral lesson, giving it religious significance, which Shaykh al-Fayumi sought to deny by claiming that it misrepresented the canon and Islamic definitions of the rights of men and women in the family. In addition to acknowledging Taymur's long distinguished career in literature, al-Nadeem recognized her contributions to the study of ethics, an indirect reference to her fictional work *Nata'ij Ahwal fi al-Aqwal wa al-Af al*, which discussed the social and moral crises facing Islamic society and their connections to the crisis of government. These considerable accomplishments explained why "the age" to which al-Nadeem and Taymur belonged, expressed pride in her. Because al-Nadeem was keenly aware of the Orientalist attacks on Islamic societies and the way they oppressed women, he was clear that Taymur's status as a secluded Muslim woman writer proved the Orientalists wrong providing a positive role model of Muslim women.

In contrast, Qasim Amin's reply to Duc D'Harcourt's Orientalist views articulated in *Les Egyptiens* in 1892 did not acknowledge the existence of any literary women writers in Egypt on the grounds that none earned their living through literary writing. Because Amin's response was written in French, it did not have the Egyptian public in mind; it showed, however, that Amin devalued Egyptian women's writings and published works in the 1890s, judging them by the standards of women's literary writing in Europe. Considering the role that Amin played in securing al-Nadeem's freedom in 1891, it is difficult to imagine that Amin did not read Nadeem's *al-Ustaz* and was therefore unaware of Taymur and her important work, which provoked public debate and then gained the praise of his nationalist idol Abdallah al-Nadeem.

Al-Nadeem's praise went as far as suggesting that God will gain from Taymur's attempt to guide her contemporaries to a virtuous life. This last point successfully neutralized Shaykh al-Fayumi's condemnation of Taymur as a misguided Muslim woman. Al-Nadeem's positive views of Taymur and her work outweighed those of the more obscure al-Fayumi, whose views were written in a pretentious religious style that made them difficult to follow. Al-Nadeem's more accessible prose and his large following among different social classes into the 1890s were likely to have more influence with the reading public.

Because al-Nadeem was a widely regarded as a multifaceted literary writer and social critic using popular poetry (*zajal*), instructional prose, and fictional vignettes in his journal, his views were more likely to attract the attention of the literary establishment. His experimentation with the use of the Egyptian colloquial meant that he reached an even larger public with many literate readers reading his writings to illiterate listeners. While al-Nadeem's early reputation was that of a primarily political writer with powerful critiques of autocratic Egyptian governments and their European allies, he also had a reputation as a social critic employing fictional characters in an expanded discussion of the specific social ills of the Westernizing and modernizing Egyptian society like the imitation of West, the corruption of the Arabic language and Egyptian social customs and the spread of drinking, gambling, and prostitution. His early interest in these social themes explained his positive reaction to Taymur's developed discussion of them 11 years later, especially in light of the fact that al-Ustaz was forbidden to discuss politics.

In response, al-Nadeem used many of the social issues raised by Taymur's *Mir'at al-Ta'mul fi al-Umur* as the focus of many of his articles in *al-Ustaz*. He began with the discussion of the abolition of slavery and its impact on the lives of the former slaves. Through the fictional characters of Said and Bekhita, he attempted to offer his assessment of slavery and freedom. Bekhita suggested that as far as she was concerned, slaves were better off under slavery since their masters satisfied their basic needs and transformed them from the status of cattle into people who knew about hygiene, proper modes of dress, and speech. Said disagreed with her pointing out that slave masters were physically abusive and that freedom made them equal to their masters. Bakhita's views might have reflected the degrading effects of slavery on men and women[65] but they also represented greater awareness of how the new freedoms coexisted with fear of continued sexual abuse that freed slave women faced in their new roles as domestic workers and the way they continued to be exploited by the middlemen who sent them to their new workplaces.[66] Both Said and Bekhita concluded that freed slaves faced a very precarious existence often facing unemployment and having to compete with other working-class groups for service jobs where wages were not secure and women continued to fear sexual abuse.[67] Bekhita ended the exchange by pointing out that contrary to views like those of Taymur, there were many freed slave women who protected their honor and men who took on their masculine roles in the family seriously. This was truly admirable in a social climate where matters of right and wrong were no longer taken seriously, men did whatever they pleased regardless of social censure and women were left to deal with new family obligations.

Another set of fictional characters, Latifa and Haneefa, described the way their husbands spent their incomes on drinking, gambling, and other women leaving them in need of money and unable to take care of the needs of their children and pushing some women to break the social rules regarding seclusion.[68] Demiana and Latifa resumed that discussion to establish that these same problems were taking place in Christian and Jewish families disputing the view that ethnic differences contributed different social practices that set them apart from Muslims.[69]

Finally, Sherifa and Bahiya discussed another aspect of what Taymur had characterized as the rebellion of respectable secluded women against their husbands: that is, leaving their homes without their husbands' permission. While Taymur described how these women ventured outside their homes (i.e., visiting parks and the shops) as a means of letting off steam, Sherifa and Bahiya expanded the discussion of this phenomenon to include the many women who went out of their homes to attend religious celebrations in the mosques of revered Muslim women like al-Seyyida Zaynab and al-Seyyida Nafisa without their husbands' permission.[70] Sherifa (whose name was translated as honorable) criticized Bahiya's (pretty) attendance of these religious activities because they exposed women to sexual harassment in the streets and even in the mosques. She declared them to be contrary to the prophetic tradition and specifically classified the actions of a wife who ventured outside of her home, visited mosques, wore her best clothes, and spent his money without her husband's permission as sinful behavior (*haram*). Not only did the absence of a husband's permission lead the angels to damn her throughout these trips, but also God could not forgive her this infraction unless her husband forgave her. If a husband did not forgive her this sin, then God could not forgive her because "this is the right of the husband not the right of God."[71] Here, al-Nadeem was making it clear that women, who overrule the rights of their husbands, could not use God and religious duty as an excuse. God respected a husband's power over his wife and would not condone the attempt by a wife to use religion to expand her freedom, right to public space, or ignore the approval of the husband. If in the medieval view of marital relations, God intervened to regulate the power of a husband by ordering him to respect his obligations to his wife and protect her interests, he was now represented in the modern views as powerless to forgive a wife who disobeyed her husband by going to the mosque without permission.

What led al-Nadeem to this conservative religious interpretation that was more in line with Shaykh al-Fayumi's partisan masculine reading of the rights of men and women under Islam? In contextualizing al-Nadeem's views, Hoda Elsadda suggested that his nationalist discourse was influenced by the colonial discursive attack on the seclusion of women as a manifestation of the backwardness of Egyptian society.[72] Al-Nadeem rejected the quest for Westernization or modernization that undermined seclusion leading to the corruption of the moral character of Muslim women. Like his contemporaries, he was ambivalent about the changing definition of femininity. He clearly supported the education of young girls (reading, writing, and learning about their religion, hygiene, and home economic), which took them outside of the home to attend public schools and/or to visit women teachers,[73] but it was a completely different matter if a wife laid claim to religion to exercise a new type of liberty at the expense of the rights of the husband. Like the more conservative al-Fayumi, al-Nadeem's response showed that he resisted any attempt by Muslim women to use or reinterpret religion for their own purposes. In the eyes of the many men of this period, the God of Islam was the God of men. Women could not or should not claim him as theirs in negotiating the basis of new rights. The expansion or the modernization of women's roles was acceptable only if it was approved by men and/or did not interfere with their power in the family. The initiatives taken by women to expand their public presence, by venturing outside the home and/or attending religious celebrations in mosques were automatically denounced by nationalist men and their discourses as the source of social corruption and/or threats to the Islamic order.

This last point could be seen in al-Nadeem's introduction of Taymur's work to the readers, which focused attention on her condemnation of the new social practices that led middle and upper-class women to leave their homes and the way freedom contributed to the moral corruption of former slave women. Whereas Taymur stressed the failure of men to shoulder their familial obligations as the larger societal problem within which women's social rebellion against existing social rules unfolded, al-Nadeem chose to ignore this context and presented Taymur as a critic of the "catastrophes" that result from the public liberties taken by women. While Taymur was indeed critical of the actions of the two groups of women that al-Nadeem cited, she was much more critical of greedy men of all classes who wasted their families' wealth putting women at risk. In providing detailed explanations of these problematic changes taking place in the family, she was trying to avoid the kind of partial reading and partisan approach that al-Nadeem offered.

Finally, because al-Nadeem was as critical as Taymur was of the men who engaged in drinking, gambling, and prostitution, he angered his male readers who objected to the way his fictional female characters detailed the scandalous degrading behavior of men. Al-Nadeem was unapologetic suggesting that this was an effective method of admonishing men. It was also clear that while the male impersonation of the voices of women was a reflection of the absence of the voices of women from public debate, it proved to be a double edged sword: it claimed to address some of the concerns of women, but clearly allowed men to parade their partisan views and agendas as those of women. This was the big difference between al-Nadeem and Taymur's discussions of what were essentially the same set of social problems: while al-Nadeem was trying to shame men into changing their behavior, Taymur was attempting in addition to clear a public discursive space for the perspectives of women on these problems. While al-Nadeem's interest in the same issues discussed by Taymur had the effect of transferring his national stature to the themes of *Mir'at al-Ta'mul fi al-Umur* and validating her role as a social critic, the fraternal agenda of his nationalist discourse, along with the fraternal religious discourse of Shaykh al-Fayumi represented doubly powerful opposing views to those offered by women. Even in 1892, gender emerged as a marker of the ideological divisions that existed between men and women about the causes and the nature of gender inequality in the community.

CHAPTER 5

Hilyat al-Tiraz

Hybridity, the Intersection of the Old and the New, and Private and Public Struggles

> With the hand of virtue I maintain my veil and with my
> chastity (`*asmati*) I tower over my contemporaries,
> And with brilliant ideas and a critical disposition, my
> literary studies/good manners are complete.
>
> —*Hilyat al-Tiraz*[1]

Taymur's collected poems (*diwan*), titled *Hilyat al-Tiraz* (the finest of its class), was published in 1892. She also published her Persian and Turkish poems with the title *Shukufeh* in Istanbul, but its date was not known. The latter lay outside the boundaries of this study, which focused on the relationship between her Arabic works to nation-building in nineteenth-century Egypt. I do recognize that the Persian and the Turkish poems most probably indicated the continued relevance of the Ottoman identity to Taymur and her aristocratic class, but the fact remains that most of her writings appeared in Arabic reflecting the development of the narrowly defined Egyptian national community.

The last two chapters addressed themselves to the broader political and social concerns of the community; her Arabic poems connected the changes taking place in her life with those of the community using broad thematic concerns like women's changing self definitions, their public roles and interest in political affairs. The novel themes and preoccupations that these collected poems introduced into Arabic poetry, the most prestigious and privileged genre of the Arabic literary tradition, underlined the adaptability of this cultural form of expression to needs of nation-building and change in general. Its hybrid form, which most modernists missed or were unwilling to recognize, led them to categorize it as "traditional" based on form.

According to Zaynab Fawwaz, Taymur's diwan were well received;[2] unfortunately, modernist literary critics dismissed the reasons behind its good reception sticking with a negative appraisal. Mayy Ziyada offered a lengthy mixed critique of Taymur's poetry in the biography she published in 1923 characterizing it as suffering from the familiar pitfalls of "traditional" Arabic poetry.

> It lacked a system of organization . . . History did not have any effect on her poems other than the inclusion of a date in the explicitly historical poems. Even though she used the metaphors of those who preceded her . . . , what intrigued me was that her personality still came through transparent veils. She avoided the emphasis that some poets put on the pride in the family and/or tribe and she did not follow the pattern of beginning with praise and ending with verbosity . . . As for sincerity, she must be ranked among the most sincere. When she spoke about herself, she drew a picture of a sincere and sweet naiveté whose style was not as geometric as that of the advocates of classicism and more in line with what the French describe as "*romantique*" which is typical of our age.[3]

While Ziyada enumerated the familiar problems that modernist critics associated with traditionalism like disorganization, ahistoricity, and continued reliance on familiar metaphors, she also conceded that Taymur's poetry avoided traditional themes, like familial/tribal pride, a verbose style of writing, describing her as having a modernist personality that broke through the old forms expressing sincere emotions and feelings that made it consistent with French romanticism. This left the reader with a paradoxical characterization of Taymur as simultaneously following and departing from the traditional canon. Ziyada, who was writing in the 1920s, could not appreciate the changes in Taymur's work and its preoccupations, a phenomenon in which M. M. Bakhtin defined much later as hybridity, a state of having "double-accented" and "double-styled" language that allow an author or poet to bring together and at the same time maintain the separation of two discursive voices. [4] The important point made here was that some texts that could be described as "transitional" move between two worlds, making it possible for them to present multiple discursive voices.

In this chapter, I am going to demonstrate why Ziyada's modernism, with its excessive preoccupation with form, made her unable to appreciate the changes in Taymur's texts and the many innovations that could be found in what on the surface looked like old, familiar themes and classifications. I am not a student of poetry by training, so my concern in this discussion of Taymur's poetry is to show how very novel preoccupations were couched in old forms. I will begin with the discussion of the layered meaning of the title of her diwan, then turning to the way its introduction offered a novel view of the relationship between religion and poetry and the different themes of the poems that reflected the social and political changes in the community. Finally, the poems offered detailed accounts of this secluded woman's personal struggles, providing a rare window on her world and a critique of modernity and her political engagement.[5]

The Finest of Its Class: Poetry's Contribution to Community

An examination of the title of Taymur's collected poems, *Hilyat al-Tiraz* offered a good starting point for an appreciation of her poetic skills and writing style, which reflected an ability to subvert the familiar. Some students of Egyptian women's history have translated the title as "Embroidered Ornaments."[6] While this was a literal translation of the title, it was a puzzling one because Taymur hated embroidery and resisted her mother's attempt to teach her that particular feminine art opting instead to learn reading and writing. So why would she choose "Embroidered Ornaments" as the title of her collected poems? Zaynab Fawwaz provided a partial answer by suggesting that the poet had the "talent of coming up with novel meanings that no one else developed."[7] This coupled with the Arabic literary writing style of the period that paid attention to play on words, creating multiple layers of meaning made the her title, *Hilyat al-Tiraz*, an example of Taymur's prodigious linguistic skills used in this instance to successfully integrate different aspects of her history and life experiences.

The benefit of this layered interpretation of the title was that it communicated different things to different readers: the emphasis on embroidery and ornaments alerted the average reader of the author's gender, but it promised the more informed that he or she could expect superior work. On the title page, Taymur explained her title in a way that supported the latter view: "This collection of poems revitalizes the mortal remains of literature through the highest level of proficiency in the arts of good style and composition. Its content reflects the most beautiful skills that distinguish it from others. This is what is meant by *Hilyat al-Tiraz*. May God prolong the life of its author in happiness and approach taking pleasure in the fame and mastery [of her art]."[8]

The above confidently informed the reader that the collected poems represented the finest of their class, revitalizing a dying form of literature and distinguishing her poetry from all others. This was why the collected poems entitled Taymur to the best wishes and prayers of her reading public. Given the above explanation, the less obvious meaning of the title of *Hilyat al-Tiraz* could be "the finest of its class, style, or kind." Fawwaz suggested that the readers and the male literary establishment agreed with Taymur's characterization of her work: "Her collected poems had a great effect on people and got a superior reception from literary writers."[9] In making poetry a new form of women's artistic creation, Taymur sought to subvert the separation of the literary interests of men and women.

The great advantage in putting her challenge of the conventional definition of women's interests in familiar gendered idioms was to successfully overcome any initial resistance that the traditional reader might have regarding change.

In the explanation of the title, Taymur arranged her words in the form of an inverted pyramid, possibly one of the popular motifs for needlework at the time.[10] She used another pyramidal form of embroidery that rested on its base to decorate the top of the first page and included another inverted pyramid on the last page. In between these embroidered ornaments that decorated the title, first and the final pages were poems that shared with the reader the poet's feelings, experience, and social and political views. Here, Taymur integrated her domestic and nondomestic parts of her life by becoming an embroiderer of words. Her use of these patterns of embroidery confirmed this.

Next, Taymur used the introduction to the diwan to offer another subversive literary idea: that poetry was where the divine and the human met. God brought out the most glorious arts of style and eloquent composition (*balagha*) in the Qur'an whose magic captured the hearts spreading the love of literature in every direction. It was important to remind the reader here how Taymur found in the Qur'an an entry to literature, a source of supererogation and a standard for the study of the Arabic language. As the messenger of the Qur'anic revelations, Prophet Muhammad was not only a religious figure but also a towering presence in the history of the Arabic language and the esteemed Meccan tribe of Abd Manaf. Faith reflected in *al-shahada* (testifying that there was only one God and that Muhammad was his prophet) provided an added religious marker to the preexisting linguistic community that was based on the Arabic literary heritage. His literary and linguistic skills, proven by the inability of other knights of the Arabic language to win their duels with him, provided an aura of purity and sacredness to his kinfolk and endowed his companions with the distinguished status of being both princes of poetry and scholastic theology (*diwan al-kalam*).

The thrust of this section is to stress the intimate connection between the religion and the Arabic language with the Qur'an serving as the literary miracle of Islam. As a paragon of Arabic eloquence, it provided poets and those interested in literature with an important source of appreciating the language. Its religious message gave literary writers, like Taymur, license to address social issues facing the community as she did in *Mir'at al-Ta'mul fi al-Umur*. While knowledge of the language gave skilled poets and literary writers the right to interpret religion, it did not confer on the interpreters of religion, the ulema, the status of the best writers or the most skilled students of the Arabic language (i.e., it did not subordinate literature to religion). More important, the intersection of literature or poetry and the Qur'an meant that a writer could reach for or realize the divine in herself or himself through linguistic excellence. This view of the divine as literary ideal for excellence contrasted with the crude interpretation offered by modern students of Arabic poetry who stressed the irreconcilable conflict or tension between revelation and a free literary imagination and expression.[11]

Next, Taymur proceeded to present herself to the readers as first and foremost a writer who was a member of the literary community that recognized poetry as the "[historical] record of the Arabs, their literary accomplishments, intellectual garden and human ornament."[12] Within that community, she identified herself as one of those who thought of poetic expression as a moral/literary obligation, not as a source of income and enjoyment. Here, she used social class to carve a special position for herself within this prestigious field. Unlike the many poets who used their linguistic skills to earn a living, she wrote out of a moral sense of obligation as a learned aristocratic woman. Poets were not to be confused with singers or musicians who did not yet enjoy social respectability. Finally, she pointed out that she followed in the footsteps of veiled women who were prominent poets, like Layla al-'Akhiliya, Walada bint al-Mustakfi, 'A'isha al-Ba'uniya (her namesake), and Warda al-Yazji, who set standards of excellence.

While Taymur explicitly identified herself with this group of women because they were literary luminaries of the Arabic language, she also developed some personal identification with their lives and accomplishments. 'A'isha al-Ba'uniya shared the same first name. Layla al-'Akhiliya, not only inspired some of the best examples of love poetry produced by Thawb ibn al-Himyar during the early Islamic period but also was a late bloomer as a poet. Because of Thawb's poems, Layla's father rejected him as a suitor marrying her off to another. Defying social conventions, Thawb and Layla continued to meet after her marriage provoking violent fits of rage by her husband who plotted to have him killed several times. In defiance, Layla warned him each time. When Thawb finally died, a mature Layla eulogized him with beautiful poetry of her own, publicly defending him against his critics.[13]

Walada bint al-Mustakfi, the leading woman poet of Muslim Spain, similarly defied social conventions by engaging in numerous polemics with male poets and literary writers. Despite her beauty, she chose not to marry considering her single status to be much better than the status of married women, maintaining loving relations with many distinguished men and poet of this period.[14] 'A'isha al-Ba'uniya, who some described as a woman of limited beauty but outstanding literary skills with knowledge of grammar, *fiqh*, and poetic meter, occupied a distinguished status among her contemporaries who considered her to be a better poet than al-Khansa,' the greatest woman poet of the Arabic language.[15] Distinguished ulema benefited from al-Ba'uniya's work reinforcing her reputation as a leading literary critic of her time.[16] Finally, Warda al-Yazji, Taymur's contemporary who was also a prominent poet, came from a distinguished

Christian literary family that made significant contributions to the revival of the Arabic language during this period. Like Taymur's father, al-Yazji's father showed similar interest in his daughter's education. The fact that al-Yazji and her family were Christians did not matter to Taymur for whom the Arabic language, not religion, was the main bond of community.

Like Taymur, each one of these women poets challenged the norms of her society, using poetry as a means of creative literary expression and a measure of independence. Their personal struggles captured aspects of Taymur's experiences. Al-Akhiliya's unhappy marriage, al-Mustakfi's value of her freedom and pride in being different from other women, al-Ba'uniya's limited beauty that did not detract from an outstanding record of learning and al-Yazji's family background and unusual literary education. They all used poetry to write their distinct gendered experiences into the literary canon and history of the Arabic language.

Even though Taymur constructed herself as part of the Arabic poetic tradition, this was an invented history. In the introduction to *Hilyat al-Tiraz*, Taymur explained that as a youngster, she learned poetry as a marker of good upbringing initially writing poetry mainly in Persian and Turkish. She wrote more infrequently in what she described as the "honorable Arabic language" because of its religious status.[17] Because the decision to write in Arabic came much later and was a conscious one, she described how she set out to collect enough Arabic poems that demonstrated her love of the language as the language of community. Behind the drive to produce Arabic poetry, she referred to her desire to leave an immortal (national) reputation and wished for mercy and forgiveness. Because of the Ottoman association between Arabic and religion , Taymur, like her father, reasserted the belief that contribution to the Arabic language also represented a source of religious rewards. The wish for divine compassion and forgiveness was another reference to the guilt she still felt regarding her responsibility for her daughter's death.

Finally, Taymur was keenly aware of the fraternal character of the linguistic and religious communities of her time that were going to judge her work. In response, she used the familiar strategy of disarming her male critics by acknowledging that her work fell short of those produced by her male counterparts, suggesting that the literary works of veiled women should be judged by a different standard that took into account the obvious obstacles that they faced in the pursuit of knowledge. Considering the title of her diwan, which she declared to be the "finest of its class," Taymur did not really believe that the poetry she produced was inferior to those produced by men. What she seemed to be doing was to remind the partisan male critics of her difference, which she felt should increase their appreciation of her poetry.

In the sections that follow, my goal will not be to evaluate the literary beauty of the poetry, its linguistic achievements, or the extent to which it compared to others produced during this period. Given her emphasis on the contextual differences that distinguished the poetry produced by men and women, I will use the rest of the chapter to stress that Taymur's Arabic poetry offered a historically and culturally specific construction of her life and how it intersected with the history of the community. Because Taymur did not for most part date her poems, I have relied on their order of appearance to (1) assign importance to their themes, (2) understand how Taymur constructed her private and public worlds, and (3) show the breadth of her interests. After noting the place of the first poem that initiated the discussion of a particular theme, I proceed to look at all the other poems in the diwan that explicitly addressed that theme as a basis for further discussion. The resulting construction of her life and work was not linear; it reflected the many discontinuities imposed on her work by life cycle changes and social and political crises facing her society and/or the different struggles she faced within and outside her family.

Poetic Themes as Historical Markers of a Changing Community

The Changing Definition of Islamic Femininity in Nineteenth-Century Egypt

In the introduction to her work of fiction, *Nata'ij al-'Ahwal*, Taymur attacked the veil and seclusion as obstacles that made it difficult for women, like her, to have access to the superior education of literary men. So it was surprising to discover that the first poem in *Hilyat al-Tiraz* celebrated the veil and seclusion. A superficial reading of the poem would suggest that after criticizing the veil and seclusion in 1887/8, Taymur changed her mind and offered a defense of them four years later. Here was another instance in which Taymur seemed to contradict herself like when she chose *Hilyat al-Tiraz*, as a title for her diwan despite her early hatred of embroidery. The fact that both her works of fiction and poetry were preoccupied with a discussion of these gendered practices and institutions and how they defined the social role of women indicated that they had become sufficiently probematized during the last two decades of the nineteenth century and that she considered the topic to be of personal importance. While appearing to celebrate the veil and seclusion, Taymur sought to subvert our understanding of them and their relationship to a changing Islamic femininity. The following were the first two lines of her opening poem:

> With the hand of virtue I maintain my veil and with my
> chastity (`asmati) I tower over my contemporaries,
> And with brilliant ideas and a critical disposition, my liter-
> ary studies and good manners are complete.[18]

In a confident tone, Taymur declared her commitment to keeping the veil on with self-conscious virtuous hands coupled with her unusual studies as bases for her elevated status among women. To the revered old values of feminine modesty, she added brilliant thoughts and a critical disposition as markers of literary education and good upbringing. She informed the reader that she wrote poetry for fun and that eloquence, logic, and writing were hobbies she shared with Bint al-Mahdi (`Aliya bint al-Mahdi) and Layla (al-`Akhiliya) who were her role models. Like Layla who did not start off as a professional poet but developed into one later in life and `Aliya bint al-Mahdi (who was Harun al-Rasheed's [the Abbasid caliph] sister)[19] who wrote playful courtship poetry, she was a mature poet from an elite background.

Taymur offered herself as a representative of a new definition of Islamic femininity, which combined pride in her veil as a symbol of virtue with a new independence that distinguished her from other women of her class. In a significant play on the word `Asmati, she combined a reference to another one of her given names `Asmat, which stood for chastity, with the legal concept of al-`asma, which Muslim women could include in the marriage contract to ensure their right to divorce their husbands giving them legal independence. During the nineteenth century, middle- and upper-class women, including Shaykh Rifa` al-Tahtawi's cousin, Karima Mohammad Farghali al-Ansari a daughter of the distinguished member of the ulema, who became his first wife;[20] and Huda Sha`rawi, the young daughter of Muhammad Sultan Pasha the prominent politician and landowner, who emerged as a key feminist figure in the twentieth century—she married her much older and already married cousin, Ali Sha`rawi[21]—enjoyed this legal right. It was hard to ascertain if Taymur also had that right, but Zaynab Fawwaz, her early biographer, suggested that the death of the poet's father and then her husband within the span of three years made her "self governing,"[22] giving her an appreciation of freedom and independence from men. It was only then that she was able to seriously resume her literary studies. Anticipating the critics who opposed Muslim women's quest for independence and freedom, Taymur used the Islamic notion of `asma as an acceptable substitute for freedom and independence, which she put in the service of virtue, education, and respect of legal rules.

Taymur also identified with other "buxom women and *spinsters*, who achieved their high aspirations weaving a lofty place for themselves"[23] within the Arabic poetic tradition. Given the widespread representations of nineteenth-century women as sexual beings defined by their relations to men, Taymur went against the grain of the tradition by celebrating buxom (*kwa`ib*) and unmarried women (`awanis), who were not primarily determined by their relationships to men but by their more lofty aspirations. In transforming these mature and unmarried women—who were not valued in a tradition that stressed youth, beauty, and heterosexual love as important social ideals—into examples of successful women, Taymur was attempting to change the tradition. In adding al-Khansa' to that group as another illustrious poet—who overcame huge obstacles working through rock (*sakhr*), the name of her beloved brother whom she eulogized with what most poets consider to be the best of that genre—she tried to suggest that they provided precedents within the tradition for the ideals she valued.

Taymur carved a distinct place for herself among this illustrious group. This was how she described her relationship to femininity and poetry.

> I have made my notebooks my mirror and the ink of my writing a sign of my fertility/productivity,
>> The ink on my fingers has decorated my face making me look like a young man with lines that looked like the first growth of a young man's beard,
>> My intelligence shows like a lit candle and the fragrance of my poetry has spread like a fine scent to the garden of the beloved[24]

Taymur's rebellion against the dominant ideal of feminine beauty dictated by her society and class was clear in the above verses replacing it with pride in her literary accomplishments. Instead of spending long hours in front of the mirror, using makeup to make oneself beautiful, and dyeing one's hair, she subverted that ideal by describing her notebooks as her mirror; the ink of her pens as her dye; and instead of applying lines to her eyes, she put them on paper or absent mindedly to her cheek, making her look like a young man whose beard was beginning to grow. Equally significant, she considered her writings, instead of her offspring, as a sign of her fertility. While she did not mind the ink that decorated her face, making her look like a man, many within her milieu considered these activities as undermining her femininity, making her masculine. Worse, Taymur found herself to be doubly masculine, not only because she was interested in writing, but also because she had to use the male voice to write courtship poetry.[25] Mayy Ziyada reported the survival of these social charges of manlike behavior (*mustargala*) leveled against women writers into the twentieth century, indicating the continued rigid social separation of the roles that men and women played in society.[26]

Taymur hinted at how these attitudes transformed her accomplishments into drawbacks in the following lines:

> My literature/good manners and education did not hurt me
>> except by making me like a flower in a breast collar,
> My seclusion, head cover and style of clothing did not
>> offend me,

> My lady like stature, the cover (*khimar*) draped over my
> body and face cover (*niqab*) have not been obstacles
> that prevented me from reaching the heights . . .
> My existence was kept as a virtuous secret, but made exotic
> among *strangers*.[27]

Taymur suggested that she faced two groups of critics in her attempt to become an educated veiled woman. In a social milieu that valued women's invisibility as a sign of virtue, her education and interest in literature were said to hurt her social standing because they made her stand out like a flower in a breast collar. There were others who viewed her seclusion and her modest clothing, most probably European critics, as clashing with education and enlightenment. To them, she said her clothing and face cover (the European concept of the veil) were not obstacles that blocked her from reaching the heights as a distinguished poet and writer. In the 1890s, Taymur gave veiling and seclusion a positive content to counter the widespread degraded European depictions of veiled Muslim as living in a backward society that crippled them and justifying continued British occupation. Not only was her mode of dress not an obstacle, but also she followed in the footsteps of a long line of veiled and secluded women making their mark on the Arabic literary tradition.

For a long time, her seclusion made her a well-protected secret, but when her published works revealed her presence, her unusual standing as a veiled and secluded writer was made exotic by strangers/foreigners. She compared her secret existence and then her public exposure to the way musk that was enclosed in a closet spreads its fragrance when it is opened and the way the seas that contained precious pearls protected them from reaching hands. Just like divers search hard for their precious pearls, she saw her public appearance as a product of a long struggle that finally illuminated the lamp of excellence with her God given skills and talents.[28]

In a recent study of this diwan, Taymur's defense of the veil and seclusion in this poem was used to demonstrate the multiple layers of her poetic personality: "On the one hand, she absolutely accepted the social requirements of the age and society and on the other, she absolutely rejected and rebelled against them . . . In this position, she demonstrated James Scott's discussion of two type of discourse used by those who suffer under the pressure of power: a general discourse that went along with power and its requirements and another that existed below the surface [and sometimes] publicly broke with it."[29] While Taymur's defense of veiling and seclusion in this poem represented the first discourse, the "poetry of opthalmia" in which she rejected eye disease that metaphorically served as a veil that separated her from the world, was an example of the second. It shed light on the tensions that Taymur faced as she pursued a general interest in change from within and the attempt to work through existing forms and institutions. A greater elaboration of this point will be presented later on in this chapter.

Taymur's enormous pride in her literary accomplishments was coupled with aristocratic contempt for those who worked for a living. As a result, she put emphasis on how she was different from other poets who earned their living from writing. It led her to describe poetry and writing as sources of enjoyment and hobbies, which were socially acceptable activities for well-to-do women. This claim clashed, however, with what we know of her serious and single-minded pursuit of literary study, which led her to risk social censure for giving up household chores and mothering. As a result, Taymur found herself in a lonely place where she did not fit among women of her class or the majority of poets and literary writers.

Finally, this poem made clear that Taymur faced opposition from different sources, not just from men who considered the activities of women writers as a transgression to masculinity but also from women in her class who took issue with her unorthodox interests and preoccupations. Because virtuous women were to avoid public exposure, some women accused Taymur of being wicked by using her interest in education and literature to gain visibility like a flower in a breast collar. Shaykh Ghamrawi, an Arabic teacher, told Ziyada that readers who were unfamiliar with the social climate of this period would not understand this negative view of education.[30] What Taymur made clear was that her embrace of a new form of education under the old social system was met with aggression from other women who felt threatened by it. Taymur's success also incited the envy of others who embarked on a campaign to discredit her achievements.

She described these women in many poems as her critics, slanderers, enemies, and the "army of ignorance." The last reference implied the large numbers of those who took part in this campaign. They used a variety of different arguments and actions to discourage her from literary pursuits. A good time friend reprimanded her for embracing such unorthodox pursuits, predicting that they were going to lead her to a bad end. Some visited her and attempted to confiscate her writings.[31] Others published their attacks using her courtship poetry, even those that praised Prophet Muhammad, to hint moral transgressions. Many took pleasure in her misfortunes,[32] casting doubt on who she was mourning during the seven years that followed the death of her daughter[33] and celebrating her opthalmia.[34] They subjected her to endless gossip, disapproving glances designed to wound[35] and transforming minor infractions into huge crimes.[36] In short, they engaged in behavior that she reluctantly compared to that of the infidels (i.e., outside the bounds of acceptable Muslim behavior) reflecting hatred like that of the ignorant kin of Youssef/Joseph, a reference to this prophet's evil brothers.[37] This last claim was the first of many references to the fact that members of her family participated in these attacks.

Despite the claims of her critics, Taymur's poetry did not separate her literary interests from the socially acceptable roles of mother, sister, daughter, and hostess. Many of her poems chronicled important family events and her feelings toward different members of her family. For example, she wrote a poem asking one of her sons to return a book he borrowed from her acknowledging and praising his zeal for learning.[38] She also used poetry in invitations she sent out for a banquet held in honor of one of her sons and the celebrations of the circumcision of her two sons. She also used it in correspondences with them.[39] She wrote poems to congratulate her father on the birth of his son and celebrated her brother's learning how to read.[40] Finally, there were the elegies she wrote mourning the death of her daughter, her father, her mother, and one of her sisters.[41]

By integrating poetry in her day-to-day interactions with members of the family, she described the popular social occasions celebrated by families in the community. She also tried to share her love of poetry with the family by positively reinforcing any interest they might have had in learning and overcoming any resentment resulting from the time she spent in her literary study away from them. This poetry showed that while the critics described her as challenging important social rules, she tried to reconcile her novel interests with her prescribed roles as mother, daughter, and sister. The only exception to this point was the glaring absence of any poem that discussed her husband or her relationship with him, which constituted a loud statement about the troubled nature of this relationship. Other than that, it was abundantly clear that unlike any other male poet of that period, her poetry attempted to integrate the literary and the daily life of this nineteenth-century woman.

Taymur also used poetry to develop a social and a public persona, which was unusual in the 1870s. These poems were used to mark various social occasions like congratulating a friend on the birth of a child, accepting a social invitation from another,[42] welcoming Khedive Ismail back from his travels (1872),[43] congratulating Khedive Tewfik on the birth of crown prince Abbas II,[44] sending greetings to some unidentified princes on the celebration of the Eid,[45] and marking the return of Hasan and Husayn Pashas—Khedive Ismail's sons—to Egypt from their travels.[46] Some of these poems, which were directed to public men in the community, identified socially acceptable situations where a secluded woman could address and have indirect social contact with men. Clearly, the princes knew of Taymur's literary interests given the long-standing government careers of both her father and husband. Given the rules of sexual segregation, one assumed that she only had relations with the women of the ruling family, especially the khedive's mother and his wives; but these poems showed that Taymur sought to establish formal (impersonal) social relations with the khedive and other princes of the royal family as well, indicating that the rules governing seclusion within the upper class and the ruling family were changing in which case upper-class women's accusations of Taymur's violation of the rules of sexual segregation and immorality would make some sense. Clearly, Taymur was attempting to break new social grounds in developing and/ or expanding these relations, which were yet to be accepted.

In addition to the princes of the royal family, Taymur also used poetry to establish relations with members of the ulema class who shared her interests in religion and literature as the elegy of Shaykh Ibrahim al-Saqqa[47] and the correspondence with another unnamed member of that class demonstrated.[48] Without sufficient information, one could only speculate about the nature and the form that these relations took: Did the elegy seek to establish her familiarity with the work of the deceased or hint that he had influence on her work? Was it intended to introduce her to other members of that class who were not familiar with her writings? Either way, Taymur was taking some bold steps that reflected increased social and literary confidence and expanding her relations as a secluded woman with men outside her family.

Personal Reflections versus Religious (Confessional) Poetry

In a chapter titled "Religious and Ethical Poetry"[49] in her biography of Taymur, Ziyada included in the religion's definition Taymur's discussion of the veil as well as confessions expressing emotional pain and/or remorse. For the Christian Ziyada, the veil and confessional poetry were associated with religion, but for Taymur they were not. She was not interested in reflecting on the religious motives behind veiling but reflected on it as a social practice as part of the definition of femininity.[50] Taymur's so called confessional poetry largely dealt with the pain of personal loss as well as living in a social environment that was inhospitable to her interests. The problematic categorization of this poetry as religious led Ziyada to draw a parallel between Taymur and the musings of the Spanish Catholic nun Teresa,[51] concluding that the former was "lacking depth and beauty, and like the rest of her poetry, dealt with the ordinary, mixing ethical feelings, confession of sins, and the desire for forgiveness."[52] Since Taymur was not a religious figure offering her views on religion, the comparison between her views with that of a nun was neither fair nor helpful.

There was no doubt that Taymur turned to the Prophet Muhammad and God as important sources of comfort in her struggles to deal with the loss of her daughter and with the hostile social climate created by women of her class. This was indicated by the fact that the second poem in her diwan titled "a Fervent Entreaty at the Prophet's Tomb,"[53] which was similar to at least three others in the first 13 pages of this volume. In contrast to the confident tone of the first poem, the second one described Taymur at a time of personal crisis. Although none were dated, the latter was most likely written during the seven years of mourning that followed Tawhida's death (1877–84). The title of the poem that dealt with the prophet as well as some of its verses suggested that Taymur might have visited the tomb of the prophet in Medina: "I extended my hands seeking your compassion as I stand in the midst of this sacred site," but regardless of whether the visit occurred in actuality or in her imagination, the poem described her loneliness at a time in her life when the loved ones were long gone.

> Is it the lightening in a dark night or the breeze that stirred
>   my feelings for those
> that I wish to hold,
> They reminded me of a time of love that is long gone and
>   the desire to see those whom I loved . . .
> My slanderers wish me to forget about those who I love,
>   but I do not care for their censure or bite . . .
> [Instead], I turn to al-Mustafa, the master of mediation to
>   God when a caller will bring to life those to whom I
>   gave birth,
> And to Taha, whose mission filled the face of the universe
>   with the light of rationality and generosity.[54]

In this poem, the past feelings of love were merged with those felt for the prophet of Islam to whom she appealed for a future meeting with her loved ones. The feeling of loss was compounded with the hostility of those who slander her, accusing her of having illicit feelings for other lovers even though the names of al-Mustafa and Taha provided reference to the other names of the prophet. In turning to al-Mustafa and to Taha, she hoped for a reuniting with those she had born and lost (a reference to Tawhida) on judgment day. The generosity and rationality of his message contrasted with the social climate she had to face.

To understand these reflective poems in which she turned to God and the prophets for help, one needed to understand the scope and the depth of her personal crisis in which she dealt with loss and bleeding eyes or the struggle with opthalmia, which undermined her sense of confidence and hope. The net result of this emotional and physical distress was considerable self-doubt. In groping for a way out, she sought strength and compassion from the prophet who was represented as a parental figure who responded to her pain with generosity. The construction of the prophet as a parental figure combined paternal and maternal characteristics. First, there was al-Mustafa's religious power of intercession to God who meted out reward and punishment. Second, Taymur described him secondarily as "the light of compassion," providing immediate comfort as a mother would for an offspring who was in pain. Recreated in this way, the prophet offered the composite characteristics of parenthood that were usually split in a gendered way.

The next two poems were without a title, but fit into this reflective mode. The first of the two was a long poem, which began with a description of her broken heart and how she had suffered as a result. Then, Taymur actually used the word "confession" to take the reader into her confidence. "I *confess* that I did not meet the *rights* [of the loved one] and I fell short in performing [my obligations]. I am asking forgiveness wrapped in my crime and wearing my shame as a belt."[55] This was an explicit statement to her failure as a mother who did not pay attention to the *right* of her daughter and her other children to her time and attention. She blamed this on her baser self: the part that emphasized her *rights as an individual* at the expense of the rights of her child.

Her guilt was compounded by the rejoicing of her enemies/the army of ignorance at her misfortune and their exaggerations of her minor infractions. In response, she again turned to God, her creator, seeking understanding. "If my rebellion and awful crime are great and I am threatened by punishment, I will depend on your vast forgiveness. You, who can see what is in my conscience, but cannot be seen, please respond to my prayers."[56] In a demonstration of how revisionist history was used by her enemies to misrepresent her deeds and goals, Taymur's rebellion against rigid social rules that narrowly defined women's interests was offered as an example of a crime that an irresponsible mother had committed against her offspring. Poetry offered an outlet to discuss this awful experience without losing face or encouraging the painful harassment she faced on a daily basis, which inflicted more psychic wounds. Her only hope was that the God who knew what was in her conscience would surely forgive her.

In the last short poem in this early part of the diwan, Taymur asked, "Suppose I had committed a lapse beyond all limits and even assault? I am a descendent of Adam, the leader of all believers. He disobeyed God, . . . but God forgave [and led him] to faith."[57]

The theme of reflecting on what she variously called her deficiency, crime, sin, or offense as a means of imploring God for forgiveness continued to be the focus of at least three other poems,[58] two of which appeared toward the end of the diwan.[59] The last two had the same title, "A Call for Help" (*Istighatha*). In locating poems that had the theme of distress at the beginning and the end of the collection, Taymur offered a device to indicate that these painful struggles continued for an extended period of time. The latter were slightly different in the sense that Taymur used them to engage in self-criticism: she only listened to herself in important matters rejecting good advice offered by others. She was, at times, ignorant and arrogant in the way she handled some things. She paid much attention to the errors of judgment committed by others and not enough to her own.[60] In an attempt to overcome these problems, she devoted a long poem to a series of questions she directed to people of discretion whose assistance she sought to reverse course so that she could still reach her desired goals. She regretted wasting many years wallowing in pain and was now more hopeful.[61]

While writing allowed her to break out of the rigid domestic roles of women, it also isolated her from others in her environment. Because she felt misunderstood by critics within and outside her family, poetry also provided a valuable outlet for feelings of anger, doubt, despair and guilt. It also offered a means of engaging in an internal dialogue. As a result, the reader was offered a record of unusual openness about the emotional world of a nineteenth-century woman that defied the purpose of the restrictions imposed by the veil and/or seclusion. These poems clearly indicated that she consciously or unconsciously wanted to challenge the closeted character of the harem.

The Critique of Modernity

Many of Taymur's poems showed how her upper-class family relied very heavily on the services of modern medicine to handle the health needs of the family. Based on these experiences, she developed a very powerful critique of modern medicine and its claims of enlightenment and scientific progress. It emerged as the third most important theme of the diwan, judging from the order of its appearance at the early part of her anthology and intersecting with the discussion of other themes especially her elegies of different family members and her struggle with opthalmia. Taymur was harsh in her critique of the profession mocking the gap between the expectations they encouraged people to have and their limited capabilities.

In providing a context for this part of her discussion, let me offer an example of the way this profession's representation of itself to the world conveyed by the official newspaper, *al-Waqa`I al-Misriyat* (*The Egyptian Gazette*) from a speech given by Mustafa Effendi Radwan, the French instructor at the school of medicine, on the occasion of the 1869 graduation ceremony:

> For each illness, there is a medicine. The science of human physiology takes precedence over that of religious sciences. If one is vigorous in body, safe in one's group and in control of one's livelihood, then good health is assured in the world.[62]

The promise of a cure for every ailment coupled with the scientific status of the study of human physiology led many doctors to make powerful claims about their ability to replace religion in the deciphering of the secrets of life and death. It was no wonder that Mustafa Radwan gave the modern science of physiology precedence over the study of religion, which had previously monopolized this discussion. In addition to a vigorous body, modern medicine underlined the importance of a sense of safety and secure livelihood as determinants of good health. Taymur took issue with this definition of good health and its relations with other medical traditions.

> You who came to heal the body of its illness,
> You think of Galen as one of your slaves,
> Your hallucinating [medical] discourses have destroyed
>   nations bringing death ever closer
> You claim that you renewed [medicine] when you have
>   wasted the old with the new.[63]

In these verses, Taymur poked fun at the pompous claims of modern doctors who discounted earlier medical traditions, confusing Galen, the name of a prominent doctor in ancient Greece,[64] with the name of an alien slave. Rather than providing a cure for hallucinations, she identified their technical discourse and/or the fact that most of doctors who practiced medicine in second half of the nineteenth-century Egypt were Europeans,[65]speaking in alien languages, which she identified as another form of hallucination. As far as she was concerned, modern medicine contributed to the death of large numbers of peoples and nations claiming all the while that it was renewing this field of knowledge/practice. In fact, what it accomplished was the destructions of older types of medical traditions.

In contrast to the hallucinations of modern medicine, Taymur provided the following broad and sensible definition of what constituted good health:

> Face of the beloved show us a good time and
> Beware, may God protect you, informing those who watch,
> Let me be because meeting the loved ones heals my heart,
> And set aside any treatment recommended by the doctor.[66]

Good health was synonymous with being happy in the company of loved ones away from the watchful eyes of the world. This happy state offered the best cure for the heart, not the treatment offered by present day doctors. Next, Taymur personalized this discussion of medicine:

> There was a time when the organs of my body were
>   nowhere near the shadow of illness, now they are
>   overwhelmed by it,
> How could it not be so when there is a moan and pain in
>   my heart and the eyes of women irrigating the sorcery
>   of Babel?

> My ill body had blocked treatment and my heart cannot
>   take in the cure . . . ,
> If you deny my grief and debility, then feel my pulse that is
>   a neutral witness,
> He said after feeling my pulse: if these symptoms are aggra-
>   vated, they could be fatal.[67]

Taymur's understanding of her illness contradicted that offered by her doctor leading her to ignore his suggested treatment. Taymur's most pointed critique of modern medicine was that it separated the understanding of the physical from the emotional. Not only was her European or European trained doctor[68] dismissive of what she believed was wrong with her, but he might have even suggested that she was suffering from hysteria. Taymur's unorthodox interests and the extended mourning of her daughter had led her family and friends to brand her as unstable. In this setting, the doctor allied himself with the family's view of his patient by declaring her hysterical. Yet his examination of her vital signs led him to agree that her distress was real and serious.

In the elegies of her daughter, father, and sister, Taymur provided accounts of other encounters with doctors that explained her lack of confidence in their abilities. She recalled the doctor who came to examine her daughter and how he arrogantly claimed that he had the cure. Very quickly, his confidence turned to resignation, failure, and weariness. In contrast, her father had complete confidence in modern medicine asking his doctor to diagnose and treat the source of his ailment promising him great rewards. Here, the patient had more confidence in claims of modern medicine than the doctor providing another indictment of the limitations of modern medicine, which advertised what it could not deliver. A third doctor failed her younger sister examining her several times, but quickly declared exhaustion and an inability to determine the right course of treatment. Only in the case of her mother's death was Taymur willing to describe a doctor as resourceful blaming her mother's demise on a history of ill health.

In the above discussion, Taymur used modern medicine as a stand in for science and modernity, which exaggerated its accomplishments but was silent on its problems and limited capabilities. The promise of treatment and the cure of illness failed to materialize. Their definitions of health were focused on disease, not health, failing to see the connection between the body and emotions. Finally, modern medicine had its own bias against women dismissing their understanding of their ailments falling short in its enlightenment toward this group.

Poetry and Popular Culture

Mayy Ziyada recalled that she first became acquainted with Taymur and her poetry when she heard one of her couplets sung at a wedding, which she attended as a young girl in Palestine.[69] She stated that many of Taymur's short poems were sung in Syria and Palestine, not only in weddings but also in parties.[70] Taymur was not the only classical poet to engage in writing popular poetry, Ziyada mentioned Ismail Sabry Pasha, another prominent poet of the period, who many credited with elevating the standard of popular singing.[71] A close examination of *Hilyat al-Tiraz* indicated that Taymur showed extensive interest in this type of popularized poetry producing many couplets, which she singly categorized as *dour*, the Arabic word for verses that could be put to music and turned into songs. These couplets helped to disseminate Taymur's poetry beyond the confines of the small literate class.

The following couplet was the one that Ziyada heard sung in the 1890s:

> Is this Kohl in your eyes or is it divine dye?
> Are your eyelids magical or do they have magical effects?
> Are your cheeks happy or dyed by God?
> You have made my thoughts lost in the eyelids and cheeks.
> God bless you what a beautiful human being (*Insan*) you
>   are.[72]

The flirtatious character of the couplet provided an idea of what the public enjoyed listening to during this period. In addition, the couplet was innovative in the way it left the gender of the beloved ambiguous treating physical attributes of men and women as important qualities that did not diminish their humanity. It challenged the representation of femininity, which privileged women's physical-sexual attributes, separating it from the representation of masculinity.

While the above couplet was written in simple classical Arabic, others like the one that Taymur categorized as an example of the "the art of the *mawal*" was written in "colloquial language, . . . to be sung with the accompaniment of a reed pipe."[73] It said,

> your eyes have triumphed over us raising their flags,
> May God strengthen them; when they speak, they pas-
>   sionately stir love;
> they make one desire the flower on your eyelids without
>   restraint.[74]

In adapting national imagery to this love poem, Taymur represented love as a battlefield where, despite claims to the contrary: affection and desire were effective weapons used by each sex to gain power over the other. If the open declarations of love defied the notions of female honor, these verses represented new levels of boldness.

Love was the dominant theme of many of these couplets because they were intended for mass appeal. It also explained why they did not adhere to the rigid formal rules of sexual segregation embraced by the middle and upper classes. So it was not surprising that most discussed the effects of seeing the face of the beloved, hennaed hands, eyes, cheeks, fantasizing about being with the loved one, thinking about him or her and suffering from rejection or inability to see him or her.[75] Others celebrated more abstract definitions of love where happy homes were described as places where hearts were open to zigzagging around the lover's limitations or happy times that were spent with loved ones away from the eyes of the world.[76] The latter reflected the concerns and experience of the secluded classes to which the poet belonged.

Taymur's attempt to produce popular as well as the formal courtship (*ghazal*) poetry collided with the social norms of her class, which emphasized female seclusion and limited social contact with men. This particular class tolerated a double standard, which celebrated the courtship poetry produced by male poets like Ismail Sabry, who in one poem asked his beloved to challenge social rules by throwing away her veil and talking to him,[77] but censured Taymur for attempting to loosen some of these rigid restraints on women's expression of the same feelings. To deflect the weight of such social criticisms, Taymur claimed in one poem "she flirted with no man, but was simply practicing this type of writing."[78] Still, Taymur found herself between a rock and a hard place: because every great poet had to explore the complexities of love as an important human emotion, she had no choice but to produce some of this poetry, which provided her critics with ammunition that they could use to slander her. In further attempt to protect herself, she used the male voice in these love poems because it was the only one that could flaunt the restrictions on amorous relations between men and women without committing social suicide. In conservatively adhering to these social and literary traditions, Taymur clearly submerged her voice in the male one. As Ziyada pointed out this device was not without cost requiring Taymur to use masculine gaze and forms of expression. According to Ziyada, the only feminine quality that betrayed the poet's gender in courtship poetry was her indirectness and the shyness that accompanied her characterizations of the beloved.[79]

While nineteenth-century courtship poetry appealed to a wide spectrum of the literate and illiterate publics, Taymur's success came with a high social cost. Because the only voices that enjoyed legitimacy in this particular genre were those of men who could challenge social conventions without suffering significant consequences, Taymur was subjected to severe social criticism from women and men of her class who accused her of flouting the social rules.

Poetry as a Form of Active Political Engagement

In the discussion of Taymur's fictional work *Nata'ij al-'Ahwal*, I explored her views of the serious political crises facing dynastic government and how they could be overcome. In *Hilyat al-Tiraz*, Taymur offered her readers concrete examples of her actual political involvement in the defense of the dynastic government of her time. She provided dates for many of these poems, which allowed one to date her relations with members of the ruling family and the important political events of this period. It is important to note here that some of these political poems were written during the seven years she spent mourning Tawhida's death (1877–84). One thing remained clear: during these difficult years Taymur struggled with an eye disease that sometimes led to periodic blindness. When this occurred, her depression became severe. During the periods in which she regained her eye sight, she regained her spirits. It was clear from her poetry that despite the emotional and other health difficulties she experienced during this period, this did not undermine her awareness of the serious political upheavals that were taking place in Egyptian society (e.g., increased international intervention in Egyptian affairs), the deposition of Khedive Ismail, the ascension of Khedive Tewfik to power and his alliance with the British leading to the defeat of 'Urabi's national revolution, which negatively impacted his authority. I was safe to assume that most of these political poems were written during the periods when she recovered her eyesight.

Ziyada described these political poems as largely concerned with flattery of the rulers, which was partially true. Unfortunately, this proved to be another one of her sweeping generalizations designed to dismiss another set of Taymur's poems on the grounds that they were traditional in character. The problem was that she did not differentiate between social poetry, which Taymur used to cement her ties with different members of the ruling family, and explicitly political poems, which were clearly part of the practical political effort to restore the authority of Khedive Tewfik and to delegitimize his opponents.

Taymur wrote ten poems about different members of the ruling family: there were two that focused attention on the deposed khedive (Ismail), five that were written specifically for Khedive Tewfik, one that welcomed a khedive back from a trip without specifying, which one was the intended recipient, two that were written about two princes: one celebrating the birth of a daughter to Hasan Pasha, another offered a greeting to a prince on the occasion of the celebration of the Eid, but without specifying which prince or which Eid was being discussed.

Taymur provided dates for two out of these ten poems, which I took to mean that she wanted the reader to make use of this historical information. Very specifically, Taymur's first poem about and for the ruling family was written in 1871, marking the birth of a daughter to Prince Hasan. The second poem for which Taymur provided a date was one that welcomed Khedive Ismail back from a trip, which was written in 1872. Even though the second poem was written after the first one, Taymur placed it first in the diwan assigning it greater importance. While I am going to discuss the two poems chronologically, I will use the importance she accorded to the second one in the explanation of the shift in her writing about the ruling family.

It was not coincidental that the two poems Taymur produced in 1871–72 focused on her relations with members of the ruling family. Her father's relations with Khedive Ismail took a turn for the better during these two years. The khedive not only gave Ismail Taymur the title of Pasha during this period but also appointed him to the court of Crown Prince Tewfik, until his death on December 27, 1872. Did Taymur's father play a role in encouraging her to use poetry to cement their ties with the ruling family just as Shaykh Ibrahim al-Yazji encouraged his daughter Warda to reply, on his behalf, to poets who corresponded with him in Lebanon during this same period?[80] Whether her father had a hand in it or not, it certainly opened a new avenue for `A'isha's talents who had resumed her literary studies during this period after Tawhida relieved her of her domestic duties.

Taymur wrote the 1871 poem, titled "Chronicling the Birth of her Highness `Aziza Hanum the Daughter of Hasan Pasha," [81]celebrating the new addition to Hasan Pasha (one of the khedive's sons) and his family whose name, Aziza, meant "the dear one." She included in this celebratory poem a discussion of Aziza's older, but still very young brother whom she described as ushering his younger sister to the world. She predicted good fortune to the brother and sister who will add to the elevated status of their family.

This light and happy poem sensitively reflected Taymur's good mothering skills through the inclusion of `Aziza's older brother in the celebration of his sister reminding the parents of the importance of the early cementing of the relations between the two siblings. In marking this social occasion, Taymur described herself both in the title and in the last verse of the poem as chronicler of the royal family.

> At the end of this verse, I wish to *historically mark*
> (*mu'arikhatan*) this clear day with its two luminary
> siblings.[82]

Taymur seemed to be positioning herself, here, to be a court chronicler, if not poet, who would historically mark the important social occasions of the family: birth of children, eulogizing the death of older ones and celebrating the marriage of young men and women. She must have already known that Shaykh Ali al-Laythi occupied the position of the "court's poet," whose role was to entertain the khedive.[83] While Taymur could not compete with him in the entertainment of the khedive, but she could, like most women in families, chronicle the history or the important social and political events of the ruling family. Given the fact that Taymur was a learned writer, her poetry would provide an elegant chronicling of the history of the ruling family from someone whose family had a long history of royal service. She reinforced her definition of this important role by marking the birth of a son, Abbas II, to crown prince Tewfik in another poem written in 1875.[84]

In another poem that Taymur wrote in 1872, she expanded her interests in the royal family to include the Khedive Ismail's comings and goings. Titled "Congratulating the Former Khedive Upon His Arrival to Egypt,"[85] the poem emphasized that Egypt was experiencing luck and good fortune following the ascent of the khedive to power. To welcome him back from his trip, Taymur described Egypt as transforming itself into a badge of honor for its ruler. On this occasion, Taymur took the liberty of calling the khedive the "the dear one" (*al-Aziz*), a form of endearment that government writers and bureaucrats, like Shaykh Rif ' al-Tahtawi, her grandfather, and her father used in addressing the rulers of the Muhammad Ali dynasty. The intended effect in this case was to remind the khedive of the Taymurs' long history of loyal and intimate service of the dynasty. She ended the poem with another verse that reiterated her desire/plan to be a chronicler of the family and/or the khedive. She said:

> The letters I have lined were proud to be part of his praise
> providing shinning pearls to his crown,
> She presented herself to his highness as a historian/
> chronicler (*mu'arkhitan*) whose loyalty goes back to
> her grandfather's time.[86]

Taymur's next poem was also titled "Congratulating the Former Khedive" on his return from another trip.[87] Egypt was again represented as feeling happy for the return of its sympathetic ruler making itself pretty as a woman would for her man. The Nile provided evidence of the khedive's good fortune by controlling itself. Taymur included herself in this happy picture at the end of the poem:

> `Asamt` became fine and pretty upon his arrival. She used
>   her ink and pens to write verses that restore and
>   shimmer
> She employed her Arabic dictionary to chronicle and
>   writing in ink that rendered this moon like figure
>   transparent bringing him honor.[88]

One should note here that these two poems did not represent Taymur's best poetry, but what she was doing with them was very remarkable by the standard of the time. She used them to personalize her relation to the khedive, bringing herself to his attention with pretty verses that demonstrate her poetic skills, which could be put in his service beyond the early narrow gendered chronicling of social history of the ruling family. The only editing that Taymur did to these two poems after the deposition of Khedive Ismail was to refer to him as the former khedive.

Taymur had a more intimate social and political relation with Khedive Tewfik. Not only was her father a member of his entourage when he was crown prince, but Ahmed Taymur claimed that his father died while praying at his palace in 1872. Four of the five poems that she wrote about Khedive Tewfik showed an increased level of political engagement in dynastic political affairs during his reign. The titles she gave to these poems were designed to explicitly describe the active role she played in the turbulent politics of the period participating in activities that no other woman in her class had attempted before. The following were the titles of these poems in the order of their appearance: (1) "She said so that they could be written on Placards that were part of the decorations used to celebrate the arrival of the Khedive,"[89] (2) "She said when the khedive returned following the revolutionary Incident,"[90] (3) "She said so it could be written on the Placards used for the Decoration of the town of Benha al-`Asal where the Khedive will pass,"[91] and (4) "She said when Khedive Tewfik Assumed the Throne."[92]

What was intriguing about those titles was that she referred to herself in the third person as though to document how her poetry addressed itself to practical and broader political questions of the day. Following the khedive's return to Cairo after the military defeat of the `Urabi revolution, he clearly began to visit different parts of the country to rebuild his badly damaged authority, which suffered from his joining the international alliance that defeated the leaders of the revolution and their quest for national independence. The titles of poems number one and three indicated that they were part of the propaganda effort to cast the khedive in a new light. They were to be placed on placards in places that he visited so that they could be read by the attendees and as was the habit of this period those who were literate would read them to those who were not.

Given their very specific purpose, most were short (five lines long at the most) with a straightforward political message, which stressed the khedive's return and the promise of happiness and good things to come. The longest of these political poems and perhaps the best was titled "the return of the khedive to Egypt following the incident of the Revolution." It celebrated the victory of the khedive expressing the joy of his allies and attacking `Urabi and his supporters.

> Lightening filled the happy horizons with moons of joy
>   and happiness,
> He appeared to eyes watchful for a missing star with bril-
>   liance that filled the four corners of the world,
> His appearance in the horizon was a delight to the eyes of
>   those who were in positions of command with hope
>   of reconciliation,
> God is Great, our dear one has returned in a great celebra-
>   tion that decorated the East . . .
> Sovereignty is yours only to be disputed by those lacking a
>   brain or a God.[93]

Taymur sometimes played with the name of the Khedive Tewfik, which meant reconciliation. In this particular poem, reconciliation was not on her mind. It described a victory parade for those who supported the khedive, wished for the defeat of the revolution and the return of their power to command and dominate the majority. Because Tewfik's name stood for reconciliation or the resolution of conflict, Taymur also used it to outline one positive outcome of his return. The defeat of the revolution reconciled the interests of British occupation with that of very weakened and unpopular khedive. No such reconciliation occurred between the rulers that those that they ruled.

In this poem, Taymur did not seem to care if she contributed to the increased political/national polarization proceeding with the Islamic chant of victory, *Allah akbar* (God is great) in the celebration of the return of an unpopular khedive. While the return of his sovereignty was a hollowed one because it was marginalized by British occupation, this did not stop Taymur from describing those who had challenged his rule as brainless and Godless reinforcing the great divide between the rulers and the ruled.

There was only one other poem that took this vindictive tone of victory over the majority, the other political poems astutely turned to the more difficult political of rehabilitating the image of the khedive in the eyes of the general public. In them, she tried to focus the public's attention on some positive signs regarding the future. People all over the world celebrated the news of the khedive's return declaring it as the inauguration of a period of happiness and well-being for Egypt. He will uphold the highest standards of knowledge and science and enlighten the hearts of those who care. Most importantly, the khedive has returned with God's support and people who were guiltless in this affair need not worry about divine punishment of those who challenged a Muslim ruler's right to govern. Because Taymur could not describe the happiness of Egyptians at this turn of events, she used international satisfaction/happiness about the military outcome to claim that the whole world shared in the joyous occasion. What was left unsaid was that international happiness was motivated by self-interest, that is, the use of British occupation to ensure that the Egyptian economy was going to be primarily devoted to the repayment of its international debts. For the skeptics within the community, she added that the khedive's triumph over his enemies provided a measure of his divine support and he, like his dynastic predecessors, will continue his commitment to the modernizing project by upholding knowledge, science and enlightenment.

In one poem, Taymur played with the name of a town that the khedive visited, Benha al-ʿAsal's (where honey was produced) suggesting that rivers of honey will flow on that occasion. Tewfik's victory demonstrated the difference between darkness and light and happiness and failure with the world wearing its best clothes in celebration, the country (*al-qutr*) was overjoyed and the people of the nation (*qawum*) were certain that their hopes would be realized.[94] Taymur established an interesting distinction between the country and its people with the land and its goods, like honey feeling happy, but the people hoping for the best.

There were two other long political poems: one dealt with the ascension of Khedive Tewfik to power providing a date for when it was written (1878), and the second dealt with the joyous celebration of his return to Egypt after the ʿUrabi revolution, which effectively suggested 1882 as the date. Both poems had one thing in common, that is, they addressed themselves to important political events of the day reinforcing Taymur's view of herself as a genuine political historian of the ruling dynasty and using poetry as a venue for the discussion of the qualities of the good dynastic ruler and the challenges he faced.

The poem that discussed Tewfik's ascent to power began by offering Egypt good tidings after a period of wrongdoing, embarrassment and slow reform. This was the only criticism that Taymur ever voiced against Khedive Ismail and/ or the Muhammad Ali dynasty. She described the new Khedive as having the qualities of a good ruler: he was a man of faith; he will govern justly and support reform. The country (*al-qutr*) hopes to reach new heights under his reign because he was largely preoccupied with the happiness of Egypt and a commitment to good deeds. The people (*al-nas*) expect good things from him and see his rise to power as an opening to end their despair.[95]

As this close examination of Taymur's political poetry showed, she offered the reader more than the simple praise of Khedives Ismail and Tewfik discussing the national aspirations of Egypt, as a country, a people and a modernizing nation state.[96] It underlined the promise of these two rulers to contribute to the happiness of their people. In this vein, Taymur introduced the novel idea that Khedive Ismail was "dear to his people" and Khedive Tewfik "enjoyed the support of the aristocracy," which suggested some acceptance of the modern notion that stressed the importance of affective relations between the rulers and those they ruled. This indicated that the ideas of government and the relations between the rulers and the ruled were undergoing changes some of which Taymur was able to capture.

In many of these poems, Taymur invoked Egypt as a national community with a shared history represented by the Muhammad Ali dynasty, a bounded geographic entity (*qutr*) and a people (*nas* and *qawum*). The references to the Nile, Benha al-'Asal, the deposition of Khedive Ismail, the ascension of Khedive Tewfik to power and the latter's victory over 'Urabi revolution provided recognizable concrete geographic, local and political markers of the national community.

In adding poetry whose preoccupations were explicitly political to her repertoire, Taymur was breaking new grounds for upper-class women. While the political involvement of nineteenth century rural and urban working class women has recently gained attention,[97] the study of upper-class women's political engagement during this same period remains largely undeveloped. Judith Tucker's work on nineteenth century women documented working class women's active engagement in the economic, social, legal and political arenas. For the major political event of this period, there was ample evidence that rural and working class women actively supported the Egyptian army, led by General 'Urabi, as it fought international forces; there was also extensive evidence that upper-class women and women of the royal family played visible and prominent roles in supporting 'Urabi's national revolution. Based on his interaction with these women, A. M. Broadly, the British lawyer who defended Ahmed 'Urabi against charges of treason, made the following observation:

> In no part of the world do women contrive to exercise so much real power as in the East and there is probably no oriental country in which their influence is so potent a factor in State affairs as in Egypt. It was in the Egyptian harems that ['U]rabi found some of his most patriotic and powerful adherents. The National cause, even in its earlier stages, was warmly espoused by the great majority of Egyptian ladies and they continued to support it till hope was no longer possible. Princesses of the khedivial family (Tewfik's mother and wife always excepted) made no secret of their strong sympathy with 'Urabi.[98]

In support of these claims, Broadly cited a report by the official *Egyptian Gazette*, which mentioned how the mother of Khedive Ismail and his daughter princess Jamila Hanim gave their horses as a free gift to the Egyptian army following the bombardment of Alexandria. They formed associations that gave succor to the wounded at Kafr al-Dawar and provided medical supplies to them.[99] Princess Injah, the widow of Viceroy Said Pasha, sent a letter to Mr. Broadly that praised him for "defending the sons of Egypt."[100] Meanwhile, Princess Zeyneb Hanim, Muhammad Ali's daughter who was mentioned earlier as resisting attempts of her brother Abbas I to divorce her from her husband Yusuf Kamil Pasha eventually settling with him in Istanbul, used her money to support Prince Halim, her brother and the senior male member of the royal family, to become khedive as was the custom before Khedive Ismail changed the line of succession into his own children.[101] Both presented themselves as supporters of ʿUrabi's ideas and bribed others to act as intermediaries in the attempt to get the nationalist leaders to support Prince Halim's claim to the throne.[102]

What the above suggested was a complex set of motivations that included personal rivalries, political ambitions and support of national politics that influenced royal women's participation in the turbulent politics of this period. Muhammad Husayn Haykal also suggested that many of the princesses of the ruling family felt contempt toward Khedive Tewfik and his mother, Shafaq Nur, who was a concubine that Khedive Ismail chose not to marry.[103] This might explain why Khedive Ismail's mother and Tewfik's grandmother, Khushiyar Khanum Effendimiz, who had a more illustrious lineage as the sister of H. M. Partav-Nihal, the Valida Sultana of Sultan Abdul Aziz of Turkey, supported the nationalist rebellion in the hope that it would replace Tewfik with one of her other grandsons.

Princess Zaynab's support of her brother, Prince Halim, and his aspirations to replace Khedive Ismail reflected the personal and political ambitions of both and the continuing resentment felt by some members of the royal family toward Khedive Ismail, who changed the rule of succession, usurping the political right of the most senior member of the family. Princess Injah's support of Broadly's defense of the nationalists was more difficult to interpret. On the one hand, her praise could be interpreted as an attack on Khedive Ismail, who showed disrespect to his uncle/her husband by failing to give him a proper state funeral,[104] on the other, she expressed the same national views that Ahmed ʿUrabi reported hearing from her husband, Viceroy Said, regarding the importance of defending Egypt and Egyptians against international incursions. ʿUrabi, who enjoyed the most rapid professional advancement within the army during the reign of Said, reported that the viceroy gave him an Arabic copy of the History of Napoleon expressing his anger about the defeat of the Egyptians at the hands of the French.[105]

In an important impromptu speech, which ʿUrabi reported in his memoirs, Said expressed sentiments that ʿArabi and other Egyptian military service men considered to be a "hopeful" basis for a new "fraternal" national order:

Brothers, I have considered the conditions that the Egyptian people (*al-sha'b al-Misri*) have faced through history. I have found that they have been enslaved by many other nations and suffered at the hands of many unjust countries including the Bedouin Arabs, the Assyrians, the Persians, the peoples of Libya, the Sudan, the Greeks and the Romans before Islam. Then, they had to face the conquering Ummayds, the Abbasids, the Fatimids, Turks, Kurds, Circassians and ending with French occupation under Napoleon.

Because I consider myself to be *Egyptian*, I think it is my duty to raise and educate the children of this country so that they can serve their country well and replace the foreigners. I am determined to translate these ideas into action.[106]

According to `Urabi, Said (1854–63) introduced the earliest articulation of the idea of the fraternity or brotherhood of Egyptian men and the bonds that brought the rulers and ruled together across different classes and ethnicities as members of an "Egyptian people." Said also identified Egyptians from other invading ethnicities and emphasized independence as the central goal of a national agenda. `Urabi and other nationalists viewed khedives Ismail and Tewfik as having retreated from these ideas. Princess Injah, Said's wife, seemed to agree treating `Urabi as cordially as her husband had done giving him a tent that belonged to Said. She was also said to have advised Khedive Tewfik to cooperate with `Urabi for the benefit of Egypt.[107] Another princess who continued to express her support of `Urabi national agenda in the 1880s was princess Nazli Fazil, the daughter of Mustafa Fazil, crediting him with being "the first Egyptian minister to force the resident Europeans to respect Egyptian law and that this was [an issue] she tried to impress on Khedive Tewfik more than once."[108] In that quote, she was referring to the importance of the exercise of Egyptian political sovereignty over all its residents, which the capitulations (international treaties that allowed western governments to regulate the affairs of their nationals in the Ottoman Empire) and British occupation undermined. What this nationalized segment of royal women appreciated the most about `Urabi was his defense of the independence of Egyptian/royal government and his attempt to restrain international intervention. They faulted Tewfik for giving away the interests of the state in exchange for international support for his formal right to rule.

These personal and national divisions within the royal family came to a head following the defeat of the revolution with Khedive Tewfik's mother and wife ordering the princesses who supported the nationalists to `Abdin Palace where some were "loudly reprimanded" while others were threatened with execution. As Broadly saw it, Tewfik misunderstood the impact that British occupation had on his ability to govern. Not only did Tewfik's support of the major powers that occupied Egypt make him the "most unpopular man in all Egypt" but also, as Broadly predicted, he "[would] be written in history as . . . the prince who brought the English into Egypt."[109] As evidence of his limited capacity to rule, the khedive's desires to punish the disloyal members of his family and/or the leadership of the revolution were frustrated by the British occupation authorities demonstrating his weakened political position.

Taymur's derogatory description of 'Urabi and his companions firmly placed her on the side of the khedive and the minority political view within the royal family. Her participation in the state's attempt to rehabilitate his political standing and to sway the feelings of the Egyptian population in his favor showed, however, that her exultations at the defeat of the revolution was accompanied by an astute awareness that important political work needed to be done to overcome the divisions within the community. The elegant poetic slogans that she wrote to greet that part of the public that showed up to see the khedive in his reconciliatory tour of the country stressed the future rather than the past. In this activity, she took on tasks that were usually assigned to the political employees of the state and/or the few political writers working for the khedive. Even if this role made Taymur an informal employee of the state for a short period, as the small number of poems indicates, this was a very unusual development. Neither the small number of the poems nor the informality of her role diminished the novelty of this particular type of involvement in state functions. Other political poems provided a record of the way she viewed some of the most important political questions of the day. It also demonstrated her sustained interest in politics throughout the 1870s and the 1880s. Finally, the visibility of royal women in the politics of the period encouraged Taymur to delve more deeply in the analysis of the challenges facing Islamic dynastic governments or communities and women's proper involvement in their reform in her fictional work *Nata'ij al-Ahwal fi al-Aqwal wa al-Af'al*.

Taymur's political poetry and her defense of khedival power, even if for a short period of time, had its rewards. British occupation and the austerity it imposed on the Egyptian government and the court for the purpose of the repayment of the international debts made material rewards unlikely. Taymur's new visibility and association with khedival government gave the poet social and political respectability underlining the contribution that a new generation of the Taymur family made in the service of the Muhammad Ali dynasty. Most significantly, royal support might have lessened the viciousness of the attacks she had suffered at the hands of women of her class. The result was an improved state of mind and a sense of hopefulness that explained the end of her mourning and the ability to produce her first publication *Nata'ij al-Ahwal fi al-Aqwal wa al-Af'al* in 1887/88.

The Elegy as a Gendered Theme in
Nineteenth-Century Arabic Poetry[110]

In Zaynab Fawwaz's nineteenth-century biographical dictionary, *Al-Durr al-Manthur fi Tabaqat Rabat al-Khudur*, the elegies of al-Khansa,' especially those that were written for her brother Sakhr, were acknowledged as the best of their kind in the Arabic literary tradition.[111] This view of women as mistresses of grief and loss was socially reinforced by the fact that in nineteenth-century Egyptian society professional female mourners (*ma`didat*) offered their services for hire in exchange for helping families process their grief through the exploration of different aspects of loss. This reinforced the gendered assumption that women in general and women poets in particular excelled in this activity more than men. Fawwaz's biography of Taymur coupled a discussion of some of the reasons that made the poet's loss of her daughter such a terrible blow (Tawhida's youth and the important role she played in ensuring her mother's independence) with an emphasis on the special temperament of women poets as explanations of their ability to feel grief more deeply.[112] This social view narrowed the scope of legitimate poetic expression among women poets undermining their aspirations to become great poets who explored a wide range of emotions and themes.

Mayy Ziyada's discussion of the two main women poets of the nineteenth century, the Lebanese Warda al-Yazji and the Egyptian `A'isha Taymur, reflected the effects of this specific narrow historical and gendered view of women. She described al-Yazji as the elegiac poet par excellence producing elegies of family members, friends and public figures that constituted the bigger half of her diwan titled *Hadiqat al-Ward*.[113] In the discussion of Taymur's poetry, Ziyada also privileged her elegy of Tawhida as the most sincere among the poems she wrote about her family and as an example of the best of her poetry.[114] In her explanation of the effectiveness of this poem, Ziyada offered a modernist abstract discussion of mothering as a woman's central role that emphasized her relationship to nature and reproduction.

"Once a woman is born, all the conditions of her life are adjusted in preparation for this important reproductive role just as natural forces directed all rivers to the sea. A mother is always compared to nature, the greatest mother of all. All ancient religions treated femaleness as the symbol of Mother Nature and its wonderful reproductive function. The Egyptian deity, Isis, was first in a long series of goddesses that represented the impulse for the divine reproduction and the divine role of the mother who gave birth to all living things. All other mythologies followed suit in considering mothering to be the symbol of the power of a woman and a representation of her natural function and connection to life. Given this overwhelming emphasis on mothering, the death of an offspring that a woman has created represented a crisis of cosmic proportion whose effects symbolized a dramatic reversal of all known things that lead parents to expect their demise before their children."[115]

The above contextualization of Taymur's relationship to mothering as an explanation of her feelings of grief over the loss of her daughter was puzzling because Ziyada knew about the poet's ambivalence toward motherhood and domesticity whose burdens she sought to escape. The biographer ignored this by placing the modernist emphasis on mothering as the primary occupation of women at the center of Taymur's life. While Tawhida's death at the age of 18 provided a sufficient explanation of the terrible blow it represented, Ziyada's association between women, mothering and nature showed the extent to which she let her modernist persuasion or discourse overdetermine her construction of Taymur's life.

Finally, Ziyada's admiration of Taymur's elegy of her daughter drew additional strength from the astonishing parallels she saw between it and that of Lord Alfred Tennyson's "The May Queen."[116] Because Taymur did not know any English and Tennyson's poem was not translated into Arabic, Ziyada praised both poets for the superb emotional effect derived from having a deceased daughter address her mother regarding the rituals of death and mourning. Here, Ziyada's critical admiration of Taymur's poem was enhanced by the fact that it mirrored Tennyson's poem. This inserted English poetry as a new standard for appreciating Arabic poetry.

Abbas Mahmud al-`Aqqad offered another modernist explanation to why Taymur's elegy of her daughter was an example of her best poetry. The social definitions of femininity placed restrictions on women's free expression of their feelings making it impossible for them to emerge as great poets who explored a wide range of emotions. The exception to this universal social rule was the license given to women to express grief at the loss of loved ones.[117]

In the remaining part of this section, I want to examine the various elegies that Taymur included in her diwan as part of the critique of the limiting modernist construction of what Taymur's elegies were about. They took stock of the lives of the figures that they mourned who were not only relatives but also acquaintances who left an imprint on Taymur. Her elegies explored a wide range of emotions showing why al-`Aqqad's view of why women could not become great poets missed the mark and why Ziyada's emphasis on mothering as a primary role and emotion fell short of in the construction of the complex emotional world of women.

Taymur's elegy of Tawhida had been singled out by most literary critics as representing the most effective description of grief at the loss of a beloved young daughter. It began with a graphic description of her mother's raw emotional and physical reactions to this traumatic event, which distorted her perception of the surrounding world.

The outpouring of a sea of tears from one's eyes protested
    the injustice of fate and the betrayal of time.
Each eye had a right to shed bloody pearls and the heart to
    experience torment and ruin.
A radiant light has been covered, the morning sun has
    chosen to veil and the beautiful moon quickly set after
    rising.
The one I love has passed away leaving me drunk with pain
    and with a inextinguishable flame in my heart . . .
If my pain were to travel back in time, no one would pay
    any attention to the losses of Qays or Kuthayyir.[118]

According to Taymur if one were to judge lost love by the level of pain, then the pain felt by the best poets in the Arabic literary tradition would pale in the face of a mother's love and loss of a daughter. Not only did Taymur insert herself here into the Arabic literary tradition, but she sought to carve a unique place for herself in that tradition that has been largely focused on the pain that male poets felt from loss of the love of a woman or in the case of al-Khansa' the loss of her brother. Hers was a doubly unique contribution to the themes of love and loss in the Arabic poetic tradition.

Next, Taymur narrated the circumstances that surrounded the illness of her daughter. The symptoms appeared in the month of Ramadan, a festive time of the year, which acquired a special sadness as Tawhida wilted like a flower and illness became her garb. Instead of enjoying the delicious juices and the deserts typically served in fancy cups during that month, her sick daughter sampled death quickly.

In a touching dialogue between daughter and mother, Taymur explained why Tawhida was special and why her loss was extremely difficult to bear. First, the ailing Tawhida asked the doctor for a quick cure for the pain, not for her own sake, but to spare her stricken mother. In this, Tawhida typically put the needs of her mother ahead of her own. Second, in this exchange first with the doctor and then with her mother, Tawhida's own poetic eloquence and skill were made clear. According to Taymur, the youthful Tawhida easily learned poetic meter and proved more skilled at it than her mother. Third, because she died at the young age of 18, her responses to her eminent demise reflected both maturity and childishness: she courageously faced death but also expressed fear at being torn away from her mother. Fourth, Tawhida's death during the preparations for her wedding and on her wedding night[119] made the loss even more tragic.

O mother, I am sorry to leave you and tomorrow you will
    see my casket march like a bride.

It will stop at a tomb, which will be my home.
Tell the God of the tomb to be gentle with your daughter
    who came here as a young bride.
Be strong at my grave and linger there for a while to calm
    my frightened soul.
O mother, our early wish had come to a quick end and
    how lovely if it could have been easily realized.
It has become like a past dream in the face of this difficult
    day of truth.
Go back to your empty home and glorious exploits that
    will now unfold in my absence.
Preserve my bridal trousseau as a memento of a wedding
    and a wish for happiness.[120]

In the above, Tawhida made clear that mother and daughter shared each other's hopes and dreams. Tawhida enthusiastically supported her mother's wish to become a poet and a writer engaged in glorious deeds and Taymur took joy in her daughter's desire for happy matrimony. While Tawhida's death aborted her dream of being a happy bride, she encouraged her mother to singly pursue her literary goals for which both had toiled. In these verses, Tawhida emerged as much more than an instrument of her mother's literary ambitions. Her relationship with her mother was a symbiotic one in which their needs were intertwined, which contrasted with the instrumental view of outsiders, like Fawwaz and others, who were unable to fathom the complex dynamics involved in a relationship that combined mutual ambition, need, love and admiration. This elegy and the seven years that Taymur spent mourning her daughter's death cast doubt on the instrumental view and supported a layered understanding of the complex psychodynamics of this mother-daughter relationship.

The remaining part of the poem painfully described Taymur's reaction to this loss and her daughter's final wishes. Her tears imprisoned her logic expressing raw grief and regret. She pledged never to forget her and never to tire from reciting the Qur'an and praying for her daughter as long as the birds continued to sing on trees. She also promised never to forget the sadness she felt when they laid Tawhida in the ground and cry over her loss until they met again.

In what was to become a significant theme of her elegies, Taymur used her name, `A'isha, which literally meant living or the will to survive, to explore the effects of the different losses on her life. When people reminded Taymur that she survived (`a'isha) the terrible loss of her beloved daughter, she replied that her life and patience were effectively over as only God would know. Along with the ability to survive, which her name signified, came the weighty obligation to demonstrate to the world the enormity of the loss through her seven years of mourning.

In this ruined life, Taymur reassured Tawhida that her mother's heart, eyes, and tongue were satisfied with her and that through them she would secure her a place of peace in heaven. Both mother and daughter made several references to the religious powers that mothers were said to possess. The daughter hoped that her mother's forgiveness and/or the religious rituals observed by families to memorialize their dead would entitle her to God's mercy. In response, her mother reassured Tawhida that her sacrifices will not be forgotten and that she will always have her prayers and religious approval. Because a Hadith declared that heaven lay under the feet of mothers, both mother and daughter drew comfort from it in the face of death.

In the second and third elegiac poems, Taymur turned her attention to the loss of important men in her life: *al-`alama* Shaykh Ibrahim al-Saqqa and her father, Ismail Taymur Pasha in that order. It was significant that she placed the loss of Shayk al-Saqqa ahead of that of her own father. According to Ali Mubarak, Shaykh al-Saqqa was a prominent member of the ulema of al-Azhar teaching Arabic, fiqh and exegesis.[121] How did Taymur know him and what kind of a relationship did they have with one another? The poem offered hints of an answer from the personal note it offered at the beginning.

> Fate has substituted my comfort with hardship and
> replaced my blessings with misery.
> Time took on such an appearance that obliged the eyes to
> mix its tears with blood . . .
> His mirror had been obliterated and its face made rusty
> after it had enjoyed a long period of clarity.[122]

In suggesting that the loss of Shaykh al-Saqqa substituted her comfort with hardship and blessing with misery, Taymur told the reader that she knew the shaykh personally and that she experienced his loss deeply.. The reference to the mirror that had been obliterated and now made rusty also offered a direct link between him and Taymur's work on *Mir'at al-Ta'mul fi al-Umur*, which discussed the rights that men and women enjoyed in Islam. Al-Saqqa might have helped Taymur select and understand the Qur'anic verses that she then reinterpreted.

She moved on to declare that the ulema would be saddened with the loss of the depth of his knowledge, which were made available to others. Meanwhile, the ignorant will be happy to continue their nightly forms of gaiety, another theme that she tackled in *Mir'at al-Ta'mul fi al-Umur*. The shaykh was such a source of religious light that it was difficult to believe during his life that *imam* al-Shafi`i, the founder of one of the Sunni schools of law practiced in

Egypt, was truly dead. He had deep religious/legal knowledge that richly guided humanity and made him one of its eloquent interpreters. He made sure that religious rituals were performed at the time of despair giving condolences to people, guarding the heart against error and from going astray. She played with his last name al-Saqqa, which meant "to water," likening his contributions to science to the watering of a colorful and splendid garden. Finally, she suggested that those who felt pain, like her, would no longer find in him a source of dampening their tormented feelings.[123] This last comment suggested that the shaykh might have served the religious needs of the family providing religious counsel to its members and performing religious services in cases of death. Taymur suggested that he provided her with religious sources of comfort in dealing with the many family losses.

> Who is going to perform the tireless rituals of the upright
> religion in the wake of anxious loss?
>
> He watered the sciences with his abundant rain contribut-
> ing to the growth of a flourishing garden . . .
> His thoughts frequently healed heavy hearts that could be
> led astray . . .
> The suffering of many will no longer be quenched by the
> careful watering by al-Saqqa.[124]

In the above account, Taymur's description of the different roles played by the shaykh supported the claim made by Mayy Ziyada that elderly religious men were often asked to teach younger women language and religion in the sexually segregated nineteenth-century Egypt. It was also possible that the elderly al-Saqqa provided moral guidance to a mature Taymur, consoled her in the wake of different family losses and discussed with her the Qur'anic verses that dealt with the rights of women in Islam in Mir'at al-Ta'mul fi al-Umur. The personal tone used throughout the poem indicated that Taymur knew him well sharing with the reader personal information about the elderly man. He suffered from a variety of illnesses, but never complained or consulted any doctors. He performed his obligations as a member of the ulema by sharing his knowledge with others from whom he received posthumous acknowledgements.

Taymur's admiration of the way the shaykh lived his life led her to conclude that he not only deserved to occupy the highest ranks of his profession but was fit to be included in the religious rank of a martyr. After having established that his was a life that was well lived and for which he will be religiously compensated, she discussed how she will miss him.

> He is in a blessed place, but we suffer greatly because of the
> distance that separates us in times of hardship.
> My heart burned for him like smoldering embers and my
> grief betrayed my misery and torment.
> I will shed tears of sorrow for him in sorrow as long as I live
> (`a'isha*) in my annihilating seclusion![125]

This ending with its personalized expression of loss was very similar to the one used in the elegy of her father, which leads one to conclude that Taymur related to him as a father figure. The above expression of loss was less burdened, however, by the strong sense of duty and the need for approval that were found in the elegy of her father. So, while Taymur considered her father to be her favorite parent, her relationship with her father, like Shaykh al-Saqqa, was a less taxing one without the clear anxiety about whether or not she was meeting his expectations. In last verse, Taymur again played with her name, as she did in other elegies. Since Shaykh al-Saqqa was a man who was not related to her, she used his loss to criticize the stifling effects of her seclusion, which he had made more bearable. Through him, she was able to maintain a link to the public world that she longed to join. Given the fact that all the other important men in her life had passed away especially her father, she promised to shed tears over him as long as she continued to live in her deadening seclusion (*madumt `a'isha bi khadr fani*). This was the only explicit denunciation of seclusion that could be found in Taymur's writing and clearly indicated her ambivalence about the seclusion of upper-class women which she also associated with virtue.

Next, Taymur directed herself to eulogizing her father in a manner that was different from the way she handled the elegies of Tawhida and Shaykh al-Saqqa, which started on personal notes. Despite her affection for her father, theirs was a formal relationship. She began with a reference to his distinguished status

> It was difficult for the inhabitants of the Earth to see him
> go like a moon eclipsed in darkness.
> It was only right that the age should mourn the loss of its
> most brilliant example of eloquence among the most
> well spoken class.[126]

The death of Taymur's father was not only a personal loss but also a cosmic and a temporal one underlining his distinguished status as a brilliant man of letters whose eloquence and brilliance stood out among the educated classes. Taymur clearly admired this part of her father's persona and sought to emulate it.

While his health had been failing affecting both his speech and then his constitution, he expressed a strong desire to live. Taymur confirmed her brother's

account of how her father died away from home. This was how she described
the news of his death.

> Calamitous news announced his loss and he was returned
>   home without hope.
> The female inhabitants of his palaces grieved as their prince
>   lay in a bed of condolences.
> The wailers spent the night surrounding him instead of his
>   friends and companions.[127]

After he was returned to his home, the mourning rituals for this wealthy man
began by the many women (wives and/or concubines) who inhabited his different
palaces. As another measure of his wealth was the very large number of professional wailing women who surrounded his corpse offering a contrast to the many
male companions and guests who used to keep him company in his literary salon.
While his daughter was not among the wailing women, female observers noted
the grief in her eyes that betrayed her misery. Here, Taymur clearly adhered to the
upper-class code of mourning that allowed women to cry, but not to engage in the
lamentations that were reserved to the professional wailing women. Taymur added
to this particular code her use of poetry to publicly articulate her feelings toward
this cherished parent. She mixed the use of the third person in outlining his formal
relationship to his children with a more personal articulation of her feeling toward
him. The former expressed the distance he maintained with his children and the
latter indicated the special relationship between father and daughter.

> She said: by the oath of fatherhood, you provided the light
>   of security to your children.
> Ever since I lost you, my gut has been on fire and my body
>   has been enveloped in pain.
> You were the treasure of my hopes, the richness of my needs,
>   my good fortune and the brilliance that filled my eyes.
> You soothed my pain, healed my sores, nourished my soil
>   and were the river of my songs.[128]

According to Taymur, fatherhood was identified with being a good provider to
one's children, a theme she also articulated in *Mir'at al-Tamul fi al-'Umur*. In
addition to providing for his children, Taymur proceeded to describe why he
was a good parent: he supported her hopes for herself, the rich satisfaction of
her other needs, her good times, the soothing of her pain, the sustenance of her
soul and rivers of songs/poems. She also added that when she felt not up to the

task, she turned to him for help. In exchange, she considered his approval to be a prized accomplishment..

> Your approval was the single most important accomplishment of my role as a daughter.
> If I felt impatient to whom shall I complain and after losing you whom shall I turn to for acceptance.
> Would that I knew when you passed on, did I have your approval or disapproval![129]

In exchange for his support of her wish to learn how to read and write, Taymur spent her life seeking his approval and good opinion. Following his death, she reported feeling haunted by whether or not he was satisfied with her or if she had disappointed him! While she considered him to have been a good parent, this was clearly a taxing relationship in which she was constantly mindful of his feelings and his opinions. She felt indebted to him and so she prayed that his soul be blessed. She was confident, however, of his immortality because she also counted him among the martyrs presumably because he died serving crown prince Tawfiq. She ended this elegy, by stating that her life without him will be tormented for as long as she lived (`a'isha`).

Taymur's elegy of her mother offered a marked contrast to that of her father as well as a different model of mother-daughter relationship than the one she described in her mourning of Tawhida. The defining event that shaped Taymur's relationship with her mother was the struggle between them over whether embroidery and needlework were more appropriate than reading and writing as the basis of the proper education for a young aristocratic girl. Mother and daughter represented two different ideals of femininity. While the former emphasized the importance of embroidery and needlework as some of the valued feminine skills that some slave women brought to their master's family, the latter sought to learn a different set of skills (i.e., to learn how to read and write). Beauty was another feminine quality associated with this old definition of femininity and one that Taymur clearly identified with her mother.

> O tomb, you must be delighted with the bright/shinning pearl that you have acquired.
> She was betrayed by destiny and had to reluctantly drink from the cups of illness that left her thin and skinny.
> She tasted bitter illness since childhood living her days in pain.
> She finally bled to death breaking one's heart with sorrow and pain.[130]

While most accounts of Taymur's life were silent on the history and life of her Circassian slave mother, the above verses volunteered some important information about this mother in contrasting bold strokes. The mother's external beauty, which was compared to a shinning pearl, hid a betrayal by fate reflected in an underprivileged background marked by a long history of illness without access to treatment. Her skinny constitution offered another piece of evidence of this impoverished childhood. Connected to this background was the experience of being sold and resold into slavery, to which Taymur made an indirect reference. Everyone who discussed her mother's slave status as a concubine of Ismail Taymur, who bore him three daughters, assumed that she had a privileged life. Taymur suggested that whatever privilege she had was too late to address the effects of early deprivation. Her mother's illnesses proliferated and got worse. Equally significant were the other unexplored wounds.

> How many nights did she stay up with the stars moaning
>   about what she held inside?
> When God's order commanded her into the tomb, the
>   order could not be reversed.
> O God, provide her with paradise as a refuge and a home
>   where she can be happy and experience joy.[131]

On the surface, her mother's sleepless nights could be attributed to her physical ailments, but Taymur also hinted that her moaning articulated other types of pain locked inside her. Like other slaves, she was taken away from her birth family, sold into slavery and had to hide her pain/illness that would have devalued her worth as the property of wealthy men. Because of the beauty of some of these women and the fact that they sometimes became concubines of wealthy masters, there was a discursive tendency to dwell only on their access to wealth and comfort and to maintain silence on the painful effects of the overall slave experience on them.[132] Taymur gently divested her readers of these romantic illusions, describing how the poor, underprivileged background of her mother led to ill health, which most probably led to her being sold many times over, highlighting a life of insecurity and the intense desire for a home.

When death came, her daughter's prayer summarized what she felt was most important to her mother: a paradise that would serve as a refuge and a home where she could be happy. The emphasis put on refuge and home as sources of happiness suggested that her slave mother might have moved from one place to another and that she was not always happy in them. While Taymur described the loss of her mother as a cause of sadness for the family provoking a stream of tears and allowing fortune to continue its torment of Taymur with more grief and loss. It was important to note, however, that this poem dealt less with

Taymur's feelings for her mother and more with the details of her mother's physical and other types of pain. Despite Taymur's sympathetic description of her mother's pain and exilic experiences, the elegy of her mother lacked the depth of feelings found in Tawhida's. The most touching verses in this poem were those in which Taymur prayed for her mother to find a final resting place/a home in paradise where she could finally be happy. The poem spoke of this loss in a very impersonal way counting it as one of many that Taymur had to face.

Finally, Taymur turned her elegiac skills to describing the emotional effects of the loss of a younger sister. Like their mother, this sister was described as a precious pearl/beautiful girl. When she died she was not old enough to put henna on her hands. In fact, she was born, and then her life was quickly snuffed by time. Fortune assassinated her in their secluded headquarter as a lion would drag a young victim into his den. Taymur used the same device she employed in Tawhida's elegy allowing her sister to speak for herself. She felt frightened when the doctor declared that his efforts had failed. She also could not understand why she was to die before any of her peers declaring herself cheated by time and defeated by her enemies and those who envied her.

In response to this early loss, Taymur suffered from severe anxiety regarding her own mortality sometimes leaving her bed ridden. She mourned her beloved sister without being able to understand the reasons for this early separation from her. She longed to hug that sister whose body now belonged to the grave, which claimed such a pearl of a sister who outdid her peers. "O my beloved how can I be reconciled with this break with a youthful sibling. This life (*'ayshati*) half lived is something I would not wish on strangers or lonely people."[133]

This early loss and trauma clearly left its imprint on Taymur as a child. It was difficult not only to understand but also to overcome. It denied her a sense of security and contributed to loneliness at an early age.

In the elegies of these female figures, Taymur provided the readers with vignettes of women of her family and the way they shaped her emotional world. Dependence and conflict provided insights into the psychodramas of these family relationships and how they affected Taymur's personal development. In contrast, men appeared to provide a link between the emotional needs and the broader literary interests and ambitions.

Opthalmia and Radical Rebellion

Taymur's struggle with eye disease occurred late in life following the loss of Tawhida. As a result, its discussion appeared late in her collected poems. According to Lamia Tewfik, this personal struggle pushed her to connect many forms of injustice constituting a bigger challenge of the existing social norms. So, even though it appears later rather than earlier, it competed in importance with the themes and struggles that opened the collection. One should also point out that many literary writings produced in the first half of the nineteenth century used the strategy of "saving the best for last" as an effective way of sustaining the attention of their readers.[134] So, while most of the dominant narratives of Taymur's life highlighted the importance of her childhood rebellion against the social rules dictated by femininity, the poetry that focused on Taymur's struggle with opthalmia during her seven years of mourning her daughter brought into sharp focus the equally important mature themes of loss and fight against an increasingly claustrophobic existence. In support of this interpretation, the first poem to document the onset of the disease was strategically placed between her elegies of her father and mother reinforcing the significance of the event and the theme of continuing adult struggles. Taymur used the poem to offer the following metaphoric commentary on the disease:

> If mortals suffer from eye disease, I only complain from
>   pain in my eyelids,
> It left me feeling worn out like a grief-stricken lover
>   reduced to calling on those who were estranged from
>   me,
> The disease left me unable to cry and without the patience
>   to eliminate my sorrow." [135]

The distinction between diseased eyes and pain in one's eyelids was an interesting one. It was directed at those who claimed that it was punishment for Taymur's not seeing clearly which should come first: literary study/writing or mothering. This led her to begin this poem by rejecting the claim that she lacked vision or judgment. Unlike many mortals, her vision was unimpaired, but she was afflicted with eye disease connected to her grief. The disease and the attacks by her critics left her feeling worn out (the verb *dhana*) compounding the grief she felt for the loss of her offspring (the noun *dhana*, which in colloquial Egyptian referred to one's child). The disease led her to turn to those from whom she was estranged, left her unable to cry and without the necessary energy to process her sorrow. The ordeal reinforced her low opinion of doctors, whose falsity, shortened peoples' long lives! She considered the despair and exhausted capabilities of these men of science a source of renewed confidence in He who was capable of curing her as long as she lived (`a'isha).

The next two poems celebrated a temporary healing of her eyes and a sense of power and confidence in her body and mind. Taymur described the passage from darkness to light as an emotional journey from despair, fear and anxiety to independence after long months of having to depend on villains and rogues. This period in the cave of isolation was unbearable and felt like being with a rival second wife (*dhora*) who resented her well being harming her in the worst possible way. In these references, Taymur was very explicit about lacking support and sympathy within her immediate family characterizing the people she had to depend on as intent on harming her. In the poem titled "A Call for Help," which signaled the return of opthalmia, she provided more evidence of her feelings of estrangement from family including her young brother:

> From the grayness of my locks, I ponder about what would
>   happen if I were to depart tomorrow,
> There will be a huge crowd, in which a brother, an uncle or
>   friend shovel dirt,
> Upon their return [from the grave site], they will behave
>   like they have never known me even though they were
>   my relatives, children and kinfolk,
> The children would busy themselves dividing the money
>   about which I was too busy to care.[136]

If she were to pass away, her family would not grieve for her loss paying more attention to what she left behind specifically money. In another poem, she expressed regret at not having left any literary production. Taymur's sense of hopelessness was exacerbated by the realization of how the loss of her sight would deal a serious blow to her legacy as a writer. She had hoped that education would open new literate doors for her instead opthalmia forced her return to the oral tradition that provided a creative outlet to the uneducated women of her family who had to content themselves with oral history and storytelling. The loss of her sight must have also reminded her of her teacher, the blind Fatima al-Azhariya, who specialized in the study of grammar as one of the limited options open to handicapped women. Even though reciting the Qur'an soothed her heart and soul, Taymur declared that she missed her books, which she lovingly touched. She mourned the loss of the happiness she derived from enjoying the beauties of reading and more significantly, the waste of the literary capital she had accumulated over the years without the prospect of earning much return.[137]

In a third poem that discussed her opthalmia, Taymur declared that her goals in life had become forbidden to her denying her what she most desired and wanted. Her books lay closed, sheets of paper remained blank, her ink was dry and her pens were split. She described these instruments of writing as reciprocating her feelings of loss: the books felt sad about her inability to read them, the blank paper mourned her absence, the ink container cried and the pens missed her touch. As a result, she was transformed against her will into an illiterate (*'omayen*) using knowledge in old familiar ways and owing a huge debt (*dayn*) to literature and religion. Taymur viewed herself as a particular type of an illiterate woman: she had access to religious and nonreligious knowledge, which made her a better person, but her education was wasted. As far as she was concerned, women who were privileged enough to have an education had an obligation to contribute to knowledge and to society.

Lami'a Tewfik argued that what she called the "poetry of opthalmia" provided the richest examples of the radicalization of Taymur's views, examples of resistance and deviation from the accepted general discourse. Whereas a younger Taymur accepted both her seclusion and its isolation, she strongly rebelled against the "prison" and "internment" imposed on her by the disease, which aggravated the restrictions imposed by seclusion. She rejected the feelings of captivity and being shut out, which she did not previously question in her celebration of Islamic femininity. Tewfik also pointed out that Taymur's attack on doctors in these poems became an outlet for an attack on men, their roles, authority and arrogance. Equally important, Taymur increasingly described writing as a central aspect of her life and existence abandoning her early claims that her interests in writing were a means of entertaining herself.[138]

These poems appeared at the end of her diwan because they had chronologically occurred late in Taymur's life. They clearly impacted on her identification with existing forms of power, which she had served and respected from childhood to adulthood. While Ziyada claimed that there was no way of identifying the historical evolution of Taymur's poetic personality, I think the struggle with ophthalmia provides us with such a marker: with the tension between the acceptance of power relations and rebellion against them as an ongoing theme in her life and work. As painful as this struggle was, Taymur emerged out of it more confident and assertive writer. It explained why she was fearless in taking on sensitive political issues like the challenges facing dynastic government and her novel interpretation of Qur'anic verses offering expansive definition of the rights that women had in the family.

Taymur characterized the healing of her eyes as a second birth. Her cloudless eyes provided a mirror to the world: seeing herself, seeing others and how they see her. In the Qur'anic story of Youssef, the eyes not only were the mirrors of beauty in a handsome face but equipped one with the ability to deal with a hostile world providing vindication for Youssef and Taymur against any charges of misdeeds.[139] It also confirmed her belief in her ability to survive, a prominent theme in the diwan that drew strength from her name, `A'isha, literally living coupled with the desire to determine how she wanted to live.

CHAPTER 6

The Finest of Her Class
Taymur on Literature, Gender, and Nation-Building

What this study of the life, literary works, and contemporaries of `A'isha Taymur has done is to shed some light on (1) the way literature played a leading role in the invention of the nation through language, fiction, and poetry and (2) how the emerging national community, in turn, provided a context that influenced the themes and approaches that literary writers developed in their works. Contrary to the dominant modernist approach, which categorized the literary works produced in the nineteenth century as either traditional or modern in a linear narrative that searched for an abrupt formal and thematic break that signaled the successful modernization of the nation and its literary forms of expression, Taymur's works combined elements of continuity and change reflected in the development of hybrid writing styles and literary forms coupled with introduction of novel perspectives couched in deceptively familiar social-political themes. As such, they allow us to recover a neglected part of the intellectual history of the 1880s and the 1890s that tested the ability of Islamic forms and themes to respond to change and contribute to the substantive debates on the problems facing nineteenth-century Egyptian society including the crises of dynastic government and the family. Taymur's works supported the development of a synthetic reform agenda whose goal was to put modernity into the service of Islamic society and its distinct forms of expression. This social and political project was neither *salafi*—that is, intent on the defense or the preservation of old Islamic traditions against the modernist innovations—nor modernist seeking to subordinate Islam and its social and political institutions to the development of modern society. It represented a third route to change, which explored the internal transformation or reform of the political, economic, and social institutions of Islamic society before years of colonial modernization effectively foreclosed that alternative.

The representatives of both of these different social and political projects met in their acceptance of the development of the nation as a fraternity, that was less determined by kinship, whose distinguishing characteristic was its contribution of a system of representation that gave men power over women through the privileging of the perspectives and views of men as a group in the civil arenas. As a result, men emerged as the major theorists and producers of modern and Islamic national discourses, which entitled them to the resources of the community. The "maleness of the nation," a phenomenon that has generally not been well theorized,[1] is explored in this study through Taymur's discussion of the modern definitions of masculinity that undermined older Islamic ones, redefined relations between rulers and ruled, contributed new competitive relations among men of different classes and dominated public debates on women. The development of modern national communities included a redefinition of the relations that men had with each other as economic and political actors and the reorganization of their relations with women. The debate that discussed the changing relations between men and women in the new communities affected men on two levels: First, it forced men to respond to external pressure by engaging in the discussion of the role that women played in Islamic society and how it compared with the role they were to play in the modern one. Second, it served to cement fraternal bonds among the male participants by underlining the new rights that they were to acquire as a civil group over the discussion of the lives of women to whom they were not related. In older patriarchal societies, kinship defined the power that each man had over women in the family, but not over women outside the family as a group. The nation as a horizontal fraternity relied very heavily on the discursive power that men as a group had over women as a group.

As a representative of an older generation of educated women, Taymur was keenly aware of these changes and how they were affecting the definition of women's membership in the nation. Modern definitions of masculinity contributed notions of male privilege that were not bound by responsibility for women and/or family. In response, Taymur suggested that women should in their caretaking capacities influence the learning of the definition of masculinity in the family. She also discussed how the development of fraternal relations among men could be used in support of less-hierarchal forms of good Islamic government that built bridges between rulers and their subjects eventually spilling into the gender arena to contribute to more egalitarian relations between men and women. In *Nata'ij al-Ahwal,* she seemed to accept that fraternal character of the nation, suggesting that women find ways to support and/or serve their gender interests from within.

In *Mir'at al-Ta'mul fi al-Umur*, Taymur contested the monopoly that men had over public debate by writing oppositional histories or discourses of the nation that represented the standpoint of women. Using gender as a marker of community during the last decade of the nineteenth century, she reviewed the dramatic changes taking place in the family, diagnosing the problem, offering a novel interpretation of the rights that men and women had in the family, and suggesting solutions. Over and above the content of the work and the responses that it triggered, it underlined the fact that for the first time during that century a woman initiated a public discussion about gender roles and rights emerging as an independent agent of women who were not simply its discursive object. As a result, it was possible to break with the old definition of nineteenth-century Egyptian women's history that was hostage to prescriptive views of the grand old men of Egyptian modernity: Shaykh Rifa`al-Tahtawi and judge Qasim Amin on women's education as a means of serving the interests of the family or men. In contrast to the discourse of the women's journals that largely focused on modern and scientific domesticity, Taymur's work offered a qualitatively broad construction of women's perspectives and interests that touched on all the changes taking place in the community's politics, economy, religion, and the family defining the interests of women in ways that went beyond the narrow domestic concerns. Taymur herself participated in the politics of the period using her poetry to prop up the authority of an unpopular khedive.

Taymur's male contemporaries generally praised her contribution to national debates as a sign of the nation's progress; very few engaged her broad views on politics or society in the discussions of the major issues of the day. When she broke new grounds in the gender arena with her *ijtihad* (interpretation) regarding the conditional character of male leadership (*qwamma*) in the family and tolerating the reversal of gender roles of men and women at a time of crisis, there was a united male effort to stop her. The owner of *al-Nil* newspaper recruited Shaykh Abdallah al-Fayumi to criticize her religious interpretations and views, which were published in a serialized form. Even Abdallah al-Nadeem, who praised her work, tried to contain the novel effects of her religious views by producing vignettes that questioned women's rights to claim their religion, which Taymur exercised, in expanding their social rights and liberties.

Taymur's adult personal experience offered other examples of disciplinary encounters with the young representatives of the new fraternal order in her family where she faced the wrath of her sons joined by at least one of her daughters, who disapproved of her ambitions and sought to punish her for them. Her doctors wittingly or unwittingly colluded in that effort by most probably diagnosing her as suffering from hysteria in the wake of the death of Tawhida. Finally, her brother showed his ambivalence to her growing reputation, which threatened to overshadow his own as well as those of his sons, as a representative of a new generation of Taymur men.

Within this fraternal order, Taymur's *Hilyat al-Tiraz* chronicled the hostility that her new interests provoked among women of her class and family. She described a virulent campaign by other upper-class women, who supported and/or benefited from the status quo, to discredit her by charging her of being responsible for the death of Tawhida, neglecting the needs of her family, and using her poetry to have illicit relations with men. Taymur's complex relations with other women during this period would not be complete without an appreciation of her efforts to develop alliances with her contemporaries, who were active in pushing the interests of women and/or writers and creating a space for their voices in the public arena. This solidarity with other women of her time, who were attempting to expand the definition of women's interests, could be traced back to the 1870s. Princess Qadriya Husayn, the daughter of Sultan Husayn Kamel who ruled Egypt from 1914 to 1917, wrote an introduction to the volume published by Taymur's family to celebrate her work that described the close relations between her grandmother and her mother both of whom Taymur visited frequently.[2] An exploration of the genealogy of the Muhammad Ali dynasty revealed that Husayn's grandmother was none other than Jesham Effet Kadin Effendi, who married Khedive Ismail in 1863.[3] Her additional claim to fame was that she used her own money to open the first general public school for girls at al-Suyufiya in 1873.[4] The genealogy of the dynasty revealed that Jesham Effet had no children of her own, which might explain her interest in the education of young girls. She eventually adopted the Circassian daughter of Admiral Hasan Turhan Pasha, Malika Hanim, during the 1870s,[5] who was Qadriya Husayn's mother. While they lost touch with each other following the exile of Khedive Ismail, when Malika Hanim became the second wife of Prince Husayn Kamel in 1887 returning to Egypt with him, she resumed her acquaintance and a relationship with Taymur.

There was no doubt that the relationship between Jesham Effet Kadin and Taymur was shaped by their mutual interest in women's education and/or poetry that reflected the changing interests and concerns of some royal and upper-class women beyond mothering and feminine crafts. The same was true of Taymur's relationship with Malika Hanum, explaining how Taymur brought some of her poetry to share with the princess during her visits to her palace in Giza.[6] As was made clear in *Hilyat al-Tiraz*, Taymur tried to share the joy of poetry with friends and family, encouraging her children to take an interest in it. Poetry served here as a unique and unusual gift to offer the members of the royal family, who have everything. In this case, it might have been designed to stimulate the princesses to take an interest in literary writing. It was safe to assume that the poetry Taymur shared with members of the royal family was written in Turkish, which was their preferred language. Sultan Husayn Kamel told Ahmed Taymur that his daughter, Qadriya, found inspiration in Taymur's Turkish diwan, *Shekufeh*. In fact, princess Qadriya Husayn eventually emerged as a Turkish writer, whose book on *Shahirat al-Nisa' fi al-'Alam al-Islami* (*Famous Women in the Islamic World*) was translated into Arabic and published in two parts in 1922 and 1924.[7]

Taymur also sent a complimentary acknowledgment of the publication of Warda al-Yazji's *Hadiqat al-Ward* (The Flower Garden)[8] and poems celebrating, Hind Noufal's, *al-Fatat*, the first women's journal published in Egypt in 1892,[9] and Zaynab Fawwaz's biographical dictionary of women, *al-Durr al-Manthur fi Tabaqat Rabat al-Khudur* published in 1894.[10] Taymur also shared material about her life and work with Fawwaz to be included it in her dictionary, making her Taymur's first biographer.

It was important to note here that published books and journals in the nineteenth century either began or ended by the listing of those who endorsed them among the literati of the period. This was a very effective device designed to persuade the reader that the book he or she is about to purchase is worthwhile. For women writers, this represented a particular problem because seclusion and sexual segregation limited their contact with male writers who constituted the literary circles of this period. While it was important to include as many endorsements as one could, Taymur's reputation as a published writer of fiction, social commentary, and poetry made her endorsement of other women writers very important. Judging from her endorsements of the work of some of the women contemporaries, she was extremely generous in effectively putting her reputation in the service of untested young women like Hind Noufal and Zaynab Fawwaz. These endorsements of the women writers of her time added, in turn, to Taymur's authority and standing. At the same time, Fawwaz and Noufal reciprocated by introducing her work to new generations of readers. In either case, the support that these women writers gave one another in the early 1890s reassured the hesitant male readers that women writers were not a novelty but had proven their metal as literary writers and were clearly part of the literary scene.

The resulting small sisterhood of women allowed the few women writers and/or those interested in women's education to contribute to the development of new forms of social solidarity among women. It served as an effective means of resisting their intellectual isolation and marginalization in the fraternal public arena. Their works provided the basis for the development of alternative constructions of the community in which women writers were visible and engaged public debate challenging the dominant fraternal construction, which represented women as silent or passive bystanders waiting for men to liberate them and/or solicit their participation in the affairs of the community. In arguing for the existence of a small sisterhood of women in the early 1890s, it would be a mistake to ignore the differences that existed among these women who belonged to different generations, nationalities, ethnicities, religions, social classes, and discourses. Taymur's relations of solidarity with women of the working classes, especially freed slaves and domestic workers, were more difficult. Even though Taymur attempted in *Mir'at al-Taʾmul fi al-Umur* to speak for women of all classes who suffered at the hands of their greedy and materialistic husbands, her relations with slave and working-class women were complicated. As the daughter of a white freed slave who chose to stay at her master's house instead of exercising her freedom, Taymur did not understand the decision of other freed slave women to choose freedom. She saw freedom in a negative light because it thrusts them into an unsafe environment that would compromise their virtue. Their decisions to leave the service of their masters disturbed the stability of the harem women, forcing them to rely on working-class women whose social values and freedoms she did not respect.

Unlike the construction of the national fraternity that was reinforced by political, social, and legal structures that prevented its fragmentation, a parallel sisterhood of women that did not have access to the same resources could not hope to maintain itself for long. There were important discursive differences that existed among different classes of women about the meaning of freedom and its relationship to modesty and virtue. This explained whey solidarity among women, informed by some sort of general romantic notion of gender interests, did not develop to challenge an equally general horizontal fraternity of men.

Two of Taymur's most daring contributions to nineteenth-century public debates remained, however, which included (1) the call for the nationalization of dynastic government through a redefinition of its relationship to the ruled, the aristocracy, and the middle classes and (2) the opening of religious interpretation of gender rights to educated women. They created new spaces for different groups, voices, and discourses. For these contributions, she earned the right to be described as the finest of her class, which was the title that she chose for her Arabic poems. She deserves this title not only for her literary, intellectual, and political contributions to the debates of her time but also for her ability to survive potentially crippling personal struggles. Unlike the sense of entitlement associated with members of her class, Taymur's gender worked against her development of this sensibility. This led her to work hard for all her achievements overcoming the opposition of her family, class, and some sections of the literary establishment.

In her work, one can see how she transferred the diligence she developed as a little girl: trying to please her father to thinking about the nationalization of the concerns of her aristocratic class to serve the interests of legitimate

Islamic dynastic government and the developing national community. While this included the right of Khedive Tewfik to govern, which was a very unpopular stance in the 1880s, she paid more attention to the fact that he needed to reclaim that important role if he was to serve as the representative of the political community. Key figures of the Egyptian nationalist movement eventually embraced that view of the khedive following his death and the ascent of his son Abbas II to power in 1892. From then on, the defense of the khedive's right to govern in opposition to Lord Cromer, the British high commissioner who was the architect of the colonial system in Egypt and the effective ruler of the country from 1882 to 1908, emerged as a central tenet of this phase of anticolonial nationalism. Abdallah al-Nadeem, the popular and older nationalist figure and Mustafa Kamil, the younger nationalist leader of the 1890s, shared this view reflected in their explicit support of the young Abbas, thus nationalizing the Muhammad Ali dynasty and its governments. These national contributions as well as the prominent position she earned in the feminist canon provided other reasons that justified the status of being the finest of her class. Curiously, far from being vain, Taymur remained very aware of the obstacles that she and/ or her work faced in creating a legitimate space for women in the fraternal narratives and structures of her society. Equally important, she never forgot the sacrifices that she and her daughter Tawhida, as representatives of different generations of women, made.

There was very little that was known about the final years of Taymur's life. Vague statements by her grandson, brother, and one of her nephews leave one unclear about her physical and mental health in the last eight years of her life. Her grandson stated that "during the last 4 years of her life she suffered from a disease that affected her mind preventing her from continuing her literary writings."[11] Ahmed Taymur supported this characterization of her last years stating, "She died after a long illness in June 1902."[12]

In a short piece published in Hoda Sha'rawi's Arabic magazine, al-Misriya, published in 1937, Taymur's nephew, Mahmud Taymur, who became a prominent writer in his own right, provided more information about what Taymur was like during her last years.

> The house of my aunt, `A'isha the poet, was across from ours at Darb Sa'ada. I remember how they would usher us into her private room where she spent the years of her old age. She would celebrate our visit and engulf us with her kindness and affection. I remember her sitting in her big chair looking very dignified and resembling Queen Victoria on her throne! Did they really resemble each other or is it my imagination that makes me represent her in this way?
>
> What cannot be disputed was that my aunt had by then become very fat and that she seldom left her chair. She surrounded herself with a group of cats, most

of whom were very old: each seated on a pillow with an individual plate in front of them for food. These animals frightened us because they were very old and did not tolerate children or their play.[13]

Even though Taymur's nephew suggested that his aunt spent her final years in her private room, he described her as taking pleasure in their visits and being very kind and affectionate toward her nephews. So whatever the nature of the illness to which her grandson alluded, it did not stop her from recognizing her visitors and welcoming them while maintaining an air of dignity. Because Taymur was the aunt whose poetry his father commanded him to "recite," it was understandable that her nephew compared her to Queen Victoria sitting on her throne. While the large size or weight of the two women as well as their frumpy look clearly led him to associate them with each other, Mahmud Taymur did not think that his aunt's size diminished her dignity. Because Mahmud wondered what role his imagination played in comparing his aunt to Queen Victoria, one could not discount other similarities that led him to make this comparison. There was the fact that like his aunt who mourned her daughter for seven years, Queen Victoria mourned her husband for more than ten years. Critics of both women, reflecting the biases of this period, accused both of being excessively emotional for engaging in such prolonged mourning and for being selfish in indulging their feelings at the expense of the needs of their children.

Finally, the cats that Taymur kept for company added an interesting note to her nephew's anecdote. Taymur clearly kept cats as pets during different periods of her life comparing her anxiety in writing *Mir'at al-Tamul fi al-Umur* to that of a frightened cat seeking to hide in a secluded household to avoid the thunderous weather outside. This observation coupled with the fact that the cats that her nephew saw in her room were old indicated she had them for a while. Taymur pampered these companions of her old age giving each its own pillow and individual plates. This seemed strange to the children whose impressions of these old cats were affected by the fact that they frightened them and that they did not really care for their childish games.

Still, the image of an old Taymur keeping the company of a brood of old cats was strange. Were they as one reading of her nephew's anecdote hinted a metaphor for Taymur in her declining years as an old, fat, and eccentric woman or did they stand for something less obvious about her life and the way she chose to live it? These old and scary cats seemed less domesticated and closer to the breed of cats that were revered by the ancient Egyptians. The "great cat" mentioned in the book of the dead was modeled on cats that lived in the wild at the boundary between the desert and the settled communities.[14] The cat goddess was not ferocious but some of its statues represented the animal in many other shapes and forms including the body of a woman and the head of a pretty cat and a queen cat who sits erect and dignified on a throne.[15]

Like the cat goddess, Taymur was undomesticated and independent, choosing to live at the boundary between the rules of her social class that required marriage and children and the freedom of her literary imagination. Even though Taymur never explicitly identified herself as an Egyptian, in surrounding herself with these old fierce cats whose worship existed in the province of al-Sharqiya where her family at some point had land suggested that she identified with the ancient history of place and/or country. The juxtaposition of these fierce cats that seemed less domesticated, refusing to tolerate children and their play, with the image of a warm aunt Taymur who dotted on her young nephews offered one final image in which Taymur tried one last time to integrate the two aspects of her life, which her contemporaries and critics felt were in permanent tension with each other.

Notes

Foreword

1. *Shekufeh* is the title of Taymur's Turkish poetry which was published in the Ottoman capital, but I could not find any bibliographic information regarding this book.

Introduction

1. Beth Baron mentioned `A'isha Taymur on pages 24 and 51 as an example of the spread of education among upper class women and her emergence as a poet who wrote in Arabic, Persian and Turkish. See Beth Baron, *The Women's Awakening in Egypt* (New Haven, CT: Yale University Press, 1994).

2. Booth's book provided examples that reviewed the various ways `A'isha Taymur's biography and work were used by different authors. Booth used Mayy Ziyada's biography of Taymur to show that biographies continued to be popular into the 1920s (xvi). Zaynab Fawwaz mentioned Taymur in support of her claim that the contemporary literary scene had many women writers (5–6). Finally, some of the women's journals used Taymur's work as an example of the local education/writing of Arab women (140) and to argue that marriage did interfere with writing (200). See Marilyn Booth, *May Her Likes Be Multiplied: Biography and Gender Politics in Egypt* (Los Angeles: University of California Press, 2001).

3. Muhammad `Amara, *Rifa' Al-Tahtawi, Ra'id al-Tanweer fi al-`Asr al-Hadith*, (Cairo: Dar al-Shuruq, 1988), 347–48.

4. Zaynab Fawwaz first offered this construction in her biography of Taymur published in her *Al-Durr al-Manthur fi Tabaqat Rabat al-Khudur* (Cairo: al-Matb`at al-Kubra al-'Amiriya, 1894), 303–4. The title of the article that Taymur published in the *al-Adaab* newspaper. was "Families Will Not Be Reformed without the Education of Young Girls." It was cited in Zaynab Fawwaz's *Al-Durr al-Manthur fi Tabaqat Rabat al-Khudur*, 306–8.

5. Al-Anisa Mayy, *Sha`-irat al-Tali`a, `A'isha Taymur* (Cairo: Dar al-Hilal, 1956), 120, 173.

6. Benedict Anderson, *Imagined Communities* (London: Verso, 1991); Juan Cole, *Colonialism and Revolution in the Middle East* (Princeton, NJ: Princeton University Press, 1993); Baron, *Women's Awakening in Egypt*.

7. Anderson, *Imagined Communities*, 25.

8. Charles D. Smith, "Imagined Identities, Imagined Nationalisms: Print Cultures and Egyptian Nationalism in the Light of Recent Scholarship," Review of *Redefining the Egyptian Nation 1930–1945*, by Israel Gershoni and James Pl Jankowski, *International Journal of Middle East Studies* 29, no. 4 (November 1997), 607.

9. Baron, *Women's Awakening in Egypt*, 24, 51.

10. Ibid., 5.

11. Samia Nassar Melki, "Palestinian Author Reclaims the Past for Generations of Arab Women, Memoir of Family History Contradicts Popular Beliefs about Pre modern Middle Eastern Society," *Daily Star*, December 9, 2004, 4.

12. Salah Issa, *al-Thawrat al-'Urabiya* (Cairo: Dar al-Mustaqbal al-'Arabi, 1982).

13. A. M. Broadly, *How We Defended Ahmed 'Arabi and his Friends* (Cairo: Research and Publishing Arab Center, 1980), 373–74.

Chapter 1

1. Afaf Lutfi al-Sayyid Marsot, *Egypt in the Reign of Muhammad Ali* (Cambridge: Cambridge University Press, 1984), chap. 3.

2. Afaf Lutfi al-Sayyid Marsot, *Women and Men in Late Eighteenth-Century Egypt* (Austin: University of Texas Press, 1995), chap. 2.

3. Ibid., 19.

4. Ibid.

5. Afaf Lutfi al-Sayyid Marsot, "Women and Modernization: A Reevaluation," in *Women, the Family and Divorce Laws in Islamic History*, ed. Amira El Azhary Sonbol (Syracuse, NY: Syracuse University Press, 1996), 44–45.

6. Al-Amir Osman Ibrahim, Caroline Kourkhan, and Ali Kourkhan, *Muhammad Ali al-Kabeer*, trans. Hoda Kourkan (Cairo: al-Majlis al-'Ala lil Thaqafa, 2005), 18.

7. Al-Sayyid Marsot, "Women and Modernization," 44.

8. Omar Ridda Kahala, ed., *'Alam al-Nisa* (Beirut: Mu'assat al-Risala, 1977), 3:162–79.

9. Khayr al-Din al-Zirikli, "Ahmed Taymur Pasha," *Al-'Alam: Qammus Tarajim* (Beirut: Dar al-'Ilm lil Malayiin, 1979), 1:100.

10. Ibid.

11. Fadwa el-Guindi, review of *Remaking Women*, edited by Lila Abu-Lughod, *Journal of Political Ecology: Case Studies in History and Society* 6 (1999): 1–10.

12. See Terence Walz, "Bakhita Kwashe (Sr. Fortunata Quasce) 1841 to 1899," Dictionary of African Christian Biography, http://www.dacb.org/stories/sudan/bakhita_kwashe.html; Eve M. Troutt Powell, "Sainted Slave: Bakhita in the Memories of Southern Sudanese," in *Race and Identity in the Nile Valley*, eds. Carolyn Fuerhr-Lobban and Kharyssa Rhodes (Trenton, NJ: Red Sea Press, 2004), 159–69; Eve Troutt Powell and John Hunwick, eds., *The African Diaspora in the Mediterranean Lands of Islam* (Princeton, NJ: Markus Wiener, 2002).

13. See Nancy Chodorow, *The Reproduction of Mothering* (Berkeley: University of California Press, 1978); Chodorow also discussed the role that culture plays in what are presumed to be universal psychological structures in "Being and Doing: A Cross Cultural Examination of the Socialization of Males and Females," in *Women in Sexist Society: Studies in Power and Powerlessness*, eds. Vivian Gornick and Barbara Moran (New York: Basic Books, 1971), 259–91. I have attempted to examine the use of this literature for the study of Egyptian Families in Mervat Hatem, "Toward the Study of the Psychodynamics of Mothering and Gender in Egyptian Families," *International Journal of Middle East Studies* 19, no. 3 (August 1987): 287–306.

14. Ahmed Taymur, "Tarikh al-'A'ilah al-Taymuriya" in *Li'b al-'Arab* (Cairo: Lajnat Nashr al-Mu'alafat al-Taymuriya, 1948), 67–68.

15. *Encyclopedia of Islam*, IV, eds. E. Van Donzel, B. Lewis, and C. Pellat (Leiden: Brill, 1978), s.v. "Ibn al-Kalbi"; *Encyclopedia of Islam*, III, eds. B. Lewis, V. L. Menage, C. Pellate, and J. Schacht (Leiden: Brill, 1978), s.v. "Ibn Khallikan."

16. Ahmed Taymur, "Tarikh al-'A'ilah al-Taymuriya," 67.

17. Geoff Simons, *The Future of Iraq: U.S. Policy in Reshaping the Middle East* (London: Saqi Books, 2003), 118.

18. Ahmed Taymur, "Tarikh al-`A'ilah al-Taymuriya," 67.

19. Dina Rizk Khoury, *State and Provincial Society in the Ottoman Empire* (Cambridge: Cambridge University Press, 1997), 44.

20. Ibid., 46.

21. Ibid.

22. Ibid., 47.

23. Muhammad Kurd `Ali, *Al-Mu`assirun* (Damascus: Matbu`at Mujama`a al-Lughtat al-`Arabiya bi Dimashq, 1980), 37.

24. Ibid.

25. Al-Sayyid Marsot, *Egypt in the Reign of Muhammad Ali*, 42.

26. Ahmed Taymur, "Tarikh al-`A'ilah al-Taymuriya," 68.

27. Ibid.

28. Ibid., 70.

29. Ibid., 71.

30. Ibid., 73.

31. Ibid.

32. Abdel Rahman al-Rafi`, `*Asr Muhammad Ali* (Cairo: Maktabat al-Nahda al-Misriya, 1951), 620.

33. Ibid., 80.

34. Ibid., 82.

35. Ibid., 84.

36. `A'isha Taymur, *Nata'ij al-Ahwal fi al-Aqwal wa al-Af`al)* (Cairo: Matba`at Mohammad Efendi Mustafa, 1887), 2.

37. Ibid., 3.

38. Al-Anissa Mayy, *Sha`irat al-Tali`a, `A'isha Taymur* (Cairo: Dar al-Hilal, 1956), 61.

39. Concubines could be white or black as William Edward William Lane suggested in *Manners and Customs of the Modern Egyptians* (London: 1860), quoted in Powell and Hunwick, eds., *African Diaspora*, 109.

40. Ibid.

41. Immanuel Wallerstein, "The Three Stages of African Involvement in the World Economy," in *Political Economy of Contemporary Africa* (London: Sage, 1985), 35–40.

42. Samir Amin, *Unequal Development* (New York: Monthly Review, 1976), 49–50, 319–26; Wallerstein, "African Involvement," 35–40.

43. Muslims could not enslave other Muslims, so enslavement was largely inflicted on non-Muslims and was rationalized as a method of converting others into Islam.

44. *Encyclopedia of Islam*, VI, eds. C. E. Bosworth, E. Van Donzel, B. Lewis and C. Pellat (Leiden: Brill 1987), s.v. "Mamluk."

45. Qasim Abdu Qasim, "Misr al-Mamlukiyya: Al-Sulta bi Quwwat al-Sayf," in *Hukkam Misr* (Cairo: Dar al-Hilal, 2005), 80–88.

46. Mervat Hatem, "The Politics of Sexuality and Gender in Segregated Patriarchal Systems: The Case of Eighteenth and Nineteenth Century Egypt," *Feminist Studies* 12, no. 2 (Summer 1986), 256.

47. Ayman Fouad Sayyid, "Amawayyun, `Abbasiyyun wa Fatimiyyun: Al-Wali Mab`uth al-Khalifa," in *Hukkam Misr* (Cairo: al-Hilal, 2005), 74–79; Qasim, "Misr al-Mamlukiyya," 80–88.

48. Fatima Mernissi mentions the point about Shajarrat al-Durr's expression of political loyalty to the Abbasid caliph in calling herself *al-Musta`simiyya* but not the flattering political gesture implied in taking on his name. See Fatima Mernissi, *The Forgotten Queens of Islam* (Minneapolis: University of Minnesota Press, 1993).

49. Qasim, "Misr al-Mamlukiyya," 82.

50. *The Encyclopedia of Islam*, VI s.v. "Mamluk," 324.

51. Mernissi, *Forgotten Queens*, 92–97.

52. Al-Sayyid Marsot, *Women and Men*, chap. 2.

53. Mary Ann Fay, "Shawikar Qadin: Woman of Power and Influence in Ottoman Cairo," in *Auto/Biography and the Construction of Identity and Community in the Middle East* (New York: Palgrave Macmillan, 2001), 95–194. In this chapter, Fay presents a very detailed discussion of these Mamluk practices.

54. Al-Sayyid Marsot, *Women and Men*, 21.

55. Ibid., chap. 3 and appendix A; Fay, "Shawikar Qadin," 95–194.

56. Madeline Zilfi, "Servants, Slaves and the Domestic Order in the Ottoman Middle East," *Hawwa, Journal of Women of the Middle East and the Islamic World* 2, no. 1 (2004), 1–33.

57. Ibid., 7, 27.

58. Al-Sayyid Marsot, "Women and Modernization," 46–47.

59. Zilfi, "Servants, Slaves and the Domestic Order," 26.

60. Ibid., 23.

61. Ibid., 18.

62. Mernissi mentions this distinction, but does not develop it. See Mernissi, *Forgotten Queens*, 92.

63. `A'isha Taymur, *Nata'ij al- Ahwa*, 76.

64. Lutfi al-Sayyid Marsot, *Egypt in the Reign of Muhammad Ali*, 206–7.

65. Al-'Anissa Mayy, *Sha`irat al-Tali`a*, 89.

66. Ibid., 58–61.

67. Ibid., 60.

68. Zilfi, "Servants, Slaves and the Domestic Order," 7, 12.

69. Shaykh Sabry al-Dessuki, "Al-Islam wa Takreem al-Mar'at," *al-Ahram*, May 13, 2010, 22.

70. Mayy Ziyada, "Katiba Tuqadim Sha`irat," in *Hilyat al-Tiraz: Diwan `A'isha al-Taymuriya* (Cairo: Dar al-Katib al-`Arabi, 1952), 79.

71. Ibid.

72. I am indebted to Denise Spellberg for an appreciation of the novelty of adding *fiqh* to the Islamic learning directed at young girls and women.

73. Ahmed Taymur, *La'ib al-Arab*, 86.

74. Ahmed Kamal Zadah, "Jidati: `Ard wa Tahlil," in *Hilyat al-Tiraz: Diwan `A'isha al-Taymuriya* (Cairo: Dar al-Katib al-`Arabi, 1952), 18.

75. Ziyada, *Sha`irat al-Tali`a*, 87.

76. Ziyada, "Katiba Tuqadim Sha`irat t," 74.

77. This section is based on two articles I published on the complex relationship between Taymur and her daughter, Tawhida, and the role the latter played in supporting her mother's literary studies and aspirations. Mervat Hatem, "`A'isha Taymur's Tears and the Critique of the Modernist and Feminist Discourses on Nineteenth-Century Egypt," in *Making Women: Feminism and Modernity in the Middle East*, ed. Lila Abu-Lughod (Princeton, NJ: Princeton University Press, 1998), 73–88; Hatem, "The Microdynamics of Patriarchal Change in Egypt and the Development of an Alternative Discourse on Mother-Daughter Relations," in *Intimate Selving in Arab Families: Gender, Self and Identity*, ed. Suad Joseph (Syracuse, NY: Syracuse University Press, 1999), 191–210.

78. Taymur, "Muqadimat al-Diwan al-Turki wa al-Farasi," in Ziyada, "Katiba Tuqadim Sha`irat" 68–69.

79. Ziyada, "Katiba Tuqadim Sha`irat," 69.

80. Taymur, *Nata'ij al-Ahwal*, 99.

81. Taymur, "Muqadimat al-Diwan al-Turki wa al-Farasi" in Ziyada, "Katiba Tuqadim Sha`irat," 73.

82. A Taymur family presentation at the Women and Memory Forum's conference on "`A'isha Taymur: Al-Thabit wa al-Mutaghiir," (Cairo, May 2001).

83. Zadah, "Jidati," 19.

84. Ibid., 18.

85. For a more developed discussion of this point, see Hatem, "Microdynamics of Patriarchal Change," 191–210.

86. In Arabic elegiac poetry, women's exploration of their emotions toward others was not only socially acceptable but was also treated as a measure of their skill in this genre.

87. `A'isha Taymur, Hilyat al-Tiraz (Cairo: n.p., 1892), 44–45.

88. Ibid., 12.

89. Hoda al-Saadi, "Changing Attitudes towards Women's Madness in Nineteenth Century Egypt," Hawwa, Journal of Women of the Middle East and the Islamic World 3, no. 3 (2005): 293–308.

90. Ibid.

91. Ziyada, "Katiba Tuqadim Sha`irat," 74–75.

92. Ibid., 75.

93. Zaynab Fawwaz, Al-Durr al-Manthur fi Tabaqat Rabat al-Khudur, (Cairo: al-Matba`t al-Kubra al-'Amiriya, 1894), 308.

94. Khayr al-Din al-Zirikli, "Ahmed Taymur Pasha," in Al-`Alam: Qammus Tarajim (Beirut: Dar al-`Ilm lil Malayiin, 1979), 1, 100; Kurd `Ali, Al-Mu`assirun, 37; Ahmed Taymur Pasha, Al-Tazkarat al-Taymuriya (Cairo: Matba`at Dar al-Kitab al-`Arabi, 1953), 450.

95. Arthur Goldschmidt Jr., Biographical Dictionary of Modern Egypt (Boulder, CO: Lynne Rienner, 2000), 208–9.

96. Fawwaz, Al-Durr al-Manthur fi Tabaqat Rabat al-Khudur, 309–19.

97. Al-'Anisa Mayy, Sha`irat al-Tali`a, 55–56.

98. Ahmed Taymur, "Tarikh al-`A'ilah al-Taymuriya," 91.

99. Mahmud Taymur, Itijahat al-Adab al-`Arabi fi al-Sineen al-Ma`at al-Akhira (Cairo: Maktabat al-Adaab, 1970), 56–57.

100. For a discussion of this argument and how it relates to late nineteenth-century Egyptian history, please see Mervat F. Hatem, "The Nineteenth Century Discursive Roots of the Continuing Debate on the Social-Sexual Contract in Today's Egypt," Hawwa, Journal of Women of the Middle East and the Islamic World 2, no. 1 (2004), 64–88.

Chapter 2

1. Taymur was said to have written another work of fiction titled al-Luqa ba`d al-Shitat that was not published. As such it lay outside the parameters of this study, which deals with her published works and how they contributed to the literary and intellectual imagining of the nineteenth-century Egyptian community.

2. Aida Nusair, Harakat Nashr al-Kutub fi Misr fi al-Qarn al-Tasi `Ashr (Cairo: al-Hay'at al-Misriyat al-`Amma lil Kitab, 1994), 162.

3. Ibid.

4. Ibid., 163.

5. Ibid., 169.

6. Ibid., 170, 56.

7. Ibid., 171–72.

8. Ibid., 491.

9. Ibid., 297.

10. Juan Cole, *Colonialism and Revolution in the Middle East* (Princeton, NJ: Princeton University Press, 1993), 113.

11. Ibid.

12. Nazarat al-Ma'rif al-'Amumiya, *Taqrir 'an al-Katateeb 'Alti Tudiyraha Nazarat al-Ma'rif min Yulyu 1889–1898* (Cairo: al-Matba'at al-'Amiriya, 1899), 6.

13. Cole, *Colonialism and Revolution in the Middle East*, 114; Sabry Hafiz, *The Genesis of Arabic Narrative Discourse* (London: al-Saqi Books, 199), 65–66.

14. Hafiz, *Genesis of Arab Narrative*, 49.

15. Cole, *Colonialism and Revolution in the Middle East*, 128–29.

16. I am grateful to the late Magda Nuwaihi, whose knowledge of the history of the Arabic language helped me see the problematic assumptions of that view.

17. Magda Nuwaihi, email message to author, February 14, 2001.

18. Cole, *Colonialism and Revolution in the Middle East*, 124.

19. Ibid., 112, 131.

20. Serif Mardin, *The Genesis of Young Ottoman Thought* (Princeton, NJ: Princeton University Press, 1962), 191.

21. Ehud Toledano, *State and Society in Mid-Nineteenth Century Egypt* (Cambridge: Cambridge University Press, 1990).

22. Mardin, *Genesis of Young Ottoman Thought*, 191.

23. Toledano, *State and Society*, 1.

24. Emine Foat Tugay, *Three Centuries: Family Chronicles of Turkey and Egypt* (London: Oxford University Press, 1963), 119.

25. Ibid., 119–20.

26. The couple's marriage ended with divorce when Zeyneb caught her husband sleeping with her slave and threatened to commit suicide. Afaf Lutfi al-Sayyid Marsot, *Egypt in the Reign of Muhammad Ali* (Cambridge: Cambridge University Press, 1984), 80.

27. Emine Foat Tugay, 122.

28. Mardin, *Genesis of Young Ottoman Thought*, 199.

29. Ibid., 241.

30. Ibid., 242.

31. Ibid., 229.

32. Ibid.

33. Ibid., 69.

34. Ibid., 257–58.

35. Ibid. 262.

36. Ibid., 228–29.

37. Ibid., 200–201.

38. Ibid., 46–47.

39. Ibid., 243.

40. Ibid., 244.

41. Ibid., 35.

42. Ibid., 38–39.

43. Ibid., 44.

44. Cole, *Colonialism and Revolution in the Middle East*, 120.

45. Mardin, *Genesis of Young Ottoman Thought*, 55.

46. Muhammad 'Amara, *Rifa' al-Tahtawi: Ra'id al-Tanweer fi al-'Asr al-Hadith*, (Cairo: Dar al-Shuruq, 1988), 128–29.

47. Rifa` Rafi` al-Tahtawi, *Takhlis al-Ibriz fi Talkis Paris* (Cairo: al-Hay'at al-Misriya al-Amma lil Kitab, 1993), 168- 184.

48. Abdel Rahman al-Rafi`, `Asr Muhammad Ali* (Cairo: Maktabat al-Nahda al-Misriyat, 1951), 518.

49. Rifa` Bek al-Tahtawi, *Mawaqi` al-Aflak fi Waqa` Telemaque* (Beirut: al-Matba`t al-Suriya, 1857), 4–5.

50. Husayn Fawzi al-Najjar, *Rifa' al-Tahtawi: Ra'id Fikr wa Imam al-Nahda* (Cairo: al-Misriyat lil Ta'lif wa al-Tarjama, 1966), 134; Ahmed Badawi, *Rifa`` al-Tahtawi* (Cairo: Lajnat al-Bayan al-`Arabi, 1950), 207–10.

51. Al-Najjar, *Rifa al-Tahtawi*, 135.

52. Al-Tahtawi, *Mawaqi` al-Aflak fi Waqa` Telemaque*, 27, 29.

53. Matti Moosa, *The Origins of Modern Arabic Fiction* (New York: Three Continents Press, 1983), 21.

54. Ibid., chap. 1; Hafiz, *The Genesis of Arabic Narrative Discourse*, chaps. 2–3.

55. Muhammad Rushdi Hasan, *'Athar al-Maqama fi Nash'at al-Qissa al-Misriyat al-Haditha* (Cairo: al-Hay'at al-Misriyat al-`Amma lil Kitab, 1974), 184; Hafez, *Genesis of Arab Narrative*, 133.

56. Anne McClintock, "'No Longer in a Future Heaven': Nationalism, Gender and Race," in *Becoming National: A Reader*, eds. Geoff Eley and Ronald Grigor Suny (Oxford: Oxford University Press, 1996), 260–85.

57. Eric Hobsbawm, "Introduction: Inventing Traditions," in *The Invention of Tradition*, eds. Eric Hobsbawm and Terence Ranger (Cambridge: Cambridge University Press, 1983), chap. 1.

58. Hasan, *'Athar al-Maqama fi Nash'at al-Qissa al-Misriyat al-Haditha*, 18.

59. Ibid., 24–25.

60. Ibid., 84.

61. Ibid.

62. Ibid., 121.

63. Muhammad `Ammara, *`Ali Mubarak: Mu'arikh wa Muhandis al-`Imara* (Cairo: Dar al-Shuruq, 1988), 181–82.

64. Timothy Mitchell, *Colonizing Egypt* (Cambridge: Cambridge University Press, 1988), 63–64.

65. Hasan, *'Athar al-Maqama fi Nash'at al-Qissa al-Misriyat al-Haditha*, 120.

66. Wadad al-Qadi, "East and West in `Ali Mubarak's `Alamuddin,'" in *Intellectual Life in the Arab East, 1890–1939*, ed. Marwan R. Buheiry (Beirut: American University of Beirut, 1981), 34–35.

67. Ibid., 30–32, 34.

68. Cole, *Colonialism and Revolution in the Middle East*, 127.

69. Ibid.

70. Peter Gran, *Islamic Roots of Capitalism Egypt, 1760–1840* (Austin: University of Texas Press, 1979), 50.

71. Ibid., 67–68.

72. Ibid., 50.

73. Ibid., 133.

74. `A'isha Taymur, *Nata'ij al-Ahwal fi alAqwal wa al- Af`al* (Cairo: Matba`at Muhammad Effendi Mustafa, 1887/8), 2.

75. Ibid.

76. Hasan, *'Athar al-Maqama fi Nash'at al-Qissa al-Misriyat al-Haditha*, 138.

77. Ibid., 4.

78. Modern psychology identifies approach and withdrawal as fundamental ways of organizing one's environment. Richard Davidson, "Affect, Health and Meditation: Perspectives from

Affective Neuroscience," Symposium on Mindfulness and Health (Bethesda, MD: National Institutes of Health, May 27, 2004).

79. Taymur, *Nata'ij al-Ahwal*, 4.

80. Ibid., 4–5.

81. Omnia Sharky, "Schooled Mothers and Structured Play: Child Rearing in Turn-of-the Century Egypt," in *Remaking Women*, ed. Lila Abu Lughod (Princeton, NJ: Princeton University Press, 1998), 127.

82. Hoda Elsadda discussed how Abdallah al-Nadeem drew on the proper behavior manuals in his magazine *al-Ustaz*. See Hoda Elsadda, "Gendered Citizenship: Discourses of Domesticity in the Second Half of the Twentieth Century," *Hawwa*, 2006.

83. Brinkley Messick discussed how the law manuals focused their discussion of childrearing on cases of parental separation. See Brinkley Messick, *The Caligraphic State* (Berkeley: University of California Press, 1996), 77–79.

84. Ibid.

85. Sharky, "Schooled Mothers," 127–28; Elsadda, "Gendered Citizenship," 10.

86. Sharky, "Schooled Mothers," 128.

87. Stefan Sperl, *Mannersim in Arab Poetry* (Cambridge: Cambridge University Press, 1989), 216.

88. Ibid., 76.

89. Ibid., 77, 79, 110.

90. John Renard, *Islam and the Heroic Image: Themes in Literature and the Visual Arts* (Charlotte: University of South Carolina Press, 1993), 203.

91. `A'isha Taymur, "La Tasluh al-`Ailat 'ila bi Tarbiyat al-Banat," in *al-Adaab* (1887), in Zaynab Fawwaz, *Al-Durr al-Manthur fi Tabaqat Rabat al-Khudur*, 306–7.

Chapter 3

1. `A'isha Taymur, *Nata'ij al-Ahwal- fi Al-Aqwal wa al- Al-Af`al* (Cairo: Matba't Muhammad Effendi, 1887/8), 23.

2. Benedict Anderson, *Imagined Communities* (London: Verso, 1996), 25.

3. Sugata Bose, "Space and Time on the Indian Ocean Rim: Theory and History," in *Modernity and Culture, from the Mediterranean to the Indian Ocean*, eds. Leila Tarazi Fawaz and C. A. Bayly (New York: Columbia University Press, 2002), 369.

4. Anderson, *Imagined Communities*, 26–30.

5. Anne McClintock, "'No Longer in a Future Heaven': Nationalism, Gender and Race," in *Becoming National: A Reader*, eds. Geoff Eley and Ronald Grigor Suny (Oxford: Oxford University Press, 1996), 259.

6. Fedwa Malti-Douglas, *Woman's Body, Woman's Word: Gender and Discourse in Arabo-Islamic Writing* (Cairo: American University in Cairo Press, 1991), 4–5.

7. Ibid., 4.

8. D. A. Spellberg, *Politics, Gender and the Islamic Past* (New York: Columbia University Press, 1994).

9. Hans Wehr, *A Dictionary of Modern Written Arabic* (Beirut: Maktabat Lubnan, 1974), 161.

10. Sabry Hafez, *The Genesis of Arabic Narrative Discourse* (London: Al-Saqi Books[0], 1993), 131.

11. Leslie P. Pierce, *The Imperial Harem: Women and Sovereignty in the Ottoman Empire* (Oxford: Oxford University Press, 1993), 16.

12. It is useful to point out here that in singling out the ministers of the treasury and defense as the villains in this narrative Taymur was embracing the partisan views of the Muhammed Ali dynasty, which blamed the international financial advisors of khedives Ismail and Tewfik and

General `Urabi, the defense minister of Khedive Tewfik, for the economic and military woes of their governments that culminated in British occupation of Egypt (1882).

13. Aziz al-Azmeh, *Muslim Kingship* (London: I. B Tauris, 1997), 159–63.
14. Ibid., 84–85; Stephen Sperl, "Islamic Kingship and the Arab Panergyric Poetry in the Early 9th Century," *Journal of Arab Literature* 8 (1997), 20–35.
15. Al-Azmeh, *Muslim Kingship*, 89.
16. Ibid., 78.
17. Ibid., 128.
18. Hubert Darke, trans., *The Book of Government or Rules for Kings, the Siyasat-nama or Siyar al-Muluk of Nizam al-Mulk* (New Haven, CT: Yale University Press, 1960), chap. 14–22.
19. Ibid., chap. 22.
20. Ibid., chaps. 4 and 17.
21. Cited in Perry Anderson, *Lineages of the Absolutist State* (London: New Left Books, 1974), 397.
22. Edward W. Said, *Orientalism* (New York: Pantheon, 1978), 153–54.
23. Taymur, *Nata'ij al Ahwal*, 4.
24. Ibid., 12.
25. Arthur Goldschmidt Jr., "The Historical Context," in *Understanding the Contemporary Middle East*, eds. Deborah Gerner and Jillian Schwedler (Boulder, CO: Lynne Rienner, 2004), 44.
26. Eve M. Troutt Powell, "From Odyssey to Empire: Mapping the Sudan through Egyptian Literature in the Mid-19th Century," *International Journal of Middle East Studies* 31 (August 1999), 414.
27. Ibid., 5.
28. Goldschmidt, "Historical Context," 48–49.
29. Taymur, *Nata'j al-Ahwal fi al-Aqwal wa al-Af'al*, 5.
30. Perry Anderson, *Lineages of the Absolutist State*, 367n13.
31. When colonel `Urabi, with army battalions behind him, presented Khedive Tewfik with the "just" wishes of the army and the nation, Tewfik replied, "'You have no rights to these wishes. I inherited this land and you are my slaves. . . .' [In response,] `Urabi said: "God created us free and not as inheritance or property. By God, we will not be inherited or enslaved from this day forward." Ahmed `Urabi, *Mudhakarat al-Za`im Ahmed `Urabi* (Cairo: Dar al-Hilal, 1989), 75.
32. Robert Hunter, *Egypt Under the Khedives, 1805–1879* (Pittsburgh, PA: University of Pittsburgh, 1984).
33. Afaf Lutfi al-Sayyid Marsot offered a nuanced discussion of justice as the rallying cry of the popular rebellion that brought Muhammed Ali to power. The populace defined the justice of the rulers to include integrity, predictable/fair taxation, law and order, and abiding by popular consensus. An unjust ruler was tyrannical and deserved to be deposed by the common people. Afaf Lutfi al-Sayyid Marsot, *Egypt in the Reign of Muhammad Ali* (Cambridge: Cambridge University Press, 1984), 40, 47, 49. During the `Urabi revolution, `Urabi called on the khedive to "restrict his power to the proper sphere." See Juan Cole, *Colonialism and Revolution in the Middle East* (Princeton, NJ: Princeton University Press, 1993), 237.
34. Taymur, *Nata'ij al-Ahwal fi al-Aqwal wa al-Af'al*, 104. This passage was translated by the author. Taymur incorporated some of these same themes in poems she wrote to celebrate the return of Khedive Tewfik to his throne after the failure of the `Urabi revolution in Egypt in 1882. They included the monarch's special relationship with God and his good fortune, honor, and virtue, noble stock and old lineage as the primary values upheld by his government. `A'isha Taymur, *Hilyat al-Tiraz* (Cairo: n.p., 1892), 15–16, 21–22.
35. Taymur, *Nata'ij al- Ahwal*, 105.

36. See Peirce, *Imperial Harem*.

37. Mardin, *The Genesis of Young Ottoman Thought* 29.

38. Ilyas al-'Ayubi, *Tarikh Misr fi 'Ahd al-Khidiwi Ismail, 1863–1879* (Cairo: Maktabat Madbuli, 1990), 2:135–44.

39. Ali al-Hadidi, *Abdallah al-Nadeem, Khateeb al-Wataniya* (Cairo: al-Hay'at al-Misriya al-'Amma lil Kitab, 1987), 45–46.

40. Iliyas Al-'Ayubi, *Tarikh Misr fi 'Ahd al-Khidiwi Ismail, 1863–1879*, 511.

41. A. M. Broadly, *How We Defended Ahmed 'Arabi and His Friends* (Cairo: Research and Publishing Arab Center, 1980), 376–77.

42. I am grateful to Denise Spellberg, who alerted me to the significance of the name and identified who Queen Boran was in Persian history and her relationship to the prophetic tradition.

43. Ehsan Yarshater, ed., *The Cambridge History of Iran* (Cambridge: Cambridge University Press, 1983), 3:171.

44. Abdel Halim Abu Shuqa, *Tahrir al-Mar'at fi 'Asr al-Risalat* (al-Kuwait: Dar al-Qalim, 1990), 2:450.

45. 'A'isha Taymur, *Nata'ij al- Ahwal*, 26.

46. Fatima Mernissi, *Beyond the Veil: Male and Female Dynamics in a Modern Muslim Society* (New York: John Wiley and Sons, 1975), chap. 1.

47. Michael Cook, *Commanding Right and Forbidding Wrong in Islamic Thought* (Cambridge: Cambridge University Press, 2000), 13.

48. While she lobbied for her son, Nizam al-Mulk supported the son of a rival wife. As a result, she threatened to influence her husband against him. See Denise Spellberg, "Nizam al-Mulk's Manipulation of Tradition: 'A'isha and the Role of Women in the Islamic Government," *Muslim World* 78, no. 2 (April 1988), 117.

49. Darke, *Book of Government*, chap. 42, 188.

50. Ibid., 185.

51. Malti-Douglas, *Woman's Body*, chaps. 1–2.

52. Taymur, *Nata'ij al-Ahwal*, 25.

53. Ibid. The translation of this passage is that of the author.

54. Abu Shuqa, *Tahrir al-Mar'at fi 'Asr al-Risalat*, 127–28.

55. Taymur, *Nata'ij al- Ahwal*, 12.

56. Stephen Sperl, *Mannerism in Arabic Poetry* (Cambridge: Cambridge University Press, 1989), 77.

57. Ibid., 78.

58. Ibid., 23.

59. Taymur, *Nata'ij al-Ahwal*, 105.

60. This discussion drew heavily upon the lessons learned from the problems faced by Khedive Ismail's government. See Hunter, *Egypt*.

61. The Turkish meaning of the names of Aqeel and Ghadur were kindly provided by Professor Muge Fatma Gocek.

62. Taymur, *Nata'ij al- Ahwal*, 17.

63. Bose, "Space and Time," 378.

64. Taymur, *Nata'ij al- Ahwal*, 33.

65. Cook, *Commanding Right*, 429.

66. Benedict Anderson.

67. Nelly Hanna, *Making Big Money in 1600: The Life and Times of Ismail Abu Taqiyya, Egyptian Merchant* (Syracuse, NY: Syracuse University Press, 1998), chap. 3.

68. Bose, "Space and Time," 381.

69. Ibid., 383–84.

70. Taymur, *Nata'ij al- Ahwal*, 80.
71. Ibid., 4.
72. Ibid., 42.
73. Cook, *Commanding Right*, 13.
74. Ibid., 15, 24–25.
75. Al-Hadidi, *Abdallah al-Nadeem*, 109–16.
76. Darke, *Book of Government*, chap. 1.
77. Muhtar Holland, trans., *Al-Ghazali on the Duties of Brotherhood* (Woodstock, NY: Overlook Press, 1976), 19.
78. Ibid., 64.
79. Ibid., 94.
80. Ibid., 22.
81. Ibid., 25.
82. Ibid., 70.
83. Taymur, *Nata'ij al-Ahwal*, 74.
84. Hanna Fenichel Pitkin, *Fortune Is a Woman: Gender and Politics in the Thought of Niccolo Machiavelli* (Los Angeles: University of California Press, 1984), 138, 140, 144.
85. Ibid., 145.
86. Cook, *Commanding Right*, 482–83.
87. Taymur, *Nata'ij al-Ahwal*, 68.
88. Mervat Hatem, "The Politics of Sexuality and Gender in Segregated Patriarchal Systems: the Case of Eighteenth-and Nineteenth-Century Egypt," *Feminist Studies* 12, no. 2 (Summer 1986), 251–74.
89. Taymur, *Nata'ij al-Ahwal*, 35.

Chapter 4

1. `A'isha Taymur, *Mir'at al-Ta'mul fi al-*Umur (Cairo: Matb'at al-Mahrussa, 1892), 7.
2. Ali al-Hadidi, *Abdallah al-Nadeem, Khateeb al-Wataniya* (Cairo: al-Hay'at al-Misriyat al-`Amma lil Kitab, 1987), 300, 315.
3. Roger Owen, *Lord Cromer* (Oxford: Oxford University Press, 2004), 270, 274.
4. Ibid., 247–48.
5. Ibid., 269–70.
6. Hoda Elsadda, ed., *Al-Fatat* (Cairo: Mu'assassat al-Mar'at wa al-Thakira, 2007), 19.
7. Hoda Elsadda, ed. "Mukkadima," *Al-Fatat* (Cairo: Mu'assassat al-Mar'at wa al-Thakira, 2007), 11.
8. Taymur, *Mir'at al-Ta'mu fi al-Umur*, 4.
9. Michael Cook, *Commanding Right and Forbidding Wrong in Islamic Thought* (Cambridge: Cambridge University Press, 2000) 506–7.
10. Taymur, *Mir'at al-Ta'mul fi al-Umur*, 2.
11. Taymur, *Mir'at al-Ta'mul fi al-Umur*, 3.
12. Ibid., 4.
13. Ibid.
14. Ibid., 4–7.
15. Afaf Lutfi al-Sayyid Marsot, "Women and Modernization: A Reevaluation," in *Women, the Family and Divorce Laws in Islamic History*, ed. Amira El Azhary Sonbol (Syracuse, NY: Syracuse University Press, 1996), 45–46.
16. Ibid., 4–8.

17. Omaima Abou-Bakr, "Surat al-Rajul fi al-Kitabat al-Islamiya: Bayn al-Tafaseer al-Qadima wa al-Haditha," `A'isha Taymur: Tahadiyyat al-Thabit wa al-Mutaghiir fi al-Qarn al-Tasi` `Ashr`A'isha Taymur: Tahadiyyat al-Thabit wa al-Mutaghiir fi al-Qarn al-Tasi` `Ashr, ed. Hoda Elsadda (Cairo: Women and Memory Forum, 2004), 161.
18. Taymur, Mir'at al-Tamul fi al-Umur, 6.
19. Abou-Bakr, 166.
20. Taymur, Mir'at al-Tamul fi al-Umur, 4.
21. Ibid., 10.
22. Ibid., 8–9.
23. Ibid., 12.
24. Afaf Lutfi al-Sayyid Marsot, Women and Men in Late Eighteenth Century (Austin: University of Texas Press, 1995), 20.
25. Ibid., 14–16.
26. Shaykh Abdallah al-Fayumi, Lisan al-Jumhur `ala Mir'at al-Tamul fi al-'Umur (Cairo: Multaqa al-Mar'at wa al-Thakira, 2002), 48–50.
27. Yaqub Sarruf, "Muqadimat," in Bahithat al-Badiya, by Mayy Ziyada (Beirut: Mu'assat Noufal, 1983), 9.
28. Khayr al-Din al-Zirikli, ed., "Abdallah al-Fayumi," in Al-`Alam: Qamus Tarajim," (Beirut: Dar al-`Ilm lil Malayiin, 1973), 4:143.
29. Al-Fayumi, Lisan al-Jumhur . . . , 48.
30. Ibid., 50.
31. Ibid., 61.
32. Ibid., 62.
33. Ibid., 56.
34. Ibid., 52–53.
35. Ibid., 56–57.
36. Ibid., 57.
37. Omaima Abou-Bakr, "Teaching the Words of the Prophet: Women Instructors of the Hadith (Fourteenth and Fifteenth Centuries)," Hawwa: Journal of Women of the Middle East and the Islamic World 1, no. 3 (2003): 306–28.
38. Ibid., 58.
39. Muhammad `Amara, Rifa`at al-Tahtawi: Ra'id al-Tanweer fi al-`Asr al-Hadith (Cairo: Dar al-Shuruq, 1988), 346.
40. Al-Fayumi, Lisan al-Jumhur `ala Mir'at al-Tamul fi al-'Umur in Mir'at al-Tamul fi al-Umur, 58–60.
41. Ibid., 64.
42. Ibid., 67.
43. Ibid., 68, 71.
44. Abou-Bakr, "Surat al-Rajul fi al-Kitabat al-Islamiya," 144–65.
45. Al-Fayumi, Lisan al-Jumhur `ala Mir'at al-Tamul fi al-Umur, 70-71.
46. Ibid., 70.
47. Mervat F. Hatem, "The Nineteenth Century Discursive Roots of the Continuing Debate on the Social-Sexual Contract in Today's Egypt," Hawwa, Journal of Women of the Middle East and the Islamic World 2, no. 1 (2004): 78.
48. Ibid.
49. Judith E. Tucker, Women in Nineteenth-Century Egypt (Cambridge: Cambridge University Press, 1985), 54; Amira El-Azhary Sonbol, "Introduction," in Women and the Family and Divorce Laws in Islamic History, ed. Amira El-Azhary Sonbol (Syracuse, NY: Syracuse University Press, 1996), 1–20.

50. See Abou-Bakr, "Surat al-Rajul fi al-Kitabat al-Islamiya".
51. Al-Fayumi, *Lisan al-Jumhur `ala Mir'at al-Ta'mul fi al-Umur* , 79–80.
52. Ibid., 80.
53. Ibid., 83–85.
54. Ibid., 88.
55. Ibid., 89.
56. Ibid., 97.
57. Ibid., 99.
58. Ibid., 112.
59. Ibid., 30.
60. Professor Hoda Elsadda's research on Abdallah al-Nadeem brought this reference to my attention. See Hoda Elsadda, "Tanaqudhat al-Khitab al-Watani fi Tanawuluh li Mas'alat al-Mar'at: Qir'at fi Majallat 'al-Ustaz' li Abdallah al-Nadeem," in `A'isha Taymur: Tahadiyat al-Thabit wa al-Mutaghayiir fi al-Qarn al-Tasi` `Ashr*, ed. Hoda Elsadda (Cairo: Mu'assat al-Mar'at wa al-Thakira, 2004), 169.
61. al-Hadidi, *Abdallah al-Nadeem, Khateeb al-Wataniya*, 243–96.
62. Ibid., 297–99.
63. Abdallah al-Nadeem, *Abdallah al-Nadeem: Al-`Addad al-Kamilat li Majallat al-Ustaz* (Cairo: Markaz Watha'iq Misr al-Mu'assir, 1994), 1:10.
64. See Abdallah al-Nadeem, "Mir'at al-Ta'mul fi al-Umur," *Al-Ustaz*, no. 33 (April 4, 1893), in *Abdallah al-Nadeeim: al-`Addad al-Kamila li Majallat al-Ustaz* (Cairo: al-Hay'at al-Misriyat al-`Amma lil Kitab, 1994), 2:775.
65. Eve M. Troutt Powell, "Slaves or Siblings? Abdallah al-Nadeem's Dialogues About the Family," in *Histories of the Middle East: New Directions*, eds. Israel Gershoni, Hakam Erdem, and Ursula Wokock (Boulder, CO: Lynne Rienner, 2002), 161–62.
66. Abdallah al-Nadeem, "Said wa Bakhita," in *Abdallah al-Nadeem: Al-`Addad al-Kamila li Majallat al-Ustaz* (Cairo: al-Hay'at al-Misriyat al-`Amma lil Kitab, 1994), 1:91, 1:93.
67. Ibid., 91–93.
68. Ibid., 132–34.
69. Ibid., 149–58.
70. Ibid., 395–99.
71. Ibid.
72. Elsadda, "Tanakudaht al-Khitab al-Watani," 177–78.
73. al-Nadeem, *Abdallah al-Nadeem*, 2:246.

Chapter 5

1. `A'isha Taymur, *Hilyat al-Tiraz* (Cairo: n.p., 1892), 3.
2. Zaynab Fawwaz, *Al-Durr al-Manthur fi Tabaqat Rabat al-Khudur* (Cairo: al-Matba`t al-Kubra al-Amiriya, 1894), 304.
3. Al-Anisa Mayy, *Sha`irat al-Tali`a,* `A'isha Taymur* (Cairo: Dar al-Hilal, 1956), 121.
4. Robert J. C. Young, *Colonial Desire* (London: Routledge, 1995), 20, 22.
5. For a discussion of this thesis, see Mervat F. Hatem, "Khitab al-Hadatha: Diwan 'Hilyat al-Tiraz' wa Ru'iyat `A'isha Taymur li Harakat al-Taghiir al-Ijtima'I wa al-Siyasi," in `A'isha Taymur: Tahadiyat al-Thabit wa al-Mutaghayir fi al-Qaran al-Tasi` `Ashr*, ed. Hoda Elsadda (Cairo: Mu'assasat al-Mar'at wa al-Thakira, 2004), 129–43.
6. Margot Badran and Miriam Cooke, Introduction to *Opening the Gates, A Century of Arab Feminist Writing*, eds. Margot Badran and Miriam Cooke (Indianapolis: Indiana University Press, 1990), xxx.

7. Fawwaz, *Al-Durr al-Manthur fi Tabaqat Rabat al-Khudur*, 303.
8. Taymur, *Hilyat al-Tiraz*, 1.
9. Fawwaz, *Al-Durr al-Manthur fi Tabaqat Rabat al-Khudur*, 304.
10. The top of the first page of *Hilyat al-Tiraz* was adorned with another pyramid that explicitly took the form of embroidered needlework.
11. Adunis, *al-Thabit wa al-Mutahawwil: bahth fi al-Ittiba` wa al-Ibda` inda al-`Arab* (Beirut: Dar al-`Awdah, 1974).
12. Taymur, *Hilyat al-Tiraz*, 2.
13. Fawwaz, *Al-Durr al-Manthur fi Tabaqat Rabat al-Khudur*, 466–79.
14. Ibid., 545–49; Elizabeth Fernea and Basima Qattan Bezirgan, eds., "Walada Bint al-Mustakfi, Andalusian Poet," in *Middle Eastern Women Speak*, eds. Elizabeth Fernea and Basima Qattan Bezirgan (Austin: University of Texas Press, 1977), 67–76.
15. Elizabeth Fernea and Basima Qattan Bezirgan, eds., "Lament for a Brother" by al-Khansa,' Poet of Early Islam," in *Middle Eastern Women Speak* (Austin: University of Texas Press, 1977), 3–6.
16. " `A'isha Bint Yussef bin Ahmed bin Nasr al-Ba`uni", in Zaynab Fawwaz, *al-Durr al-Manthur fi Tabaqat Rabat al-Khudur*, 293–94.
17. Taymur, *Hilyat al-Tiraz*, 3.
18. Ibid.
19. "`Aliya Ibnat al-Mahdi al-`Abbasiyya", in Zaynab Fawwa, *Al-Durr al-Manthur fi Tabaqat Rabat al-Khudur*, 349.
20. Rif`at al-Said, "Wathiqat Jawaz, Rifa`," in *al-Mu'alafat al-Kamila* (Cairo: Dar al-Thaqafa al-Jadida, 1978), 34.
21. Hoda Sha`rawi, *Mudhakarat Ra'idat al-Mar'at al-`Arabiya al-Haditha* (Cairo: Dar al-Hilal, 1981), 82–83.
22. Fawwaz, *Al-Durr al-Manthur fi Tabaqat Rabat al-Khudur*, 303.
23. Taymur, *Hilyat al-Tiraz*, 2.
24. Ibid.
25. Al-Anisa Mayy, *Sha`irat al-Tali`a*, 64-65, 148.
26. Ibid.
27. Taymur, *Hilyat al-Tiraz*, 4.
28. Ibid., 3–4.
29. Lami`a Tewfik, "Sijin al-Rammad wa 'Afaq al-Hawwiya fi Shi`r `A'isha Taymur," in `A'isha Taymur: Tahadiyat al-Thabit wa al-Mutaghiir fi al-Qarn al-Tasi` `Ahar, ed. Hoda Elsadda (Cairo: Mu'assassat al-Mar'at wa al-Thakira, 2004), 115.
30. Al-Anisa Mayy, *Sha`irat al-Tali`a*, 102.
31. Taymur, *Hilyat al-Tiraz*, 54.
32. Ibid., 6.
33. Ibid., 8.
34. Ibid., 12.
35. Ibid., 10.
36. Ibid., 6.
37. Ibid., 42–43.
38. Ibid., 11.
39. Ibid., 33, 37, 50, 62.
40. Ibid., 34, 21.
41. Ibid., 17–18, 28, 31, 32.
42. Ibid., 13, 34.
43. Ibid., 14, 17.

44. Ibid., 23.
45. Ibid., 35–36.
46. Ibid., 58–59.
47. Ibid., 19–21.
48. Ibid., 34.
49. Al-Anisa Mayy, Sha`irat al-Tali`a, 156.
50. A discussion with Dr. Lamis Jarrar, psychologist and colleague at Howard University's Counseling Center, helped me realize how the Christian Ziyada transposed a Christian definition of religion on the poetry of the Muslim poet (June 30, 2004). See Salma Al-Haffar al-Kuzbari, Mayy Ziyada Aw Ma'ssat al-Nubugh, vol. 1 (Beirut: Mu'assasat Noufal, 1987), chaps. 2–3 for a discussion of Ziyada's family's religious background and her religious education.
51. Al-Anisa Mayy, Sha`irat al-Tali`a166–67.
52. Ibid., 165.
53. Taymur, Hilyat al-Tiraz, 4.
54. Ibid.
55. Ibid., 6.
56. Ibid.
57. Ibid., 7.
58. Ibid., 13, 46, 53.
59. Ibid., 53-56.
60. Ibid., 46.
61. Ibid., 53.
62. Al-Waqa'I al-Misriyat (March 15, 1869), 1 in Sabah al-Khayr (January 13, 2004), 43.
63. Ibid., 9.
64. Professor Joyce Zonana of the English Department at the Manhattan Community College was very helpful in identifying this Greek physician. He lived in the second century BC and his medical treatises were very highly regarded. He was also supposed to have said that a physician was like a god. Professor Joyce Zonana, email communication with author, September 9, 2004.
65. Zaynab Hamdy, "Ali Pasha Ibrahim, Ba`ith al-Nahda al-Tibiya fi Misr," Rose al-Youssef, January 23, 2004, 70.
66. Taymur, Hilyat al-Tiraz, 11.
67. Ibid., 12.
68. Ali Pasha Ibrahim, who graduated at the top of his class, opened a private practice with another Egyptian doctor after his graduation in 1901. He eventually had to give up the practice because of the dominance of foreign doctors and the general lack of confidence in Egyptian doctors. See Hamdy, "Ali Pasha Ibrahim, Ba`ith al-Nahda al-Tibiya fi Misr," 70.
69. Mayy Ziyada, Sha`irat al-Tali`a, 24–25.
70. Ibid., 152.
71. Muhammed Husayn Haykal, Tarajim Misriya wa Gharbiya (Cairo: Matb'at Misr, n.d), 173–74.
72. Ibid., 63.
73. Hans Wehr, A Dictionary of Modern Written Arabic (Beirut: Maktabat Libnan, 1974), 932.
74. Taymur, Hilyat al-Tiraz, 61.
75. Ibid., 31.
76. Ibid., 11.
77. Haykal, Tarajim Misriya wa Gharbiya, no. 172.
78. Taymur, Hilyat al-Tiraz, 36.
79. Al-Anissa Mayy, Sha`irt al-Tali`a, 148.

80. Mayy Ziyada, *Warda al-Yazji* (Beirut: Mu'assat Noufal, 1980), 17.
81. Taymur, *Hilyat al-Tiraz*, 23.
82. Ibid.
83. Abdel Rahman al-Rafi`, `*Asr Ismail* (Cairo: Dar al-Ma'rif, 1982), 1:266.
84. Taymur, *Hilyat al-Tiraz*, 23.
85. Ibid., 14.
86. Ibid, 14–15.
87. Ibid., 17.
88. Ibid.
89. Ibid., 21.
90. Ibid., 21–22.
91. Ibid., 24.
92. Ibid., 25.
93. Ibid., 21–22.
94. Ibid., 24.
95. Ibid., 25.
96. Hatem, "Khitab al-Hadatha," 138–41.
97. Judith E. Tucker, *Women in Nineteenth-Century Egypt* (Cambridge: Cambridge University Press, 1985), chap. 4.
98. A. M. Broadly, *How We Defended Ahmed `Arabi and His Friends* (Cairo: Research and Publishing Arab Center, 1980), 373.
99. Ibid.
100. Ibid., 374.
101. Ibid., 259–60; see also Haykal, *Tarajim Misriya wa Gharbiya*, 87.
102. Broadly, *How We Defended Ahmed `Arabi and His Friends*, 261–70.
103. Haykal, *Tarajim `Arabiya wa Gharbiya*, 74.
104. Ibid., 50.
105. *Muthakirat Ahmed `Urabi* (Cairo: Dar al-Hilal, 1989), 17.
106. Ibid., 18; italics are mine.
107. Muhammed al-Khafif, *Ahmed `Urabi, al-Za`im al-Muftra `Aliyhi*, in Raja' al-Naqqash, "Amirat Nabilat," *Al-Ahram al-Dawli*, February 13, 2003, 13.
108. Ibid.
109. Ibid., 378–79.
110. This section is based on Mervat Hatem, "Writing About Life Through Loss: `A'isha Taymur's Elegies and the Subversion of the Arabic Canon," in *Transforming Loss into Beauty*, eds. Marle Hammond and Dana Sajdi (Cairo: American University in Cairo Press, 2008), 229–52.
111. Fawwaz, *Al-Durr al-Manthur fi Tabaqat Rabat al-Khudur*, 110.
112. Ibid., 304.
113. Mayy Ziyada, *Warda al-Yazji*, 40, 43.
114. Al-Anisa Mayy, 131.
115. Ibid., 133–34.
116. Ibid., 134–35.
117. For an expanded discussion of Al-`Aqqad's views of Taymur as a poet, please see Hatem, "Writing About Life Through Loss," 235–36.
118. `A'isha Taymur, *Hilyat al-Tiraz*, 17–18.
119. This piece of information was offered by the family representative attending the Women and Memory Forum's conference celebrating the centennial anniversary of `A'isha Taymur's death held in Cairo in May 2001.
120. Taymur, *Hilyat al-Tiraz*, 18.

121. Ali Mubarak, *al-Khitat al-Tawfiqiya al-Jadida Li Misr al-Qahira* (Cairo: Al-Hay'at al-Misriyat al-'Amma lil Kitab, 1982), 2:163.

122. Taymur, *Hilyat al-Tiraz*, 19.

123. Ibid., 19–20.

124. Ibid., 20.

125. Ibid., 21.

126. Ibid., 28.

127. Ibid., 29.

128. Ibid.

129. Ibid.

130. Ibid., 31.

131. Ibid., 32.

132. As an example of this dominant discursive tendency, please see Fadwa el-Guindi, review of *Remaking Women*, edited by Lila Abu-Lughod, *Journal of Political Ecology: Case Studies in History and Society*, 6 (1999).

133. Taymur, *Hilyat al-Tiraz*, 33.

134. Peter Gran's analysis of the cultural production of the first half of the nineteenth century offered this very important observation about how writers organized their presentations and their materials. Please see Peter Gran, *Islamic Roots of Capitalism, Egypt 1760–1840* (Austin: University of Texas Press, 1979), 87.

135. Ibid., 30.

136. Ibid., 46.

137. Ibid., 52.

138. Tewfik, "Sijin al-Rammad wa 'Afaq al-Hawwiya fi Shi'r 'A'isha Taymur," 116–25.

139. Ibid., 44–46.

Chapter 6

1. Geoff Eley and Ronald Grigor Suny, eds. *Becoming National: A Reader* (New York: Oxford University Press, 1996), 259.

2. Al-Amira Qadriya Husayn, "Tahiyat wa Taqdeer," in *Hilyat al-Tiraz* (Cairo: Lajnat Nashr al-Mu'alafat al-Taymuriya-Dar al-Kitabl al-'Arabi, 1952), 4.

3. http://www.dreamwater.net/regiment/RoyalArk/Egypt/egypt.html.

4. Abdelrahman al-Rafi', 'Asr Ismail (Cairo: Dar al-Ma'arif, 1982), 1:203.

5. http://www.royalark.net/Egypt/egypt.htm Please provide a working URL or delete.

6. Qadriya Husayn, "Tahiyat wa Taqdeer," 4.

7. Omaima Abou-Bakr, "Taqdeem," in *Shahirat al-Nisa' fi al-'Alam al-Islami* (Cairo: Muassasat al-Mar'at wa al Thakira, 2004), 9.

8. Zaynab Fawwaz, *al-Durr al-Manthur fi Tabaqat Rabat al-Khudur*, 308–9.

9. Hoda Elsadda, ed. *Al-Fatat*, 100–101.

10. Fawwaz, 3.

11. Ahmed Kamal Zadah, "Jidati: 'Ard wa Tahlil," in *Hilyat al-Tiraz: Diwan 'A'isha al-Taymuriya* (Cairo: Dar al-Katib al-'Arabi, 1952), 19.

12. Ahmed Taymur, *La'ib al-Arab* (Cairo: Lajnat Nashr al-Mu'alafat al-Taymuriya, 1948), 89.

13. Mahmud Taymur, "Lamha min Hayati," *al-Misriya* 1, no. 3 (March 15, 1937), 34.

14. Amin Salama, trans., *Mu'jam al-Hadara al-Misriya al-Qadima* (Cairo: al-Hay'at al-Misriya al-'Amma lil Kitab, 1992), 208.

15. Ibid.

Bibliography

Articles

Abou-Bakr, Omaima. "Teaching the Words of the Prophet: Women Instructors of the Hadith (Fourteenth and Fifteenth Centuries)." *Hawwa: Journal of Women of the Middle East and the Islamic World* 1, no. 3 (2003): 306–28.

`Amara, Muhammad. *Rifa` al-Tahtawi: Ra'id al-Tanweer fi al-`Asr al-Hadith.* Cairo: Dar al-Shuruq, 1988.

Al-Dessuki, Shaykh Sabri. "Al-Islam wa Takreem al-Mar'at." *al-Ahram,* May 13, 2010, 22.

Elsadda, Hoda. "Gendered Citizenship: Discourses of Domesticity in the Second Half of the Twentieth Century." *Hawwa, Journal of Women of the Middle East and the Islamic World* 4, no. 1 (2006): 1–28.

Guindi, Fadwa. Review of *Remaking Women,* edited by Lila Abu-Lughod. *Journal of Political Ecology: Case Studies in History and Society* 6 (1999): 1–10.

Hamdy, Zaynab. "Ali Pasha Ibrahim, Ba`ith al-Nahda al-Tibiya fi Misr." *Rose al-Youssef,* January 23, 2004, 70.

Hatem, Mervat. "The Nineteenth Century Discursive Roots of the Continuing Debate on the Social-Sexual Contract in Today's Egypt." *Hawwa: Journal of Women of the Middle East and the Islamic World* 2, no. 1 (2004): 64–88.

———. "The Politics of Sexuality and Gender in Segregated Patriarchal Systems: The Case of Eighteenth and Nineteenth Century Egypt." *Feminist Studies* 12, no. 2 (Summer 1986): 251–74.

———. "Toward the Study of the Psychodynamics of Mothering and Gender in Egyptian Families." *International Journal of Middle East Studies* 19, no. 3 (August 1987): 287–306.

Melki, Samia Nassar. "Palestinian Author Reclaims the Past for Generations of Arab Women, Memoir of Family History Contradicts Popular Beliefs about Premodern Middle Eastern Society." *Daily Star,* December 9, 2004, 4.

Al-Naqqash, Raja'. "Amirat Nabilat." *Al-Ahram al-Dawli,* February 13, 2003, 13.

Powell, Eve M. Troutt. "From Odyssey to Empire: Mapping the Sudan through Egyptian Literature in the Mid-19th Century." *International Journal of Middle East Studies* 31 (August 1999): 401–27.

Al-Saadi, Hoda. "Changing Attitudes towards Women's Madness in Nineteenth Century Egypt." *Hawwa, Journal of Women of the Middle East and the Islamic World* 3, no. 3 (2005): 293–308.

Smith, Charles D. "Imagined Identities, Imagined Nationalisms: Print Cultures and Egyptian Nationalism in the Light of Recent Scholarship." Review of *Redefining the Egyptian Nation 1930–1945,* by Israel Gershoni and James Pl Jankowski. *International Journal of Middle East Studies* 29, no. 4 (November 1997): 607.

Spellberg, Denise. "Nizam al-Mulk's Manipulation of Tradition, `A'isha and the Role of Women in the Islamic Government." *Muslim World* 78, no. 2 (April 1988): 111–17.

Sperl, Stephen. "Islamic Kingship and the Arab Panergyric Poetry in the Early 9th Century." *Journal of Arab Literature* 8 (1997): 20–35.

Taymur, Mahmud. "Lamha min Hayati." *al-Misriya* 1, no. 3 (March 15, 1937): 34.

Walz, Terence. "Bakhita Kwashe (Sr. Fortunata Quasce) 1841 to 1899." *Dictionary of African Christian Biography*. http://www.dacb.org/stories/sudan/bakhita_kwashe.html.

Al-Waqa'I al-Misriyat (March 15, 1869), 1 in *Sabah al-Khayr* (January 13, 2004), 43.

Zilfi, Madeline. "Servants, Slaves and the Domestic Order in the Ottoman Middle East." *Hawwa, Journal of Women of the Middle East and the Islamic World* 2, no. 1 (2004): 1–33.

Books

Abu Shuqa, Abdel Halim. *Tahrir al-Mar'at fi `Asr al-Risalat*. Vol. 2. Kuwait: Dar al-Qalim, 1990.

Adunis. *Al-Thabit wa al-Mutahawwil: Bahth fi al-Ittiba' wa al-Ibda` inda al-`Arab*. Beirut: Dar al-`Awdah, 1974.

`Ali, Muhammad Kurd. *Al-Mu`assirun*. Damascus: Matba`t al-Mujama` al-Lughtat al-`Arabiya bi Dimashq, 1980.

Amīn, Qāsim. *The Liberation of Woman*. Cairo: American University in Cairo Press, 1992.

Amin, Samir. *Unequal Development*. New York: Monthly Review, 1976.

`Amara, Muhammad. *`Ali Mubarak: Mu'arikh wa Muhandis al-`Imara*. Cairo: Dar al-Shuruq, 1988.

———. *Rifa' Al-Tahtawi, Ra'id al-Tanweer fi al-`Asr al-Hadith*. Cairo: Dar al-Shuruq, 1988.

Anderson, Benedict. *Imagined Communities*. London: Verso, 1991.

Anderson, Perry. *Lineages of the Absolutist State*. London: New Left Books, 1974.

Al-Anisa Mayy. *Sha`irat al-Tali`a, `A'isha Taymur*. Cairo: Dar al-Hilal, 1956.

Al-Ayubi, Iliyas. *Tarikh Misr fi `Ahd al-Khidiwi Ismail, 1863–1879*. Vol. 2. Cairo: Maktabat Madbuli, 1990.

Al-Azmeh, Aziz. *Muslim Kingship*. London: I. B. Tauris, 1997.

Badawi, Ahmed. *Rifa` Rafi` al-Tahtawi*. Cairo: Lajnat al-Bayan al-`Arabi, 1950.

Baron, Beth. *The Women's Awakening in Egypt*. New Haven, CT: Yale University Press, 1994.

Booth, Marilyn. *May Her Likes Be Multiplied: Biography and Gender Politics in Egypt*. Los Angeles: California University Press, 2001.

Broadly, A. M. *How We Defended Ahmed `Arabi and His Friends*. Cairo: Research and Publishing Arab Center, 1980.

Chodorow, Nancy. *The Reproduction of Mothering*. Berkeley: University of California Press, 1978.

Cole, Juan. *Colonialism and Revolution in the Middle East*. Princeton, NJ: Princeton University Press, 1993.

Cook, Michael. *Commanding Right and Forbidding Wrong in Islamic Thought*. Cambridge: Cambridge University Press, 2000.

Darke, Hubert, trans. *The Book of Government or Rules for Kings, the Siyasat-nama or Siyar al-Muluk of Nizam al-Mulk*. New Haven, CT: Yale University Press, 1960.

Eley, Geoff, and Ronald Grigor Suny, eds. *Becoming National: A Reader*. New York: Oxford University Press, 1996.

Elsadda, Hoda, ed. *Al-Fatat*. Cairo: Mu'assassat al-Mar'at wa al-Thakira, 2007.

———, ed. *Tahadiyat al-Thabit wa al-Mutaghiir fi al-Qarn al-Tasi` `Ashr*. Cairo: Mu'assassat al-Mar'at wa al-Thakira, 2004.

Fawwaz, Zaynab. *Al-Durr al-Manthur fi Tabaqat Rabat al-Khudur*. Cairo: al-Matba`t al-Kubra al-Amiriya, 1894.

Al-Fayumi, Shaykh Abdallah. *Lisan al-Jumhur `ala Mir'at al-Támul fi al-Umur*, Reprinted in *`A'isha Taymur, Mir'at al-Támul fi al-Umur*. Cairo: Multaqa al-Mar'at wa al-Thakira, 2002.

Fernea, Elizabeth, and Basima Qattan Bezirgan, eds. *Middle Eastern Women Speak.* Austin: University of Texas Press, 1977.

Goldschmidt, Arthur, Jr. *Biographical Dictionary of Modern Egypt.* Boulder, CO: Lynne Rienner, 2000.

Gran, Peter. *Islamic Roots of Capitalism Egypt, 1760–1840.* Austin: University of Texas Press, 1979.

Al-Hadidi, Ali. *Abdallah al-Nadeem, Khateeb al-Wataniya.* Cairo: al-Hay'at al-Misriyat al-'Amma lil Kitab, 1987.

Hafez, Sabry. *The Genesis of Arabic Narrative Discourse.* London: Saqi Books, 1993.

Hanna, Nelly. *Making Big Money in 1600: The Life and Times of Ismail Abu Taqiyya, Egyptian Merchant.* Syracuse, NY: Syracuse University Press, 1998.

Hasan, Muhammad Rushdi. *'Athar al-Maqama fi Nash'at al-Qissa al-Misriyat al-Haditha.* Cairo: al-Hay'at al-Misriyat al-'Amma lil Kitab, 1974.

Haykal, Muhammed Husayn. *Tarajim Misriya wa Gharbiya.* Cairo: Matb'at Misr, n.d.

Holland, Muhtar Holland, trans. *Al-Ghazali on the Duties of Brotherhood.* Woodstock, NY: Overlook Press, 1976.

Hunter, Robert. *Egypt Under the Khedives, 1805–1879.* Pittsburgh, PA: University of Pittsburgh Press, 1984.

Ibrahim, Al-Amir Osman, Caroline Kourkhan, and Ali Kourkhan. *Muhammed Ali al-Kabeer.* Edited by Huda Kourkan. Cairo: Al-Majlis al-'Ala lil Thaqafa, 2005.

Issa, Salah. *Al-Thawrat al-'Urabiya.* Cairo: Dar al-Mustaqbal al-'Arabi, 1982.

Kahala, Omar, ed. *'Alam al-Nisa.* Vol. 3. Beirut: Mu'assat al-Risala, 1977.

Al-Khafif, Muhammad. *Ahmed 'Urabi, al-Za'im al-Muftra 'Alih.* Cairo: Dar al-Hilal, n.d.

Khoury, Dina Rizk. *State and Provincial Society in the Ottoman Empire.* Cambridge: Cambridge University Press, 1997.

Al-Kuzbari, Salma Al-Haffar. *Mayy Ziyada Aw Ma'ssat al-Nubugh.* Vol. 1. Beirut: Mu'assasat Noufal, 1987.

Malti-Douglas, Fedwa. *Woman's Body, Woman's Word: Gender and Discourse in Arabo-Islamic Writing.* Cairo: American University in Cairo Press, 1991.

Mardin, Serif. *The Genesis of Young Ottoman Thought.* Princeton, NJ: Princeton University Press, 1962.

Mernissi, Fatima. *Beyond the Veil: Male and Female Dynamics in a Modern Muslim Society.* New York: Wiley and Sons, 1975.

———. *The Forgotten Queens of Islam.* Minneapolis: University of Minnesota Press, 1993.

Messick, Brinkly. *The Caligraphic State.* Berkeley: University of California Press, 1996.

Mitchell, Timothy. *Colonizing Egypt.* Cambridge: Cambridge University Press, 1988.

Moosa, Matti. *The Origins of Modern Arabic Fiction.* New York: Three Continents Press, 1983.

Mubarak, Ali. *Al-Khitat al-Tawfiqiya al-Jadida Li Misr al-Qahira.* Vol. 2. Cairo: al-Hay'at al-Misriyat al-'Amma lil Kitab, 1982.

Al-Nadeem, Abdallah. *Abdallah al-Nadeem: Al-'Addad al-Kamilat li Majallat al-Ustaz.* Vol. 1. Cairo: Markaz Watha'iq Misr al-Mu'assir, 1994.

Al-Najjar, Husayn Fawzi. *Rifa' al-Tahtawi: Ra'id Fikr im Imam al-Nahda.* Cairo: Al-Misriyat lil Ta'lif wa al-Tarjama, 1966.

Nazarat al-Ma'rif al-'Amumiya. *Taqrir 'an al-Katateeb 'Alti Tudiyraha Nazarat al-Ma'rif min Yulyu 1889–1898.* Cairo: al-Matba'at al-'Amiriya, 1899.

Nusair, 'Aida. *Harakat Nashr al-Kutub fi Misr fi al-Qarn al-Tasi' 'Ashr.* Cairo: Al-Hay'at al-Misriyat al-'Amma lil Kitab, 1994.

Owen, Roger. *Lord Cromer.* Oxford: Oxford University Press, 2004.

Pierce, Leslie P. *The Imperial Harem: Women and Sovereignty in the Ottoman Empire.* Oxford: Oxford University Press, 1993.

Pitkin, Hanna Fenichel. *Fortune Is a Woman: Gender and Politics in the Thought of Niccolo Machiavelli*. Los Angeles: University of California Press, 1984.

Powell, Eve M. Troutt, and John Hunwick, eds. *The African Diaspora in the Mediterranean Lands of Islam*. Princeton, NJ: Markus Wiener, 2002.

Al-Rafi`, Abdelrahman. `Asr Ismail. Vol. 1. Cairo: Dar al-Ma`arif, 1982.

Al-Rafi`, Abdelrahman. `Asr Muhammad Ali. Cairo: Maktabat al-Nahda al-Misriya, 1951.

Renard, John. *Islam and the Heroic Image: Themes in Literature and the Visual Arts*. Charlotte: University of South Carolina Press, 1993.

Said, Edward W. *Orientalism*. New York: Pantheon Books, 1978.

Al-Said, Rif`at. *Al-Mu'alafat al-Kamila*. Cairo: Dar al-Thaqafa al-Jadida, 1978.

Salama, Amin, trans. *Mu`jam al-Hadara al-Misriya al-Qadima*. Cairo: Al-Hay'at al-Misriyat al-`Amma lil Kitab, 1992.

Al-Sayyid Marsot, Afaf. *Egypt in the Reign of Muhammad Ali*. Cambridge: Cambridge University Press, 1984.

———. *Women and Men in Late Eighteenth-Century Egypt*. Austin: University of Texas Press, 1995.

Sha`rawi, Hoda. *Mudhakarat Ra'idat al-Mar'at al-`Arabiya al-Haditha*. Cairo: Dar al-Hilal, 1981.

Simons, Geof. *The Future of Iraq: U.S. Policy in Reshaping the Middle East*. London: Saqi Books, 2003.

Sonbol, Amira El-Azhary, ed. *Women, the Family and Divorce Laws in Islamic History*. Syracuse, NY: Syracuse University Press, 1996.

Spellberg, D. A. *Politics, Gender, and the Islamic Past*. New York: Columbia University Press, 1994.

Sperl, Stefan. *Mannerism in Arab Poetry*. Cambridge: Cambridge University Press, 1989.

Al-Tahtawi, Rif`a Bek. *Mawaqi` al-`Aflak fi Waqa`Telemaque*. Beirut: Al-Matba`t al-Suriya, 1857.

Taymur, Ahmed. *La`ib al-Arab*. Cairo: Lajnat Nashr al-Mu'alafat al-Taymuriya, 1948.

———. *Al-Tazkarat al-Taymuriya*. Cairo: Matba`t Dar al-Kitab al-`Arabi, 1953.

Taymur, `A'isha. *Hilyat al-Tiraz*. Cairo, 1892.

———. *Mir'at al-Tamul fi al-Umur*. Cairo: Matb`at al-Mahroussa, 1892.

———. *Nata'ij al-Ahwal fi al-Aqwal wa al-Af`al*. Cairo: Matb`at Mohammad Effendi Moustafa, 1887/8.

Taymur, Mahmud. *Itijahat al-Adab al-`Arabi fi al-Sineen al-Ma`at al-Akhira*. Cairo: Maktabat al-Adaab, 1970.

Toledano, Ehud. *State and Society in Mid-Nineteenth Century Egypt*. Cambridge: Cambridge University Press, 1990.

Tucker, Judith E. *Women in Nineteenth-Century Egypt*. Cambridge: Cambridge University Press, 1985.

Tugay, Emine Foat. *Three Centuries: Family Chronicles of Turkey and Egypt*. London: Oxford University Press, 1963.

`Urabi, Ahmed. *Mudhakarat al-Za`im Ahmed `Urabi*. Cairo: Dar al-Hilal, 1989.

Wehr, Hans. *A Dictionary of Modern Written Arabic*. Beirut: Maktabat Lubnan, 1974.

Yarshater, Ehsan, ed. *The Cambridge History of Iran*. Vol. 3. Cambridge: Cambridge University Press, 1983.

Young, Robert J. C. *Colonial Desire*. London: Routledge, 1995.

Al-Zirikli, Khayr al-Din, ed. *Al-`Alam: Qammus Tarajim*. Vol. 1 and 4. Beirut: Dar al-`Ilm lil Malayiin, 1979.

Ziyada, Mayy. *Sha`irat al-Tali`a, `A'isha Taymur*. Cairo: Dar al-Hilal, 1956.

Ziyada, Mayy. *Warda al-Yazji*. Beirut: Mu'assat Noufal, 1980.

Chapters in Books

Abou-Bakr, Omaima. "Surat al-Rajul fi al-Kitabat al-Islamiya: Bayn al-Tafaseer al-Qadima wa al-Haditha." In `A'isha Taymur: Tahadiyyat al-Thabit wa al-Mutaghiir fi al-Qarn al-Tasi` `Ashr, edited by Hoda Elsadda, 144–68. Cairo: Muassasat al-Ma'at wa al-Thakira 2004.

Omaima Abou-Bakr, "Taqdeem", in Shahirat al-Nisa' fi al-`Alam al-Islami (Cairo: Muassasat al-Mar'at wa al Thakira, 2004).

Badran, Margot, and Miriam Cooke. Introduction to Opening the Gates, A Century of Arab Feminist Writing, edited by Margot Badran and Miriam Cooke, xiv–xxxvi. Indianapolis: Indiana University Press, 1990.

"Walada Bint al-Mustakfi, Andalusian Poet," in Middle Eastern Women Speak, eds. Elizabeth Fernea and Basima Qattan Bezirgan (Austin: University of Texas Press, 1977).

"`A'isha Bint Yussef bin Ahmed bin Nasr al-Ba`uni", in Zaynab Fawwaz, al-Durr al-Manthur fi Tabaqat Rabat al-Khudur

Bose, Sugata. "Space and Time on the Indian Ocean Rim: Theory and History." In Modernity and Culture, from the Mediterranean to the Indian Ocean, edited by Leila Tarazi Fawaz and C. A. Bayly, 365–87. New York: Columbia University Press, 2002.

Chodorow, Nancy. "Being and Doing: A Cross Cultural Examination of the Socialization of Males and Females." In Women in Sexist Society: Studies in Power and Powerlessness, edited by Vivian Gornick and Barbara Moran, 259–91. New York: Basic Books, 1971.

Elsadda, Hoda. "Tanaqudhat al-Khitab al-Watani fi Tanawuluh li Mas'alat al-Mar'at: Qir'at fi Majallat "al-Ustaz" li Abdallah al-Nadeem." In `A'isha Taymur: Tahadiyat al-Thabit wa al-Mutaghayiir fi al-Qarn al-Tasi` `Ashr, edited by Hoda Elsadda, 169–97. Cairo: Mu'assasat al-Mar'at wa al-Thakira, 2004.

Goldschmidt, Arthur, Jr. "The Historical Context." In Understanding the Contemporary Middle East, edited by Deborah Gerner and Jillian Schwedler, 33–78. Boulder, CO: Lynne Rienner, 2004.

Fay, Mary Ann Fay. "Shawikar Qadin: Woman of Power and Influence in Ottoman Cairo." In Auto/Biography and the Construction of Identity and Community in the Middle East, edited by Mary Ann Fay, 95–194. New York: Palgrave Macmillan, 2001.

"Fayumi, Abdallah," al-`Alam, Qammus al-Tarajim, IV, ed. Khayr al-Din al-Zirikli (Beirut:Dar al-`Ilm lil Malayiin, 1979).

Hatem, Mervat. "`A'isha Taymur's Tears and the Critique of the Modernist and Feminist Discourses on Nineteenth-Century Egypt." In Making Women: Feminism and Modernity in the Middle East, edited by Lila Abu-Lughod, 73–88. Princeton, NJ: Princeton University Press, 1998.

———. "Khitab al-Hadatha, Diwan 'Hilyat al-Tiraz' wa Ru'iyat `A'isha Taymur li Harakat al-Taghiir al-Ijtima'I wa al-Siyasi." In `A'isha Taymur: Tahadiyat al-Thabit wa al-Mutaghayir fi al-Qaran al-Tasi` `Ashr, edited by Hoda Elsadda, 129–43. Cairo: Mu'assasat al-Mar'at wa al-Thakira, 2004.

———. "The Microdynamics of Patriarchal Change in Egypt and the Development of an Alternative Discourse on Mother-Daughter Relations." In Intimate Selving in Arab Families: Gender, Self and Identity, edited by Suad Joseph, 191–210. Syracuse, NY: Syracuse University Press, 1999.

———. "Writing About Life Through Loss: `A'isha Taymur's Elegies and the Subversion of the Arabic Canon." In Transforming Loss into Beauty, edited by Marle Hammond and Dana Sajdi, 229–52. Cairo: American University in Cairo Press, 2008.

Hobsbawm, Eric. "Introduction: Inventing Traditions." In The Invention of Tradition, edited by Eric Hobsbawm and Terence Ranger, 1–15. Cambridge: Cambridge University Press, 1983.

Husayn, Al-Amira Qadriya. "Tahiyat wa Taqdeer." In *Hilyat al-Tiraz*, 3–5. Cairo: Dar al-Katib al-`Arabi, 1952.

"Ibn al-Kalbi"; *Encyclopedia of Islam*, IV, eds. B. Lewis, V. L. Menage, CH. Pellat, and J. Schacht (Leiden: E.J Brill, 1978).

"Ibn Khallikan", *Encyclopedia of Islam*, III, eds. B. Lewis, V.L. Menage, CH Pellat and J. Schacht (Leiden: E.J. Brill, 1978). "Lament for a Brother" by al-Khansa,' Poet of Early Islam," in *Middle Eastern Women Speak* (Austin: University of Texas Press, 1977).

"`Aliya Ibnat al-Mahdi al-`Abbasiyya", in Zaynab Fawwa, *Al-Durr al-Manthur fi Tabaqat Rabat al-Khudur,*

"Mamluk": *Ecyclopedia of Islam*, VI, eds. VI, eds. C.E. Bosworth, E.Van Donzel, B Lewis and CH. Pellat (Leiden :E.J. Brill, 1991).

McClintock, Anne. "'No Longer in a Future Heaven': Nationalism, Gender and Race." In *Becoming National: A Reader*, edited by Geoff Eley and Ronald Grigor Suny, 260–85. Oxford: Oxford University Press, 1996.Powell, Eve M. Troutt. "Sainted Slave: Bakhita in the Memories of Southern Sudanese." In *Race and Identity in the Nile Valley*, edited by Carolyn Fuerhr-Lobban and Kharyssa Rhodes, 159–69. Trenton, NJ: Red Sea Press, 2004.

———. "Slaves or Siblings? Abdallah al-Nadim's Dialogues About the Family." In *Histories of the Middle East: New Directions*, edited by Israel Gershoni, Hakam Erdem, and Ursula Wokock, 155–66. Boulder, CO: Lynne Rienner, 2002.

Al-Qadi, Wadad. "East and West in `Ali Mubarak's `Alamuddin.'" In *Intellectual Life in the Arab East, 1890–1939*, edited by Marwan R. Buheiry, 21–37. Beirut: American University of Beirut, 1981.

Qasim, Abdu Qasim. "Misr al-Mamlukiyya: Al-Sulta bi Quwwat al-Sayf." In *Hukkam Misr*, 80–88. Cairo: Dar al-Hilal, 2005.

Said, Rif`at, "Wathiqat Jawaz, Rifa`a," in *al-Mu'alafat al-Kamila* (Cairo: Dar al-Thaqafa al-Jadida, 1978).

Sarruf, Yaqub. "Muqadimat." In *Bahithat al-Badiya*, by Mayy Ziyada, 9–14. Beirut: Mu'assat Noufal, 1983.

Sayyid, Ayman Fouad Sayyid. "`Amawayyun, `Abbasiyyun wa Fatimiyyun: Al-Wali Mab`uth al-Khalifa." In *Hukkam Misr*, 74–79. Cairo: al-Hilal, 2005.

Al-Sayyid Marsot, Afaf. "Women and Modernization: A Reevaluation." In *Women, the Family, and Divorce Laws in Islamic History*, by Amira El Azhary Sonbol, 39–51. Syracuse, NY: Syracuse University Press, 1996.

Sharky, Omnia. "Schooled Mothers and Structured Play: Child Rearing in Turn-of-the-Century Egypt." In *Remaking Women*, edited by Lila Abu Lughod, 126–70. Princeton, NJ: Princeton University Press, 1998.

Taymur, Ahmed. "Tarikh al-`A'ilah al-Taymuriya" in *Li`b al-`Arab* (Cairo: Lajnat Nashr al-Mu'alafat al-Taymuriya, 1948)

Taymur, `A'isha. "Muqadimat al-Diwan al-Turki wa al-Farasi," in Ziyada, "Katiba Tuqadim , Sha`irat" in *Hilyat al-Tiraz: Diwan `A'isha al-Taymuriya*, 33–148. Cairo: Dar al-Katib al-`Arabi, 1952.Taymur, Mahmud. "`Amati." In *Hilyat al-Tiraz: Diwan `A'isha al-Taymuriya*, 11–13. Cairo: Dar al-Katib al-`Arabi, 1952.

Tewfik, Lami`a. "Sijin al-Rammad wa 'Afaq al-Hawwiya fi Shi`r `A'isha Taymur." In `A'isha Taymur: Tahadiyat al-Thabit wa al-Mutaghiir fi al-Qarn al-Tasi` `Ahar, edited by Hoda Elsadda, 108–28. Cairo: Mu'assassat al-Mar'at wa al-Thakira, 2004.

Wallerstein, Immanual. "The Three Stages of African Involvement in the World Economy." In *Political Economy of Contemporary Africa*, edited by Peter Gutkind and Immanual Wallerstein. London: Sage, 1985.

"Wathiqat Jawaz, Rifa`a," in Rifa`at al-Said, *al-Mu'alafat al-Kamila* (Cairo: Dar al-Thaqafa al-Jadida, 1978), 34

Zadah, Kamal. "Jidati: `Ard wa Tahlil." In *Hilyat al-Tiraz: Diwan `A'isha al-Taymuriya*, 15–19. Cairo: Dar al-Katib al-`Arabi, 1952.

Zirikli, Khayr al-Din. "Ahmed Taymur Pasha," in *Al-`Alam: Qammus Tarajim* (Beirut: Dar al-`Ilm lil Malayiin, 1979).

Ziyada, Mayy. "Katiba Tuqadim Sha`irat(please revise the spelling of sha`irat)." In *Hilyat al-Tiraz: Diwan `A'isha al-Taymuriya*, 33–148. Cairo: Dar al-Katib al-`Arabi, 1952.

Index